# GHOST TIME

*For all the artists*
*who have made this possible.*

Text copyright © 2013 by Courtney Eldridge

Amazon Publishing
Attn: Amazon Children's Publishing
P.O. Box 400818
Las Vegas, NV 89140
www.amazon.com/amazonchildrenspublishing

ISBN-13: 9781477816578 (hardcover)
ISBN-10: 1477816577 (hardcover)
ISBN-13: 9781477866573 (eBook)
ISBN-10: 1477866574 (eBook)

Book design by Katrina Damkoehler and Susan Gerber
Editor: Ed Park

Printed in the United States of America (R)
First edition
10 9 8 7 6 5 4 3 2 1

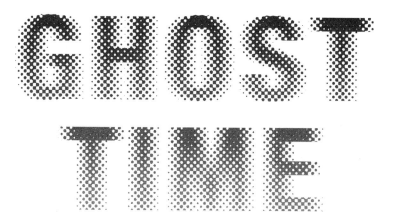

# GHOST TIME

BY **COURTNEY ELDRIDGE**

**SKYSCAPE**

## MONDAY, APRIL 4, 2011

**5:27 PM**

What's funny is I used to think I made him up. Seriously, it's been six months, but even now, like this afternoon, looking at him, the light was so amazing, I almost ran back in to get my camera, but I didn't, because I didn't want to miss it. I mean, it was the goldest golden-hour light, shining all around him, and looking at his face, I was just like, *You are so beautiful, what if I did make you up in my head?* And you know what he said? Right when I was thinking that, Cam looks up at me, grinning, and he was about to say something else, but he goes, Hey, Thee, maybe you should put some clothes on? Then I looked down, and my jaw just totally dropped, because it didn't even occur to me.

Honestly, we'd already said good-bye, but after I closed the door, I was just like, No, wait, I've got to watch him leave, because I always watch him leave, so I went back outside. And I should've put some clothes on, I know, but I was right outside our door, and I only thought I'd be out there for a second, and none of our upstairs neighbors were home yet. We live in this L-shaped two-story building that doesn't really look like an apartment building, probably because it used to be a Super 8 Motel, but anyhow. The highway's right on the other side of the parking lot, and there I am, in a T-shirt, sticking my ass out, leaning over the rail, showing the whole world my crack. Just what the world needs, another teenage exhibitionist, right? So Cam was looking at me, like, You gonna stand there half-naked all night? I go, All right, all right, but tell me what you were going to say before that, and Cam goes, Oh, yeah.

He looked over at this old beater truck that belongs to Al, the building's super. I don't know if it even runs anymore, but it has stickers all over the back window, like, Think Globally, Act Locally, whatever. Cam goes, What I was going to say is, you know what your name means, Thee? I smiled and I go, Of course, I do, and he goes, *Bzzt!* Wrong answer! Like I was supposed to play dumb, right? So I put both hands on the side of my face, and I go, Why, no, Cam, what does my name mean? He smiled, wagging his finger at me, and he goes, Believe it or not, *Theadora* is Greek for *God's gift.* And I go, Hey, Cam, you know what Socrates said? He ignored me, even though he was grinning, and he goes, And that got me to thinking. You know those bumper stickers that say: God is coming back and is she pissed? I go, Please tell me you aren't getting your mom one of those? Cam goes, No, but what I was thinking is, what if God wasn't a man or woman? What if God was a teenage girl? And when he said that, I was just like, *Whoa!* because I'd never heard anyone say that before, so I had to think about it for a second.

But then I was just like, I go, Well, no wonder the world's so fucked up, huh? And Cam laughed, shaking his head at me, before getting in his car. It was cold, and I was just like, *Brrrr!* totally nipping out, completely covered in goose bumps. But I still waited until he honked and turned around before I went back inside and closed the door. Except then all I could do was lean against our front door, rattling it with my fists and screeching *Eeee!*

Seriously, I just stood there, leaning my back against the door, before I slid down to the ground, laughing, because I could still hear Cam's voice. I could still hear him and feel him next to me from when we were in my room, before he left. We were in bed, and he was there, but he wasn't there—I don't know where he was. Cam was so spaced out all afternoon, and I could even feel it in his body, you know, so finally I had looked up and I said, Where are you?

He was staring at my ceiling, and he nodded, smiling, and he said, I was just thinking how, when I was a kid, we used to have this telescope, and every night before bed, my dad would show me the stars, explain about planets and gravity and light—those were my bedtime stories, he said. And I'll never forget the time Dad told me that given the incredible distance light must travel, any star I saw shining in the sky might actually be dead. So right away, I said, But then how do you know *we're* alive, Dad? Doesn't it work both ways? What if there are stars looking at us, thinking the same thing right now? I didn't understand why, but my dad was so proud of me, he told my mom what I said at dinner. That night he got this idea, because I always hated going to bed. I used to kick and scream every night at bedtime. So the next day, my dad put those glow-in-the-dark stars on my ceiling. Remember that star wallpaper, Thee? he said, and I nodded my head yes. I never had it, but I remember it, and Cam said, After he hung up the Milky Way, the first night, tucking me in, my dad said not to tell anyone, not even my mom, because I had the secret of the whole universe right on my ceiling, where no one would ever think to look—except me.

It made me smile, listening to him, because Cam never really talked about his family. So I kept quiet, hoping he'd keep talking, and he did. He said, From then on, my mom never had to force me to go to bed again, because I could look at my stars all night. I did, too—they used to keep me up at night, he said, kissing the top of my head. Because stars made me think about time, and time made me want to learn about physics and math, and once I found math, he said, his muscles tensing beneath me. I had to bite my tongue, because he was on such a roll, I didn't want him to stop talking, when he said, Who's to say that time is any one thing? Who's to say that time moves in any one direction, and that the only direction is forward? What if time isn't one thing, but many, Thee? What if time is plural, and time can move forward and backward? What if there are two times, moving forward and backward, simultaneously, like two men in a duel? Think about it: what if time can play tricks on itself, sneak up on itself—Ghost Time, he said. What's that? I said, and he said, That's what I call it, the equation I'm working on: Ghost Time.

I had my head on his chest, looking at his skin, so white, such perfect skin, and then I looked up and said, Cam? I felt him snap back like a rubber band, and he looked down at me. I said, Tell me this isn't what you think about when we're having sex. *Ghost Time?* He started laughing, making my head shake, and he said, Would that offend you? And I cocked my head like, tell me that's not what you think about, and he grinned. Well, the forward and backward part, maybe, he said, and I was just like, You are such a perv! You are such a pervy *nerd*! I was about to grab a pillow and hit him when his phone chimed again, and I was like, Ohmygod, who is having an algebra meltdown? I didn't mean to snap, but he kept getting texts all afternoon, and he suddenly looked so stressed out about it, reading the message. Which is weird, because Cam never gets stressed out about anything, but I know he takes his tutoring really seriously, so I rolled over to let him get up.

He kissed my shoulder, and then he goes, Listen, Thee. I know you can't keep your hand off my pervy nerd bod, throwing the covers off of us. But I'm late, he said, standing up and putting on his jeans in one jump, while I propped my head on my hand, and then I said, Then again, who knows. If you're late in one time, maybe you're early in another, right, boy genius? Hearing that, he immediately stopped buttoning his jeans, looked up at me, surprised, and then he goes, Aren't you clever! See what a good influence I am on you? Then, of course, I had to laugh. *You?* You're the good influence? Cam ignored me, cocking his head behind him, all business. Walk me out? he said. So I threw on a shirt, while he zipped up his jacket, and he took my hand, leading me to the front door . . . then I snapped back, too. Returning from some other time, the one moving us backward, while I moved forward, alone.

Happy—that's when I realized what was going on—I was happy. Talk about will wonders never cease, because I was so happy, I fell on my side, giggling, and then there was this voice in my head that was just like, *Would you* stop? *Stop it, you're disgusting!* We are, too—ohmygod, Cam and I, we're so sickening, we make my teeth hurt. But then I was just like, *So?* I mean, seriously, how many times in your life do you get to feel like that, much less for the first time? Once, right? You get that maybe once in your whole life, so why would you ever take that away from yourself?

I mean, unless you're afraid, and I'm not—not anymore. I used to be, I used to be so scared, if anyone had told me six months ago that I'd meet this boy and my whole life would change, that *I* would change, I never would've believed it, no way. But I did—it's all true—I met a boy, and I have changed. Just to prove how fearless I am, I opened the door again, and Cam was just about to pull out, on the highway, so I screamed it, loud as I could. Top of my lungs, I go, I love you, Cam Conlon! I waited, watching his car drive past our building, and I don't know if he heard me or not, but it didn't matter, because I know he knows, and I know he feels the same about me. And for the first time in my life, standing there, I thought, *I am the happiest girl in the whole wide world.* Then I saw my mom pulling in, and I groaned, *Ugh. Mom's home,* and I ran inside to get dressed.

## MONDAY, APRIL 4, 2011
## (TWO HOURS LATER)

I don't know what's going on, but my mom's been really stressed out lately. Like every day when she gets home from work, she's so bitchy, and I know she hates her job, but it's like, get off my case, you know? Seriously, it's not my fault money's so tight and we have to live in this shitty little apartment. That's mean, I know, because my mom's done what she can, but it's still a dump—I'm sorry, but this place is a dump, at least compared to our old house. I mean, we used to have a nice house, with a garage and a garden and a front yard and a big backyard and two guest bedrooms. We even had a separate dining room we never even used, and now, sometimes I walk in the door, and I know how it happened, but I look around, and I'm just like, *How did we fall so far?*

I wish she'd take money from my dad, but she won't take alimony. Child support, but not alimony. We've gotten into it a couple times because I'm like, Mom, why won't you take the man's money? It's the least he can do, you know? And she goes, Thea. You don't even speak to the man, and you want me to take his money? I go, Mom, taking his money and not speaking to him is a much better deal, trust me. But she won't do it, she won't take his money, and it's so dumb. Then again, I really admire her for not taking a nickel from the guy—I just wish pride didn't require we live in a dive, you know?

So I know the money thing stresses her out, and I feel bad, I really do, but still. She kept yelling at me from the kitchen about turning off the TV and doing my homework, and I didn't say anything, but I was just like, *Mom, please, you know this is my show, I only watch it every night.* But I was in such a good mood, I didn't want to get into it, so I said, Soon as *The Simpsons* is over, okay? Please, Mom? Because this is the best *Simpsons* ever, I said, whimpering—totally laying it on, right—and she actually bought it. I heard her close the oven, then she poked her head in and she goes, Which *Simpsons* is the best *Simpsons* ever? And I go, *Me back is frontward*; the one with the Buzzcocks, I said, knowing that would get her, and it did. She goes, Which one is that? I go, Mom, the Sid and Nancy one, where Lisa's Nancy and Nelson's Sid? Come see.

She walked in, drying her hands with a dish towel, right at the point where Lisa's realizing maybe she's not cut out for the life and death of a punk-rock junkie girlfriend, and I go, Poor Lisa, I wonder if she ever meets the man of her dreams. And walking past me, my mom goes, *Poor Lisa?* What about poor Mom and the man of her dreams? she said, sitting down on the couch, beside me. And I go, What, you mean Rain Man's not the man of your dreams? She looked at me, like, don't start, and I tried not to, but I couldn't help laughing, thinking about Raymond being the man of any woman's dreams, and then Mom looked at me and goes, Come here—get over here, you, and she pulled me over by my arm, resting my head in her lap during the commercials. She started playing with my hair, and I let her, that's how happy I was.

## MONDAY, APRIL 4, 2011
## (TWO HOURS EARLIER)

**3:32 PM**

I took pictures this afternoon. I threw on this old shirt of Cam's that used to belong to his dad. It's Hang Ten, this brand from the seventies, and it has these big blue and yellow horizontal stripes with a floppy white collar, I love it. We went to the kitchen to get something to eat, and I didn't feel like getting dressed, but my feet are always cold, so I threw on a pair of white knee-high tube socks, and then Cam snapped his fingers at me, doing this little shimmy with his shoulders, acting all groovy, and he goes, Rockin' the seventies. And then I shook my hips, pulling out my imaginary guns, shooting him down: *bang! bang!* And I go, That's right, baby. I'm too foxy for your love, and then he said something totally rude, but anyhow.

Cam was wearing his boxers—he's so skinny, they were almost falling off his hips—and there was still a red outline of my lip gloss on his left hip bone, from when I'd knelt down, kissing him, because his hip bones drive me crazy. And just above his elastic band, you could see this thin brown line, like this sliver of gold-brown pubic hair, shining in the light beneath the kitchen window. Oh, but when I say skinny, I don't mean it in a bad way—I love Cam's body. All the time. He's perfect, if you ask me, and that's why I took pictures of him, standing at our kitchen sink, holding a glass of milk in one hand and this humongous double-decker PB&J—like, three pieces of bread, stuffed in his mouth, and this big dab of raspberry jelly on his chin, like he hadn't eaten for weeks or something. And I said, Don't move, and I ran to my room.

Cam's so used to it by now, me taking his picture all the time, he didn't move a muscle. Yeah, just like that, I said, focusing, and then he goes, Just look at the camera? And I go, Yeah, look at the camera, and I ended up taking a whole roll—real, honest-to-goodness film, too. Don't ask me how I'm going to pay to get it printed, but anyhow.

Cam took all the other photos. Those are just digital, all the ones of me, jumping on my bed, in front of my window. That was just before Cam left, and the curtains were drawn, but the light's so bright, it's like it's taking an X-ray of the whole room. There's this one photo he showed me, and at first, I was like, Ohmygod, *delete!* Because it's a picture of me, lying facedown, on my bed, and all I'm wearing are those ugly tube socks. But before I could ask for my camera back, Cam got another text. Someone kept calling and texting all afternoon, and I was so annoyed, I told him to turn his phone off when he walked over to check the message.

When he picked up his phone, he looked at it like, *WTF?* And he had such a strange look, reading the message, I said, What's wrong? He shook his head no, then he looked up and smiled, and he goes, Nothing, babe. It's fine, but I can't stay for dinner—I've got to work, and when he said that, I was just like, *Tonight?* Seemed kind of late to be calling for a tutoring session, but Cam goes, No, not now, five thirty, and I started whining, *No!* and I threw myself on the bed. So I'm lying there, facedown, legs spread wide apart, squeezing my fists. And you can't tell by looking, but the moment he took that picture, what I was saying was, Don't leave! I turned over, and I go, What do I have to do to get you to stay? And Cam goes, Thee, look at this. Look how beautiful you are, as he showed me the picture he took.

The thing is, I really hated that picture when he first showed it to me, but now I kind of like it. Not because it's the best picture of my butt, definitely not, but because . . . because it's true, you know? It's so true. I mean, I'm not beautiful—I never really feel that way about myself, on my own. But when I look at Cam, when I see me the way he sees me, I don't know what happens, but I'm the most beautiful girl in the world.

## MONDAY, APRIL 4, 2011
## (FOUR HOURS LATER)

I called him twice, and I texted him, too, like, three or four times before I went to bed—he couldn't still be tutoring after ten o'clock, right? Usually he calls right back, but I don't know, I figured maybe he was working on his car—sometimes he'll stay out in the garage, working on his car until, like, two, three in the morning. Cam's a total night owl—he'll stay up half the night, working on his car, or taking drives, or writing equations in our notebook: part geometry; part hieroglyphics; part graffiti tags. Cam has a written language all his own that he shares with me— it's crazy and beautiful, in no particular order. Anyhow, he loves to work at night, so I didn't worry about it, really.

And since I figured he was working, I decided I better get some work done, too. Not homework—please, instead of talking to Cam all night, I spent the night working on some drawings

I'm making for him. For the past couple months now, I've been designing something I like to think of as our Barbie Dreamhouse. Which looks like a five-thousand-square-foot downtown loft in New York pretty much. Except that in Thea and Cam's Barbie Dreamhouse, we've got this enormous wooden half-pipe, so Cam can skate anytime he wants, rain or shine. And we have also got all these projectors mounted that project wall-size skateboard and surfing and old BMX movies all day, and I have this huge walk-in closet that's bigger than our whole apartment. It's not serious or anything—I mean, it's not like I think we're going to get married and I've already named all our unborn children or whatever—it's just a place I'm making for the two of us. Like if I could stop time and go anywhere I want to go, I'd be with Cam, and that's where I'd take him, to our home.

I've gotten used to it, the way people look at him all the time, because he's such a pretty boy. He's tall and thin and has this ruddy skin, never gets any zits. Sandy-blond hair, thin eyebrows, thin nose, long eyelashes that almost look like he uses a curling wand, with these big gray eyes—and his bone structure, like his cheekbones, are *to die*. And I'm not just saying that because he's my boyfriend, either. Everyone notices, even guys.

Seriously, Cam started shaving his head last year, and it makes his cheekbones stand out even more, so I started calling him Hitboy. Like the video game *Hitman*, right? So we cut last period, and on our way to my house, we pulled over to get some gas. Cam was about to get out, and I go, Wait—I've got to rub the Buddha. What I mean is, Cam's got really thick hair, so after he shaves his head it gets all soft and bristly, and I can't stop buffing his head with my hand 'cause it feels so good.

So he leaned over, and I rubbed my hand back and forth a couple times. Okay, I said, but he's such a smart-ass, he goes, Anything else you want to rub? I was just like, Keep your pants on, Buddha, and he goes, You know, Buddha was quite a lady's man, and I rolled my eyes, and I go, Just fill 'er up, will you? And then Cam goes—never mind. I don't know what it is, but boys and crudeness, it's like a pig in mud, you know what I mean? Like, they just love to cover themselves and everyone else in it, right? Anyhow.

I used to be so self-conscious, like if we were out in public, I always felt like people looked at me and looked at Cam, wondering what he was doing with me. But I've gotten over it pretty much, and now when people look, especially if it's an older guy, I know it's the car. Because Cam has this really cool old car—it's so *boss*. He inherited his car from his dad—this gold color they don't even make anymore. Seriously, they don't make that color of paint anymore; it's probably toxic or something. Anyhow, Cam's dad died when he was a kid, and he'd bought the car for Cam because Cam was already working on cars by then. So his dad bought this old Dodge Dart for him to fix up, and he did, after his dad died. Took him two years to find all the parts, but he got it running, and now men check it out all the time. It's a dude thing, you know?

So, yeah, we were at the gas station, and this man walked over, and I got scared for a second, thinking he was going to scold us about not being in school, because he looked all uptight, but Cam didn't get flustered at all. He was just standing at the pump, filling up, when the guy walked over and said, What is that, a sixty-nine? And Cam said, Sixty-eight, and the guy whistles, nodding at the car. Then the guy goes—he was well-dressed, too, it's not like he was a hick or anything—he goes, I don't suppose you'd be interested in selling it, would you? Cam stopped pumping, and he put the pump back, and he goes, You don't suppose right, and I'm in the car listening, but the guy goes, Well, if you should change your mind, and then he takes out his wallet and gives Cam his card.

Cam took his card, and right then, his phone started ringing, so I handed it to him when he opened the door. I wasn't really paying attention, but the man walked away, and I saw Cam start talking to someone on the phone, leaning his butt against the rear end of the car. Then he looked up and his head fell back, like he couldn't believe what he was hearing. When he got back in, he had this look on his face, like he was somewhere else, and he checked the rearview mirror, watching the man pull away. What's wrong? I said, turning, but the car was already on the highway. He'd been acting really weird all day, and he said, Nothing's wrong, babe. I didn't believe him, but he reached over and squeezed my thigh. Really, I just didn't sleep much last night, he said, and then I started telling him, I told you so! but I stopped, because I've already told him he needed to sleep like a hundred times, and it's no use.

I'd been sitting there, with our notebook in my lap, looking through Cam's last entry while he was gassing up the car. It was page after page of 1s and 0s, but done in all these different styles, like twenty different graffiti artists had tagged and retagged this endless wall. It's so cool—I'd never have thought of that, I said, thinking out loud while he started the car. All information can be rendered in 1s and 0s, so I wrote you a note in code. *In code*, I said, like, yeah, right, and he cocked his head and raised his brow all Spock-like. Okay, then, tell me, what's this say? I asked, showing him the last page, and he said, Forever. It's *Forever* written in 1s and 0s, and I said, Ha!, cocking my head back at him, and he said, I'm serious—that's exactly what all those pages say: Forever. Then he smiled, reaching over and squeezing my hand, like he'd never let go.

## TUESDAY, APRIL 5, 2011
## (TWELVE HOURS LATER)

I was having this really bizarre dream where I come to, and I see Cam's car—like the first thing I see is Cam's car, parked in front of this two-bedroom house in the middle of nowhere. And there aren't any other houses around, just this little white house, and the grass is so overgrown, it's waist high, except for the yard right around the house. It's not like I'm scared or anything, but it's weird, so I walk over to Cam's car to see if the keys are in the ignition, and they are.

I get in, and just as I'm about to turn over the engine, I hear Cam—like, his voice starts calling my name. And it sounds like he's in the house, waiting for me, so I get out, and I walk over and knock on the front door, but nobody answers. So I stick my head inside and say, Hello? but no one answers. And then I see that there's nothing in the house; it's empty, and Cam's not there. I turn around, and he calls me again: Thee, come here! It sounds like he's out front, right, so I go back outside, but he's not there, either. So I walk around the house, looking for him, but I can't find him anywhere, and then I start to hear pounding, and he keeps calling me, Thea!, Thea! His voice gets really loud, too, and I'm just about to yell at him to stop knocking and come out, when I realize it's my mom's voice—I'm dreaming—I was just dreaming.

I have no idea what's going on, and I can barely open my eyes, but I told her to come in, and when my door opens, it's not just Mom, Karen's there, too—Cam's mom, she's standing at my door, looking all crazy. Seriously, I've never seen Karen look like that, and then she looks behind me, in my room, and she goes, Where is he? And I'm just like, I don't know. I mean, I actually turned and looked around my room, too, like . . . I don't know, maybe there was some way Cam was in my room, and I didn't even know?

Cam? Karen says, and my mom looks at me, and I look at my mom, like, I have no idea what's going on. I said, Karen, Cam's not here. I don't know where he is. And she goes, He didn't come home last night, and then I was just like, *What the fuck? Is he okay? Was he in an accident? Where is he?* I said, He left right before my mom came home, and Karen goes, His car is here. I said, Karen, I'm telling you, I never saw him after he left yesterday, and Mom nodded, agreeing with me, and right away, I started feeling woozy, like when you lose cabin pressure.

I sat up and I go, Wait a second, and I got my phone, and I tried calling him, but he didn't answer. Not only that, there was no message—his voice mail didn't pick up, the line just went dead, disconnected. I looked at my phone, and then I tried again, and the same thing happened again. By that point, I was totally awake, and Karen and my mom were standing there. But when I looked at Karen, the way she looked at me, I knew she'd already tried and experienced the same thing: no answer. His car is here—it's out front, in your parking lot, she said again, and I go, I'm telling you, I watched him drive away last night, and I haven't seen him since, Karen.

We walked into the living room, the three of us, and Karen said she'd called the police, and they said to give it a day, twenty-four hours, since he's eighteen and legally an adult, but that there hadn't been any car accidents reported. My mom offered to make her coffee, but Karen said, No, thank you, heading for the front door. She apologized for overreacting, and Mom and I walked her out, but I could tell something was going on by the look on her face, something she wasn't saying. After Karen left, I tried calling Cam again, and then I texted and I e-mailed, too, and I thought maybe he'd gone camping or . . . I don't know. I sat on the side of my bed after I got out of the shower, staring at the ground, the same way Karen had, and all I could think was, *Where the hell are you?*

I haven't taken the bus once in six months, but before I left for school, I tried again. I called, texted, e-mailed. I went to his site, but even his website was gone. No, not just down, gone—it was *gone*. No address, nothing: vanished. I swear, when that happened—I mean, I tried three, four times, then I searched on Google, and when nothing came up, every hair on my arms stood up and my hands got all clammy. He wasn't at school, either—I kept looking for him, expecting him to walk around the corner any minute, but no. So I texted him all day, until finally, I was just like, *Okay, three things: one, this sucks; two, you suck; and three, where the hell are you? I'm really pissed, so get back on the grid!* It wasn't until I sent the message that I had the strangest feeling about the grid.

It's this running joke. Because Cam loves to talk about getting rid of everything—his cell phone, credit cards, going off the grid and disappearing completely. So all day, I kept remembering how he'd just said that, the day before, on our way to school, and I just rolled my eyes. Then he goes, You laugh, Thee, but watch: One day, I'll go off the grid. And you'll be like, Where's Cam? Every time I thought of him saying that, I texted him, like at least fifty times. No answer.

He picks me up every morning, and that's the only thing that gets me out of bed, Monday mornings. And Tuesday, and Wednesday, but anyhow. I kissed him, and then I sat back, shaking my head at him, like, *What have you done now?*

You know how a little kid will spaz out after a birthday party, all jacked up on sugar? Well, that's how Cam is after he pulls an all-nighter, trying to figure something out in his head. I call it the geek tweak when he goes on these rants about the laws of physics and the space-time continuum. Like, say, what if time's a double exposure, or a multiple exposure, or even an infinite multiple exposure? Seriously, last week, he was going on about how the perfect model for a time machine is a song, and he was, like, What if a song is a time machine, Thee? Think about it—it's mathematical, it's coded, you're transported every time you hear that particular equation, right? But, see, for Cam, the point isn't coming up with an answer, the point is the possibilities.

Sometimes you can almost see sparks shooting out of his ears when he gets going, talking about time travel and time codes—Cam's *obsessed* with the idea of time codes, of identifying exact moments in time. He has this theory that if time has a code, then you've just got to hack the code. Because if you figure out how to hack the code of a specific moment in time, you can change the entire course of history. And looking at him, as we pulled out on the highway, heading into town, I knew that's why he looked so tired. Cam gets insomnia, which is normal, I guess, but this is the sort of stuff that keeps him awake at night.

Oh, wait, let me guess, I said. Did you stay up all night hacking the code again, babe? I mean, since you are the world's foremost hacker and all, right? I said, trying so hard not to laugh, but I couldn't help it. Oh, laugh all you like, little missy, but one day soon . . . , he said. Yeah, yeah, yeah . . . , I said, wishing we could just keep driving—right through town, and the next town, and the next.

Three percent. That's the other thing—Cam drives me crazy with talking about how we can only see 3 percent of reality with our eyes. Like, he's always going on about the other 97 percent, about how, if you think about how much can be seen with a microscope, that's the tip of the iceberg. So he started in again, first thing Monday morning on our way to school, and I go, Cam, if I had a dollar for every time you've mentioned this, and he goes, All I'm saying is, can you imagine what the other 97 percent looks like? And go, Cam. I imagine it all the time—what do you think I do when I draw?, thinking, *Me—of all people, how did I end up with such a geek?*

The other thing Cam always talks about is the grid: he loves the idea of this world, this underworld with all these revolutionaries who live entirely off the grid, preparing for the Internet Apocalypse or whatever; I don't know what. But Cam always says the next Che Guevara is going to be a hacker, and that hacker Che will have to use guerilla warfare tactics, always on the move, hiding out in the virtual jungles. According to Cam, hacker Che is out there—maybe even driving me to school, and I'm just like, *Dude*, you are no Che Guevara, okay? Anyhow.

Just before we got to school, I asked Cam, Which would be easier to hack into, NASA or Facebook? Facebook, he said, pulling into the parking lot, and I go, What makes you say that? Because I've done it, he said, turning off the ignition, patting my thigh, and I started laughing, and he goes, Don't believe me? I looked at him and go, *No.*

He grabbed his bag from the back, and he goes, Listen, Thee. I know you love me for my rugged looks and scorching hot bod, but, for your information, missy, I am one of the world's foremost hackers, and ohmygod, I totally lost it, laughing at his rugged bit, forget the scorching bod part. Deep down, he's the most humble guy in the whole world, but you wouldn't know it, hearing him talk smack. Then he goes, I'm telling you, one of the world's foremost hackers is living right here, in a quiet little town in upstate New York. Really, why do you think we had to move here, of all the places in the world? he said, and then first bell rang.

Cam's such a goof, I couldn't stop laughing, getting out of the car, and he goes, You think I'm kidding, huh? Then he grabbed my arm and started swinging me around, and I almost tripped, and Cam had to grab me to keep me from falling on the ground. I thought he had me, too, but he didn't, and we both fell down. Smooth, right? So we're on the ground, right in front of school, with all these kids walking past us. And even though it's Monday morning, and we still have an entire semester to go before summer vacation, I don't care about any of it, because I don't want to be anywhere but exactly where I am. That's the first time I realized that it's all the moments I don't have pictures of that stay with me the most.

## TUESDAY, APRIL 5, 2011
## (TWENTY HOURS LATER)

Like it wasn't bad enough, being worried sick and completely pissed off, barely able to sleep all night, the next day, Tuesday, Mr. Jenssen took my phone away in sixth period. It wasn't my fault, either. What happened was, right after he took attendance, someone's phone went off, and he stopped writing on the board, and he turned around with this exasperated look. He's this small-ish guy and very beige—when I think of Mr. Jenssen, I think of beige. Like he always wears Dockers and beige button-down shirts and brown shoes, and he probably has a beige wife and a couple beige kids, too. Anyhow, you could tell Jenssen was in a mood, because he turned around and said, Whose phone is that? Because they're really coming down; we've got all these new rules about phones, so we're not even allowed to bring them to class. But of course I did, because if Cam called, I wasn't going to miss his call, no way.

Thing is, I wanted to know who it was, too. Because as soon as I heard this eerie tap-tapping snare drum sound, I knew it was Bauhaus—someone in class had Bauhaus for a ringtone, and I was like, *Wow. Is there actually someone cool in this class?* I mean, that was strange enough, but their phone kept ringing and ringing, and each ring, the ringtone got louder, and by then, the whole class was looking around, and Jenssen was about to pop a vein in his neck. But by the looks on everyone's faces, you could tell no one knew whose phone it was, so Jenssen started walking around the room, everyone watching him, and then he goes, *I said*, whose phone is that? Who brought their phone to class?

No one answered. Everyone just stared at their hands, and by the fifth ring, it stopped, but he was *really* annoyed. He waited for like thirty seconds, and then, finally, Jenssen goes, We'll wait to start class when someone tells me whose phone that is, and he started walking up and down the rows, waiting. Then it went off again, same song, and then I was like, *Oh, shit*, because it sounded like it was coming from my phone, beneath my desk. I reached for it, thinking someone must've put my bag on top of their phone, but when I pulled my bag over, it *was* my phone. I reached inside my bag, trying not to let Jenssen see, and I felt it in my hands, ringing—I didn't know what to say, because that's not my ringtone—I *swear*, that is not my ringtone.

I mean, yes, it was my phone, but I'm telling you, my ring-tone is the Cramps' "Goo Goo Muck." I just changed it last weekend—it's another inside joke—it's this shirt of Cam's, see. Cam has this old shirt, and because it's so shrunk now, he's been letting me wear his dad's old Cramps *Bad Music For Bad People*

T-shirt: so fucking cool. Before that ringtone, I had the Ting Tings' "That's Not My Name"—still love that song. And before that, it was "Black Balloon" by the Kills: love. And before the Kills, I had Bowie's "Life on Mars?" for ages, because it was my theme song, but anyhow.

I spaced out for a few seconds, thinking about that, and then Jenssen goes, Miss Denny, give it to me: here, holding out his hand, so I gave him my phone, and he turned it off before he put it in his desk drawer and went back to the board. I heard one of the guys in the back of the room make some sort of joke, and I was so embarrassed. And a minute later, there was this guitar riff, coming from the front of the room. Jenssen turns around with this look, like, not again, and says, What is that? And Ricky Meyers—he's such a goof, he goes, I think it's Bauhaus, and everyone starts laughing. No, Ricky's not a goof. What I mean is goofs are the kids who try to be class clowns or whatever, and doofs, they don't try. Ricky doesn't have to try, that's what I'm saying.

Anyhow, Jenssen goes, Who now?, and his neck started turning red, so I said, I think it's my phone. In your desk. We all watched him, too—everyone saw Jenssen turn it on and turn it off. So he took my phone out of his desk and turned it on, waiting, then he turned it off and went back to the board. A minute later, it happened again: Bauhaus. But this time, it was loud, like, really loud. Maybe it's broken? one of the guys said. I think it was Josh Bolton. I don't know who said it, but then Mr. Jenssen curled his finger at me, saying, Thea, please take your phone to the office.

So I grabbed my bag and took my phone and I walked out. I started heading for the office, down the main hall. It's this long hall with a glass case that runs the whole length, with all the statues the school has ever won. It's crazy, because the school was built in the fifties, the main building, at least, so there are photos that go back to the days of black-and-white, like ghosts of teenagers past. I was looking at some of their faces, and all of sudden, I heard this . . . it was a chorus of cell phones. Rounds—that's what it's called, like when you sing, "Row, Row, Row Your Boat" in rounds. Except that every face I passed in the glass case, a phone went off with the exact same ringtone, all playing "Bela Lugosi's Dead." You know how the bass line goes, *Doo . . . doo . . . dooooooo*, right? Like how it sounds all sinister, with that Goth snare echoing, and I was just like, *What the fuck is going on?* By the time I got halfway down the hall, it was so loud, I felt like if I turned around, it would pull me under, like an avalanche coming straight for me.

I don't know why, but I broke out laughing, giggling, thinking, *Ohmygod, it's going to get me! Bela Lugosi's going to get me!* And then I just took off, running for the principal's office, like I was running for my life. I couldn't even hear my footsteps on the linoleum, that's how loud it was, and I don't know why, but I started screaming—I'm running and laughing and screaming, and even then, you couldn't hear my voice over the music. I got to the office, I had to stop and lean over to catch my breath, and before I opened the door, I turned around, and I swear—I swear, this gust of wind blew my hair, and I stumbled, getting knocked over by it, like a wave. I know it sounds crazy, because it was, but after the wave passed, a second later, every cell phone stopped. Dead silence for five seconds, and then the fire alarms went off, and then you could hear people going crazy, every room in the entire school, everyone just lost it.

On the bright side, I didn't get in any trouble, because of that. Because it wasn't just my phone, and then everyone was talking about it for the rest of the day. Like as soon as the bell rang, the halls were *insane*: people shouting, and all the teachers had to come out, telling everybody to get to class, because everyone was freaking out. I knew then—I knew it was a sign from Cam. I mean, I have no idea how he did it, but that was the first time. The moment after that wave hit, I turned around and I thought, *What if Cam wasn't kidding? What if he was actually telling the truth?*

I've been having episodes again. I had a fever all weekend, draw-ing in tongues—that's what my grandmother called it. Not Gram, my mom's mom. No, it was my dad's mom, Nanna. She said I used to throw fits, drawing, the way some children threw fits, kicking and screaming on the floor. She said it wasn't normal—I heard her, telling my dad that. She said I should see a doctor, a specialist, and I heard my dad try to play it off, asking her what sort of specialist treats drawing in tongues? Really, Mother, it's not epilepsy, he said, and she goes—I'll never forget this—Nanna goes, Don't be so sure.

Of course I didn't know what epilepsy was at the time, and I could tell it wasn't nice, what she was saying about me, but it's one of my favorite memories about my dad, because I heard him sticking up for me. I'll always remember him saying, Mother, Thea's *artistic*, and Nanna didn't say anything for a minute, thinking about it, and I could hear ice being dropped into a glass. Then she said, She's got a bad head, Michael, and Dad goes, Oh, please, Mother. Enough with the bad head, and I heard her lift her glass, mixing the drink, taking a sip. Then, Mark my words, she said, and I swear, it sounded like a curse. I was about four or five, and hearing that, their entire conversation, I almost blew my cover, pretending I was the CIA's youngest girl spy ever, crouching on all fours, hiding behind the couch in Nanna's sitting room. It took every ounce of self-control I had not to get up and march into the living room, because I was just like, *My head didn't do anything bad, so don't say that!*

Seriously, I got so angry, because I didn't understand what a bad head meant, and I was trying to be so well-behaved, too. Every time we visited Nanna's house in Chicago, where she lived in this huge apartment on East Lake Shore Drive—I'm talking like twenty rooms, the place was so big. And of course my mom stayed home, in New York, making up some excuse, but she'd send me off with my dad for long weekends, always telling me to be on my best behavior. I know why, too, because this other time, I heard Nanna tell some friends of hers that my mother was very pretty, but she simply wasn't cultured. I remember hating that word, *cultured*, because I knew it was being used against my mom, and against me, too, or at least half of me.

Also, it's like Nanna had all sorts of wack ideas about what art was and wasn't. Seriously, she used to love to say, Imagination is a wonderful thing—just so long as you don't get carried away. She said that all the time, and I was about eight or nine when it finally occurred to me, and I asked her, point-blank, Then what is the point of imagination, if you don't get carried away? Then she told me I was *impudent*, and I didn't know what that meant, either, but even then, I knew, deep down, she was afraid of my drawing, how I could get so lost in my own world.

After I got my first camera, I found out she didn't consider photography art, not like painting and sculpture are art—fine art, she always said, photography is not *fine art*. She said, Thea, pay attention. Because if you paid attention, you wouldn't need to take a picture of every last thing, now would you, dear? Nanna said people were taking pictures before they'd taken a moment to look at what was right in front of them, all these special moments they were trying to capture for all eternity. Well, how's this for irony? After all her talk about remembering, after all her rants, Nanna lost her memory. Alzheimer's.

That's what I was thinking, holding my pencil in my hand, when I finally heard him: Thea? Thea . . . yo? I didn't hear him before—I didn't hear Cam saying my name, three, four times, and then I about jumped off my chair like, Oh! He'd been watching me, sitting at my desk, drawing, and he goes, You didn't hear me, did you? I go, No. What's up? And he goes, Can we listen to something else? I said, What's wrong with Bauhaus? I love this song, and Cam goes, I know you do. Because you put it on repeat two hours ago, before you started drawing. Then he goes, I hate to have to tell you this, Thee, but Bela Lugosi's dead. He's dead, he's dead, he's *dead*, Cam said, standing up, walking over to my iPod.

I looked at him and made this face, like, Ha, ha, ha, but come on, two hours? I'd been out of it for two whole hours? I was just like, *Nuh-uh*, then I looked at the clock, and it was almost eight—it really was two hours. Poor Cam, it must've been like Chinese water torture listening to "All We Ever Wanted Was Everything" over and over and over, not wanting to bother me while I was working.

So I told him, Sorry, I was just thinking about my grandmother, Nanna, how she used to say I had a bad head, and he said, That's not true. And it was so sweet of him, I go, I wish she could hear you say that, and he stopped twirling the dial, picking a different playlist and hitting play. Then he walked over, and he goes, Nope. Good head, but you've got a . . . bad *ass*! Then he grabbed my arm and pulled me over on my bed, and he put me across his legs, saying, A very, very bad ass, and he was about to start spanking me, so I started screaming, Stop it, Cam! Stop! And then, out of nowhere, my mom starts knocking on the door: Thea? Thea, what's going on?

Then, when she opened my door and stuck her head in, ohmygod . . . the look on her face, seeing me, spread across Cam's lap, and Cam's hand in the air, and she looked at us, and we both looked at her, no one saying a word. Then, finally, Cam goes—his hand still in the air, right—he goes, S'up, Renee? I had no idea what was about to happen, and my mom goes, Just checking, and then closed the door! I couldn't even believe it—I go, Mom, come back! Mom, help!

No word. No call, no text, no e-mail, nothing. For twenty-four hours, I kept checking every ten seconds. Couldn't eat, couldn't sleep, and then, finally, Wednesday morning, Karen called before I left for school to let me to know she was calling the police. And I knew—of course she had to call the police, it'd been two days. But somehow, I couldn't believe she'd actually make the call, because that would mean Cam was really missing. Until then—even then, after she called—I kept expecting him to walk in the door any second. But all I could do was nod, and tell her I was here if she needed me, and then I hung up the phone. Sitting on my bed, I was just like—numb. I kept staring at the ground, thinking, *This isn't happening, this isn't really happening. . . .*

When my cell rang again, ten seconds later, I was sure it was her, but instead it was an e-mail from Cam. I was so relieved, ohmygod, I didn't know if I was going to scream or cry, and I checked the message, but it didn't say anything. It was a link—there wasn't any message from him, nothing, so I just stared at the phone, thinking, *What are you doing? What is this?* And I was furious, you know. I was so worried about him, it's no time for fun and games, but that's all I had. So I went to my computer, and I clicked the e-mail, and it was a YouTube link. So I clicked and it started, and at first, it was so fuzzy and grainy, I couldn't make out what was happening. I mean, it looked all night-vision *Blair Witch* herky-jerky motion, green crotches and . . . penis—ohmygod, it was a guy's penis—and I looked up and my mouth fell open. Because it wasn't just some guy, it was *us*. Only it wasn't us—me and Cam—it was a sex video someone made of us. All I could do was cover my mouth.

Because it was a video of the two of us from Monday afternoon . . . having sex. It was only fifteen seconds, but I couldn't shut my mouth, so I just got up, off my chair, and I stepped away from the desk, shaking my head no. No, no, no . . . denying it—I don't even know who I was denying it to. I mean, yes. Yes, yes, it was my face, my body, my—my pussy. God, what word do you use to talk about your own sex? I don't know, especially since it's not true. I mean, even if it was real—yes, that really happened; yes, we really had sex, but it still wasn't true. What I mean is that there are things that cannot be shared, no matter what you see, but watching, I felt tingly all over, then numb, and then my mouth started watering like I was about to heave. *That's not us*, I thought, swallowing back.

Then my phone rang again, and I almost jumped out of my skin, checking. It was Karen again, so I didn't know if I should answer or not, because all I could think was that she was about to tell me she was watching the video, too. So my hands were totally shaking when I answered, and then Karen said, It's me, Thea. Just wanted to let you know that I spoke with the police and I'm filing a missing person report. Okay, I said, still staring at my computer screen, and Karen said, They'd like to talk to you, as well. Is that all right? My stomach let out this huge gurgle, but I said, Yes, of course. I waited, holding my breath, but she didn't say anything about the video, and then I asked her if she wanted me to go to the police station with her, and she said no, they'd be in touch.

So after we hung up, like two seconds later, I turned back to my computer, and the video was gone. No, seriously, it was gone. There was an error message, and I tried checking the history, but it wasn't in the history. So right way, I reached for my phone, but then Cam's e-mail was gone, too—both the video and his e-mail were gone. Honestly, I clicked and clicked, looking for it, like, *What the fuck?* Nothing. I must have been dreaming—a waking dream, delirious, I—I don't know. Too little sleep, too much stress—I don't know what. But I swear, it was real: I saw it. So I sat down again, and I sat there, until my mom knocked, telling me to get a move on or I'd miss the bus. I mean, seriously, I felt like I was losing my mind, and I was this close to shouting, Mom, there's a video of me and Cam having sex on YouTube, you think I care about *the bus*? But I didn't say a word.

The cops came right before lunch. I got a pink note at the end of fifth period that said I needed to go to the principal's office, soon as the bell rang. So I went to the office, and the secretary told me Cheswick was waiting for me in the conference room. So then I walked to the conference room and knocked, and Cheesy, Principal Cheswick says, Come in. So I walk in, and Cheswick's standing there in front of the door, and he says, Thea, shut the door, please. So I shut the door, and Cheswick says, Thea, sit down please, and there's this guy, standing there at the end of the table, smiling at me, and Cheesy says, Thea, this is Detective Knox, and the man says, Hello, Thea. He's old, but kinda good-looking, I guess: tall, dark hair, dark eyes. Anyhow, the cop, Knox or whatever, he goes, Thea, I'd like to ask you a few questions, if that's all right? I couldn't even answer. I mean, can you believe they say that? Like when he said that to me, I was so weirded out, because that's what you hear on TV, and I kept thinking, *This isn't happening, this isn't really happening. . . .* But it was.

Is this about Cam? I said, and Detective Knox nodded and he goes, Have you seen or spoken to him since Monday night? I said, No, and he said, Cameron hasn't contacted you at all? I said, No. And he goes by Cam—nobody calls him Cameron. He nodded and smiled, like he genuinely appreciated me telling him, then he goes, Do you have any idea where Cam is, Thea? I said, No, and he said, You don't have any idea where he could be? I go, No, I have no idea. But is it true that if you don't find someone in the first twenty-four hours, you probably won't ever find them? It just came out, and Knox balked, then he tilted his head side to side, yes and no. He goes, In child abduction cases, yes, but Cam's not a child; he's of legal age. And as far as we know, he hasn't been kidnapped.

I didn't know what to say, so I just stared at my feet, and Knox waited before he said anything. Then he goes, Thea, I'm sorry to have to ask you so many personal questions, but how long have you two been dating, you and Cam? I could feel Knox shoot Cheesy a look, like, whatever he was hearing in this room, it went no further. Knox wasn't asking Cheesy, either, he was telling him; confidential. I said, Since the beginning of school, last year, and he goes, Did you know each other before then? And I said, No, and he said, So you never spoke before that? No, I said, and he goes, Never saw each other around? I go, No, I'd never seen him before that, and he goes, It's not a very big school. Big enough, I said, and he's new. Knox said, His mother told me they moved here from California, and I nodded yes.

Then he said, Cam's a senior? And I nodded yes, and he goes, What year are you? I go, Sophomore. He goes, And how did you two meet? So I told him, I said, He was my geometry tutor, and Knox goes, I'm told he's some sort of math whiz, is that right? And I said, Yeah, that's what Cam keeps telling me, too. Knox smiled, and he said, So Cam was your tutor, and then you started dating? I said, We were friends, then we started going out, and he smiled, trying to put me at ease, I think.

Then he goes, Does Cam have many friends in school? I said, Cam gets along with everybody, and the cop goes, What about you? And I go, Me? I can't stand anybody, I said, and he smiled. Opposites attract, he said. Guess so, I said, shrugging. So there was no one Cam had any fights with, no one who had any grudges? And I said, No. No one. I told you, he got along with everyone. Knox goes, And Cameron—Cam, sorry—he never talked about running away? I go, All the time, but not without me, then he kind of perked up and he goes, So you two talked about running away together? I said, We talked about traveling together, all over the world. That's not running away, that's running to, I said. And where did you talk about going, running to? Knox asked, grabbing the back of the plastic bucket chair in front of him with both hands. Everywhere, I said, shrugging again, because that was private, you know? I didn't have to tell him that.

Last bell for sixth period rang, and I was going to be late, so I looked at him like, Anything else? Knox shook his head no and said, Why don't I walk you out? I nodded okay, and he followed me out of the office. There was no one in the hall by the time we walked out, then he looked at me and said, One more question. Did anything unusual happen that day, when you last saw him? No, I said, not that I can think of, and he said, You two didn't have a fight that night? I almost said it, too. I almost said, Cam's a hacker, not a fighter, but I didn't.

I said, No. I mean, we've had fights, but who doesn't?, and he nodded, like he agreed with me. I go, But why did you think we had a fight? I just had to ask, he said, pulling out his card and handing it to me. Please call me if you need anything, or if you think of anything? Okay, I said, and then Knox said, Thank you, and he turned toward the doors.

That afternoon, after school, I just kept staring at his card, the whole way home—second time I found myself taking the bus home, feeling . . . *so alone*, you know? I mean, I couldn't get any homework done, I couldn't concentrate, I couldn't do anything. I just sat at my desk, staring at Hubble all night—our notebook, that's what we call it, Hubble.

Cam gave it to me for Christmas. It's got this thick, beautiful paper, and it's oversized, it's perfect, and we share it. Like I take one page, and he takes the opposite page, and we swap, back and forth. But I take the left side, because Cam's left-handed, so he has to write upside down, otherwise. Because it's spiral, he'd have to write over the spiral, you know what I mean? The reason we call it Hubble is because, well, after he gave it to me, Cam said, What should we call it? And I said, You mean give the notebook a name? What, like Betty? And Cam goes, *No*. I mean, yes: not Betty, but something. Because *notebook* seems so . . . impersonal, you know?

He was right. I didn't even need to think about it, because he was right; we had to call it something. I looked at the page where he'd already written an entry, and it looked upside down to me, even though it was right-side up to him. It made me think about the stars, how Cam always loved to say the amazing thing about looking at the stars is you're looking into the future and the past at the same time, and how, somewhere up there, in the sky, the Hubble Telescope is taking pictures of things we can't imagine. What about . . . I started to speak, and then felt kinda stupid, so I shut my mouth. Tell me, he said, and I said, What about Hubble? Cam balked, hearing that, then he smiled this big, big smile. And his smile said yes: perfect. Then, of course—I mean, I didn't say it, but I was just like, *Ohmygod, I just named our notebook Hubble? That has got to be the geekiest idea I've ever had in my entire life.*

Anyhow, we've been working on it since Christmas, and Hubble's everything: it's photos, collage, pencil sketches, ink drawings, inside jokes, our entire universe. Cam even writes these ridiculous formulas—talk about hieroglyphics, don't ask me if they're real or he's screwing around—our video game ideas, our scripts, everything. Everything starts here, goes here, belongs right here. Because it's our own world, you know? It's a world just big enough for two, and the day he left—the day he *disappeared*— god, that's so hard to say, the day Cam disappeared. Anyhow, that day, for the first time, I couldn't put anything down. Cam handed Hubble back on Monday afternoon, and it was my turn, left side—except that both sides were these huge blank white pages, and I had this pang in my chest, thinking it might be that way from now on. For the first time, those two blank pages really fucking scared me.

I kept staring at it, completely spaced out, like somehow the notebook would tell me the answer, solve the mystery of my universe, let my boyfriend know I was going to kill him if this was some sort of joke. *Because trust me, I'm not laughing, Cam. You hear me?* I don't know if I said that out loud or not, but then I looked up and saw that I'd written it, in our notebook; these big block letters: **I'M NOT LAUGHING!!!!!!!!!!!!**

Well, I'm not what you'd call a party girl. I mean, I used to love going to parties, but now, it's like, binge drinking with jocks just isn't my scene. Crazy me, right? I mean, it's like when you're in junior high, you think a high school party will be *so cool*, right? Well, hate to break it to you, but watching a bunch of junior and senior girls chugging vodka and Red Bull is so far from cool, you stand there thinking, *Is this it? Really?* But then, I don't know, somehow you figure you might as well join them, because the truth is so sad, and that's exactly what you were trying to avoid with all your daydreaming.

But the thing is, Cam gets invited all the time; every weekend he's invited to two or three parties, and it'd be rude if he didn't stop by once in a while. So Saturday night, he wanted me to join him. And when he asked me, on Tuesday or whenever, I said I'd go, thinking, if I'm with him, I can do anything, right? I thought

I'd be fine, but by Saturday night, when he picked me up, god, I didn't want to go. But then again, I did, because Cam wanted me there, with him, and wherever he is, is where I want to be.

Cam said it again, when we got there. He was just like, Thee, try to have a good time, all right? And I was like, That's what I'm going to do, and I did, too. I did try. And it was fine, it really was. I talked to a few people, and everyone was cool, but honestly, I didn't know what I was doing there, standing in somebody's parents newly redecorated colonial Americana kitchen, drinking Coors or whatever.

Cam can't see it, but I'm telling you, people still look at me like I'm this pixie thing—on a good day—they don't get what Cam sees in me, when he could have any girl in school he wanted. Like there are still people who call me Addams, short for Wednesday Addams, because they think I'm so Goth. But the thing is—I mean what annoys me most is that they don't even know what Goth means. Seriously, they look at my hair, and I'm just like, Dude, it's a Louise Brooks bob, okay? We're talking silent-film star and one of the original It Girls, not the Sisters of Mercy. Except I can't even say that, because they don't know who Louise Brooks or who the Sisters of Mercy are, drr.

Anyhow, there we are, crammed into the kitchen with a hundred other bodies, and I look over, and it happens again. It's not like making time stop, it's more like the world's a merry-go-round, but just the two of us, me and Cam. Like the world keeps spinning, but we stand still. So I look over at Cam, thinking, *It's happening—it's happening again*, and there's this huge smile on his face, and I know exactly what he's thinking, because we're thinking the exact same thing. It's private, and it's ours, and we're grinning at each other, thinking the same dirty thought, like there's no one else in the world.

And then none of it mattered. Everything, all the shit that happened last year, the kids from school, all my old friends, it doesn't matter what people think, what they do or don't know about me; none of it matters. Because Cam knows me, and he loves me, and I know him, and I love him more than anything in this whole world. And for a second, like a fraction of a second, the ground disappeared beneath my feet.

## THURSDAY, APRIL 7, 2011
## (THREE DAYS LATER)

It's not just me, okay? Things have been happening all over town, and at first, people thought it was random, but not me. I never thought it was random, and whether I was right or wrong, everything related to Cam, like he was sending me signs. The first sign was Thursday morning, and it was so strong, it felt like a magnet pulling us off the road. Seriously, I was sitting next to the window, with Hubble open in my lap, when the whole bus swerved, knocking me on my side. When I looked up, every head was turned, looking out the left-side window, because someone had driven right through the dividing wall, along the opposite side of the highway. It's just a tall, orange plastic net, nothing that could hurt anybody, but it had been there as long as I'd been taking the bus.

I had my headphones on, so I don't know who saw it first, but in two seconds, every kid on the bus was jumping out of their seat, trying to get a look at the gash in the wall, and instantly, each little brain on the bus started trying to solve the crime. Because the strangest thing was, the car's tire marks went on and on, like they must have crashed right into the horizon, because there was nothing out there, it was this empty field that went on for miles. One look, and you knew it was no accident—someone did it on purpose, and then they just kept right on going.

So there I was, gawking with everyone else, trying to piece it together. I mean, really, who did it, and what would possess them, and where the hell did they go, and most of all, why? And then, on second thought, *Why had it never happened before?* It was like someone cut a hole in something bigger than the wall, and it was a revelation to all of us, everyone on the highway, every driver slowing down to look, all asking the same question. Who knew you could just get up and do something crazy like that and get away with it? And now that they had, what were the rest of us supposed to do?

You could feel it, too, you know. All morning, you could just feel it, like when teachers talk about barometric pressure or things that affect the moods of kids in their classes, it was like that, like something weighing you down or something just not right. All day, the whole school, every class, no one was screwing around, no one was raising their hands, like we'd all been waiting for that knock on the door. And when it finally came, everyone looked up, and the room was so still that Linda Friske, the office aide, looked spooked, sticking her head in the door, holding up a pink slip like it was a white flag. I knew it was for me: everyone knew it was for me. I'd already grabbed my bag and I was halfway to the door before Mrs. Friske called out my name. She waited, holding open the door, and she nodded as I stepped into the hall, then she headed off in the opposite direction, delivering some other message.

The school office is at the end of the main hall, in clear view of the front entrance, and the sun was shining like a spotlight through those thick double doors. I felt this sense of dread, despite the light, and no one had to say it: I knew there was someone to see me. Even stranger, I knew it wasn't Detective Knox. I don't know how; I could just tell it wasn't him, so I took my time. There was no one else in the hall, and I don't know how to explain it, but the building felt scared. I swear, even the electric current quit humming—you know that awful buzzing of fluorescent lights overhead, extending in every direction? Well, for once it was quiet.

When I walked in, the secretaries didn't say anything, not a word. They both just looked at me, and then they quickly looked away, like they knew something and didn't want me to see it in their eyes. Thea, Principal Cheswick said, stepping out of his office, hearing the front door open. So weird: he never stepped out; he never waited; one of the secretaries always buzzed him first, and you were told to take a seat. So something was definitely wrong, and then he said, Come in, opening his office door for me.

Cheswick didn't close the door, but he lowered his voice, telling me there was an agent there who needed to talk to me about Cam. Then, in this voice, like he was trying to stay calm, he goes, FBI, and I looked him in the eye. He has a few questions for you, Thea. You can have a lawyer present or I can go in there with you, whichever you prefer, he said. And if I didn't know any better, deep down, I knew Cheesy was scared. I recommend an attorney, but that will be a few hours, and you'll have to wait here, in the office, he said. And I shook my head no. I said, If you can come in with me, that's fine, and he nodded gravely. So we walked down the hall, and when he opened the conference room door for me, there was a man, standing at the end of the room, in front of the blackboard, with his hands clasped.

And the way he looked at me, it's like he knew me or he'd seen me before, but I didn't know him. And I felt like I should remember him, but I didn't—I'd never seen this guy in my life— really strange. So we walked in, and Cheesy goes, Thea, this is Special Agent Foley, and the man looked at me and said the same thing: Hello, Theadora, I'm Special Agent Foley, FBI. He took out his badge, showed it to me, and then he said, I'd like to ask you a few questions, if that's all right? Where's Detective Knox? I said, looking around, and he goes, Detective Knox, yes, I'm told you spoke. But the FBI will be taking over the case from here, he said, and I swear his voice, it—it *slithered*. The guy had this snake voice, I'm not kidding.

Not only that, he did this thing, it was like—*ugh* . . . he claps his hands, then he presses his thumbs together, and then he slowly gyrates thumb against thumb, 'round and 'round—so disgusting! Like he's jerking his thumbs off—I'm sorry, but it's true. Seriously, I don't know if he's into little boys or girls or animals or what, but there was something so wrong about this guy. Twisted. And he looked at me like he could read my mind or something, so I couldn't even look at him. Then he goes, Please, pointing one hand at the chair. Sit, Theadora.

Just as we stepped into the conference room and sat down, one of the secretaries knocked on the door, and Cheesy got up to answer. He leaned out, and said, Would you two excuse me for a few minutes? Behind me, I could hear a woman's voice whisper. Then Cheesy said, It's Superintendent Phelps. I need to take this call, and then I'll be right back. The FBI guy smiled, folding his hands, and said, Of course. Take your time, principal, and the door closed. And then the guy just stared at me, smiling. Twenty seconds of that was about all I could take, because there was something really creepy about him, before I said, Go ahead and ask me whatever you want. He said, Wouldn't you like a lawyer or some advocate present? No, I said, no lawyers, and he smiled like he understood what I was saying. Well, the problem is—one of many problems is, I should say, that you're a minor, Theadora. I said, You bring in a lawyer, and I will never ever talk to you. The guy looked at me for a moment, didn't blink, and then, suddenly, he relaxed and said, Of course.

All right, Theadora, he said, and he removed a computer and pointed the camera toward me while he pressed an audio program, recording our conversation while the video's lens stayed focused on me. Again, he moved so quickly, it almost felt like he knew everything I was going to say, before I said a word. This is Special Agent Foley; it's 8:37 a.m. on Thursday, April 7, 2011, and I am interviewing Theadora Denny, who has stated in no uncertain terms that she will not speak on record if a lawyer is present. Is that correct, Theadora? he asked, and it's so weird, feeling yourself being recorded that way, knowing other people are going to watch this tape, hold you to it. Yes, I said, that's correct. If you a bring a lawyer in here, I won't say one word. Good, Foley said, and please, sit down, Theadora. And I didn't look at him, but I could feel his eyes, watching me pull out a chair and take a seat. In that case, I will record our conversation for the purposes of our investigation, as it will not be admissible in any court of law, and I said, Fine. So, he said, given the circumstances, we will proceed with the interview and expect Principal Cheswick to return to the room at any time. The way he looked at me, though, I'm telling you, there was something not right about this guy, and not just his hands. His suit, too.

It was hard to look at him, but physically, he's got a little nose, and thin lips, tidy, short hair, parted on the side, and beady eyes—kind of reminds me of a weasel. Actually, that's exactly what he looks like, a weasel man in a fancy suit. Seriously, I took one look, and I was just like, *Who knew the bogeyman wore bespoke?* Besides, like, how could he be FBI and afford a suit like that? Then he smiled, like he knew what I was thinking, but I just looked at him. I go, So you're here because you think Cam's been kidnapped? Not exactly, he said. No, I'm here because we believe Cam's been kidnapped because he was breaking into top-security government sites, and then he disappeared the very day that the NSA was about to arrest him. I go, NSA? And he goes, National Security Agency, and I didn't mean to, but when he said that, I go, Oh, *bullshit*, and I started laughing, but he just stared at me until I stopped.

Honestly, I was speechless. Because it was so totally and completely outrageous, but Foley just stared, and then my heart stopped. It stopped for, for I don't know how long. Then it started up again. Beat. Beat, beat. Beat, beat, beat, thump, thump, thump, like my heart was going to pound right out of my chest. Then my stomach made a fist so tight, I couldn't swallow, I couldn't even move. Theadora, did John ever mention any work he was doing, anything special he was working on? Yes, I said, looking up, not knowing why he called him John. All the time, I said. Oh? he said, raising his brow, tilting his head to the side. Can you tell me about that work? he asked, smiling at me like we had all the time in the world. Yes, I said, smiling back and then leaning forward: his car. He likes to work on his car. Cam stays up all night working on his car sometimes, I said. *Yes*, Foley said, almost drawling the word. I see, he said, winking like we had some inside joke. Interestingly enough, he said, We're looking through his car now, and I almost shivered at the idea of that guy touching Cam's car. Speaking of his car, it seems his mother found it at your house, is that right? Yes, I said. But you didn't see him after he left your house Monday afternoon, is that also right, Theadora? Yes, I said. Strange, don't you think? he said, and I just bit the inside of my lip. I wonder if maybe he returned to see you again or he had something to tell you . . . ? I don't know, because I didn't see him again, I said, locking my jaw and looking away.

He goes, Tell me, did John ever talk to you about hacking? I looked up at him, shocked to hear him say the word, but then I covered, and I go, No. And he goes—he raised his brow, because I think he knew I was lying, he goes, Never? And I go, No. *Never.* And Foley goes, How odd, considering you two seemed so close, and I said, How would you know? Foley cocked his head and he goes, Yes, you have a point, Theadora. How would I know that?

Foley sat there, staring at me, until I looked up at him like, *What? Say it, if you have something to say*, and he said, What I do know is John's computer is also missing. Do you know where it might be, Theadora? I said, It's probably with Cam, and then he smiled that twisted smile of his, and Foley goes, Indeed, his voice sidewinding across the table, totally creepy. In any case, Theadora, I need to ask you a few more questions about John—. Cam, I said, correcting him, and Foley smiled. Ah, you call him Cam. Yes, he said. Well. Trust me, Theadora, I want to find John just as badly as you do. And I will find him, he said, swirling a black leather portfolio with his index finger before opening it, fanning it out with both hands. And then, like he'd been practicing this move his entire life, he pulled a silver pen from his inside pocket and removed its cap with an expensive popping sound. Then questions, the same questions over and over again: How long have you two known each other? How did you meet? Over and over . . .

When I got outside, right before second bell, the whole school was buzzing, and when I walked past the library, heading to my locker, I saw there was a crowd gathered. I could tell something *big* was going down, and honestly, my first thought was a terrorist attack or something, but when I finally got a peek and saw the television on the movable AV stand, it was a broadcast of the Albany news. They sent a crew to report on the hole in the dividing wall on the highway, and if that isn't enough, they even sent in a helicopter to show an aerial view of the tire tracks. And the really bizarre thing is that from the air, you can see these big, thick black tire tracks, all the way from the highway, into an empty field that looks like it goes on forever. Then, about a half mile from the highway, the tracks end. They just end, like the car disappeared through a black hole or something.

The reporter, this woman, was broadcasting live, from the highway, and she was laughing at something the guy reporter, back in the studio, was saying about it being as big as a baseball field and how it was one of those mysteries like those crop circles. All of a sudden, I got the chills and started shivering, like so frickin' weird. And then Hicky, Tyler Hendricks, goes, Holy shit! They flew in a *helicopter*? Then Toby Brock turns to him and he goes, *Dude*, we're famous, and I don't know why, but all the hair on my arms stood up, and I got the chills.

It's pretty weird that me and my mom both have boyfriends now. I mean, I don't know that Raymond's really her boyfriend, they're so on-again, off-again. I keep hoping she'll end it, but she doesn't, and I just don't get it. They're nothing alike, and they don't have anything in common, really, and Raymond—ugh, has *the worst* taste, okay? Just the shittiest eighties music you've ever heard. Like, sometimes I'll be sitting in my room, drawing, and I'll hear this awful guitar riff, like a song that's so bad, I have to cover my nose like, *What is that smell?* And then, sure enough, I hear Rain Man pull into the parking lot, blasting Bad Company or whatever with his windows down, and I cover my face, like, *Ohmygod, that's who my mom's going out with?*

Then there are times when it works in my favor. Like Sunday, when they went to see one of Rain Man's friends in Albany. Mom said they wouldn't be home until seven or eight, at the earliest, and I should make myself a sandwich for dinner. So I about pissed my pants when I heard "The Boys Are Back in Town" blaring out front—you know that song from *Toy Story*? "The boys are back in town, the boys are back in town," ugh—I love *Toy Story*, but I hate that song; I hate it. Anyhow.

It was about two-thirty, and we were in my bed. I mean, we're totally naked, but I was under the sheet, lying on my stomach, with my head at the foot of the bed and my feet in Cam's lap. He was drawing high-tops on each foot, using one of my silver metallic pens to draw rivets, and I don't know what made me think of it, but I go, Cam, can I ask you something? I got up on my elbows and I turned to look up at him, and he just smiled at my feet, inspecting his work. Hold still, he said.

So I waited, watching him, until he put the pen down, and then leaned over, blowing on my ankle to make the ink dry, and then he looked at me, waiting to hear what I had to say. I wasn't sure I should ask, but then I did. I said, How did your dad die? You've never told me, I said, sitting up, on my elbows. In almost six months, all he'd ever told me was his dad died when he was a little boy, and in all that time, I never asked. Finally, lying beside him, naked, I just felt like we'd reached the point I should know, you know? Cam didn't say anything at first, he just looked at me, and then he started twisting my ankle to get me to turn on my stomach, so he could draw the back side of my high-tops.

When he first started drawing shoes on my feet, when we first started going out, I used to be *so* self-conscious. Like whenever Cam'd twisted my ankle, trying to turn me over, so he could draw the back, I wouldn't turn over, because I didn't want him to see my butt all . . . *butt.* I'll never forget the first time he tried to get me to turn on my stomach, and I wouldn't do it, and he goes, Turn over, and I go, Why? He goes, Because I want to look at you, and that was it. I didn't want to, but he asked, so I did.

I turned over, on my stomach, and then I spread my legs. I felt so, so—scared, you know? So I turned around, looking at him, and he was staring. Just kneeling on my bed, staring at me, like that, and then, seeing the look on my face, he smiled and spanked my butt, then he fell on top of the bed, beside me, putting his face right up next to mine. He leaned forward, and I closed my eyes, because I thought he was going to kiss me, but then he took my nose in his mouth, sucking my nose, and I screeched. Stop it! Stop, you dirty nose-sucker! Gross!

Anyhow, Sunday, I turned over, resting my chin on my hands, and I always think about how we share everything, but I couldn't help thinking maybe I shouldn't have asked that. Then he said, Heart attack. My dad had a heart attack in the shower, he said, and I figured he wasn't upset that I asked, because I could hear him giving the silver metal pen a good shake, stirring up the ink. I wasn't going to say anything more about it, but then he said, I don't remember, except that at the funeral, I heard somebody say that it's quite common for men to have heart attacks in the shower. I don't know if that's true, but for a couple years, I was afraid of taking a shower. I go, What's your excuse now? like the words just started coming out, without my thinking about them. Ohmygod. I felt so terrible, too, because we were talking about his dad, and I shouldn't have made a joke. Awful, I know. And I turned my head to look at him, wincing, and then he just stared at me, didn't say a word for like a minute. I really started worrying, too, and then he goes, Oh, Thea made a funny, and I go, I am so sorry—I didn't mean it like that, and he goes, Are you? Are you really sorry? And I said, Yes, I am. And he goes, Well, then, let's have a look. Stand up for me. Because he knew I wouldn't say no, you know?

But when he said that, I got all tense. I still get embarrassed, being naked in front of him, and I was trying to think of an excuse not to get up. Up, he said. I want to see my latest masterpiece. So I got up and stood on my bed, and I was ready to get under the covers again, and he says, Turn around, and I'm like, Cam, no, kinda whining, you know? He goes, Let me see the back, and I said, That's the problem! Why do I always have to be the one to turn around? Thee, please? Two seconds, he said, crawling forward, crouching right behind me, inspecting his work—wasn't even really looking at me, either—like he was more into his work than me, and I was like, *Cam. What's up with that?* Then he goes, Yep. I think they're done, looking at the new style of shoes he'd drawn on both feet. Come on, he said, getting up and holding out his hand for me. We'll take a picture.

We always take a Polaroid of the shoes he draws, so I got up and got my camera out of the closet. I used to keep notebooks— well, I still keep notebooks with all these collages I make of pictures I rip out of magazines. So one time, I was showing one of my notebooks to Cam, telling him how I fantasize about having a closet full of shoes, all stored in their original boxes, with a Polaroid tacked to each box, so you can see a picture of the shoes. And then Cam said, Why don't you do that now? I said, Because

I don't have a closet full of amazing shoes, that's why. So then, one day, we were hanging out, and I don't know why, but Cam started drawing a shoe on my foot. And it was cool; it was like this paisley high-top, so I asked him to draw me another, and he did. And when he was done, he had me stand on the kitchen table so he could take a picture.

So that's what we were doing on Sunday, when I hear this whining guitar solo out in front of the building. Seriously, I'm standing there, naked on our kitchen table, while Cam's working on the best angle for the shot of my shoes, and just as the Polaroid ejects the picture, I hear Ray's car pulling up front. And I screamed, *They're home!* holding out my hand for Cam to help me down. So we sprinted to my room, started throwing our clothes on, knowing we had like twenty seconds, and Cam held up my shirt, shaking it at me, like, You're wearing my shirt, give me my shirt, and I was just like, Let me put my pants on! So I threw his shirt back at him at the same moment he threw my shirt at me, and we ran to the living room, jumped on the couch, and I turned on the TV the second—I mean, the *very second* Mom and Raymond walked in.

Hey, you two, Mom said, and I was just like, Hey, Mom, and Cam goes, Hey, Renee, hey, Raymond. Totally normal, right? And I grabbed the remote from the coffee table, because the news was on. What's up? I asked, meaning, like, why are you home already? Look at this, she said, showing me where she spilled coffee all over her blouse. Just want to change, and then we're going to get a bite to eat. She goes, You two want to join us? And I go, Nah, thanks, we're going to do some work.

So Mom went to change and Ray took a seat on the chair, across from the couch, and I have to say, I was pretty pleased we managed to pull it off in time, just like, damn we're good. Then Rain Man looked over and he goes, S'up Theadorie? And I hate it when he says *S'up*, and I really hate it when he calls me Theadorie. I said, Not much, Ray. What's up with you? He goes, Hanging in there. Great, I said, staring at the TV, and then, fortunately, my mom came right back, wearing jeans and a T-shirt, and I have to say, she looks really good for her age. All right, then, Mom said, putting on her jacket. Shall we? she says, smiling at Ray, and he says, See you, and holds out his hand to Cam, who does a hand slap with him. Have a good night, Cam said, smiling at my mom, and I said, Bye, giving a little wave.

I waited a second, after the door closed, and then I breathed this huge sigh of relief, and I almost bust out laughing. Good thing I didn't, because like a second later, Mom opened the door again and stuck her head in, and I'm just like, *What now?* Mom smiles and goes, Oh, one other thing. You might want to turn your shirt around, the right way, before you take it off again, and then she closed the door. Cam waited to be sure she was gone— both of us just held our breath, waiting to hear her open the car door, and then, after we heard her shut her door, Cam started laughing at me. *Shush!* I said, but I couldn't help laughing, either, I was so busted. Because she knew: ohmygod, the whole time, my mom knew exactly what was going on, but she still left us alone. Well, I have to say, she has her moments. Not many, but some.

But you can't keep anything secret in school. So right away, by the end of the week, all these rumors started flying around. People were saying Cam had run away, that he'd joined a cult, that he was a drug dealer, all sorts of crazy shit, and the thing is, what could I say? And I'm not being paranoid, everyone was looking at me, whispering in the halls when I walked by. People thought I knew where he was, and I was like, Trust me, I have no clue where Cam is, or I'd find him myself. And strangle him.

Detective Knox called again, Friday morning. He asked if he could speak to me; he had a few more questions, and I was like, Wait. I thought you were off the case, and he goes, What gave you that idea? And I go, Agent Foley told me, and he goes, No. FBI's in charge, but I'm still on the case. And I was just like, Good, because I'd so rather deal with Knox than Foley, so I said I could meet him at three, if he could give me a ride home. God, I hate the bus—*I hate it, hate it*—and Knox said that would be fine.

After school, I saw him, two blocks away, standing, leaning on his car, and I walked over, and he opened the door for me. So I got in his car, and I thought we'd have to make small talk: How was school, Thea? Fine, thank you. How was your day, Knox? But no. Right away, soon as he pulls out, he goes, Thea, you didn't tell me you and Cam missed last period Monday afternoon, and I was so busted, I started giggling. I didn't mean to be a smart-ass, really, but right away, I said, Honestly, Knox, I didn't miss last period at all, and he smiled for a second, biting the inside of his lip. Then he goes, What did you do? And I said, We went to my house. Is that a crime? He goes, You were at your house that entire time? And I said, Yes, and he said, And nothing unusual? Nothing Cam said that struck you as odd? I go, Everything Cam says strikes me as odd: that's what I love about him.

So you said you two have been dating since September, he said, pulling out on the highway. And I said, No, we started dating in October, we met in September. September 23, 2010, 3:00 p.m. And then Knox whistled and he goes, Wow. You remember the date and the time, and I actually started blushing. Then, thankfully, his phone rang, and Knox goes, Sorry, one second, and he pulled out his phone. He even answered like you always see them on the TV shows. He goes, Yeah, Knox here— that's exactly what he said. And then I heard a woman's voice, and she sounded upset, and then Knox goes, I'll be right over. He looks at me, and he says, I'm sorry to do this, Thea, but our sitter has to pick her son up from preschool. So I need to stop by my house, before I take you home, and I was just like, Oh, no, what happened to her son?

Knox pulls a U-turn, heading back to town. To be honest, I was relieved not to have to go home, and he says, Guess he stuffed a box of raisins up his nose, and I was like, An entire box of raisins? And Knox just sighed again.

I was cool, but it was awkward for some reason, like I got this feeling there was something he wasn't telling me, and then he says, Do you mind? I said, No, no, that's fine. So you have a kid? He nodded yes. A daughter. How old is she? I said, and he goes, Oh, about your age. After my last comment, I should've just kept my mouth shut, I know, but I didn't. I said, She's my age and you still have a babysitter? Knox didn't say anything: awkward. What's your daughter's name? I said, changing the subject, and Knox looked surprised, and it took him a few seconds before he answered the question: Melody, he said. Her name is Melody.

## SUNDAY, MARCH 20, 2011
## (FIFTEEN DAYS EARLIER)

Karen invited me over for sushi, and of course I should've known that she'd make it herself, but I was so blown away, because I don't know anyone who makes their own sushi, you know? I was like, Karen, you are the coolest mom in the whole world, and she started laughing. More? she asked, seeing me finish everything on my plate, including the pickled ginger, and I said, No, thank you, I'm full. It was delicious, sitting back, realizing I'd made a total pig of myself, but it was so worth it.

Karen reached for her sake glass and she sat back in her chair, smiling, then she goes, That reminds me, and then she left the room and came back with a picture. Something I wanted to show you, she said, handing me a picture, sitting down again. It was a picture of Cam as a little boy. He was so young, with all this long white-blond hair; I don't think he'd ever had it cut. His face was skinny, too, like a kid who's just lost all his baby fat, and he was wearing this red and blue striped shirt, sitting on a cement floor, with all this junk around him, and something on his hands.

What's on his hands? I asked, leaning in, trying to get a better look. Gloves, she said. He's wearing gloves, and just then, Cam walked in, coming back from the bathroom, and he rolled his eyes. I could tell he knew the picture, because the way he nodded his head, like, let's get this over with already. Karen reached for the sake bottle and poured herself another glass, then she goes, One year, just before he turned four, we bought Cam a bicycle for Christmas. Cam was *so excited*, he literally peed his pants, and Cam goes, Is this necessary? Karen waved him off: He loved it—he was over the moon, so happy with his new bike, she said, talking to me. And because he'd woken us up at five o'clock in the morning to open Christmas presents, by ten, we all took a nap. At least I thought we were all taking naps, but, turns out, when we woke up, we found him, sitting in the middle of the living room, with his new bicycle in pieces all over the floor.

I looked at Cam, and he knew I was looking at him, scratching his chopsticks across the pat of wasabi on his plate. It's so funny when I see him like that, like I forget sometimes that there's another side of him, the person he is with his mom, in private. A boy, a son. What happened? I asked, and Karen took another sip, and she goes, Well. I looked at his dad, and then his dad said, Cam, you did a great job taking that bike apart. Now you have to put it back together, and I didn't think either of us took him seriously. But then the damndest thing happened: he did. Took him two days, but that's exactly what he did: Cam put the bike back together. Soon after that, he discovered the vacuum cleaner, and the television, the DVD player, and my computer—. All right, Cam said, and we both smiled. Well, Karen said, pushing her chair out. Listen, you two, it's getting late. Cam, you take Thea home, and I'll clean up, she said, standing.

We got in the car, and he pulled out, and then, when we reached the end of the block, he goes, Thee, I want to show you something, and he turned left instead of right, heading back into town. We passed the high school, and at first, I had this crazy thought that he might want to break in—Cam has a devious side, trust me. But a minute later, we pulled in behind the town baseball field, about eight blocks from school, on the other side of town. It wasn't lit, because they never light the field during winter, and Cam pulled around back, behind these big metal trash bins, which is where a lot of kids drink and get high on weekends. Look at this, he said, turning his high beams on this big gaping hole in the chain-link fence. Isn't that beautiful? he said, staring at this blown-out hole the size of a baseball like it was a double rainbow.

I could tell, just looking at him. I mean, you could see the numbers he was writing on the chalkboard of his brain, computing the pitch, velocity, angles of the baseball bat, writing the whole story of how a single ball tore a hole right through time and space. It turned him on, I could just tell, but it was a little violent, too, almost like he wanted to get his fingers in the gouge and tear it wide open. If the fence was made of flesh, you'd call it carnal, but it was exactly the same, the way his brain hummed, like something you feel in your gut, but deeper, between your legs, just looking at this hole. What are you thinking, Thee? he asked, catching me studying him, and I said, Guess someone hit a home run. Looks like it, he said, smiling, grabbing my hand. Except that no one's played a game here all winter: I asked the groundskeeper. Then someone must've snuck in, I said, shrugging my shoulders.

Cam goes, Thee, did I ever tell you about the bird in the bottle? And I shook my head no. It's an old riddle, he said, and the riddle is this: There's a bird trapped in a bottle. So how do you get the bird out of the bottle without harming either the bird or the bottle? And I thought about it, but shook my head, no idea. One day, I'll figure it out, he said, reaching over, and I go, But that's not the point is it? He didn't answer, and he was so spaced out, staring at the hole in the fence, I actually wondered if we'd sit there all night.

Finally, he said, You know, when I was a little kid, my dad took me to a baseball field, just like this one, near our old house. He brought a kid-size bat for me and this, you know, like, ancient baseball, he said, wrinkling his nose, wrapping his hand around an invisible baseball. It was so heavy and gnarly, he said, and then my dad told me it used to belong to his grandfather, my great grandfather. And that his father had taught him to swing with that same old baseball. Family tradition. So we got started with batting practice, and I kept missing and missing, and I was getting so frustrated, but my dad calmed me down, telling me that's exactly how it was when his dad taught him. And he kept explaining the finer points of hitting, and then, out of the blue, I hit that damn ball so hard, I knocked it out of the field. I'm not kidding, he said, and I couldn't say anything, because he never talked about his family, especially his dad. I just waited, hoping that wasn't the end of it, and it wasn't.

I guess what I'm saying is that when I saw that hole in the fence, it reminded me of that time with my dad, and how, at some point when you're a kid—like every kid in the world, you know, whatever it is, running or jumping or swimming, swinging a bat, at some point, you give it all you got. And when you connect, you honestly believe you are the fastest kid or the kid who jumps the highest or whatever. You are the best of all the kids in the entire world; no one is better, he said. The thing is, that has to be true for at least one kid, right? Some kid really *is* that kid, and I said, Is this leading back to you by any chance? He laughed, biting his tongue between his molars, and then he said, All I can say is—. This should be good, I said, and he said, We never found that baseball. I thought I'd done a terrible thing, but my dad, he . . . he was so proud, said it was the best swing he'd ever seen in his life. He said it was a tribute—I'll never forget that. So, yeah, what I'm saying is that it's hard to be the best kid in the world, and just as I reached to slap him, he grabbed my arm. I said, This is why you brought me out here at ten o'clock on a Sunday night, so I could feel your pain? And he said, You wanna feel something else, you're saying? And I just locked my jaw, snatching my hand back, thinking, *No, no, no, not gonna say it.*

But then I did. I said, You know, sometimes, I actually forget you're a boy, and Cam said, Come again? And I said, No, really, there are times when you can go three, four hours without saying anything rude or crude, but then it just wells up inside you, doesn't it, and you have to let it out. Come on, he said, cocking his head toward his window and opening his door. I'll show you the other reason I brought you here. Where are we going? I said. I didn't want to get out—it was *freezing*, and dark. Cam goes, It's a surprise, holding out his hand for me. Oh, and bring your camera, he said, so I did, walking over to him. This way, he said, taking my hand and leading me down, around the edge of the fence, down this old cobblestone walkway, with no idea where we were going.

I thought I knew this town, but I don't. Every time he shows me something, takes me somewhere, I realize how many hiding places, just how many secrets this town has. Especially because there are all these abandoned tunnels, from when there used to be a different rail line with these underground tunnels that were just left here to die. I've been here three years, had never even heard of them before, and Cam's barely been here six months, and he knows a hundred places I've never seen. One of the first things he'd ever told me was how he takes drives sometimes in the middle of the night, when he can't sleep, and I've never asked where, because it's private, you know? That's probably how he found this place.

Here, he said, leading me around this old brick wall, reaching these steps, leading down into a cave or something. There's a tunnel here, he said. Did you know that? he asked, and I shook my head no. Don't be scared, he said, squeezing my hand, and I said, I am—I am scared, not wanting to go down there. I'm right here, Cam said, and then he reached into his coat and pulled out a big flashlight. I'm here, he said, and you stay right behind me, okay? I nodded yes, but I couldn't even speak, I was so afraid. I mean, who knew what was down there—there could be people, stray dogs, anything.

It's blocked off about a hundred feet in, he said, pointing the flashlight down the tunnel so I could see it wasn't very deep, the space. They built all these tunnels back when the town was a military base, then closed them up when they built the new rail line. But if you could get through the wall, I bet it would lead all the way to the river. Every time I come down here, I imagine what would happen if you could walk to the other side, only to find yourself in some other dimension, a parallel universe. Or what if it took you back in time, this tunnel right beneath some small town, he said, and I shivered. You okay? he said, and I nodded yes, but I was trying to breathe, while my eyes adjusted.

I wanted you to see it, because I was thinking maybe you'd think up a story, he said, and I said, A story about an old tunnel? And he said, Yeah, maybe a story about a group who go underground, tunnel rats who discover other dimensions. Like *The Twilight Zone*, but with teenage kids. Think about it, that's all I'm saying, he said. Could be good, you know? It could, I said, but tell me, what was the first thing that came to mind when you imagined reaching the other side of the wall, the other dimension? Cam shook his head no, he didn't think of anything, but right away, I did—I saw it—I knew.

Cam knew I saw it, too, because he goes, That's why I brought you down here, Thee. What do you see on the other side of the wall? And I told him. First thing I thought of was a street, some main street in a small town that's covered with this film, like snow, but maybe four inches thick, right? But you don't know what it is, and it sort of looks like confetti, like there's been some victory celebration, Super Bowl, who knows what. When you first see the street, it's a perfectly tidy, pretty main street, except then you see this strange trash, all over, and then you see that the street is littered with the corpses of every balloon every kid in the world has ever let go of by accident. You know how kids always wonder what happens to balloons, where they go? Well, that's where. Not just balloons, either. Every soccer ball, baseball that's ever gone over a fence and been lost. Or through it, I said, smiling at him.

Is there more? he said, and I said, Don't know. I'd have to draw it first, and he goes, Then draw it, Thee, and even in the dark, I could see he was smiling, so pleased. All right, I will, I said, because I liked that idea of a town just past this brick wall, a town identical to ours, but with a main street littered by tons of balloons and balls, and what would that town be, you know? Like what was the story of that town that had to be the grave-yard for all those things that kids miss so much? I better get you home, Cam said, holding up his hand for me, again. See? Told you, nothing to be afraid of, he said, and I took his hand, smiling at how scared I'd been, but not completely convinced.

## FRIDAY, APRIL 8, 2011
## (FOUR DAYS LATER)

*God*, I wish I'd had my camera with me. Seriously, when we walked into her room, I swear Melody Knox was the prettiest girl I'd ever seen. Like the kind of pretty that makes you catch your breath—that's how I felt, looking at her. And you know what she said? Before I even had a chance to say hello, she goes, *I love your hair.* That was the very first thing she said to me. Like I walked right into her voice, saying, *I love your hair,* and I stared at her, agog. Because I was like, *You're the prettiest girl in the whole world and you love my hair? Ohmygod, I love you.*

And then, before I could even say thank you, I realized who she reminded me of. I said, Ohmygod, you know who you look like? I turned to Knox, and I go, You know who she looks like? Melody said, *Who?* And I said, Brooke Shields in the movie *Pretty Baby.* Except for the way Melody was dressed. I really don't mean to be mean, but Melody was wearing this pink knit shirt and velour sweatpants, kind of like Juicy Couture but more like Cheapy Couture, and I was like, *What's up with that?* Also, her hair was pulled back in a ponytail, like a six-year-old—I didn't get it at all.

So I said, If you did your hair, you'd look just her, and she goes, *Pretty Baby? I've never seen it.* We'll have to rent it, I said, because she's *gorgeous.* Your eyebrows are thinner, and your hair's lighter, but otherwise, you could be twins. I didn't say it, but I was just like, *Wow, I can't believe she doesn't know who Brooke Shields is,* and she goes, *I want to get my hair cut like yours,* and I go, You should—you'd look great with a bob. Or maybe with bangs, like Siouxsie Sioux in "Spellbound"? And she smiled and she goes, *Who's that?* I looked at Knox, and then I looked back and said, You're kidding, right? I mean, I'm standing there, thinking, *Knox, you dress your teenage daughter like she's five, and you have someone babysit her, and she doesn't know who Siouxsie Sioux is? What sort of parent are you?* I felt something behind me, and just as I turned, I saw Knox's jaw drop like a bowling ball.

All of a sudden, looking at him, it's like the whole scene replayed from when we got to Knox's house. I mean, we got there, and we went inside, and he introduced me to his babysitter, who gave me this weird look, like what were we doing together, right? But then she didn't have time, running out the door, and Knox sighed this heavy sigh, then he said, I'll take you upstairs to meet Melody. So I followed him upstairs, and their place is nice enough, but it's not my style at all; it's very cozy, all these frilly touches, whatever. Anyhow, I followed him upstairs, and Knox knocked on Melody's door, and I heard her voice say, *Come in*, and we walked in, and that's the first thing I remember: so beautiful, and, *I love your hair*.

Then Knox goes, Thea, I'd like you to meet my daughter, Melody, and then he turns to her and says, Mel, this is Thea. I'm working with her—it's business. And I said, You didn't need to put it like that. Excuse me, he said, it's for work. Then I remembered that I hadn't even acknowledged her, so I said, Thank you, smiling at Melody, and Knox goes, Sorry? I said, I wasn't talking to you. I was talking to Melody, and he looked at me. I don't understand, he said, and I go, I said thank you, because she said she liked my hair. That's when I realized Melody looks exactly like Brooke Shields, and I told her so, then everything stopped moving, and Knox stared at me with his mouth open.

It was getting weird at that point, and I was losing my patience. It'd been a long, long week, and I didn't have time to play Who's on First? So I said, Knox, what did you want me to say? She said she liked my hair, and I said thank you, and Knox looked at her, then he looked at me, and then I saw her, Melody, as she really is. Melody was a different girl than the girl I saw at first, and that girl, the girl he sees, she was sitting in a wheelchair in the middle of her bedroom. Detective Knox's daughter in a wheelchair.

The whole thing replays in my head; exact same scene, only not with the perfect girl, with the girl Melody really is. That's why she has a babysitter, because she's in a chair and she has palsy or something like it; I don't know what. I could tell right away, too, that when she gets excited or when she's trying to say something, she flails, because she can't move her arms or legs.

Like when she saw us walk in, she looked so excited, but all Melody could do was moan and flail. She can't speak—I heard her talking, but she can't speak a word.

I didn't understand what was happening, and I didn't know what else to do, so I held out my hand, and she tried to move, to reach for my hand, so I shook her hand, and it was like . . . it was like being shocked. Except it didn't hurt—it wasn't like that at all. It was like, it was like hearing this voice—just the most beautiful voice, and Melody said, *I'm so glad you're finally here.* Knox's mouth started to open, then she did it again—she said, *Will you tell him I want to get my hair cut?* I didn't think about it, I just did as she asked. I said, She said she wants to get her hair cut, and then Knox took a step back, and he goes, Thea, this isn't funny—. For her birthday, I said, because that's what she said, and he was like, Please, Thea. *Tell him about this morning*, she said, so I told him. She says you asked her what she wants for her birthday this morning, when you were putting on her shoes, and she wants you to take her to get her hair cut, I said.

Knox's face—I've never seen that look on anyone's face before. Then, finally, he closed his mouth, and he had this look like he was getting angry, and he goes, Thea, why don't we go downstairs? All of a sudden, Melody starts yelling at me: *I'm here! I'm right here!* She goes, *Don't go! Please don't go!* I turned back and I said, I won't—I won't go. Knox looked at me, like, Are you out of your mind? So I told him: Can't you hear her? She's shouting, I said, plugging my ears.

Knox covered his face with both hands, and seeing him like that, seeing Melody, hearing her, I almost started bawling.

Because I got so scared, and I didn't know what the hell was going on, and the whole time, Melody kept begging me not to leave. I looked at her, and I kept seeing the beautiful girl, and all I could do was nod my head, because I was so confused. She just kept saying, *I'm here, please believe me, Thea*, and I said, I do. I know you're here. I know, but I—I don't understand what's happening, and then the real Melody moaned, out loud, and you could almost hear a syllable, and I said, I'm sorry. . . .

Knox stood, perfectly still, and he grabbed my arm, like he was about to walk me outside, then he said, You understand? You know what she's saying? I said, Yes. Yes! She's saying, I'm here! I'm here! I was almost shouting, so I could hear myself over her. I even put my fingers in my ears, but it didn't help, because she was inside—her voice was *inside* my head, not out. *Baby blue*, she said, almost yelling. *Thea, tell my dad I said, Baby blue*, and I said, Baby blue, and I looked at her, wondering what that meant, and Knox froze. He goes—almost hissing—he goes, What did you say? I didn't know what to say, and Melody goes, *Tell him, "It's All Over Now, Baby Blue"!* Knox grabbed my arm, and I go, She said to tell you it's all over now, baby blue, and Knox stared at me, and Melody goes, *Sing, Thea—sing the song! Sing "You must leave now, take what you need, you think will last," and I go, I can't sing, but Melody wouldn't listen to me. She goes, *Tell him, please—sing the song, he'll know—he'll know you're telling the truth if you sing it to him, I swear! Sing, Thea.* And she started singing, and I tried to tell her no, no, I don't want to sing, and my throat was contracting, but she kept singing. I couldn't even hear my own voice, so I had to sing as loud as I could: You must leave now, take what you need, you think will last! But whatever you wish to keep, you better grab it fast! I said, almost shouting so I could hear myself over Melody. Knox's mouth fell open, and he looked at her—and then he saw it—he saw that she was there.

I looked at him, Knox, and swear to God, I felt so dizzy for a second, I reached out, and then I fainted. I mean, I always thought it was bullshit, like who really faints? But it's real—seriously, the whole room started spinning, and I felt my legs giving, and then I blacked out. Knox reached over and caught me just in time, and he goes, Hey, hey, Thea? Thea? holding on, making sure I was all right, while I got my legs back under me. It was only a second, though, then I stepped away, nodding that I was fine.

Right then, the bedroom door opened, and a woman walked in: There you two are! she said. At first, she was smiling, and then, looking at us, Knox holding my arm, Melody twisted in her chair. And her eyes kept moving from me, to Melody, to Knox, and back again. The woman didn't say anything, but she gives me this look like, Who the hell are you and what the fuck are you doing in my house? Then she goes, Oh, hello, I'm Heather—it's Knox's wife, right?—and I wiped my nose on my sleeve, trying to smile, and I said, Hi, I'm Thea. And she goes, Oh. *Thea* . . . of course! How nice to meet you.

She's being perfectly nice, but right away, I can tell she doesn't like me at all, and me, I'm just like, Of course what? So I tried smiling, but I was as obvious as she was, and I had to look away, smiling at Melody. His wife, Heather, she's really pretty, and you can totally see the resemblance, too, but she's got strawberry blonde hair and freckles. They have the same eyes, though, Melody and Heather—they have the same blue eyes. God, talk about awkward; Heather smiling at Knox, waiting for some explanation, then Knox goes, I was driving Thea home when Shelley called. Guess Dylan stuck a box of raisins up his nose, and Heather goes, A whole box? I almost started laughing, because it was the same question I asked, you know, but I didn't want to have anything to do with her. We don't know yet, he said, and she turns to me and goes, I'm so sorry I couldn't leave work, Thea, and I said, It's fine. He was just telling me Melody's birthday is coming up. When is it? I said, and Heather smiled, stepping between us—almost like she wanted to get me away from Melody, I could tell. But Melody goes, *June 16*, and I go, June 16? That's my birthday! Melody goes, *It is?!* And I almost said yes, but I caught myself, and I just nodded. It was really nice meeting Melody, I said, seeing the shock on Heather's face, then she looked at Knox, like, *WTF?* Nice meeting you, Thea, she said, ushering us toward the door, and I go, You, too, and I walked out, hearing Melody calling to me, *Bye!*

So Knox pulls out, and we drive a few blocks, not a word, no communication. We made it to the highway, and then a light went on, on his dash, and he said, I need to get some gas, and I didn't say anything. So we pulled into the first station on the highway, and he got out, and I sat there, turning in my seat. I could still hear her voice in my head, Melody's voice. I could still hear her begging me not to leave, that she was in there, right there—I know what I heard. Knox got in, but he couldn't even look at me. Look, I said, I don't care if you believe me or not, but why would I tell you something so crazy? You think I *asked* for this? And my ears are still ringing, just so you know, I said, plugging one ear with my middle finger. I mean, seriously, Knox, and then I just looked out my window, never mind. So let me . . . I'm trying to—let me just, he said, struggling, covering his mouth with his left hand. Did you, do you have to look at her to hear her? No, I said. I don't think so—no more than I'd have to look at you to hear you talking.

Finally, I go, Is it palsy? Is that what Melody has, palsy? Knox nodded yes, and I said, How long's she been in a wheelchair? And he puffed up his cheeks, thinking about it, then he said, Twelve years. She's never talked? I said, and he started to answer, then he just shook his head no, staring straight ahead. I said, You don't believe me, do you? He didn't answer—for like a whole minute, he didn't say anything—then, finally, he goes, I don't know what to believe anymore, and I go, Yeah, me, neither.

We were just about to pull out on that highway, when Knox said, Thea, look! Look, look, he said, pointing up at the sky. There was a yellow balloon, floating, like it had all the time in the world. Sad kid, he sighed, smacking his gums, like, tough luck. And I thought about it, watching the balloon move through the air, just so proud, so free, you know? Sad kid, but happy balloon, I said.

Knox pulled up to the building, parking below our door, and I said, Thanks for the ride, unbuckling my seat belt, and he said, You're welcome, and then I got out of the car, but before I closed the door, Knox leaned over and he goes, Thea? I leaned in, and I was just like, Yeah? I could tell he wasn't sure he should tell me, but then he did. He nodded once, like he couldn't believe it, and then he said, I used to sing that to her, when Melody was a baby. That song "It's All Over Now, Baby Blue." I didn't know any lullabies, so I sang the songs I knew, and she loved that song—I mean, I think she did, he said. Then I knew what she was saying, why she told me to tell him that. I go, She did love it—you should sing it to her again—she knows all the words, you know? He looked down, not knowing what to say, so I closed the door.

Turning around, I almost jumped out of my skin, because I heard a woman's voice calling me. Like so many voices, I felt insane—I didn't know if it was Melody or what, and this woman goes, Excuse me, are you Thea Denny? I turned around, and this woman was standing there, over near the stairs. She was pretty, but in a television-pretty way, with lots of hair spray and heavy makeup and a gray pantsuit. She looked so familiar, too, and then I realized who she was, and no wonder there was something TV about her! Her name's Jenna Darnell, and she's one of the reporters from WVOX, out of Albany. She's the reporter they sent here to do that story about the hole in the barrier on the highway and the tire tracks that stop in the middle of the field.

She smiled, introducing herself, and then she said she was hoping she could ask me a few questions. She said she'd heard about Cam and wondered if his disappearance had anything to do with some of the weird shit that was happening around town—she didn't say it like that, but that's what she meant. I looked at Knox for help, and he got out of the car, leaning over his hood. Jenna Darnell looked at him, and you could tell he was going to step in, and then she hands me a card and says, I'm sure this is an incredibly difficult time for you, Thea. But if you ever want to talk about it, publicly, she said, and I took the card. Thanks, I said, and I looked at Knox. You're the woman from the news, right? he asked her, and she smiled. Yes, WVOX, and Knox said, Crazy about the wall, isn't it? She smiled at me, and then she said, Almost like someone ran right into . . . nowhere, and I shivered, crossing my arms. Huh, Knox said, smiling. That's one way of putting it. Nice meeting you, he said, letting her know she could leave now.

I should go inside, I said to them both, and Knox nodded, opening his door, and Jenna Darnell headed for a white rental car, parked beside our super's old truck. I went upstairs, unlocked our door, and went inside, and then I just stood at the window, peeking outside, thinking, *WTF?* I mean, first Melody, and then I literally turn around, and there's a reporter who wants to talk to me?

I sat down on the couch, folding my arms around my bag, and then I got a text. I checked my phone—my hearts stops every time I hear my phone—but it was only Karen. She asked if I wanted to have dinner at her place, and I texted her right back: How soon is now? I waited at the window, and when Karen pulled in, I ran downstairs and got in, but we didn't say anything the whole way. Which is something I love about Karen, that you never have to fill the silences, not at all. I was just happy to be with her, because I feel like she's the only person who really knows what this week has been like.

We got to their house and went inside, and first thing, walking into Cam's house, without him there, my chest just went oomph! I was like, *Ohmygod, Karen, how did you get through this week, living here?* She saw it, too, the look on my face, but she didn't say anything. She goes, Dinner'll be ready in half an hour; why don't we go sit outside? So I followed her outside, and it's a little run-down, their house, but they have a big screened-in porch in the back with a porch swing, and I took a seat.

You know, some nights, doing something as simple as sitting on a porch swing, when the first cricket begins to chirp, getting warmed up for the season, and the air is so clean, it's almost enough to make you believe people are that clean, too. Of course you know better, but you still give in: you breathe the air; and in that moment, you believe in goodness in your bones. It was chilly, though, so Karen pulled out a blanket and covered me, such a mom, tucking the blanket in along my thighs, before sitting down next to me.

So. How are you holding up, kiddo? she asked, brushing my bangs back with one hand. I don't know, I said, shrugging. I guess I don't believe it most days, I said, looking at her: I don't believe he's gone, that's how. Because if I really believed that I'd never see him again, I'd be a total basket case, I said. She nodded, like she understood, and I said, All day long, I think he's going to text or call or walk through the door, you know? But when he does, I think the first I'll do is kill him, I said, looking at her, and she smiled. You'll have to beat me to it, she said, inhaling and then flapping her lips as she exhaled this heavy sigh. Staring off, she started to say something else, but she stopped.

Karen's beautiful. Like what you imagine some classic California beauty looks like, tall and thin, with ruddy tan skin and a few freckles across her nose, just like Cam's, and beach-blonde hair, and it took me a while to get used to how pretty she was; it kept surprising me, when I first met her. But now she looked so tired, or something worse than tired, not haunted, just the opposite. I keep seeing this look in her eyes, almost like she knew what was going on, like she'd been waiting for this moment for such a long time, and finally, here we were.

When he was little, she said, looking over at the garage, Cam had such an ugly temper, and my mouth fell wide open. *Cam?* I said, The guy who barely raises his voice to sing in the shower? Oh, *the worst*, she said, raising her eyebrows, No: demon child. Still, I said, Karen, I'm sorry, but I cannot imagine him with a temper—that wouldn't be Cam. People change, Thea, she said, turning to look at me, but really looking at me. Like when someone says something that's a place marker, and then, one day, they'll finally tell you what the hell they were talking about, what they weren't telling you at that moment, you know? I don't know, I just had this feeling it would be a while before she told me what she actually meant by saying that people change.

But then I felt so guilty, like I was hiding something from her, that I just blurted it out. I go, Karen, this reporter showed up at my house this afternoon, then she frowned and she goes, A *reporter?* I nodded, because I couldn't believe it either, and I said, Right before you texted, then her face relaxed and she goes, Did you speak to him? I go, It was a woman, but no. I mean, I took her card, because she handed it to me, but I didn't say anything about Cam. Karen nodded, then she patted my thigh, about to stand up, heading to the kitchen, and she goes, I trust you, Thea. You don't have to ask me for permission: you do what you need to do, all right? Which sounds great, at first, right, but on second thought, I was just like, *You trust me? I'm glad one of us does.*

It was so stupid, but we got in this huge fight a few weeks ago, after Cam gave me my first driving lesson with a stick. In his car. And maybe I overreacted, but Cam kept snapping at me, like, Do this! Do that! Don't do that! You're going too fast! Slow down! Speed up! More gas! Don't shift so hard! Shift now! Stop riding the clutch, Thea! Thea, you're riding the clutch! Finally, I stopped and I was just like, I don't even know what that means, Cam, riding the clutch! But stop yelling at me! I yelled back, and then Cam goes, I'm not yelling, Thee. All I'm saying is slow down or you're gonna drive through the barrier.

We were in this huge parking lot they'd built on the back side of another strip mall before the money fell through to finish it. Now it's hidden behind this big plastic barrier they put up along the highway, I don't know why. Maybe it's so people can't see all the failing businesses in town, but there was no one else there, and on the other side of the parking lot, it's just this endless field. Anyhow, that's what he said, that I was driving so fast, I was going to tear a hole in the plastic wall, and that's when I stopped the car and my mouth fell open, like, *Seriously?*

I turned off the ignition, and I go, Cam, what am I going to hit? He goes, Thea, you were headed straight for the wall, and I said, I was headed in that direction, because it's in front of us. What am I going to run into here, Cam? It's nowhere, there's nothing here. You can't run into *nowhere*, I said, so annoyed, and he tilted his head, raising a brow, saying, I must disagree, because you can most certainly run into nowhere, and I said, Oh, whatever. He goes, Fine, but all I'm saying is that you weren't following instructions, Thee—. I go, I was trying to follow instructions, Cam, but I have to *learn*, and I can't learn if you're yelling at me, and he goes, I wasn't yelling. I said, Yes, you were. And if I had known you'd get so snippy, I would have told you not to bother trying to teach me how to drive, and Cam goes, Thee, don't give me that, *you know* I'm a good teacher—in fact, I'm an excellent teacher. I said, When it's geometry, maybe. And please, I didn't hurt your stupid car, okay? I knew I shouldn't have said that, that it was mean of me to call his car stupid, and then, when he didn't even look at me, he just stared straight ahead and he goes, Yeah, well, I bet my car could pass geometry.

My mouth fell open, because I was just like, you are *such* an asshole for saying that! I couldn't even believe he made that dig, you know? So I go, You know what, Cam? Here, I said, taking out the keys and tossing them across the seat. Then, opening my door, he goes, Come on, Thee, what are you doing? I said,

My lesson's over—feel free to teach your car geometry, and I got out and started walking away. It's at least five miles back to my house, but I was like, screw it, I'd rather walk than talk to him, so I started walking.

Cam waited, and I could totally feel him watching me, trying to figure out what just happened, and then, a minute later, he rolled down the window and yelled after me, telling me to come back, and he even said please, but I kept walking. I heard him start the car, then he drove over and pulled up, driving alongside me. He leaned out the window and he goes, Can I give you a ride? I said, No, thanks, not even looking at him.

He was leaning out his window, and he goes, So you're going to walk the whole way home? I go, That's right, and then he pulled up beside me, driving with one hand, leaning out the window: Can I walk with you? he said, and I said, No. And he said, Why not? And by that point, I could tell he thought he was being suave. I go, Because I want you to leave me alone, and he goes, Why, because I got impatient with you for grinding my poor—. I go, Cam, *I told you* I don't know how to drive a stick and you said you'd be patient and you weren't patient at all. First you tell me I have to try things I'm afraid of, but then, when I try—. Okay, okay, he goes, no need for yelling, is there? I stopped and I just looked at him: Go away, I said turning, trying to walk in a different direction.

No, he said, turning the car and circling around, following behind me. It was getting so dark it was almost time to turn the headlights on. I walked all the way to the highway, before I turned around: Quit following me! I said, and Cam goes, Okay.

But I want you to know I accept your apology. I go, That's funny, because I didn't apologize, and he goes, Yes, you did. Remember when you said, Cam, I love you so much and I'm sorry for being bitchy and making a big drama out of nothing, please forgive me?

And then, it snapped, and I stopped, cold. The drama, I mean. Why was I throwing such a fit? Why that moment and not the moment before, I don't know. Just that my feelings get ahead of me sometimes, and I don't even realize what I'm doing. Or why.

So when he stopped the car, I walked around, behind the car, but when I got in, I just stared ahead, because that's as far as I could go. I waited for him to start the car, but he didn't. He just looked at me, waiting. I don't know why, but then and there, it finally clicked in my head. He was right: throwing tantrums, creating this whole huge drama, for what? I didn't even understand why, but I finally got it, that there's no need. I felt so stupid, too, dumber than his car, and that made me smile. Cam goes, What are you laughing at? I just shrugged, and I go, Can we go back to the parking lot? And he goes, You want to learn to drive in the dark? I looked over, and I gave him this smile and I said, That's not what I want to go back for.

Saturday, I didn't want to go out, because I didn't want to run into anybody, and Mom went to the grocery store, and I just didn't know what to do with myself. It's like I've forgotten how to be alone, which is so strange, because I was alone for so long, until I met Cam. Now that he's gone, I can't remember how I used to pass the time.

Sometime around three, I couldn't stand being in my room anymore, so I got up and I walked outside, and I was right outside our door, staring at the spot where Cam's car was parked—Tuesday. Karen drove over, that morning, when she came to my house, looking for Cam, and that night, someone dropped her off and she drove Cam's car home. But I didn't tell her I had a set of keys, because I didn't think about it, and she didn't ask.

Finally, staring down at some empty, grease-stained parking lot, afraid of being alone anymore, I was just like, *WTF?* All of a sudden, I knew what I had to do, so I went back inside, grabbed Cam's keys and my jacket. I got on my bike and road over to Cam's house, and I knocked, but Karen didn't answer. I looked inside, and I didn't see any sign of her, and her car was gone. So I pulled my bike around, leaning it against the side of their house, and I walked over to the garage, behind their house, and peeked inside the window, just to be sure. Then I went back to the front door, and I tore a piece of paper out of one of my old notebooks and wrote her a note:

> Karen,
> I'm taking Cam's car.
> I'll bring it back in a few hours.
> Please don't worry.
> xx, Thea

I pulled open the garage door—it's an old garage, and you have to be careful, opening the door with both hands, because it'll spring on you, but anyhow. I backed out the drive, and their driveway made me so nervous, the gravel crunching beneath the tires, like the whole neighborhood knew I was taking Cam's car without asking permission. I made it all the way out of town, though, and pulled out, onto the highway, before it even occurred to me that I had no idea where I was going.

The thing is, there are so many back roads, upstate, so many places a person can get lost. I just drove, like we always drove together on Saturdays, and I kept thinking I'd turn around at the next exit, but I didn't. I was on the highway for about twenty minutes before I turned off on this road, heading north, and I drove another fifteen minutes, taking a dirt road along this creek bed. A few miles down, the road came to an end, and I had to stop. So I rolled down the window, and I sat there, listening to the creek, the leaves, and then, for the first time all week, I started crying. I mean, I fought it, hard as I could until finally I started sobbing.

It was at least ten minutes before I calmed down and blew my nose on a rag I found beneath the seat. Then I got out of the car and sat on the hood, staring at the creek, like it had an answer. But what can you say when there's nothing to say, except, *Where are you? Where the hell are you?* It's worthless, but I said it anyway. I shouted it, even, as if Cam could hear me: Where are you?! My throat hurt, I shouted so loud, and a few birds flew off, scared, and then the creek was still again.

A moment later, like two seconds later, my phone rang, and I jumped—I was sure it was Cam. For a moment, I truly believed he knew exactly where I was, that he'd heard me, that he was coming to get me. Then I checked the number, but it was Karen, so I sat there, and I debated answering, because I couldn't take her yelling at me about the car, but then I figured I might as well get it over with. I answered and she goes, Hey, you, and she didn't sound angry, and I said, Hi, clearing my throat. She goes, Where are you? I go, I don't know, and she said, Are you hungry? I said, No, not really, because I wasn't at all, and she said, I'm making dinner. Do you want to join me? I said, Honestly, I don't think I can eat anything, and she said, Me, neither. But I'd much rather not eat with you than not eat alone, she said, and I had to smile.

All right, I said, looking up at the trees, and it was so beautiful, but I just wanted to hit something, you know? I can't explain, but Karen goes, Good, then I told her I might be a while. And she said, That happens when you don't know where you are, and I said, Guess so. She said, We'll eat when you get here, whenever that is. Or we won't eat when you get here, how's that sound? Karen? I said, and she said, Yes? And I told her, I go, Karen, I'm just . . . I'm just really angry, and I meant it, but soon as I said it, I didn't feel angry, I felt like crying again. She didn't answer for a moment, and I wasn't sure if she heard me, and then Karen said, I'll set the table, take your time, before she hung up.

I sat on the hood a few minutes longer, looking at this bridge, because I couldn't seem to move. There was an old bridge, downstream a ways, and it was so rusted, it was completely orange, with these barnacles of chunky rust all over it and half of the bridge was missing in the center. I kept thinking if Cam were there, he'd have to climb that old bridge, all the way across, stand there, right over the water. For a moment, getting up off the hood, I got the feeling Cam had been there before. In that very spot. I looked around—I just had this feeling, like he might come walking down the road at any moment, but he wasn't there, of course. It was just me and the birds I was scaring.

Standing there, staring at the rusty bridge, downstream, the slow creek passing by, all I could think was, *You should be here*, as if he could read my thoughts, feel the fist in my chest, come back. I think I even said it out loud. Come back, please come back, but he didn't come back just because I was thinking of him. So I got in the car, and turned the engine over. Now all I had to do was find my way home. Seemed like I should just be able to head back the same way I came, right? But it never works that way, does it?

We went to Silver Top after school, *Fort Marshall's oldest diner*, just like the sign said over the cash register. We go there all the time, and believe it or not, I actually get homework done there now. Doesn't hurt any that I've got my very own tutor, 24/7, but Cam doesn't do my homework for me. Honestly, he's such a smart-ass, he always says doing my homework for me would be cheating me of an education, and he'd never cheat me. Anyhow, Sharon came over to check on us, ask if we needed refills—I love Sharon, she's like our diner mom.

Sharon must have been a bombshell thirty years ago. She has that about her, the way she carries herself, holds her head. But there's something a little hard-living about her, too. Like those sixties country-music women, so brilliant and beautiful, but always hooking up with the worst possible men. I don't know anything about Sharon, really, but it's just a vibe you get, looking at her. I mean, even though she's gray and nicotined, the woman's got chutzpah—isn't that what you call it when you meet a woman who has balls?

Anyhow, I don't know why it never occurred to me before, but when I looked over, at the Elders, this group of old men who practically live at Silver Top, the way their heads were turned, it reminded me of the painting *The Last Supper*. So I decided to draw a picture and call it *The Last Cupper*, and right away, I started drawing the long table and Jesus, and then I started filling in each Elder in place of the apostles or whoever it was that showed up for the Last Supper.

It was just a sketch, but I turned the notebook to show Cam, and he ducked his head down, so the Elders wouldn't see him laughing. I didn't put them in white robes, I put them in their usual duds, their jeans and plaid and madras shirts. I let a couple of them wear their hats, too. Come here, Cam said, leaning forward, curling his finger at me, so I did. What? I said, and Cam kissed me, grinning, and I leaned back.

You know what I want to draw next? I said, and Cam smiled this big smile, so proud. Cam always encourages me—he encourages me more than anyone, really, even my mom, because he's always telling me not to be afraid. No, what he says is not to be so afraid that I don't let myself follow the pictures in my head, draw the things I see. Never censor my imagination, because it's the cardinal sin of creativity, and of course I know that, but when someone's behind you, 100 percent, and they tell you that, it means so much more than you can mean, alone. So I started giving myself permission to draw anything at all, and I never really let myself do that before. Letting someone else really see me—the things you create, like your art—it's just like being naked, only with a different skin.

## TUESDAY, APRIL 19, 2011
## (FIFTEEN DAYS LATER)

When we got to school, everyone was standing around the flag-pole, out front. Bus after bus of kids were getting off, and without even thinking about it, we all head straight for the flagpole, looking up, because everyone was standing there, looking up, and for a second, you know something's wrong without knowing what. Like one of those things you feel in your gut. And then you saw it, just a glimmer of too much sky, too much blue, and then, piece by piece, we all saw it: someone had cut every single star out of the American flag, flying in front of our school.

One by one, everyone's jaw dropped, speechless—everyone was speechless. Looking at each other like, How could it be? Who did it, and how? Really, how did they do it? Because you couldn't climb up a hundred feet above ground, and cut up the flag, holding on to the pole. So how did they do it? Did they pull the flag down? That was the only explanation, right, but even that would take a long time, cutting out every single star. So, what, did someone deface, de-star, whatever, an identical flag and then take the school's good flag down and swap them out?

Completely bizarre, okay. And it was windy, too, so the wind kept blowing the flag like a kite, practically showing it off. It was eerie, too, the way you could see all that sky through fifty empty stars. Looking at it, I felt like we were . . . I don't know how else to put it, except that it felt like our town was being invaded by some parallel universe. As if there was another country, another America, shining through that flag. An America that we'd never thought about because we're all so hopelessly American, it'd never even occurred to us that there could be two of us, you know?

Well. Before you knew it, Cheesy, Vice Principal Gray, all these teachers, the school counselor, and the whole office staff were out front, ordering everyone to get inside. For a minute, it threatened to become a mob scene, too, but of course the teachers managed to get everyone inside. Still, all day long, everyone kept asking, How? Who could pull that off? It was the prank to end all pranks, and one by one, everyone turned to look at me, thinking the same thing: *Cam. Did he have something to do with this?*

After first bell, the janitorial staff, all three of them, was out front, trying to take the flag down, but then the chain got caught at the top of the pole, and they couldn't get it down. So then they tried to cut the chain with these huge bolt cutters, and what happens? They cut the chain in a way that the flag managed to stay in place, with this whip of loose chain blowing in the air, ringing the flag pole like a little bell with every gust of wind. So then they had to call the mayor's office—this is what I heard—the principal's office called the mayor's office, and the mayor's office sent a crane to take the remainder of the broken chain and the flag down. After all, it's a crime to deface the flag.

But wait, it gets better—because the crane showed up at lunch, when everyone was on the front lawn, eating. Everyone just sitting there, watching, while this huge crane started stretching upward, and then Mr. Gray walked out, barking, clapping: Inside! Everyone inside! Now! practically blowing a rape whistle at us. For two weeks, things had been so slow to boil, and then, in that moment, you could feel it simmering, everyone was so amped up.

The next day, it really hit the fan. Because someone posted a video, like everyone in school got a text with this video link, and it was time-lapse photography of the first starless flag, blowing in the wind, with sped-up blue sky and puffy white clouds passing behind it. Which was weird, yes, but the thing was, the time code on the video was dated for the day before, Monday, April 18, the day *before*. I mean, it must have been a trick with the date, right, but how'd they do it? And what really upset people was, could it be possible our flag had been defaced for an entire day and *no one noticed*? I kept thinking about that all day, listening to all the chatter in the halls, between classes. *Because if it wasn't a trick, what other explanation could there be unless*, I thought . . . and then I heard my answer, right behind me. A voice, clear as day said: Unless someone hacked the code, and practically jumping out of my skin, I turned around, and no one was there. The bell had rung, and it was just me, alone in the hall.

Everyone kept going on and on about the flag, and it's like I couldn't even hear myself think. So I didn't even go to the library at lunch, I just wanted to find a quiet corner where I could be alone, but of course who do I run into but Ricky. Hey, I said, raising my hand. He was sitting on the window ledge—it's wide enough, it's like a window seat, and he was just about to pull something out of his lunch bag. Mind if I join you? I said, and he raised his brow, meaning sure.

Last year, after I moved here, Ricky gave me a red rose for Valentine's Day, and it was so sweet—he was the first boy to ever give me a rose, but the thing is, I just didn't like him that way, you know. And of course my friends—my ex-friends made fun, and it was so embarrassing, I just avoided him as much as possible. I've always wished I hadn't done that, treated him like that, but then he started avoiding me, and then, by summer, it seemed for the best.

People go after me, but they used to be so mean to Ricky. One of the junior guys, Tyler Hendricks, used to call Ricky *Special Needs* right to his face, like it was his nickname, then he went and told everyone Ricky has Asperger's, when he doesn't, he's just different. Last year, I got in all this trouble after I got drunk at a party and there were all these pictures of me and all my so-called friends quit talking to me, but Ricky was always nice to me—that's what I mean by different. That's what's truly special about Ricky: he'd never do or say anything hurtful to anyone, and how many people in this world can you say that about?

So all last spring, we'd eat lunch together—not in the cafeteria, in this little window seat under the staircase next to the

Chemistry lab, in the east wing. It always smells sulfuric, but it's a good place to be left alone. That's where I found Ricky, just like old times. I got up in the window, across from him, watching him shove his hand back in his bag, and pull something out. And then he threw his head back, practically pounding it on the brick wall behind him. Why? he said, staring at the ceiling, holding a sandwich in his hand. *Why, why do you do this to me?* he said. I looked at him, waiting for him to finish, and then he showed me. She does this *every day*, he said, more annoyed than I've ever seen him, because his mom had cut his sandwich into four triangles.

I know his mom, Blanca. She's Honduran—her family was dirt-poor, like ten kids, and then they came here and built a business from nothing, total American success story. Now his parents own a title company, land deeds, something like that—my mom's done some work with them before. Anyhow, Ricky huffed, rolling his eyes, then he goes, What, like my life isn't hard enough without my mom mothering me to death? I think it's sweet, I said, trying not to laugh. Here: have a turkey sandwich triangle, he said, so I took one. I didn't know what else to say, so we didn't say anything, we just shared his sandwich, sitting in silence until the bell rang. It was just what I needed, actually.

Hey, Thea? he said, sounding shy, and I said, What's up? standing up from my seat. He stared at his feet, like he wasn't sure whether or not to tell me, and I said, Ricky, is everything okay? You okay? I wasn't talking about Cam or school, I was talking about his health. Ricky's epileptic, and maybe because of what Nanna said about me, I always felt we had some sort of connection—I know that's strange, but it's true. Also, Ricky hid it for a long time and no one knew, but then he had a seizure in school once, right after I moved to Fort Marshall. Now they have him on these new drugs, and I think that's why he seems a little doped up sometimes, because he is.

It's just that—I don't know, but something weird happened last week, he said, and I braced myself, thinking it was Cam. Then he said, I had a seizure, and hearing him say that, I felt so relieved—I know that's a terrible thing to say, but it's true. I haven't had a seizure in almost a year now, he said, nothing, but this was different—it wasn't like any I've ever had. Different how? I said, and he said, Like I—I can remember. You remember what was happening around you? I said, and he said, No, I remember things that didn't happen. Like a dream? I asked, and he said, Yes. But not my dream, like someone else's dream, he said, his face looking so pained, so embarrassed, and he said, Never mind, then second bell rang.

I looked at him, waiting for him to finish and then he said, Better get a move on or we'll be late, he said, stuffing his rumpled up paper bag in the trash and walking off. Hey, Ricky? I said, looking back, and he turned around. Thanks for the sandwich, I said, and he shrugged, like no problem: Mi triangle es su triangle, he said, giving a wave. For the first time all week, I could feel it, a smile on my face.

It didn't last long. Because of course my very next thought was to tell Cam, thinking how much Cam would like Ricky's line, and how I'd probably never hear the end of it. Then I remembered a day last year when we were in Cam's car, leaving school, and we saw Ricky walking out the front door. You know the Greeks believed epilepsy was a sign from the gods, that you were touched, Cam said, and I tilted my head, like, What's up with you and the Greeks anyhow? Cam raised his eyebrow, like, What can I tell you? Well, I don't know about that, I said, and even if it's true, I doubt that's any consolation to Ricky. I felt so bad for Ricky, because I know how he hates being on the drugs they have him on, and I get it. Believe me, I totally get it. For what it's worth, Ricky Meyers is one of the smartest kids I've ever known, Cam said, and I said, He's flunking Algebra I. Cam tutored Ricky, too, that's how they knew each other, and then Cam said, So? That doesn't matter. Look at you, and I was just like, Oh . . . that's *low*. I'm telling you, Thee, he said, honking and waving at Ricky as we drove by: That kid's going to surprise you someday. Big time. You just wait, he said, looking in the rearview. Remembering that, I could hear Cam's words as if he were standing right beside me, and watching Ricky walk down the hall, readjusting his backpack over his shoulder, it looked like someday was coming after all.

Anyhow. By the end of the day, the air in the halls turned to static and started spreading through town. By Wednesday, the next morning, you got shocked, practically, stepping out your front door. Everything started wobbling, like someone was holding up one of those circus mirrors to the whole town, and suddenly, it seemed like anything could happen. It got everyone's wheels spinning, kids started smiling at each other, like we were all in it together—we're talking loser freshman boys and all the other outcasts, everyone, united.

Thing is, those tire tracks that end in the middle of that field, the missing stars in the school flag, it wasn't about someone getting away with vandalism or destruction; this was different. This was the kind of rejoicing you imagine they must feel in prison when one of the prisoners escapes. Because someone had figured a way out, and the rest of us, maybe we never thought about it before, but now we all knew there was a way out. And for better or worse, nothing would ever be the same.

One day, I was sitting at my computer, and I was wearing this baggy sweatshirt, and when I leaned over, the shirt fell off my shoulder, right? I didn't even think about it, because I was looking at my notebook, and Cam goes, Thee, can I write you something? He got up, walking over, squeezing my shoulders, and I go, Write *on* me, you mean? And Cam goes, If you insist, and I go, What, a love letter? He goes, You read my mind, and I knew he was up to something. But I handed him a Sharpie, then he pulled the sweatshirt down some more and started drawing on my shoulder blade, and it was long, too. Like on and on, and it tickled, and he goes, Hold still. And five minutes later, he finally waved his hand over my back, drying the skin, and then he goes: *Voilà!*

So I went to the bathroom to read it in the big mirror, and you know what it was? *Pythagorean Theorem*—all over my back— ohmygod. I was just like, Cam, you are such *a geek*! That's not a love letter, I whined, and he goes, It is, too—I love it, and I ignored him, trying not to smile. Help me wipe it off, I said, so he grabbed the sponge from the shower and helped me scrub all the ink off. Then, of course, he just happened to spill a sponge full of water over my chest: Oops! he said, putting his fingers over his lips. Then he goes, Oh, you're all wet, Thea, better take off your shirt, and I go, If I take off my shirt, will you write something nice? Cam held out his hand: Deal, I said, shaking, and we went back to my room and I took off my shirt.

He kissed my ear, and then he put the pen in his mouth and pulled the pen out, and he drew something in like ten seconds. I go, Done? Already? And Cam goes, Done, and I got up and went back to the bathroom to look again, thinking, like, *What is it this time? The Transitive Property?* And then I saw what it was. He'd drawn over my scar—this scar I've had since I was a kid, on my shoulder blade. Cam had used it as an arrow that shot through a big heart, and in the heart, he wrote TD + CC = TLA. He was leaning against the door frame, watching me read, and then I looked at him. What's it mean, TLA? I said, and he grinned, then he leaned forward and whispered, *True. Love. Always.* And at the moment, I would have given anything to stop time, just the two of us, and stay right there, forever.

Every day now, when all the kids got off the bus, everyone looked up at the flag, making sure it was all there, that all the stars were still there. It was, too, far as we can tell. But the thing is, deep down, we're all hoping they'll disappear again. We all wanted to see if all hell would break loose, if it does. Really, what better place for hell to break loose than a small-town high school like ours?

Well, I knew something was up, next time they called me to the office. I mean, one look at Cheswick, and I knew Agent Foley was back, for one thing, but something more than that. Because when I passed Cheesy's office, I stopped, and he said, Special Agent Foley is here. He stood up, joining me, and I nodded yes. I know, I said, and he followed behind. If I didn't know any better, I'd think he was dreading it more than I was.

When I knocked and walked into the conference room, Foley was sitting across the table from the door, with some sort of laptop I'd never seen before, open. It was black, and it had this huge screen, and when I walked in, Foley was watching something, totally entranced. So I pulled out a chair and sat down, and he goes, *When grown people speak of the innocence of children, they don't really know what they mean.* But it's like he was saying it to the screen, not to me, so I just looked at him, not sure I heard him right. He kept watching whatever it was, but then he goes, In any case, thank you for coming in, Theadora, but then I couldn't stop staring at the computer, because it looked like a MacBook, but a lot bigger. And for some reason, it gave me the chills, almost like he was watching us, or—I don't know, it's hard to explain.

Cheesy closed the door, and he said, I'll stand in the corner—pretend I'm not even here, Special Agent Foley, and Foley smiled and said, Of course, and I pulled out a chair, taking a seat across from him at the table. Then Foley goes, Tell me. Do you do well in your classes, Theadora? And I knew he knew I'm not the greatest student, but I said, Some. And he goes, Oh, really? Which? And I go, Art classes, and he goes, Yes, I'm told you are quite gifted, Theadora, so I took a look for myself. I must say, you are extremely talented—I'm particularly fond of this drawing, he said, removing a print from a black folder, behind his computer, pushing it toward me. I picked it up, wondering how the hell he'd seen any of my drawings, and then I just froze: because it was the drawing I'd done at Silver Top. That one of the Elders, *The Last*

*Cupper.* Looking at it, I was shocked, because that's in Hubble—I didn't show that to anyone but Cam, and my first thought was that someone must've broken into my house or something, and I was trying not to panic.

This one, too, Foley said, pulling out another drawing, and my mouth fell open. Because it was the same drawing, exactly the same, except that the Elders weren't wearing any clothes. They were just four old men, hairy and short and tall and saggy and skinny and fat men, sitting in a red leather booth at Silver Top, and the only thing attractive about them were their elk heads—I drew each old man with their own crazy crown of antlers. But what's really screwed up is that I didn't draw that one—I only thought it. What I mean is that I thought of it, but I never actually drew that picture.

I don't know why, I just thought it'd be funny, but looking at it, it's scary. Where did you get that? I snapped, suddenly feeling, I don't know, angry? No, not angry, worse: violated. Foley acted surprised, and then he goes, On Flickr, Theadora. On John Cameron's Flickr photostream. I looked through everything of yours he posted there, and, again, I'm quite impressed, he said, smiling and folding his hands. And when he said that, I thought I was going to puke, like something was so wrong, my bowels felt like spaghetti. But I pulled it together, and I said, I go, Cam never posted those on Flickr—I'd know if he had. Foley raised his eyebrows and he goes, How odd. Then he turned the computer around and hit a key, turning the screen to face me: and there was Cam's Flickr account, NaturalBornNinja. With all my work on it—sets and sets of my drawings and photos, thousands of them, and seeing it all, seeing the name *Cam Conlon*, I had to cover my mouth, gagging.

That is your artwork, is it not? Foley asked, tapping again, scrolling through an entire gallery of my sketches. Every single drawing I was working on the day we met, when Cam came up behind me in the library, back when I was working on this whole American Apparel series. I hate those ads so much, all the girlies sticking their asses at the camera. So I started by drawing animal heads on them, making them as photorealistic as I could, because that's what I always do, but then I decided it would be even better if I drew famous figures, like figureheads, get it?

So I started drawing Gandhi and Malcolm X and the head of JFK on American Apparel models, Bill Clinton in a mesh thong leotard, that sort of thing. They were mine—they were definitely my drawings, but I couldn't answer, because I had no explanation. The only person who'd ever seen those drawings was Cam, but that still didn't mean . . . Then Foley goes, What, if I may ask, inspired this series, Theadora? I didn't even think about it, I just go, Political activism, and he smiles that awful Foley smile and he goes, Indeed. Indeed, Theadora—god, it drives me crazy how he's always calling me Theadora.

Then he goes, There are videos, as well. Would you like to see them, Theadora? I go, What's your point, Foley?, doing everything in my power not to get up and run away, and he goes, Theadora, I have to ask, how long have you and John been having sexual relations? My mouth fell open—couldn't, could not believe he asked me that. I go, That's none of your business, and Foley goes, Actually, Theadora, that is very much my business.

So let me ask again, how long have you and John been having sexual relations? I go, What does that have to do with Cam's disappearance? He goes, Theadora, that is precisely what we are trying to figure out. Now, tell me about the videos, he said, and that's when I started to lose it. I go, What *videos* are you talking about, Foley? And he said—I'll never forget this, either—he goes, The sex tapes, and I was really starting to lose it, but I go, What sex tapes? And then Foley goes, Yours, Theadora. The videos you and Cam made, and I swear, I couldn't breathe for a second.

He kept staring at me, waiting, and then, finally, Foley goes, You mean he didn't tell you? I go, Tell me what? What are you talking about? Foley had this concerned look on his face, tilting his head, and then he said, Theadora, I'm so sorry to tell you this, but it appears that John Cameron has posted videos of the two of you—. *Nuh-uh*, I said. No. I don't believe you. I just started shaking my head no, like no way. There was no way.

He thought it over, tried another approach: You two are sexually active, you have had sex? I go, I told you that's none of your business, and Foley goes, Do you want to see them for yourself? I go, No, I don't, and then Foley goes, Well, Theadora, unfortunately, we don't have much choice. And he pushed another button, playing a YouTube video. I didn't know what was about to happen, and then it started, and it was a video of us in the parking lot where I had my driving lesson. Cam was teaching me how to drive a stick, and we got in a fight, but after our fight, we went back and we had sex in the parking lot—not in the car, on the cement, right beneath the headlights, and . . . That's not me, I said, looking away.

Foley turned the computer around again, pressing a button, and then he goes, No? You have to admit that it certainly looks like you, and I said, I don't care how it looks, that's not me. Foley smiled and he goes, I see. So what we have here is a video of a boy approximately eighteen years of age, who bears a striking resemblance to your missing boyfriend, John Cameron Conlon, having sex with a girl approximately fifteen years of age, who bears a striking resemblance to you, Theadora, in the front of a gold 1968 Dodge Dart with Cam's license plates? he asked, clicking a few keys, turning the computer back around, showing me a frame of the enlarged license plate. It's true; you could see Cam's vintage yellow and brown California plate, clear as day.

I realized I was biting my thumb, and I took my finger out of my mouth. I go, I don't know what to tell you, and he goes, You don't? What about this one, he said, and then he hit another key, playing another video of the two of us, having sex in my room on the day Cam disappeared. It was my room, I'm sure of it, and I knew it was me, because I was lying on my bed, facedown, wearing those stupid tube socks, and Cam was behind me, spreading my legs apart, just like he did that day. Foley was watching me the whole time, and he goes: Again, I'm sorry to have to ask you this, but do you recognize either of these two, Theadora? I couldn't look at him, I was so freaked out, but I go, No. I don't. And Foley goes, You don't recognize either of them? Look again, he said, and then he hit another key on his computer, freezing the image, and I had to look away. I told him again, I go, No, I don't, and I wasn't lying—I mean, it happened, but it's not possible. Because the thing is, that day, at the time, I wanted to see Cam's face—I didn't, but that was how I imagined his face—that's what I imagined—you can't capture that. No one could have taken that film: it was in my head.

I said, You're enjoying this, aren't you? And then my stomach gurgled, and I crossed my arms, looking away. I couldn't speak for I don't know how long. And then, finally, all I could say was, I told you, it's not us. The smile left his face, then he leaned forward, and he goes, I'm telling you that all these videos were traced to John's website, and I cut him off. I said, Cam's website is down—I checked. And Foley goes, Maybe it was. But it's not anymore, and then he turned the computer toward him and he goes: See for yourself, and before I could say no, Foley pressed a key, pulling up Cam's homepage. And then he pressed another key, and pulled up the same videos that were on YouTube. Foley stared, waiting, and all I could do was stand and say, Can I go now? Or do you want to watch it again? I pushed the chair in, and he goes, Theadora, *please sit down*, and there was something so hard and cold in his voice, I did.

I go, Anyone could've hacked into his account, and Foley goes, Agreed. But it's quite a coincidence, don't you think? That he goes missing, and then these videos appear? I go, I seriously doubt Cam ran away so he could post sex tapes on the Internet, and Foley goes, Theadora, do you know Cam's IQ? I said, No, and he goes, One hundred sixty-nine, like it was three separate words. Smart, I said. Genius, actually, he said. As a matter of fact, and I don't mean to be rude here, Theadora, but what do you think John—Cam, sorry—what do you think Cam saw in you? I go, I'm sorry, but what part of that isn't rude? He goes, What

I'm asking is, what do you two have in common, Theadora? I go, Why don't you ask him that? When you find him, I said, and he smiled, and he goes, I'll do that, and I looked away.

Now, he said, trying to act all pleasant again, given your age and the sensitivity of this case, we contacted YouTube. We told them to take the video down, and they have not yet complied. That's one of the reasons we need to speak to your mother, as well, he said, and so many thoughts started rushing through my head. Your mother should be here any minute, he said, and I was just like, *Ohmygod*. I go, No, please. Please—please don't tell my mom! I'm so sorry, he said, looking up, a second before there was a knock at the door. I just looked at him, pleading, and then he goes, Come in, and he stood up, smiling, and I just hid my face in my hands: *Why me? Why is this happening to me?*

When my mom walked in, I couldn't even look at her, while Foley held out his hand, saying, Hello, Mrs. Denny, asking her to sit down, so she did, right beside me. Then he showed her my drawings and the videos. With me, sitting right there, and then, finally, Mom held up her hand, blocking the screen: That's enough, she said, and she turned to me. I was staring at my hands, trying not to cry, but I could feel her looking at me, expecting some sort of explanation, but all I could say was, It's not me, and she goes, *Thea*, and I go, It's not me! And out of the corner of my eye, I could see Foley folding his hands again.

I nodded, disgusted, then I caught Cheesy, nodding his head, too, standing guard at his perch in the corner of the room. I'd gotten so used to him being there, I didn't think about it anymore. And I could tell Cheswick wanted out of that room almost as badly as I did. Because it might have seemed all sexy and *Law & Order*, but, in reality, it was some fucked-up shit you really didn't want to know about, ever, and now Cheesy had to carry it around, just like I did. Then and there, our relationship as principal and student changed. Cheswick nodded at me once, in resignation, and I knew that from then on, the rule was, You stay in your corner, and I'll stay in mine. I break a rule, skip a class, from now until Cam comes back, so long as I don't kill anybody, let's stay out of each other's way. And that's how we'll get through this.

Then Foley goes, Actually, Mrs. Denny—we don't need to watch any more, no—but what's particularly alarming is that every time this video plays, it becomes sharper, a clearer image. And seeing as it's become an Internet phenomenon, the video has quickly gone from the likes of Super 8 quality to high-definition— it's going viral, as we speak, he said, and I felt like I'd been kicked. For a second, I couldn't breathe, like someone had kicked me in the gut, and I really thought I was going to hyperventilate.

Also, he said, while Mom was still trying to form the question in her mouth, How? How is that possible? One other thing, he said, and then, at that second, someone knocked on the door, and Foley goes, Come in, and this nurse's aide walked in, carrying a briefcase. Foley removed a piece of paper from behind the computer, and he goes, As I explained to your mother on the phone, Theadora, we need to fingerprint you, and we need a blood sample, and I nodded, not understanding. The woman started opening her leather bag, and my mom grabbed my arm, steadying me, and Foley goes, I'm sorry to do this to you, Theadora, but we need to take a sample of your blood, court order, he said, but I didn't care. No, I said, trying not to panic. No way—don't even think about it, I said, and Mom squeezed my arms, like she was trying to give me strength, soothe me.

Foley removed a digital fingerprint scanner, sliding it across the table. If you would put your right palm flat on the screen, please, Theadora? I placed my hand on the black scan, that was fine, but blood, no. No blood: I just kept shaking my head, no blood sample. Foley tilted his head in one of his stock concerned looks, then he said, Unfortunately, the local police were extremely sloppy in their handling of this investigation, and we have since found blood in the trunk of John Conlon's car. So we need to make sure it's not your blood, Theadora, and I said, I'm telling you, it's not my blood, and I tried to keep from panicking, seeing the woman start removing things from her bag—that's what it was, a doctor's bag. That's what she was there for, and I saw the needle, and right away, I thought I was going to puke, and my mom said, Don't look. I didn't look, but I almost passed out, just thinking about it, and after the woman put the Band-Aid on my arm, I stood up, almost stumbling, and then I ran for the bathroom.

## THURSDAY, MARCH 3, 2011
## (FIVE WEEKS EARLIER)

I try to talk to my mom, I really do. Sometimes. Like a couple weeks ago, I got this idea, reading about the earliest days of photography, back when people tried using photography to help treat the mentally ill. I'm not sure how they thought it would help, but that's why there are all these collections of photographs of patients at all these mental institutions in the U.S. and England from the 1800s, right?

Well, so my idea was that this handsome photographer is commissioned to take portraits, create this whole collection of pictures of the patients of an asylum. And while he's there, he meets one of the patients, this young woman, and of course she's beautiful and she comes from a good family, but she never talks, and it's like she never sees him. She's completely in her own world, and when he tries finding out why she's there, no one can tell him for certain what happened to her or what the problem is.

So the photographer gets this idea that maybe he can treat her or heal whatever's ailing her by taking her picture; maybe he can draw her out and give the girl her voice back through his photography, but it doesn't work. Turns out, the Native Americans were right, that the camera does steal a piece of your soul, and he knows that myth, because he's been to the West, and he's taken pictures of different tribes; he's been warned. But then he keeps taking her picture, trying to find her, reach her, trying to love her. But most of all, he's trying to make her love him back. That was as much as I knew, but I started drawing the things I could think of. Like this scene in the hospital gardens, and then, later, this scene in a forest, where he takes her to photograph her.

But that's all I know so far, really. I mean, I think maybe he finds out the real reason she's there, and maybe, whatever the truth is, it's much better and much worse than he ever could've imagined. Maybe the girl starts speaking; she tells him her deep, dark secret, and it turns out she's really not crazy at all, and he wants to help her escape or to run away with her. I don't know, maybe he thinks she'll love him, that she could love him, and finds out that she can't; she'll never love him, and that's why he keeps taking her pictures, knowing he's capturing her soul, frame by frame.

I was thinking about calling the story "Ambrotype," but I'm thinking I'll just call it "Sepia," because it's easier. Still, I thought it could be a really beautiful period piece, but it could also be about modern photography and all the things we deal with today, becoming obsessed with people we don't even know just because we have a picture of them on our desktop. I felt like it could actually work, and so I kept writing everything that came to mind. I was just trying to finish a first draft to give to Cam for Valentine's, right? So one night, I took a break and I went into the kitchen to get something to drink, and my mom looked up at me, smiling, sitting at the kitchen table, and she reached out to grab my arm, just like she used to, and I don't know why, but I told her my idea.

I took a glass out of the cupboard, and then she asked what I'd been up to, and I said, Hold on, I'll show you, and ran to my room and got our sketchbook and took it back to the kitchen. Her car broke down and she had to put all our money into getting it fixed, and things had been so stressful, I just wanted it to be like it used to be, when I'd show her my drawings. I know it hurt her feelings that I share so much with Karen now, and not with her. And that's partly because Karen studied art and film, you know, but I think I also share so much with Karen exactly because she's not my mom. That's the point, you know?

Anyhow, I told her the whole idea, and Mom goes, That's an amazing idea, Thee. How's it start? Like this, I said, sitting down and opening to the first drawing, turning the sketchbook so she could see. I said, It looks like lapse photography of storm clouds, right, but it's actually steam, you see? I think it should start, like the credits start with one of the patients, sitting in a chair, sitting still, staring at the audience. Someone attractive, not one of those crazy women without teeth who looks like she's from Appalachia. Because back then, you'd have to sit still for five, ten minutes, even, for daguerreotypes. Like they had neck braces and all this equipment to keep people from moving, because it was so expensive, and you'd have to sit perfectly still for such a long time.

Mom shook her head and said, Braces? Yes, I said, these huge braces, I said clasping my hand behind my neck, so happy to see she was totally into the idea. And at one point, Mom, I was thinking of circling the camera around, showing the metal braces from behind the sitting models, so you'd feel how uncomfortable it was, having your picture taken, like the things people were willing to do, but anyhow. Credits don't take ten minutes, but like a good three or four minutes of this person staring at you, while names appear in old-fashioned handwriting, and then, at the end of the credits, the model finally blinks, and then a flash goes off, and then there's a cloud of smoke. And then, I don't know, maybe cut to another cloud of smoke, when a train stops at the station, and the photographer gets off, carrying all his equipment, all these leather bags and old tripods. Cam will know how to make it work, I said. I guess it's not really very developed yet, but we'll see, I said.

Mom smiled, not saying anything, and I had to smile, thinking how Cam always says, You're color, kid, and I'm play by play. Like baseball announcers, you know? How one announcer handles the technical, and one does the song and dance, entertaining. And I liked being color, too. So how's it end? Mom said, propping her chin with one hand. I could tell she was genuinely interested in the story; she wasn't just being nice because she's my mom. We were having such a good time, hanging out together, then who walks through the door? Hey, girls, Rain Man said, waltzing in, and I rolled my eyes—seriously, what timing. Hey, Mom said, smiling, and then he leaned over to kiss her, and I had to turn away, thinking, *Never mind me and my gag reflex. . . .*

Ray goes, Hey, Theadorie, and I go, Hey, and he goes, Don't let me interrupt, heading straight for the fridge. And I said, Easier said than done, Ray—I said it under my breath, but my mom cocked her head at me, even though I don't think Raymond heard, because he'd already grabbed a beer and was fishing for a bottle opener in the silverware drawer. Mom kept looking at me, though, telling me to watch myself, because Ray's been behaving lately.

I know she was trying to be nice, to show me she was proud or something, make peace, I don't know. But then she goes, Thea, tell him about the script you're writing, and I just looked at her, like, *Why did you have to say that? That's private: this is why I don't tell you anything anymore, because for some reason, you think you have to tell Raymond, who never even gets it.* I didn't say anything, and she goes, It's such a great idea for a movie, Thea, tell him.

It's hard when you're being flattered that way, but there's a price, you know? So I sighed out loud, and I said, I have an idea about a photographer in the 1860s who falls in love with a beautiful girl in an insane asylum, who he's commissioned to photograph, and then he steals her soul because she doesn't love him back. Or maybe he breaks all the plates, killing her, but freeing her soul, I'm not sure yet, I said. And Ray goes, Wait, a little girl? furrowing his brow, before tilting his head way back, taking a drink. I said, A young woman, trying not to clench my jaw so tight I'd never be able to open it again.

Ray goes, This is a movie idea? opening the cupboard and taking out the can of nuts, and I go, Yes. It's a movie script for a movie, Ray. By the way, did you wash your hands? I asked, watching him shove his hand in the tin of mixed nuts Mom keeps for him. And then my mom goes, Thea, don't be rude, and I looked at her, like, I'm being rude?

Ray could care less. He takes a sip of beer and goes, Well, if you ask me, and I go, Actually, I wasn't asking you, and Mom cocked her head, and Ray goes, I'm just saying, it's a little twisted, is all. Really, who wants to watch a love story that takes place in a nuthouse? he said, grabbing another handful of salted nuts. I looked at him, and then I go, Whatever, slapping my sketchbook shut, and I got up to leave the room. Of course Mom called after me, telling me to come back, and I ignored her, slamming my door as quietly as I could get away with without being scolded about slamming my door. I'm sorry, but I was having a good talk with my mom for once, and then Raymond has to walk in, and it's just like, *Ugh. I can't stand you.*

Anyhow, I fell on top of my bed and opened up to the page again, the one with the picture of trees, the pictures of everything the girl sees in her silent world, all the beauty in her mind, no matter that everyone takes it for darkness. I mean, it's called *crazy love*, after all, so what better place to set a love story than an insane asylum?

## THURSDAY, APRIL 21, 2011
## (SEVENTEEN DAYS LATER)

12:58 PM

Then I just started crying. I mean, not in the conference room with my mom and Foley—I didn't have anything to say to either of them. No, I made it to the fountain in the hall, before I retched, and then I went back inside. I sat there, staring at the table, while Foley told my mom everything he'd just told me. When he finished, Mom said the same thing I did, that she didn't believe Cam would ever do such a thing, but she turned white as a sheet—only time I've ever seen my mom that pale was when she got food poisoning, that time we were on vacation in Mexico. When sixth period bell rang, Mom stood up and said, Agent Foley, I'll need to speak to my daughter about this, so Foley nodded his head, like he was overflowing with compassion, liar, and he gave her his card, and then we walked out of the office.

When we got to the hall, Mom offered to take me home, but I said no, because I didn't want to talk—I couldn't, and she was as shell-shocked as I was, so I knew she'd wait until she got back from work. She turned and walked out, and I went to my locker to grab my books, and last bell rang, and I was late already, but that's when I went to the bathroom, and I went into one of the toilets, locked the door, and then I just started sobbing. When I couldn't cry anymore, and I don't even know why, but I called Knox. I just needed someone to talk to, and who can I talk to anymore? He picked up right away and asked what was wrong, and then I started blubbering all over again, so he couldn't understand what I was saying when I told him someone put tapes of me and Cam having sex on the Internet. And Knox goes, Thea, where are you? I go, The girls bathroom, where do you think? Then he sighed and goes, I better come and get you, so I told him, I said, Knox, I don't want to talk about it anymore, okay? He goes, Good: me, neither.

When he picked me up, out front, I got in, and he didn't say anything. I couldn't tell if he was being for real or not, so I said, I feel like you aren't saying something. And he said, I'm not. And I go, You saw the videos, didn't you? He nodded yes, and I said, Speak up, then, and he goes, That afternoon, you two cut class and drove to your house? And I said, Yes, and he said, And then what? I was so annoyed. And we had sex, I said, okay? And he goes, I'm sorry, Thea, but I have to make sure I'm understanding you. You're telling me that you and Cam did have sex that day? I said, Yes, we did, but it's not us in the video, Knox. He goes, How can you be sure? And I go, Because we didn't tape ourselves, that's how! I yelled it at him, too, and he held up his hand, holding me back, and I sat back in my seat.

12:58 PM

He looked in the rearview, and then he goes, I'm sorry to have to say this, Thea, but look at the facts, and I go, He *didn't. Do it.* Okay? It's impossible, I said, and he said, Anything is possible, and I said, Not in this case. And he goes, How can you be so sure, Thea? I said, One, because I know Cam, and two, because it never happened. Knox goes, What do you mean it never happened? I said, You won't believe me if I tell you, and he raised his brow, and he said, Try me. I go, Okay, then. The last video, that one that looks like us from that Saturday night, the one that looks like us having sex in the bathroom at that party? It never happened. I'm telling you that it can't be us in that video, because it *never happened*—it was just something I thought, and then Knox's head started shaking, and he pulled over. He stopped the car, and then he turned to look at me like, let's get this straight. Knox goes, Thea, you're telling me . . . you're telling me you two didn't have sex in the bathroom that night; you only thought about it? What, like a fantasy? You're saying it's a video of your fantasy? I looked over at him, and I go, *Exactly.*

## THURSDAY, MARCH 3, 2011
## (FIVE WEEKS EARLIER)

Cam's hands were all black from Magic Marker, helping me scrub the ink off my feet, before we got back in bed. I put my arm across his chest, and he was looking at one of my scars, and he didn't say anything. He was just looking, turning my biceps to the light, and I told him, I said, Craziness is genetic, you know? I come from a long line of crazy people, and he goes, Hard to believe.

I go, I'm not kidding. One year, when I was about five or six, they had a family reunion on my dad's side, and it was this big, big deal. Like even my mom came, and she never went to Nanna's house. Anyhow, I just remember everyone whispering about one of my dad's cousins who was there. I guess he got special permission to be there, because he'd had some sort of breakdown, and they had to commit him. I didn't really understand that at the time, but I remember overhearing some of my relatives talking about how it all started. David, my cousin, when he was a teenager, I guess he had such bad insomnia that he could barely go to school, then he started seeing things. So one morning, he walked down to the breakfast table, and told his parents there were ghosts in their house, and then it got worse, the hallucinations, whatever, until he was diagnosed as schizophrenic.

He was about my dad's age, and he was really handsome, too, David. I remember seeing him sitting in a chair, alone, at the back of the room, during the big party. I stopped to look at him, and I was young enough, it didn't occur to me how rude I was being, staring. I couldn't help it, though, because I thought, *He doesn't look any crazier than anybody else*, and then, right on cue, David smiled and curled his finger for me to come over to him. So I walked over, and he goes, You're Thea, aren't you? I nodded yes, then he goes, Do you want to hear a secret? And I did— ohmygod, I wanted to hear a secret so badly, because I knew he must have some really good secrets, because crazy people always do, right? I nodded, so serious, and I said, Yes, and then he cupped his hand, leaning over to whisper in my ear, and he goes: There are angels all around you. Did you know that?

I remember opening my eyes wide, because I believed him, and I started looking all around for them. And the thing is, he's all dressed up, and he was so handsome, but I knew he was living in some completely different reality from the rest of us—kids can tell, you know? Then he leaned toward me, and he said: Thea, I've been watching you all night, and the angels have been following you everywhere, he said, running his index and middle finger all over the room, and then, out of nowhere, my dad swooped in.

Dad goes, Is Thea giving you any trouble? leaning over, smiling at me. And I could tell my dad was afraid, but I had so many questions I wanted to ask David, because I'd never met anyone who could see angels, I said, looking up. Then Cam tucked my hair behind my ear and I felt so close to him, like we shared our skin. I said, Maybe it's silly, but I think we can become our own ghosts, when we stop living in the present, when we can't let go of the past. I don't know what that has to do with David, exactly, but I think he knew. Because I think all the angels and ghosts he saw, I think they told him things, secret things, and he got stuck in between now and then. I said, But see, that's the difference between kids and adults. Because adults look at that, and they say, How *could* there be angels and ghosts? Kids look at that like, How could there *not* be angels and ghosts?

Cam hugged me, and I laid my head on his chest, while he stroked the inside of my bare arm with one hand. It was so calming in a way, but at the same time, I could feel his hand running over all my scars, reminding me how strange my skin must feel to the touch. Just then, he said, Shhh, like he could read my mind, and I couldn't help grinning, hiding my face, because I think he did.

I don't talk about the hospital much, not even with Cam, really, even though he knows the whole story, but I did then. I said, You know I thought about David a lot for those months when I was in the hospital, because I was where he was. I mean, we weren't in the same hospital, but I felt like I was in the same position he must have been in for all those years. And because I hadn't heard anyone mention him in so long, I had to wonder if he ever got better, or if he ever got out. Because I was so afraid I wouldn't get better, that I'd never get out, I said, looking up, realizing I was talking about the hospital, not even thinking about it. Cam never talks about his dad, and I never talked about the hospital, but looking at him, I knew he would let me tell him as much as I wanted, or as little. I wanted him to know everything about me, but at that moment, all I could say was, Isn't a ghost just someone trapped between two worlds? But Cam just smiled, looking at me for the longest time.

## FRIDAY, APRIL 22, 2011
## (EIGHTEEN DAYS LATER)

2:51 PM

Knox called Friday afternoon, right in the middle of class. And because of my *special circumstances*, as Principal Cheswick called it, I was allowed to keep my phone on vibrate in all my classes. So I was sitting in seventh period, when my phone started buzzing, and of course, soon as I saw the number, my heart stopped. All I could think of was Cam, that they'd found him, or—I don't know. Because the thought stopped there. Like it just cut off. The idea of him . . . the thought of Cam being dead, it, it's not possible. Hurt or in a hospital, maybe. That was as far as I could go. Because I'd know if something happened. I can't explain it, but I knew I'd feel something if he weren't alive. I don't know how, but I swear I'd know.

I asked for permission to go to the bathroom, and I was so worried, I didn't even listen to Knox's message, I just called. He answered, and right away, I go, Is it Cam? And he goes, Thea, you didn't get my message? I said, I didn't have a chance. What's wrong? And he knew what I was thinking, because he goes, No, it's not Cam, Thea. I'm sorry, I left a message saying that it was a personal matter, he said. And I go, Personal? Listen, he said. Do you have a minute? and I looked around the girl's bathroom. Sure, I said. Well, I wanted to ask you something, and I realize it's a little unusual, given the circumstances, but I wanted to talk to you about—. Melody, I said, thinking out loud. Yes, he said, and I said, Is she all right? She's fine, fine, he said, like he was waving his hand. It's nothing, and then I heard it in his voice. Okay, I just have to come out with it, he said: I was wondering if you had plans tonight? Plans? I said, laughing for the first time all day, What, like a kegger? Knox goes, I don't know, a party, or whatever you do. Not really, I said. Why?

Well, Melody was smiling all night, after you left, and to be honest, it's kind of an emergency, because I have to work tonight, and my wife's out of town, and our babysitter just called and she has the flu, so I don't want her near Melody, and you know what? He goes, It's probably a bad idea, and I go, Yeah, well, that's never stopped me before. I'll meet you at your house a little after three? Knox goes, That'd be great, thank you. Really, he sighed. Not because he got a sitter, though. I could tell that wasn't what he was most worried about, but something else. Like she wasn't the one who needed me, he was.

He acted kind of nervous, too, when I showed up. Thea, hello, come in, he said, stepping back, ushering me in with his arm, come in, come in. He was wearing his work clothes, and seeing me, he suddenly looked really stiff in his own house. Melody's in the living room, he said, so I followed him in. Melody, look who's here, sweetheart, he said, picking up the remote and turning down the volume. There were Nickelodeon cartoons on, looked bad. What are you watching? I asked, not really asking, just curious, and Mel goes, *He does this to me every day.* Hey, I said, stepping in front of her, so she could see me. Her hair was in braids, and I'm sorry, but once again, I was like, *Would you people please quit dressing her like she's five?*

*Nickelodeon. All. Day. Long,* she said, and I smiled, and Knox looked at me, curious. I go, I can't believe you make her watch this, Knox. And he goes, *Make her* watch this? I love Nickelodeon, he said, and I go, You're a *dad*! And he goes, What's that mean? And Mel goes: *Means no one cares what you think, Dad,* and I looked at her, *Right?* Ugh, I said, and Knox looked at me, then he looked at Melody, and then he looked at me again, and he goes, I'm right here, you know? And Mel goes, *Trust me, we know,* and I started laughing—she's very funny. Knox gave us this little nod, and he goes, All right, that's about enough out of you two.

Then his phone rang, and he held up his finger, answering. I watched him for a moment to be sure it wasn't Cam, and it wasn't. I could tell. Sorry about that, he said, I have to get a move on. Thea, help yourself to anything in the fridge. I'll be home in a few hours, he said, speaking to Melody. She's all set, he said, and if you need anything, call me, okay? I go, Just one thing, and he goes, What's that? opening the door. I go, Melody says to tell you she doesn't like Nickelodeon, and Melody goes, *Hate—I hate Nickelodeon*, and I go, Hate. She said she *hates* Nickelodeon cartoons.

Knox goes, She smiles whenever I put cartoons on, and he looks at me with that stunned dad face, all hurt and bewildered to learn a little truth about their daughter. Then he looked at Melody, like it couldn't possibly be true, and she didn't care. Melody said, *That's not smiling*, so I told him: No, she doesn't. And Knox goes, Let's talk about this later, and he walked back over and gave her a kiss, and she goes, *Yeah, that sounds great, Dad, we'll talk*, and I started laughing. Knox looked at me, and I nodded my head. All right, then, you got my number? he said, and I nodded yep, got it, and he closed the door.

*How was school?* she asked, watching me sit down on the couch, dropping my book bag. It was heavy, and I'd run the whole way. Same. As always, I said, starting to smile, and then feeling it clipped, remembering, thinking, *Same, as always, only a million times worse without Cam. I'm sorry*, she said, and only then did I realize she must know everything, maybe more than I do. Does he talk about it? Your dad? I asked, suddenly paranoid they were talking about me, about us. And she goes, *No, it's nothing like that. But I heard him tell my mom that a boy from town was missing—Dad doesn't talk about work, don't worry*. I go, It's fine. Really, the whole world knows, why shouldn't she?

*What's in your bag?* she asked, changing the subject. Books, I said. *That's all homework?* she asked. Most of them, I said. I have one from the library, but I haven't started it. I haven't been able to read. Like I start reading a line, and my eyes move, but then, two pages in, I realize I don't remember a word, I said, pulling the book out. *Thea*, she said, sounding so shy: *Can I ask you something? A favor?* Sure, I said, really curious what that could be. *Would you read to me?* she said, and I was so surprised, I said, You want me to read to you? That's the favor? *Yes*, she said. Course, I said. Of course I'll read to you. But I only have this with me now, I said, showing her my library book. You want me to read this? I asked, and she inhaled. *Will you? Just a few pages?* she asked, so excited. All right, I said, smiling. I'd never read to anybody, really. Well, Cam, but he didn't count—in a good way, I mean. So I turned her around, pushed her over to the couch, and took a seat. Then I opened the book, and I tried to do it all proper, reading the title, saying, Chapter One, and then I read to her.

We read almost forty pages before my throat got sore, and then we decided to watch TV for a while, but there was nothing on. So I pulled out my sketchbook, and I showed her some of my drawings, and then Knox got home. Early, like nine, even. What have you two been up to? he asked, and I told him. I read to her, I said, standing, reaching for my bag. That's nice, he said, smiling. What did you read? *The Lovely Bones*, I said, showing him the book, before I put it back in my bag. *Ah*, he said, like he knew it. And then he said, What's it about? I said, It's about a fourteen-year-old girl who's raped and killed by her next-door neighbor, then her ghost returns to help her dad find her killer. But we haven't gotten that far yet, I said, zipping up my bag, standing up from the couch, throwing it over my shoulder. He just stood there, looking at me.

*I like it*, Melody said. Yeah, I don't know, I said, because I was reading, and when I'm reading, I'm thinking about saying the words, reading it right, so I'm not sure. Then Knox goes, Thea, can I speak to you for a sec? I go, Sure, looking at him, waiting. And he goes, In the other room? Mel goes, *What's the problem?* So I told him, I said, Knox, Melody wants to know what the problem is? No problem, baby, he said, looking at her, like he'd heard her, then realizing he hadn't. *Then say it*, she said, and I go, She said to say it, and Knox exhaled through his nose. It's just, don't you think that's a little morbid? he said, and I go, Look, I didn't write it, Knox. And she asked me to read it to her, I said, shrugging.

*Tell him I like it*, she said. She said she likes it, I said. Listen, Knox said, I really appreciate you helping me out, but I don't think it's appropriate, all right? Have you read it? I asked. *Exactly*, she said. No, and I don't need to, he said. *So what's appropriate in your opinion?* Melody asked, and I told him, She asked what you think is appropriate? And Knox goes, I don't know, something, something happy and positive? I was like, Happy and positive? I said, Obviously you've never been a fifteen-year-old girl, Detective, and Knox goes, Obviously not. I go, You don't get the reference, do you? And Melody goes, *I don't get it either*, and I go, *What?* I turned to her and I go: You've never seen *The Virgin Suicides*? Okay, this is getting a bit much, he said. It's such a great movie, I said, ignoring him. Ohmygod, I can't believe you've never seen it! And I just looked at him like, *Shame*.

So Knox goes, Listen. I'm sorry, but rape and killing of teenage girls, virgins killing themselves, anyone killing themselves, it's just *not* appropriate, and then Melody goes, *What world are you living in?* I go, Seriously, and he goes, What did she say? looking back and forth at us. I go, Oh, so now you believe me? Knox goes, Thea, I told you, I don't know what to believe, but if you think she said something, I'd like to know. Mel goes, *Tell him if he doesn't like it, don't read it. Really, who was asking you, anyhow, Dad?* I repeated what she said: Who's asking you, anyhow? Knox goes, I'm her *father*, and Melody goes, *Dad, please. I'm fifteen—almost sixteen.* I go, She said she's almost sixteen. Knox did one of those big dad inhale-through-the-nostrils things, then he goes, Listen, it's getting late. Let's get you home, Thea, and Melody goes, *Because he knows he's wrong.* I go, I know, but it's not worth fighting about, and she goes, *I want to see the movie,* and I go, I'll bring it next time, and Knox gave me the eye, but I ignored him, opening the front door.

Their minivan was in the driveway, and it only took him a couple minutes to get Melody situated in the back. I could tell Knox was irritated, and so was Melody, but I didn't have anything to say, because I didn't do anything wrong. Seriously, don't kill the messenger, you know? Besides which, worse than treating her like an invalid, he was treating Melody like a child. And she wants so badly to be a girl, you know? God, you don't have to hear her to feel it. But I have to say, one thing I really like about Knox is that he doesn't make small talk, probably because he doesn't know how, but I wasn't complaining.

Here we are, he said, pulling into the parking lot in front of my building. It was dark, and the lights from the strip mall across the highway reminded me of something, while he parked and turned off the ignition. Here, he said, twisting in the seat, removing his wallet from his back pocket, and I shook my head no. Please, he said, you really helped us out, and I just looked at him, like, Dude. I go, I did it because I wanted to hang out with Melody, grabbing the door handle. Thank you, he said, seeing I wasn't going to take it.

Best Friday night I've had in weeks, I said, speaking to Mel. I go, We'll make it a double feature: *Pretty Baby* and *The Virgin Suicides*, and Mel goes, *You're on*, and then I caught this look on Knox's face, and I thought of the saying, Seeing is believing. But in his case, it was the opposite, like seeing us together, he couldn't or he wouldn't let himself believe, maybe because he wanted it to be true so badly, I don't know. 'Night, I said, holding my hand against Melody's window, and she said good night, and then I walked upstairs.

Knox waited for me to open my door, and then I waved down at him, but when he pulled away, I swear Melody did everything in her power to turn her head and smile, to raise her hand and wave, and my chest went, Oomph! And then I remembered the line. It's from a short story by Amy Hempel that begins *My heart—I thought it stopped*. I read it last year, in the hospital; someone left it behind and I guess the nurses must've thought it was a self-help book, because it's called *Reasons to Live*. I've always remembered it, because it's like, in one line, the whole story could go either way, you know? Like maybe it's only a fraction of a second, but still, there are always moments when even the heart doesn't know one from the other, good from bad.

## SATURDAY, FEBRUARY 26, 2011
## (SIX WEEKS EARLIER)

We took a drive and then we went to Silver Top, Saturday afternoon, and at first, it was just like any other day. What I mean is that I didn't see it coming, and I guess I chose to block it out, but still. Once we sat down and Sharon brought our drinks and a plate of fries, just as I was reaching for the red plastic bottle of ketchup, Cam leaned over and grabbed his backpack. I was wondering why he brought it in, then I had the strangest sensation, hearing him unzip it, and I didn't know what was wrong, until he pulled out a big white envelope and set it flat on the table, between us.

I froze. Because I knew right away. I knew by the size and the font and the pink postage in the corner—one look, and I knew he'd been accepted to MIT, and honestly, I felt a little upchuck in my mouth. Like I actually touched my fingertips to my throat for a second. I know that's awful of me, but it just hit me so hard, and before I knew it, my tongue was twisting in my mouth, and I had to bite to hold it down.

Of course I knew what it was. I mean, okay, I can barely pass half my classes, but come on, I know what a big envelope means. It means he's got a ticket out of Fort Marshall, means Cam was leaving. Seeing it there, inches from my hands, I didn't feel the wind knocked out of me, I felt punched in the gut, and I couldn't speak. I just waited, punishing myself, staring at the envelope like it was the enemy, cursing a piece of paper in my head. But it was his job to tell me, so I sat there, waiting, thinking, *Say it. Go on. You brought me here to tell me, so tell me.*

Finally, he reached over, pulling my chin up, so I'd look him in the eye, and I still looked at him—and even then, even when I'm angry, he's so beautiful, I think, *What are you doing with me?* But I still threw a fit, pushing him away, because sometimes that's the only thing I know how to do. I did; I looked away, acting all, whatever. Cam goes, I wanted you to be the first to know, pressing his hands across the table, reaching for my fingertips, and I pulled away.

He pulled back, and I go, Tell me what, Cam? And he knew I knew, but he said it anyway. He goes, I wanted you to be the first person I told that I got into MIT. I looked away again, at our fries, and I said, Does your mom know? Not yet, he said, spreading his fingers, pressing his hands against the table like he was going to reach for me. Told you I wanted to tell you first, he said, licking his bottom lip, and I go, Gee, thanks, but I couldn't look at him. I couldn't help feeling so angry, so . . . alone.

Then and there, I could feel it: I knew what was coming. He'd leave for school, and I'd stay, and we'd be one of those memories you grip on to for dear life, knowing you're the only one gripping. I was becoming the one left behind. My throat started swelling into a fist, and he goes, Thee, it's a long way away, a whole year, and I said, *Don't*, biting my lip: don't say it. He goes, Don't say what, Thea? I go, Don't give me the, Oh, I'll come back and visit. Or, Oh, we'll see each other on vacation, any of that bullshit people say, I said, looking out the window, clenching my jaw. He goes, I wasn't going to say that, and I go, Good, because it wouldn't be true, I said, but only after I swallowed to get the words out.

Thea, he said, reaching for my hand, I don't know what's going to happen, and neither do you. I go, Well, you're headed to MIT. That's what's going to happen, I said, sighing, crossing my arms, and he goes, Yes, I am. Well, congratulations, I said, raising my eyebrows, like, lucky you! Because that's about as much of a bigger person as I was capable of being at that moment. Thank you, he said. You're welcome, I said, twisting my tongue again. At that moment, I knew I was being such a bitch, but so what. He was leaving me: I had every right.

We just sat there for I don't know how long, but finally, he leaned forward again, and he goes, Look at me, and I tried, but I couldn't hold his eyes. Just out of curiosity, when did you find out? I asked, taking a sip of my Diet Coke. Last night, he said. Mom was at the store, so I got to the mailbox before she did. I go, Last night. And you didn't tell me? He goes, I didn't want to tell you on the phone, Thee. Was there a better time to tell you? Nope, I said.

Then he goes, You want to fight, don't you? And he was right, but so what? I go, Honestly, I don't want anything, Cam. Except to be alone, I said, reaching for my coin purse, pulling out a couple dollars and getting up to leave. And I did. Just like that, I got up and walked out, making up my mind to walk the entire way home. I had to: it wasn't a choice. I mean, for the first time in my life, I felt like someone had reached into my chest, taken hold of my heart, and ripped it clean, like it was nothing more than a chain around my neck. I wanted to be happy for him, because he's my best friend, and I was happy for him, but I was sad for me, I was so sad, all I could do was . . . feel angry. Cheap, I know, but easier than bawling, realizing I didn't know how to do this anymore: this, this town, these people, school, my mom . . . none of it made any sense if he wasn't there, and I didn't know how I'd ever get through.

I made it a couple hundred yards, and then I felt Cam pull up behind me. In his car, yes. Just before sunset, and he was driving about five miles an hour, on the side of the road, following right behind me. He didn't honk, he didn't roll down his window or anything, but still. At first, for like the first mile, I wanted to turn and yell, scream at him to leave me alone, let me be, I needed to walk. Alone! I didn't, I just made fists with both my hands, and he knew what I meant, and I knew he knew, and he knew I knew he knew, but he followed behind me anyhow.

I could see him like I had eyes in the back of my head, calmly driving, and one by one, the highway started lighting up with people turning on their headlights. And then it crossed my mind, how I must look, but I wasn't getting in. And if he wanted to follow the whole way, let him follow. And he did. Three miles, all these different cars slowing down on the highway, drivers honking to make sure I was all right, was this guy bothering me? Then, seeing it was obviously some sort of lovers' quarrel, whatever, they drove on.

I walked the whole way, too. Sometimes Cam could talk me down—just about all the time, but not now, not this time. I remember the sound of the gravel crunching behind me, as he slowly turned, pulling into our parking lot, but I didn't turn around even then. But he still waited out front—Cam waited until I got inside, and then, after I closed the door, he flashed his lights three times, shining through our curtains. Standing there, in our living room, alone, there were so many words, banging around in my chest, working their way up to my throat, choking me, and all I could think was, *Why am I such a spaz?* It was so embarrassing, because I knew what I was doing, and I knew it was wrong to behave like that, but I just couldn't do any better. And my eyes welled up, because it was his big day, that envelope was his ticket, and he earned it. Cam worked so hard, and I felt awful, so awful, seeing myself like that: small.

So I went back outside, fast as I could, and just as he was about to pull a U-turn, I leaned over the ledge, over the rail. I didn't even know what to say for myself, behaving like that, but he stopped and looked up at me. I could see him perfectly, too, because of the big overhead light that shines down on the parking lot; it'd just turned on. Still, all I could do was hold up my hand, press it flat against the air. That was all I had to say for myself, really. Cam looked at me, through the windshield for a moment, and then, he did the same, waiting as I moved my hand, aligning it, so it fit, pressing against his.

I didn't see him again until Monday morning, because he went with Karen to do some work on the properties she owns, somewhere in the Catskills. I worried for a second whether or not he'd pick me up Monday morning, but he did. I was so happy, too, when I saw him pull into the parking lot. I had an apology all prepared, when I got in the car that morning, then he leaned over and kissed me, soon as I closed the door. He goes, Before you say anything, I want to ask you something. He looked so serious, too, like he'd been thinking about it all night. All right, I said, bracing myself, taking a deep breath. Then he goes: Have you ever seen a thunderstorm in the desert? No, I said, waiting, thinking, *I'm the storm or the desert or where are you going with this? Natural disaster, what?* And he goes, No? I said, No. I've never seen the desert. Pictures, I said, shrugging. You've seen pictures, he said, smiling. I was just like, Yes. Looks cool. Very, um, mystic, I said.

He looked out his window, thinking it over, and then he goes, Thea, Thea, Thea . . . , squeezing the steering wheel with both hands. What are we going to do with you, Theadora Denny? I go, Is that a rhetorical question? Then he turns and looks at me: You've got to see the desert, Thee. You just gotta see it to believe it. And it is mystical, it's . . . it gets in your blood. It's like, I don't know. Corny, but it's just one of those places that make you feel so damn small, so completely insignificant, but in the best possible way, he said. Which is what? I said, and he said, Humbled.

And then, when it rains—I mean, it almost never rains, but if you're there when it does, it's like watching the earth and sky going ten rounds. *Awesome*, he said.

Someday, I said, still waiting for the gist. By that point I was just like, *Okay, let me have it already, you're making me tense here with these weather reports.* No, listen, we need to go, he said, and I said, I know: first bell is in ten minutes. Cam goes, I meant the desert, friendo, and I was just like, Oh. Right, I said. Why not? he said. We could road trip, end of the year, we could just hit the road, he said, and I was like, Oh, right, like my mom would ever agree. And he goes, She likes me, babe, and I go, Yes, she does, but but not that much. Cam goes, Leave the talking up to me, pulling out. You'll love it, he said. Joshua Tree, Death Valley. And I go, I'll love Death Valley? Thea, you wouldn't believe the flowers there, after it rains, he said. Fields of purple flowers like you've never seen. I want to take you to the desert, he said.

I thought about it, and then I said, Cam, don't tease, no longer amused. Thea, he said, reaching the stop sign, right before the highway. Do I look like I'm teasing? he said, turning to look at me, all serious. I looked at him, but I didn't answer. Well? he asked. No, I said, and then, pulling out, he goes, That's because I'm not teasing. I've decided you need to see the desert and we need to take a road trip. You've decided, I said, and he goes, I think what you meant to say was, Oh, thank you. Or maybe, Cam, you are the greatest boyfriend in the whole world, he said, and I started laughing.

Thing is, he's so forgiving. It's one of the qualities I admire most about him, how he could watch me screw up in some completely stupid, hideous, shameful way, and he'd forgive me, too. And I just kept spazzing out, since the day we met, and I kept waiting for him to see how ugly I was, inside, and if he saw it, well, all I know is, he never looked away. We just sat, quiet, all the way to town, until we pulled into the school parking lot, and he turned off the ignition.

Then he turned to me and he goes, You still getting your head around that, or you need some help, there, Sparky? I started laughing, trying my hardest not to laugh, but once in a while he'd throw out some nickname. And I am so not Sparky, trust me. Yeah, I need something, all right, I said. You're telling me, he said, because I need something, too. So maybe we could work something out, you and me, he said, winking at me. *Now*, he sighed, sitting back, so he could get a good look at me, his head freshly shaved, grinning as wide as the day is long, as my grandpa used to say. About that apology? he said.

I felt the blood heading straight for my cheeks, and then, almost as though it was ringing from the heavens, the bell! I raised my arm in V for victory, practically punching the top of the car. And that, friendo, that is what we like to call saved by the first bell, I said, taunting him, still holding my arms up high, and his face. Oh, what I'd give to have a picture of Cam's face at that moment, but, then again, who knows. I guess Nanna was right: there are times when you just have to look at what's right in front of you, take it in, and hold on as tight as you can, every last detail.

## FRIDAY, APRIL 29, 2011
## (TWENTY-FIVE DAYS LATER)

I have no idea how I made it through the week, but Friday, after school, standing on the front steps, I couldn't stand the thought of getting on the bus again, and I didn't want to go home. After everything that's happened, I didn't want to be alone any longer than I absolutely have to be. Which is not me at all, I know, but it was getting lighter out, every night, and I just wanted to sit somewhere I'd be left alone for a couple hours. Not school, not home, so I went to Silver Top.

It felt so strange, because it was the first time in six months that I'd been there without Cam. It was past three, but the Elders were still there. I've always called them that, because they're like a tribal council, the Elders. The first time Cam saw them, he said it looked like they must have called shotgun on the big booth in the back sometime in the sixties, and it's true—no one dares sit in the back booth if they're around. You know Silver Top has been open since 1963, and it hasn't changed one bit since then. Like it's still got the long row of round chrome and red leather stools at the counter, padded booths, and a rotating glass pie case. It's a time capsule, and it's definitely not Starbuck's. Which is another reason I love it.

And the Elders, they all wear a matching uniform, more or less. It's like this old-timer's dress code, and there's a little bit of variation, but their favorite look is something like a red and white checkered shirt, black Justin boots, and, of course, baggy-assed Levis, which they still call *dungarees*. I'd never been close to any of the four of them, but I just knew they smelled like the old man cocktail of whiskey, Old Spice, and Marlboro Reds, with the faintest whiff of engine oil, even though they scrubbed their nails spotless with Lava soap.

Anyhow, this is where they come, it's their home away from their homes, and they come every day, talking, not talking, like men who've known each other fifty years do, I guess. But sometimes, the way they look out the window, you'd think it was the silver screen. And when you walk in—doesn't matter if you grew up here, doesn't matter if you were here yesterday and the day before and every day for the past month—you'll hear growling in their stares. They're like the watchdogs of a time past, and they know it's passed—the Elders know better than anyone that it's gone, that their time has come and gone, and that's what makes it all the more valuable, their padded booth at the back, their clear view out the window. It's one thing that will never change, so they hold on to it for dear life.

Anyhow, I couldn't bring myself to sit in the same booth where we always sat. I just couldn't do it, so I sat a few booths away, looking at our booth longingly, with this pang in my chest, like, *Ugh, there's our booth, where we like to make fun of people who have things like Our Songs.* . . . Seriously, I caught myself getting all sentimental, but we spent so much together, right there, with nothing in the world between us but that Formica tabletop. Honestly, I was so out of it, I didn't even think about the fact I'd opened my old notebook to some sketches of Cam's hands that I'd drawn months ago, and I spread the spiral notebook open. I thought I was in the clear, too, but then my ears started burning, because I knew the Elders must have been talking about Cam, when I walked in, not sure whether or not to keep talking. Then one of them said, You hear the news? Then another one of them said, Hear what? FBI's involved now, one said, and another Elder said, I'll be damned, and another one of them said, In that case, you better get in line, and he took a lazy sip of coffee, slurping out loud.

I know because I saw the whole thing in the window's reflection. My ears were beet red, and then, sure enough, the bell rings above the diner door, and I know who it is, without even looking: it's Agent Foley. It happened so quickly, I didn't think to grab Hubble when I heard the bell, and a second later, he was standing over me. I could feel him, so I didn't look up, and he waited, and I ignored him, until, finally, Foley goes, Hello, Theadora. Would you mind if I joined you? I didn't look up, because I was too afraid to look him in the eye, and the whole place went quiet. I knew the Elders were listening, but I told him, I go, Yes. I would mind very much, reaching for my sketchbook. Of course: you're working, he said, in that annoying pleasant tone that makes me want to stab his hand with a pencil, *ugh*. So what's he do? He walked straight over to our table in the corner, directly in front of me, then he goes, Wonderful drawing, by the way. Those hands are so *lifelike*, Theadora, he said, sitting down, removing a discarded newspaper from the seat beside him, putting it on the table.

I tried ignoring him, and at the same time, I tried not listening to the old men, but the blood started in again, and I could feel it moving straight for my cheeks. Still, at that moment, trapped there, between two worlds, I couldn't care less who drove through the net on the highway or who defaced the school flag, and then, looking down at what I'd drawn, realizing my hand hadn't stopped moving the entire time Foley approached me and walked away, at that very moment, I began outlining and shading the words I'd written, *But what did they do with all those stars?*

From the moment she laid eyes on Foley, Sharon, the owner of Silver Top, didn't trust him. It was so obvious, too, when she walked over, just how stiff she was and how she stood back, saying a dry, curt hello, before she asked what she could get him, holding the plastic menu like a shield over her chest, not even setting it down for him to look at. Sharon wasn't having anything to do with him.

Coffee, please, he said, and she goes, Anything else? her voice as flat as a board. Just coffee for now, thank you, Foley said, and I could feel him smiling. Then he just sat there, with his hands folded on top of the table—I could see his hands, touching our table, and it grossed me out. I could feel him watching me, studying me, like he did in the conference room. So I had him in front of me, and behind me, I could feel the Elders staring at him, right through me, and they didn't like him, either. No, I could feel their stares like a furnace blowing behind me, and sitting there, between them, I felt like I was caught in a cross fire, until Sharon brought Foley his coffee. Then she came over, blocking his view. Fill 'er up, darlin'? she asked, looking at my glass. I shook my head no and looked up, smiling at her, so grateful for her protection, and I practically grabbed her wrist when she stepped away, hearing something drop in the kitchen, leaving me, like a sitting duck.

In all that time, I bet you no one blinked. It was so tense, and when it was clear that neither side was backing down, the old men started talking, like Foley was invisible. They were upping the ante, see, staring right at him, but really, looking right through him, just daring Foley to speak. I knew he knew what they were doing and he wasn't going to fall for it, but that wasn't the point. Territory, that's what you have to understand about people around here, the way they look at the whole world is about territory, and Silver Top belongs to the Elders.

I heard it was clean, too, said one of the old men. It was Del, I think, and they were back to talking about the school flag again, about the missing stars. I hear it looks like a seamstress cut them out, one by one, all fifty stars, but sewn up so there wasn't one loose thread, he said. What do you make of that? he asked. Dunno, why go to all that trouble? said Frank, who was the tallest and had the highest voice of the bunch. Did you see it? Del asked. I saw it, Frank said, Everyone's seen it. School might as well charge tickets, don't have any money in their budget. Well, there you go, Del said.

I almost jumped out of my skin when my phone rang. I mean, I tried to play it off, because everyone must've noticed, it spooked me so bad. The strange thing is—I mean, aside from the fact no one ever calls me, and thinking it's Cam every time my phone rings—when my phone rang, just then, I felt it in my bowels. Gross, I know, but it just twisted me up and made me so nervous for some reason. And I tried to play it off, checking, but I didn't know the number, so I ignored it, sighing, like, whatever. So I put my phone away again and acted like I was too busy to care. But Foley was smiling—I could feel it, and to be honest, between the phone call and the vibe he was giving me, I started sweating. My hands got all clammy, and I was afraid I'd smudge both pages of my sketchbook. So I pulled my phone out again, acting like I was texting someone, just to keep my eyes busy, but then my phone rang again. I thought maybe it was the same number, the same person calling back for some reason, but it was a New York number, 212. I don't know anyone in New York, but I was curious.

So I waited for both voice mails to come through, and then I turned to the window, looking away so Foley couldn't see my face, listening to the two messages, both from reporters. Can you believe that? Both calls were from reporters; one was a man, and the other was a woman, and they both said they wanted to speak to me. I couldn't imagine why some missing teenage kid would be big news, seeing as he's a legal adult, and no one had any information. I mean, people go missing all the time, right, so I nodded my head, looking at my phone, like, *Really?*

Foley knew—I could tell he thought he knew something about the calls or maybe he even knew who was calling. But I just ignored him and turned to look for Sharon, give her the sign. I caught her eye through the short-order window, and she put her hand up, so I left my money on the table and grabbed my books, trying not to look like I was running out. It's just beginning, you know, Foley said, speaking to me, but loud enough for everyone to hear, and I knew it then. They smell blood, he said, and hearing that word, the Elders stopped talking, and it was like the scene in a movie where there's the popping and cracking of shotguns and pistols, and everyone's got their finger on the trigger. I couldn't see either side, but who needs to see a gun to feel a trigger being pulled?

All I knew was I had to get the hell away from Foley, because if I didn't, he was going to say something else. So I walked out, and I knew Sharon would stall Foley if he tried to follow me—she always said she'd worked in a diner long enough to know a bad egg when she smelled one. Foley must've left cash on the table, because I heard the bell above the door chime twenty seconds after I got outside. Not even thinking about it, I grabbed my phone to call my mom and tell her I'd meet her at her office, but when I heard footsteps behind me, I had this feeling that Foley was about to say my name, and I swear, if I had to hear him call me Theadora one more time, I was going to scream. So I turned my phone off, and just started walking as fast as I could. Then, when I heard a car start, knowing it was him, I bolted.

I don't know how long I ran or where the hell I was going. I didn't know that part of town at all; I just kept cutting across people's back lawns, trying to stay away from the road, dodging a couple of spotted terriers who were looking for a fight. And then, at one point, I was so out of breath, I stopped and hid behind a tree along the dividing line between these two big backyards that must've been like two miles from town, at least. There I was, hiding behind a pine tree, my heart and lungs pounding like timpani drums in my ears, trying to remember the last time I ran like that. When I looked up, catching my breath, in the next house over, in this backyard, I saw this blue dome—a tent or something. There were cars parked in the driveway, but I didn't see anyone moving around inside the house.

At first, I just wanted to get a better look, see what was beneath the blue dome. I knew Cam would've been so proud of me, too, sneaking over to take a look, and it hurt for a second, not having him there. Then it felt like the only way to find him, to be close to him, was to touch the thing, like you have to touch home base in a game of tag: it had to be done, that's all I can say. Still, the whole time, I kept expecting someone to come out and ask me what the hell I was doing in her backyard, but no one did. And then, once I reached the dome, I don't know what got into me, but I had to get in, because it reminded me so much of the forts I used to play in when I was a kid. Really, what is it about kids and forts? I guess it's about having a place in the world we can believe is safe, even if the roof is made of a felt blanket with baby blue teddy bears on it, you know?

So I got in. And, then, once I was inside, kneeling down, I

had this wonderful and terrible feeling I was going to get caught. I laid flat on my back, and then I felt the hair on my arms stand on end as I thought, *What if Foley knows where I am?* Because at that moment, it really felt like he might walk straight into these people's backyard and knock on the walls of their blue fort, and say, Why, hello, Theadora. What are you doing here?

At the time, though, watching the light fade through the dome's opening, I was safe from Foley. I was in a fort, after all, and nothing bad happens to you in your own fort. Most of all, I just needed to close my eyes for a few minutes, and I didn't think I'd fall asleep, right there, but I did. I totally conked out, and when I woke up, my hands and feet were numb, I was so cold, and I had no idea where I was or what happened. When I remembered what happened, and I knew I was okay, my next thought was, *Mom. Ohmygod, my mom's going to kill me.*

I felt bad, because I knew my mom must've shown up at Silver Top right after I ran off, and that she'd be looking for me, and she'd be worried, but then again, you know what? Join the club, lady. So I fished out my phone and called her, and the first thing she said was, Where the hell are you? But how she said it was, *Where. The hell. Are you?* I go, I'm in a tent in someone's back-yard, and she goes, Are you *drunk*? I go, I wish, and she wasn't amused. She goes, Get home. Right now. Better yet, she said, tell me where you are and I'll come get you, changing her mind. Oh, I was going to get it, all right.

I'll be there soon, I said, and then I just turned off my phone. So I got on my knees, crawling out, getting up. There were lights on in the house, but no one was in the kitchen, so I walked to the road, in front of the house. I really needed to go home, but I couldn't. And then I had a thought. I turned my phone back on, ignoring the incoming messages, and I dialed Karen. I didn't think she'd answer, but she did. She goes, What's going on, sweetheart? I go, I have a big favor to ask you.

Okay, she said, and I go, I'll understand if you say no, but I hope you'll say yes, and she goes, Thea, tell me what the favor is, and we'll find out. So I took a deep breath, and I said, I was just wondering . . . and then I had to clear my throat, because I couldn't say it. Could I sleep in Cam's room tonight? I asked. She didn't say anything for a minute, and then she said, Yes. Thank you, I said, able to breathe again. Do you need a ride? she asked, and I said, No, I'll walk. Well, I'll be here, she said, and then, as she was about to hang up, I said, Oh, wait, Karen? Karen? And I just caught her.

One other thing? I asked, wincing. Now you're worrying me, she said. Out with it, and I said, It's just that, would you call my mom and tell her I'm spending the night at your place? Karen didn't say anything, and I thought maybe she was angry with me, then she started laughing. I said, What's so funny? But then I started laughing at her laughing, reaching the street, heading toward town. Then Karen goes, No wonder Cam loves you. I couldn't help smiling, because, I don't know, you don't throw that word around, but at the same time tears came to my eyes, and I thought I was going to start crying again, right in the middle of wherever the hell I was. So I rolled back my eyes, and I said, Karen? Her voice got all soft, and she goes, Yes, darling? And I go, So you'll call my mom? I could hear her nodding her head at me, unbelievable. See you soon, she said, hanging up.

It took me about ten minutes, but I made it to the highway, to the gas station. It's the easiest way to Karen's, cutting across town, so I walked to the station, coming from behind, where the toilets are. The station looked deserted, and I was looking at the fluorescent lights over the pumps, when I noticed something out of the corner of my eye. On the wall, behind the gas station, in these huge letters, like four-feet tall, someone had graffitied: **NBN**.

I stepped forward to touch the cement, because it was dripping—the paint was still fresh. I rubbed it into my fingers, but then I couldn't breathe, because it was Cam's handwriting: it was his. Right away, I reached in my bag and pulled out Hubble, flipping through, looking for one of the pages where he'd signed one of his equations—last winter, he got on this kick, signing all his equations with this ridiculous *NBN*, Natural Born Ninja, right, like he was Picasso or something—and when I found one, I held it up to the wall: same. Exactly the same. It was Cam's hand-writing, his tag: he was here, right here. I looked around, turned around, yelling, Where are you? Cam, where are you?! Then the guy came out, the cashier—same guy that was working the night I started crying about the dog, and when the guy saw me, he was like, *whoa*. He looked like he almost didn't believe himself, say-ing, It's you, and I go, Hey, raising my hand. He stepped around the corner, then he saw the wall and he balked, seeing the graffiti. Then he looked at me and he goes, Did you do that? I go, Do I look like a tagger? And he goes, Just asking. I said, No, I just got here—it's still wet. Then he goes, I heard screaming. You okay? I thought about it, then I said, Not really, but thanks for asking, and I put the notebook back in my bag, walking back to the road, before I started running again.

I have no idea how I did it, but I was way, *way* across town. It took me forty-five minutes to get to Cam's house, and when I did, when I knocked, the door flew open, like Karen had been waiting for me with her hand on the door the whole time, since I called. Oh, man . . . when I saw her—I mean, the way she looked at me, opening the screen door, I almost wished I'd gone home to face my own mom. You could have called, Karen said, opening the door, and I practically whimpered, I'm sorry, I didn't know where I was, and I just wanted to walk, and I didn't think it'd take so long—. Inside, she said, giving me the mom look, and I walked in and turned around, looking at her, trying to show her how sorry I was with my eyes, if I couldn't really tell her so. But once I was inside, I realized how cold I was. I didn't dress for being out after dark, and it was still cold at night. She just stood there, looking at me, and I was just like, *Please? Say something. This is awful.*

I'll get you a sweater, she said, walking up, rubbing both my arms to get the circulation flowing, and then walking to her bedroom. I loved the sweater she brought me. It was an old fisherman's sweater, and it was so big, it fit me like a dress. It was my father's, she said, smiling. You can wear it anytime you're here, Thea. Thank you, I said, hoping she could read the look on my face, see how bad I felt. You're welcome, she said, reading it. But trust me, I won't get suckered into calling your mom again without asking for more details. She's furious, she said, and I knew, but I couldn't help rolling my eyes. Save it, Karen said, she's worried. And I go, I'm sorry, and Karen goes, Don't tell me, tell her. I will, I said. Can I still stay? Of course, she said. You hungry? she asked, and I didn't even realize I was famished until she asked. Smells so good, I said, because Karen cooks, like really cooks. Cam and Karen, they ate dinner together. At the table. Every night. At my house, we save that for special occasions, when we're on our best behavior.

Stew, she said, shrugging, and that was the first time I noticed the dark circles under her eyes. You're free to go hang out in his room while I finish, she said. Thanks, I said. I won't touch anything, I said, and she goes, Believe me, between the police, the FBI, and me, everything has been touched. Fortunately or unfortunately, Cam kept his room spotless, and practically fingerprintless, too, they say. Anyhow, go on in, she said, so I walked down the hall, and I knew, from all the times I'd snuck in and out, which floorboard creaked. I tiptoed over them, because it was a habit, and then I realized I might never sneak out of Cam's house again. It made my throat get blocked up, and when I got to the door, I almost didn't want to open it. But I did, and the room was so empty. Nothing had changed, and everything looked just like Karen said, but without his computer, without his body, his spirit, the room was sad. Seriously, how can a room be sad?

It was so dark, my shadow was at least ten feet tall. I just stood there, at the door, looking in, thinking about him. Thinking about the last time we were there together, two weeks before he disappeared, and it seemed like a lifetime ago. And it was—it was a lifetime ago. I went to his closet and opened it, taking out one of his old jean jackets. Another hand-me-down of his father's, a seventies-style Wrangler denim jean jacket with thick shearling lining. I held it to my nose, smelling his collar. Thea? Karen called, and I jumped, quickly put the jacket back, closing the closet. I shouldn't have touched—I said I wouldn't, and I was sorry, and I whispered it to him, as if he could see me: I'm sorry, I'm sorry. . . .

You all right, Thee? Karen asked, walking down the hall as I stepped out of Cam's room. Yeah. Just needed a moment, I said, trying to smile. Time to eat, she said. They searched his room? I asked, following her back to the kitchen. Top to bottom, she said. Three times. Nothing? They didn't find anything? I asked. Nope, she said, pulling out a chair at the table for me. Then she goes, I have something for you, holding a box. When I saw what they were, she said, I didn't look. I know it's private, so I took it before the police came, she said. I thought you'd want it.

I opened it, and they were pictures I'd given Cam. Scraps of paper, notes from our first tutoring session, a sketch I was working on, the first day we ever met in the library, after school. It was a drawing I did of Stephen Hawking, wearing an American Apparel gold lamé leotard. Can I have this? I said, closing the lid and looking up. Of course, she said, it's yours, isn't it? And for the first time all week, since the day I took his car, I felt like crying. Karen walked over and kissed the top of my head. Want to hear a secret? she asked, touching the back of my head, taking her seat. Honestly, Karen, I don't know if I can take any more secrets, I said, swallowing to keep from crying. This one you can, she said: Sit down. So I did.

She took a sip of wine, then she told me. She said, The first day you two met, he came home and told me all about you. Cam would kill me if he knew I told you that, but that's what he gets for leaving the two of us alone, right? she said, setting down a big bowl of stew in front of me. I couldn't help smiling; it smelled so delicious, but I didn't know how I was going to eat a bite. I picked up my spoon, but then I just had to know: What did he say about me? I asked, and Karen started laughing. Took you long enough, she said, grinning. Cam said . . . she said, picking up the wine bottle and pouring a glass of wine for me and refilling her glass. Cam said that you were the most beautiful girl he had ever seen, Thea.

Then something in me snapped, finally, and tears came rolling down my cheeks. All this time I'd thought maybe it'd been a trick, or that I'd find out some joke was being played on me all, all because it scared me too much to think maybe it was true, all those times he'd told me that himself. Hearing it from Karen, I knew it was just me being too afraid to trust him, to believe he loved me, and it was so sad. Not like I felt sorry for myself, but to see what he'd been trying to tell me all along, and now he wasn't there when I finally figured it out. So I sat there for five minutes, and Karen just let me be.

We stayed up, sitting at the table until after midnight, talking. And Karen's . . . well, honestly, I don't know what Karen's doing here, in this town—I mean, she's so smart. Like Karen went to

Berkeley, and she studied film, and she's traveled all over the world. She knows all about art and music and, god, it's, I mean, she wears Black Flag T-shirts, listens to *Carmen*, the opera. And Karen *reads*. Books, yes. They have books all over their house, and artwork, and photography, and she follows all the design mags. So why would she move here? If it was Woodstock or one of those places, maybe, but *here*? I'm sorry, but I just don't get it.

So I finally asked her, straight-out, what would possess her to move to a town like this. And she looked at her wineglass, holding it between her thumb and middle finger, thinking it over, smiling that half smile, like Cam smiles when he's making an effort. We needed a change, she said, with this expression like she'd thought of all reasons she could give and that was most sensible. She looked up at me, smiling wide this time, but mostly to tell me the discussion was over. Time for bed, she said, getting up, taking her bowl and mine, and then I cleared some things from the table, following behind her.

After we cleaned up the kitchen, she turned out the light, heading down the hall, and I said it again. I won't touch anything, I promise, I said. I know I'd told her before, but I had to say it. I just wanted to be in his room; I'd never spy on him or anything like that. And she goes, Thee, you can touch anything you like. But one thing, she said, stopping to open the hallway cupboard: we'll need to change the bedding. Between you and me, I slept in there a couple nights ago, she said, and I guess my face gave me away. You don't need to do that, I said, seeing her arms loaded with sheets and pillowcases. You're right, Thee, she said, and then she loaded the stack on my arms: you know your way around that bed, right? And *bam!* Ohmygod, instant blush—like a raging forest fire just tore across my face. I swear, I almost reached to touch my eyebrows, just to make sure they hadn't been singed by my own blush. I mean, I knew she must know something, but that was so bad, I couldn't even look at her, and I didn't know if I'd ever be able to look her in the eye again, and then she started laughing at me.

Come here, she said, pulling me to her, but not that close, given the stack of bedding between us. You're going to be all right, she said, leaning over, kissing the top of my forehead. Whatever happens, she said, you're going to be all right, Thea. I go, You believe that? Really? I asked, looking up at her, hoping it was true, thinking, *Promise? Promise me?* Yes, she said. I do. Because I don't give myself any other choice, she said, cupping the side of my face with one hand. Karen is the only woman who I can stand looking at me, like actually stand still, looking back at her. And to be honest, that was the first time I thought about what she must be going through, having lost her husband, and now, no idea if she'd ever see her son again. But there she was, comforting me.

Good night, she said, and I said, Good night, turning to the door. Thea, she said, turning back, your mom will be here to pick you up first thing in the morning. Oh. Right. My mom, I said. Right, she said, and you owe me one—*oh*, do you owe me big time. I know; I know I do, I said, wincing again, sorry again. 'Night, she said, grinning at me, at the end of the hall, before turning off the hall light, opening her bedroom door.

I sighed, opening Cam's door again, but I didn't turn on the light, I just closed the door behind me. Then I sat on the side of his bed for a minute. I dumped the bedding on top of his bed, letting my eyes adjust, and then I just looked around at his desk, his bookshelves, all the pictures I'd given him, that we'd hung, together. Everything was there, exactly where he'd left it, but I didn't feel him. I mean, I felt better there than in my own room, but I couldn't figure out how Cam managed to take it all with him, his whole spirit.

I really didn't want to bother, so I made the bed as fast as I could, and then, very carefully, as if Karen could hear me, I opened up his shirt drawer and pulled out one of his shirts to sleep in. Changing in the dark, it was cold, and I climbed in, thinking, *What a week . . . what a crazy week,* realizing I was covering my forehead with my hand, rubbing my cold feet, sawing them together, trying to get warm. I sighed, tired, so tired, but safe, warm, blood flowing in my feet, even, so I pulled the duvet under my chin. I was just about to shut my eyes when I saw it. Looking up, it took a few seconds to register what I was seeing, on the ceiling, and then, one by one, five, ten, twenty, thirty . . . and I realized what it was: stars: fifty white cloth stars on Cam's ceiling.

Cam was lying on my bed, working on his computer, and I was sitting at my desk, working on another installment of *The Lola Crayola Chronicles*. So I didn't notice when he stepped up, behind me, and then, when he put his hands on my shoulders, I screamed, he scared me so badly. After I calmed down, I slapped him, and I go, Don't do that! You scared me! He goes, You didn't hear me saying your name, did you? And I said, No, and he said, I'm sorry, Thee, I'll shout louder next time. What I said was, can I see?

He meant the drawing I was working on, so I showed it to him. I said, That's the famous Lola Crayola. She was my best girl. Then I told him the whole story, about how, when I was little, I had a doll. I mean, I had lots of dolls, of course, but my favorite was Lola Crayola. I'd dress her, feed her, pose her in different costumes, and then I'd draw her for hours. She was the best model I ever had, my muse, my best friend. I wrote stories about her and all her adventures—I still do, sometimes.

When he left, when my dad left us, I threw her away. I threw her out just to prove I could. To show them all, to show the whole world I could always hurt myself worse than it could, worse than *anyone* could possibly hurt me. So I threw Lola in the kitchen trash, with coffee grounds and gristle. I remember so clearly, stepping on the black piece, the step of the trash can, and its mouth opening, and seeing all that trash, and throwing her in. I can still feel that in my toes, too. That was my first cutting.

I watched my mother take out the trash the next morning, and I watched as the garbageman threw her into the back of their garbage truck and drove off. Why? *Because I can. Because you will never hurt me as much as I can hurt myself, so try all you like*, I thought. Still, I had nightmares after that, all the time. And in my nightmares, I heard Lola crying, alone, in the dark. A couple weeks later, right before we moved here, my dad woke me once, hearing me crying for her. He turned on the light and he told me he'd get me another doll, even better than Lola, but that only made waking worse than the nightmare. I started yelling at him: How can you say that? You don't understand: you'll never understand! I screamed even louder than before. I was hysterical by that point, so he called my mother at two, three o'clock in the morning, waking her up. He told her it was an emergency; she needed to come and pick me up; there was nothing he could do for me.

When my dad drove me home, he took me inside, and I heard him whispering, talking to my mom in the other room. Dad said they needed to do something, and my mom said exactly what I was thinking, Do something? What should we do? Like what? she said. Dad snapped, Renee, Thea was hysterical—she threw away a doll for god's sake. It's not normal, he said, and for the first time in my life, my dad sounded like Nanna, his mother. I came so close to walking in and telling him to his face, What's normal, exactly? Besides, it's not about whether her heart was as real as mine, it's about my heart—*my* feelings were real. I loved her. My love made her real.

How could I explain it any more plainly to the man? She was my favorite doll, you understand? She was my *best girl*, and I threw her away. Just to prove I could. To prove there was nothing my dad could do to me that was worse than what I could do to myself. I told Cam everything about her, everything I could remember; I confessed all my sins. People talk about pouring their heart out, and I did. I'm just not sure if I opened my mouth that whole time. But, really, does it matter if I said it in words or a drawing of Lola Crayola, standing in a truck-stop parking lot in the middle of nowhere, no place for a pretty little doll with a girl's bloody heart?

## MONDAY, MAY 2, 2011 (FOUR WEEKS LATER)

6:47 AM

In my dream I open my eyes, and I'm standing in a green field, in front of a small white house, and Cam's car is parked in the grass, and he's calling my name. At first, it sounds like he's inside, calling me, so I run inside the house. There's graffiti all over the walls, endless rows of 1s and 0s—just like the pages of our notebook that Cam used to fill with 1s and 0s, and it all seemed so random and garbled and insane, but he'd say he was just tagging reality. All the walls, the entire house is tagged, and it's exactly the same as what he wrote in Hubble, only bigger, much bigger. I know his writing—I even know his writing when it comes out of a spray can—I can see his left hand from a mile away. *He's here*, I thought. *Cam's here! It has to be him*. Cam! Cam, where are you? I check every room, but he isn't there. I can feel him everywhere, but he isn't there, and I keep wandering around, knowing I just have to keep looking, and then he calls my name again.

Now it sounds like he's outside, and I start laughing, running to find him. I run back to the front yard, I run all around the house, but he's not there. It's dark by then, and in the distance, I see this car approaching, and I can't make it out, but it looks like an SUV, coming straight for me. I think maybe it's Cam, but then, as it pulls up the drive, I can't see who's behind the wheel, because the lights are so bright, I have to shield my eyes, and I try to cover my face, but I can't block out the light. . . .

Bright—too bright—there's light, shining in my eyes. It's annoying, too, like I fell asleep with the light off, but then I turned over, opening my eyes, and it was pitch dark. I had no idea what time it was, but I was awake. So I stumbled to the bathroom, and sat down to pee, and I opened my eyes a crack, and there it was again, the light, this green light, shining in the bathroom mirror. But I couldn't see where it was coming from, so I stood up, and then I almost started screaming, because the light wasn't behind me, it was *on me*. There was this thing, this, this—it was like a tattoo—that's exactly what it was. It was a tattoo, on my shoulder blade. And it was *glowing*.

I tried scrubbing, and it wouldn't come off, whatever it was. So I just sat in bed, staring at it in the hand mirror, and then, when it started getting bright, it started to fade. The fluorescent light went out, and you couldn't even see it. I've been so tired, I've been so stressed out, I thought . . . I thought maybe I dreamt that, too. I didn't say anything to my mom, of course, but when I got to school, I called Knox, right away, and he goes, What is it, Thea? I go, I have to see you, and he goes, When? And I go, Now. He goes, I'm still at home, and I said, Knox, it's an emergency, and he said all right. I go, I'll be there soon as I can, and I ran all the way over, couldn't even breathe, when I rang their doorbell.

He opened the door, and I walked in, catching my breath. I looked in the living room, but she wasn't there. I said, Where's Melody? He said, She's got physical therapy this morning, and I was really disappointed to hear that. I wanted to see her, I said, and he said, I'll tell her you stopped by. So what's this all about, Thea? I said, I have to show you something—you've got to see it with your own eyes, and he goes, What is it, Thea? Tell me what's going on, and I go, Do you have a basement? Somewhere dark? Knox nodded, not understanding. I go, Knox, I just need a dark room, okay? And he goes, Oh. How's the guest bathroom? I go, Perfect.

So we walked to the end of the hall, I went in, and he stood there, at the door, and I said, You have to come in. So he came in, with me, and it was tight, like big enough for a sink and a toilet, and I said, You aren't going to believe this, and I started unbuttoning my shirt. And he goes, Whoa—whoa, don't, don't—what are you doing? I go, Please. I have to show you my shoulder. Now turn out the lights; give me a little privacy. He goes, Thea, tell me—tell me this isn't going to look as bad as it looks right now? I go, No, it's not. It's going to look a lot worse. Now would you just turn out the lights? So he did, leaning as far away from me as he could, and then I pulled my shirt down, showing him my shoulder blade.

I couldn't even see him. You couldn't see anything except my tattoo, glowing even brighter than I remembered it in the middle of the night. Then, finally, Knox goes: What, what, what is that?

Is that like some sort of highlighter or paint? I said, It's not a highlighter or paint. I have a scar on my shoulder, and it's a heart with an arrow drawn through it. It's a glow-in-the-dark tattoo, right through my scar. He goes, *Wow*, I never heard of a glow-in-the-dark tattoo, and I go, Probably because they don't exist! You saw it, right? And he said, I saw it, all right. I go, Good. Now look, I said, turning on the light and pulling my shirt down again, so he could see. He leaned forward, looking, and I go, You can't see it now, can you? And he goes, Calm down, and I go, Knox, don't tell me to calm down, you aren't the one who's fucking glowing in the dark here!

He winced, and then he goes: Does it hurt? And I said, No. No, I can't feel it at all, and then he said, Thea, we need to take you to a doctor—. No, I said: no doctor, no lawyers, no trouble. And he said, Thea, please, we—. I said, We what, Knox? He shut his mouth. No means no, I said, ending the discussion. All of a sudden, he snapped his fingers, and he goes, Hold on, hold on a second, shading my shoulder, then he goes, Holy shit. And he turned out the light, and I go, What are you doing? The bathroom flickered green a bunch of times, and then he turned the light back on. That's what I thought: dash, dash, he said. Morse—it's Morse code, Thea. I said, You know Morse code? And he goes, Used to. I was in the military. I go, You were in the military? Knox goes, Iraq, one, and I go, Can you read it? He goes, I'm a little rusty, but let's see. Dot dash; dot dot dot; dash dash dot dash . . . A, S, Q, he said, and I said, U? A, S, Q, U, right? And he said, Yes, how'd you know? Then I turned on the light, and Knox goes, I'm not done, and I go, No, but I know what it means, and he goes, You do? And I said, A, S, Q: A squared plus B squared equals C squared, and if the length of both A and B are known, then C can be calculated as follows. . . . Knox nodded his head, with no idea what I was talking about. I said, It's a message, and he goes, What's the message? Then I pulled up my shirt and opened the door. He's alive. For the first time, I felt happy again, this surge in my chest, because I knew it was true. I go, It means Cam's alive.

Let's get lost, that's Cam's favorite game. I'm serious, he's in love with the idea of getting lost. Like, I'd get into his car, and he'd give me a kiss, and then he'd say, You know what we should do today, babe? We should get lost—let's just get lost, huh? And then I'd smile and nod my head, like, sounds great, Cam. Give it your best shot. Because, see, the problem is, Cam has this innate sense of direction. Cam's never gotten lost in his life. Seriously, he has no idea how that feels, how scary it is, not knowing where you're going or where you are. For him, it sounded like a great time, like what a blast.

We were in their kitchen, talking, once, and Karen told me about this time they took him to London when he was a little boy and his dad had some conference there or something. So Karen and Cam had the day to explore, and the first day they went out, they got on the Tube, and it was so crowded, Karen got confused and they missed their stop somehow. So they got out at the next stop, and Karen tried turning around, but she was so disoriented, she got on the wrong train. So they got off at the next stop to turn around, and she walked them over to check the map, and Cam couldn't even read the names of the stations, but he read the map, following the lines, and he got them right back to their hotel. Karen said he was really happy, because he got to save the day.

Close as you ever got to being a Boy Scout, I'm sure, I said, laughing, seeing he was still proud of himself for saving the day. *NBN*, he said, looking all smug, and I just nodded, refusing to take the bait. Go on, ask, he said. Ask me, Thea—ask me what NBN stands for? I was just like, No, it's all right, and Karen got up from the table, mumbling, Oh, here we go, and Cam goes, Natural Born Ninja: invisible. Even when I'm standing *right behind you*, he said, before standing up straight, fanning both hands at himself, like, what can you do? Then he stood up from the table and did a jujitsu punch-block move or something, then bowed at Karen, and then bowed at me. I mean, for all his humility and his quietness, sometimes, he's just too much, you know?

Saturdays, whenever we'd go for drives, sometimes he actually tried to get us lost, taking random back roads, no GPS, no map in his car, nothing—almost like he wanted to know how it felt, because he couldn't do it. Kind of reminded me of all the times in the ocean, when I'd lay back, floating, and I'd try to sink to the bottom, but couldn't sink in the saltwater. Really, when they moved from California, Cam drove almost the whole way, Karen said, and he didn't look at a map once. Got the GPS right here, baby, he'd say, tapping his temple, and I was just like, *Ohmygod*.

Anyhow, he'd just stop at a stop sign on some dirt road, and he'd say, What do you think, Thee? Left or right? I hated him asking me that, too, because I knew I'd get us lost, except I'd be the only one in the car who was lost; Cam would be fine. In the woods, too, when we'd park somewhere, get out to hike around a bit, I always let him lead. I'd follow behind, with my camera, able to space out, watch the trees, the leaves, the back of his head, his neck.

Then this one time, we were walking on this hilly path; it was pretty narrow, and there were bushes on both sides of the path, and I stopped, because I was shooting film, and I wanted to check on something. But when I looked up, Cam was gone—vanished. There was this hill, and he'd been walking up it, like fifty feet in front of me, so I walked to the top of the hill, up the path, and I called his name, and he didn't call back. I started walking, and I told him to come out, because it wasn't funny, but it was silent. It was only two minutes, maybe, but I kept calling him, and then he jumped out at me, scaring me half to death. So I screamed at the top of my lungs, and then I couldn't even hear my own voice, my heart was pounding so fast.

Cam was so pleased with himself, too, I wanted to punch him, but I didn't, I just glared at him. He goes, You want to hit me? looking at my fist, still clenched, and I said, Yes, and he goes, Go on, stepping toward me, offering his arm. I go, No, I'm not going to hit you. Because violence is not the answer. Deeply satisfying, but not the answer, I said, turning around and walking away. I'm sorry, he said. Thea, come on—I'm sorry, okay? I didn't think it'd scare you so badly, but I was still so scared, all I could do was be angry, while he kept calling me. Finally, I just wanted him to be quiet, so I turned around and I go, What? What, Cam, what do you want?! And he goes, You're going the wrong way. The car's this way, he said, cocking his head in front of him. Oh, I said.

I walked past, quiet the whole way. When we got in the car, closing both doors, I just sat there, staring straight ahead. Still, watching him back out, heading back down the dirt road, wherever we were, I realized something. One of the differences between us is getting lost has never been a problem for me, really. My problem is getting found.

I can't figure out what it is, exactly. I mean, is it really just chemicals that give you that giddy, tingly feeling when you meet someone, when you make a new friend? I felt that for Cam, but it's totally different with girls. It reminds me of that cotton candy smell that you never think about, and then, out of nowhere, when you smell that sugar in the air and you see the man spinning a big pink cloud on a white cone, it's the happiest smell in the whole world. That's how I felt, and I just couldn't stop thinking of Melody all week, and I kept wanting to give her something, share something.

So I called Knox a few days later and asked him if there was a time I could drop by their house, because I had something for Melody. It was just a picture I found, but I wanted it to be a surprise, I told him. He said that was very thoughtful of me, and I could stop by on Wednesday, after five o'clock, so I went over, right after school. He let me in, and I go, You didn't tell her I was coming, did you? He goes, I told her you were coming, and she's been waiting for you since Sunday, he said, and I just looked at him, like, that's so mean. Now I feel bad, I said, and he said, She's in her room, go on up. I didn't even make it to the door before I heard her, yelling my name: *Thea?!*

She sounded so excited, I almost started laughing. Because no one ever gets that excited to see me. It's me, I said, knocking on the door and walking in. I was afraid you weren't coming, she said, and I go, It was supposed to be a surprise, walking in, smiling as I stepped around her chair, so that she could see me. There's always that moment she strains, when she tries to move, but her body just won't cooperate. I try to smile through it, seeing her like that, because I want to fix it, and I can't. It's something I can't fix.

Surprise! I said, bending over, and she goes, *Hi!* and her body got all stiff with excitement. Her hair was in braids, and they were cute—I wanted to screw them up, twist them like a milkmaid, but I didn't want Mel to feel like I'm always trying to change her. She's perfect, really, exactly as she is—just not the way Heather dresses her. I said, Here, I brought you something, and I took the picture out of a folder in my bag, holding it up for her to see. It's a picture of this girl, and you don't know if she's jumping off a ledge or a trampoline, or what, but she's wearing shorts, and she has these long, long legs, and her blonde hair is in a ponytail, and it looks like summertime, but it's a world where it's always summer.

Melody goes, *Did* you *take that, Thea?* gasping, twisting in her chair, she was so impressed. I love that about her. It's like some people wear their hearts on their sleeve; well, Melody wears her heart on her voice. No, I said, I found it on Flickr. And she goes, *What's that?* And I go, Flickr, thinking she hadn't heard me. You know, Flickr, I said, and she shook her head no, and I go, You mean you've never seen *Flickr?* She goes, *No,* and I was just like, Ohmygod, I said, Seriously, Mel, you've been living in a cave, and she goes, *Uh, what have I been telling you?* I said, Listen. We've got to fix this immediately, Mel, but she wasn't listening, she was staring at the picture.

Do you like it? I said, trying to guess what she was thinking, and she goes, *I love it. Will you hang it up for me?* Yes, I said. Where do you want me to hang it? *Anywhere,* she said. *No, wait,* she said, *will you put it on the wall, by my bed? So I can see it when I wake up?* And I go, Of course. Do you have any tape? I asked, looking around. *Yes, but I don't know where my mom keeps it,* she said. I'll ask your dad later, I said, looking at the picture again. Do you really like it? I asked again, realizing I'd asked her once already, but I couldn't help it. Because I chose it for her, and I spent all weekend, trying to decide.

I sat down on her bed, and turned her around to face me, and I go, I'll bring you more pictures. I have thousands of pictures, so just give me some direction, and she goes, *What do you mean?* And I go, Well, what do you like about this picture? And I held it up for her again, and she goes, *I don't know,* sounding shy all of a sudden. Then she goes, *I like the . . . well, her legs. God, look how long and straight her legs are! I like how strong she is, the way she's just firing into the sky. Is that stupid?* she asked, seeing me smile, and I go, No, no! Why would you say that? And she goes, *Well, because you looked like I made a joke or something.*

I go, No, Melody. I was smiling because I couldn't have put it that way. Honestly, and she goes, *You want to know why I like it? Really?* I go, Yes. Tell me, and she goes, *I like it, because I want to be her, and I want to jump into the sky like that. Because I look at her, and it's like seeing the best part of being a girl. It's the part I'm not,* she said: *free.* When she said that, I didn't know what to say, you know, but my throat clenched, so I stared at the picture, not saying anything. And then I felt like, like I'd screwed up. Like I tried to bring her this gift, and all I thought about was the freedom of the picture, or the way I saw it, at least, and I didn't think that she'd feel more trapped, not less.

Then she goes, *It's all right. Really, it's okay. I'm so happy you brought it,* she said, smiling at me, and then her eyes moved back to the picture again. I go, Wait, did you hear that, can you hear what I'm thinking, Mel? I suddenly felt paranoid she could read my mind, too, and Melody goes, *No,* laughing at me. *But I can read the look on your face,* she said. *Honestly, it's the nicest gift anyone has ever brought me,* she said. We sat there a minute, quiet, and then she said, *Thea, do me a favor?* Course, I said, what's that? *Show me that, what's it called, Flickr?* she said, and I laughed. I'll show it to you, next time I come over, and she goes, *Promise you'll come back soon?* I go, Promise. I'll ask your dad when I leave, and she goes, *Yeah, definitely don't ask my mom,* and then I said, Why does she hate me, Mel? And Mel said, *She* doesn't hate you, Thea. I think it's just because she knows something is up, and we can't tell her, okay? Ever.

I didn't know what to say, and then I go, What about the picture? Will your mom take it away? And she goes, *No, it's not like that. But just in case, tell my dad*, and I go, Tell him what, exactly? *Thea, tell him to step up and put his foot down*, she said in this tone, like, *drr*. She goes, *What did God give him legs for, you know?* I started laughing, thinking about telling Knox to put his foot down, and I go, All right. Listen, I said, I have to go. I just wanted to bring this by, and she goes, *Thank you, Thea. It's beautiful*, and I started to say, Just like you, but I didn't. The thing is, I knew then—I knew perfectly well that I'd wish I had for a long, long time. I'd wish I'd spoken up, that I'd been as brave as Melody was, looking at a picture of a girl jumping into the sky, free as a bird, straight as a board, and saying exactly what she thought and felt.

Standing there, in the middle of Melody's froufrou room—it was like those people who love to boast how they've lived their whole life without a single regret, and I don't know what that means. Seriously, why is that something to boast about? Because at that moment, I felt like maybe there are some regrets worth having, because they're the kind you learn from, the kind you'll be so happy to leave behind. Who knows when, but the day you're finally ready to jump, when the sky calls your name, it'll be so sweet. When I left their house that day, heading home, I knew when that day comes for me, just before I left all the regret behind of not speaking up like I should have, I knew I'd remember that picture and standing beside Melody, and that whether she knew it or not, she was more like that girl then than I could ever be.

When their sitter got there, Knox gave me a ride home, and he saw me unzip my bag, rearranging some things. I pulled out a script, and he goes, What's that? You writing a novel? And I go, It's my script—well, our script—Cam and I were working on it, and I've been carrying it around. Oh, he said, raising his brow. So you're working on a script together? And I shrugged, why not? We have a few different scripts, I said, and he goes, Can I ask what it's about, your script? I go, Yes, but I won't tell you, and he looked over at me and he goes, Why not? And I said, Because that would be telling, Knox, but he didn't get it. I said, That would be telling, *The Prisoner*? Information! Information! He just stared, and I go, You've never seen *The Prisoner*? Never mind. I go, It's a script about an arsonist in a wax museum. It's about this guy, this mastermind arsonist who decides the crowning achievement of his brilliant career would be burning down Madame Tussauds—the one in London. He gets totally obsessed, too, like he fantasizes about watching them all burn—Marilyn, Liberace, Cher, Posh Spice, everyone is going to melt.

So he's got it all planned, I said, every last detail, but then, when he gets there, he falls in love with this girl working at the gift store. So it's all about this guy fighting with his demons, because what could top burning down Madame Tussauds? I said, It's such a perfect crime, he almost wants to get caught, so people will know, you know? So it's all that, watching this woman from afar, and then Knox goes, Do they have a gift shop at Madame Tussauds? I said, Of course they do. I mean, how could they not have a gift shop? He goes, Just asking. To be honest, I don't know if they do, so I said, Well, maybe that will be fictional; we'll figure it out. That's why we're going to go and research the place, and Knox goes, *London?*

He didn't believe me, I could tell by the look on his face. I said, As my graduation gift, then Knox goes, But that's more than two years away, and I go, What's your point? Knox could tell he'd hit a sore spot, because he goes, So what happens to the arsonist? Honestly, I was so relieved to be able to talk about something besides sex videos of me and my boyfriend, I told him the whole story. I go, Keep in mind, this guy isn't just any old arsonist. We're talking totally sexy, totally hot arsonist—. Knox goes, A hot arsonist? trying not to laugh at me, and I go, You know what I mean. Stylin', wearing Savile Row suits, like James Bond. Like, imagine Daniel Craig as the greatest pyromaniac in history. Imagine that he's an arsonist for hire, instead of an assassin for hire, right? Knox goes, Daniel Craig, huh? I shrugged and said, The role calls for a sex symbol, what can I say? After all, Knox, arson *is* a sexual crime. Where'd you hear that? he asked, looking like this was news to him. I go, I don't know, *Law & Order*, maybe? And he goes, Well, in that case, it must be true, raising his eyebrows, and I said, Isn't that strange, though? That they say rape isn't about sex, it's about power, but arson isn't about power, it's about sex? Very strange, he said, as in, no further comment.

He goes, Okay, so the Daniel Craig arsonist character falls in love with the girl in the gift shop, and then he kills her? I go, Yes, but it's an accident, and Knox goes, But he sets the museum on fire on purpose? And I go, Yes, but Daniel Craig doesn't know she's in the building when he sets it on fire, see? And Knox goes, So she dies? The girl dies, he says, looking at me, making sure he's got the story right. I go, Of course: it's a love story. Somebody has to die in a good love story. Then he goes, Well, it sounds very interesting, and he sounded like such a dad, saying that, I was just like, Gee, thanks. Sometimes, the way Knox looks at me and the questions he asks, it's like he's never talked to a teenage girl before. Seriously, Knox looks at me like I'm from a distant galaxy, and here he is, the very first earthling to ask me questions about where I came from, what our planet looks like, what food we eat. And maybe all old men are like that; I don't know. Fortunately or unfortunately, I don't know many old men.

Then he said, The arson story, do you have a title for it? I said, Yes. It's called "Pyroglyphics," and he raises his eyebrows, and he goes, Catchy. Can I read it sometime? he said, and for once, I was the one who was surprised. It was sweet of him to ask, you know, and I said, Sure. Then I thought it over for a second, and I said, But I'll have to ask Cam, first. It's his script, too, and Knox looked at me: Of course, he said, sitting upright again.

He sighed again, still staring straight ahead. Honestly, Knox has about as many varieties of sighs as Eskimos have for the word for snow. And then, completely out of the blue, Knox goes, Thea, tell me about your dad. I was like, What? And he goes, I asked about your father, and I said, Speaking of love stories that end in death, you mean? No, he said. No, because you never mention him. Yeah, well, what was your first clue? I said. Go on, he said, tell me what happened. Okay, well . . . I sighed. Let's see, I said.

Once upon a time, he was a prick, and that's it in a nutshell, pretty much. I shrugged, nothing else to add, and Knox goes, Yes? He wasn't asking for his job, he was asking because he truly wanted to know, and no one besides Cam ever really asked me anything genuine anymore, so I told him.

He left my mom for his secretary, I said, feeling angry all over again. Seriously, Knox, who does that? Men who buy sports cars and have comb-overs, that's who, and Knox goes, Does he have a comb-over? I go, No, he has good hair, actually. But he does have a sports car and a wife who's half his age, I said, before pointing my finger down my throat: gag. Knox didn't say anything; he just looked out his window. My mom was such a mess, too, I said. And you? he said, and I said, And me what? He goes, How were you? And when he said that, so many things came to mind, but all I could say was, Not good. I'm sorry, Thea, he said.

I just nodded, pursed my lips. Finally, I said, Why are you sorry? You didn't do anything, and Knox goes, Don't have to do a thing to be sorry, do you? Guess not, I said. Men are just so fucked up, I said, and it was stupid, but it's true. Knox raised a brow at my language, but I'm sorry, that's how I really feel sometimes, and then he said, Thea. He started to say something else, then he dropped it. Instead, he said, When was the last time you two spoke, you and your dad? I said, Four months and two years, actually: Christmas, 2008. *Thea*, he said, and I go, What? He had this paternal look on his face, too, and then he goes, Well, I don't know, but he is your father. I go, You should remind him of that, not me. He didn't say anything for a minute. Then he goes, So why don't you tell me how it is? I go, Knox, he didn't call to wish me a Merry Christmas; he called to tell me that his new wife was pregnant. Knox balked: Two years ago? Yes, I said. And did she have the baby? he said. Apparently, I said, because he sent a birth announcement. Boy or girl? he asked, and I said, Don't know. I never opened the envelope, and just then, we reached my house, our building. Well, Knox said, pulling up, under our apartment, not knowing what else to say: here we are. I looked up, seeing the light on, and I go, Thanks, and I got out. I waited outside our front door, waving Knox off, and then I turned back around and sat down on the top stair.

I didn't want to go inside, so I sat there, watching cars drive by on the highway. You know, I remember our old house, our old life, all the time. I try not to, because it hurts, but without even closing my eyes, I can still see every room in our house, and I remember exactly how my room looked when I woke up in the morning, how the living room looked at sunset. I remember falling in love with light, there, sitting on the couch in the living room, trying to draw the window or a chair.

I know my mom feels the same, even if she never says anything. I mean, I don't understand when I see women talk about starting over on TV, like it's this big adventure, this new chapter of life, right? Because they make it sound so easy to start over, but when it's just me and mom at night, eating dinner on the couch, watching TV in that dinky little apartment, it's like we haven't started over, we've false-started. Like we started running, but we got called back, and now we're just waiting for something to fire the gun again.

## MONDAY, FEBRUARY 14, 2011 (SEVEN WEEKS EARLIER)

**1:47 PM**

I can't even believe I'm saying this, but for once in my life, I loved Valentine's Day. Honestly, long as I live, I'll never forget it, because we had this snowstorm, and it dumped like three feet in two days, so we got the day off from school. Cam called me at six thirty—it might've even been six, he was so excited to go out and play. I'm in bed, cocooned in my covers, half-asleep, so my voice cracks. Hello? And he goes, Snow day! Thee, isn't that the best Valentine's you can imagine? Let's go play in the snow! And I go, I've got a better idea. Let's play in bed—let's play the sleeping game, huh? And he goes, I'm on my way, and I was just like, *Ohmygod, what am I going to do with you?* Cali boy had never had a snow day before he moved to Fort Marshall, so it was like Christmas to him.

So he came right over, after we hung up, and we made French toast and screwed around for a while, watching *Battlestar*

*Galactica*. After I got dressed and bundled up, we drove to this abandoned parking lot halfway between my house and town. There was no one there, and the parking lot and the field beyond, it looked like it was a mile long, mile wide, covered in three feet of snow. Just a powder-white sky, powder-white ground, and this curtain of snowflakes. I reached for my camera, and I looked at Cam, like, *Isn't that the most beautiful thing?* He grinned, nodding, then he goes, Virgin, the smart-ass, and I slapped him with the back of my hand, *Be quiet.*

Cam brought Karen's car, her new Audi, because it has four-wheel drive and obviously he can't drive his car in these conditions. When we got in the car, I took a deep breath, inhaling that new-car smell, and I was like, *I remember that smell, I remember having new cars*, and the snow was still coming down, hard, but it was amazing. It was like our town was in one of those snow globes, with these huge, fluffy flakes, and dry, not slushy and gross. It was so quiet out, just the two of us, and it felt like we had the whole world all to ourselves, and the world was such a beautiful place, I didn't even recognize it.

So we parked and got out and we had a snowball fight and made snow angels, and then, after we drank the hot chocolate I brought. We were sitting in the car, warming up, and then Cam looked at me and goes, You ready to go skating? I was like, Now you want to go skating? I said, I haven't been on skates since I was, like, ten. I don't even know if I can stand up on skates anymore, and he goes, Not a problem. We'll stay seated, he said, then he rolled down all four windows, and I was like, Cam, what are you doing? Just lean back, and enjoy, he said, so I pushed my chair back, and I got all comfy. Then he goes, Ready? I was laughing, still no idea what he was about to do, and I was. Am I ready? I barely got the word out when he floored it—he hit the gas, gunning for the middle of the parking lot, and I started screaming, and he turned the wheel, hard as he could, whipping a kitty or doughnut, whatever they're called, and then he took his foot off the gas, and the car just started gliding across the parking lot.

It was so great, because we couldn't hit anything, and there was just enough ice on the ground that he was able to keep spinning around, and we kept running into these waves of powder, just crashing into the car. It was the best amusement park ride I'd ever been on, like playing bumper cars with the clouds, so I grabbed my phone and took some video, because it reminded me so much of those old sleds, carriage sleds or whatever they were called. We car-skated for maybe an hour, then he stopped. My face and my neck and hat were sopping, and I was like, Oh, man, Karen's going to be so pissed her new car's soaking, but then Cam stopped, and he turned off the car. He held his finger to his lips and he goes, Listen, and I held my breath, listening, and all you could hear were the flakes, falling, so sweet and warm, just the faintest tinkle.

He reached over and took my hand, and I looked out my window, and the world looked so white, so pure, and I turned back, grinning, because he was watching me. I go, What are you thinking? And then he mouthed it: I love you. He mouthed the words, and I said, *Don't tease*, and I threatened to point my camera at him, if he didn't stop. But then he didn't stop, just the opposite: Cam leaned closer and said, I'm not—I'm not teasing. So I hit video and I said, Then tell me again, for the record, Cam, and he said it again. Well, he mouthed it again, and I got up real close, like I was going to kiss him with my phone. Then he said it out loud: I. Love. You.

When someone disappears, when someone you love vanishes into thin air, you imagine the worst, while trying to hope for the best. And it's exhausting—it's so fucking exhausting. It's not like grief—when my grandpa died, I remember how I cried and cried. But at least you can cry, because you know they're dead. But when someone disappears, you're just stuck in limbo, getting jerked all around all day, all night, awake, asleep, same difference. Every sound, every single time a phone rings or a car drives by or a door opens, I think: *It's Cam! He's back!* But it's not him; he's still gone; he's still missing. Then you have to start all over again, so every morning, I take it from the top, asking myself: *Who am I? Where am I? What day is it? How do I do this?*

So I cover my eyes for a moment, letting my mind fill up like a tub, and piece by piece, things fall into place: bed; bedroom; morning; sunlight; awake in bed, and, finally, *Thea: my name is*

*Thea.* The thing is, of course you don't know who you are any-more, when you wake up, when you get out of bed, and every time you blink your eyes, all day long, because that person who's gone, he took part of you with him. Maybe even the best part, and who knows if you'll ever see either of you again, you know? I know it must sound silly or inane, whatever, but how do you live in the present when the best place you've ever been is in the past? I'm serious, why would you want to be here, now?

Mom started knocking on my door, making sure I was up, and I said, I'm awake, but she didn't hear me, so she banged, Are you up? And I go, I'm *awake*! And she goes, That's more like it, and I heard her walk to the kitchen. Thank god she leaves me alone, pretty much, but I can see it in her eyes, that she remem-bers how much of this is beyond my control. A rite of passage that's just not right; there's nothing right about this passage: she knows it; she understands. And she cuts me and my lip a lot of slack, too. Sometimes. I mean, it was a long time ago, but she was me once. Fifteen, at least.

But what I see, that look I see in her eyes isn't disappoint-ment, or anger, or even sadness, it's resignation. That's what it is: my mom's resigned herself. Because, stupid as it may be, she couldn't help hoping that we'd be different, the two of us, that we'd be the exception to the rules of nature. She always hoped we'd be like those shiny mothers and daughters, living out those glossy lives that slip through your fingers like the pages of the magazine in which they appear. And the trick is, you can touch, but you're never touched back. And I would say it, too. I mean, there are times I would tell her how sorry I am, but that's not what Mom wants, that's not what she's looking for.

No, she's just looking through the telescope of time, seeing us, here and now, as we really are, sad, but true, and at the same time, she's wondering how it's possible that only yesterday she was me, wearing a punk shirt, itching for a fight with her mother. And now, in a flash, here she is, on the receiving end of the glare and rolled eyes, just another lonely woman, known to run for her phone, hearing a text message, only to discover it's the public library, calling to say the Suze Orman book she reserved has been returned, she can pick it up anytime. Cruel.

After I got dressed, I heard her humming to whatever she was listening to, singing along, and I knew the song. It took me a minute, but I knew it: *Angel came down from heaven yesterday, she stayed with me just long enough to rescue me . . .* Hendrix. Mom's big on Hendrix before work—she calls it soul power—as if that'll help her get through the day, and I guess it does. But me, I couldn't seem to move, and listening to her sing, I thought, *You have such a pretty voice, Mom.* I almost said it, too, called out, until I realized I was standing there, with my mouth open. No: I shook my head no, heading to the living room. I put on my jacket and opened the door to leave, but Mom called me, stepping into the living room, holding a tea towel in her hands, with this look like I'd forgotten to do something.

*What?* I said, waving the door once for good measure; meaning, say what you have to say. Good-bye, she said. Bye, I said, realizing that was all she meant. She was just saying good-bye;

she just wanted me to say good-bye. I felt so bad, closing the door behind me, heading for the bus stop, then I swallowed it back. Just like that, it was gone again.

When I got to the stop, the designated spot about two hundred yards down the road, at the turn off, between the country road and the highway, a group of kids were waiting, having formed a line. I walked around them, standing back, and then I balked, seeing the freaky little twins—Cam always calls them the IV Twins or InVitro Babies—they were there, too. Something must have been wrong with their eighty-year-old mother's car or hip, because the twins never ride the bus. Whatever the problem was, there they were, in their matching red wool winter coats, with their matching red winter caps, pulled down over their freaky little twin eyes, that look like black marbles swimming in saucers of skim-milk-blue skin. Looking at them, I remembered how Cam always said if you can create life in a petri dish, why couldn't you travel back in time? It's all just code, he said. Code, Thee: reality, everything—*everything* has a code.

The very thought made me sad—our mean nicknames almost brought tears to my eyes—and I could feel my face fall, giving me away, before I pulled it together, shaking it off. But they were all eyes, the twins, gawking at me. I stared back at them, waiting, until finally, I cocked my chin, threatening: Was I talking to you? I said, irritated, and they looked down in tandem. Fortunately or unfortunately, the bus came a minute later, and I was last on, saying hey to Mason, the driver, before bracing myself, knowing I was about to be hit again by the heinous sound of the bus door vacuum-sealing our fates for another day, as Mason gripped the handle, pulling the door closed behind me. Everyone was waiting for me, and I sighed and took a seat halfway, making this little second grader move over, so I could have the window.

My bones felt so heavy, I thought, *God, do I have mono? What's wrong with me?* And then, once again, I remembered, No, I don't have mono: I have boyfriend. Or worse, had: I *had* a boyfriend. All of a sudden, I felt sick to my stomach. For a second, I thought I was going to puke, and I squeezed my bag, trying to breathe. Thankfully, I swallowed, and it passed. But the light: *Where is all this light coming from?* I thought, looking up. I unzipped a pocket and pulled out my sunglasses, resting my head against the window, but there was no escape. Finally, I looked up at the morning sky, at the sun, thinking, *Is that really necessary?*

The day was just—thick. I don't know how else to describe it. Not just slow, you know, but more like, like you were trudging through water up to your knees, and you had to be careful with every step, pushing yourself forward, tugging to get through it. I was in English when the knock finally came, and then, hearing Linda knock, the scariest sound you can ever hear in a high school classroom: quiet.

I knew it was Foley, too. I just knew he was waiting for me with something dirty, something I'd never want to see, and I got as far as the office door, and then I stood there. I mean, I had my hand on the office door, and then I was just like, *No. I don't have to do this. I don't have to go in there. I don't have to talk to him. I don't have to watch any more sex videos of me and my boyfriend that can't possibly be real, nothing—none of it.* Then I let go of the door handle, and I walked to the front doors, and I walked out. First time in my life, I walked straight out the doors, didn't even turn around to get the rest of my books.

I walked into Silver Top and Sharon's head snapped—even the Elders stopped talking. Everyone looked at the clock on the wall. I just shook my head no, you don't want to know, and I went to my booth. Not our booth, my booth, and I sat down. I took my phone out, and Sharon brought me some coffee, and she did the sweetest thing. She didn't ask if I was okay, because clearly I wasn't. But for the very first time, she leaned over and kissed my head. I don't know why it made me all teary, but I looked up, smiling, and I looked away, before I started crying.

I just sat there for an hour or two, watching this video of us that I took on our last snow day. I had to hide my head, because I didn't want the Elders to see me wiping the tears away, and then I noticed something weird. My video looked kinda strange. I played it again, and it started to, I don't know, like it started to fade, like someone poured bleach into my phone. I started the video again, and it got worse every time, so finally I called and I got Knox's voice mail, so I left a message. I said, It's Thea. I'm at Silver Top, and you've got to get over here, and he called me back two minutes later, and I said, Knox, something weird is happening, and I heard him sigh, but then he said he was on his way.

He took, like, twenty minutes to get there, and when he walked in, he slid into the booth with me, and I go, What took you so long? He goes, Thea, I've got other work—. I go, Yeah, listen: something really strange is going on. And he goes, You don't say. I said, No, with my phone *and* my computer, both. Look, I said, patting the seat beside me, telling him to slide over, so he sighed again, then he did. See: this is a video we shot a few months ago in my room. Cam's got a brand-new video camera, too—he got it for Christmas, I said, holding up my phone. Now, look, I said, pressing play. Look at how it's all grainy and queasy.

He watched the whole thing all the way through, and then his head pulled back, like, Whoa. I go, *Right?* Have you ever seen anything like that before? And Knox said, Wow. It's like it's disintegrating, and I said, It can't disintegrate—it's digital, digitized, whatever. It can't fall apart, and Knox said, Well, of course it can fall apart—. I snapped, Knox, you know what I'm saying. Knox said, Wait, you know what it is? *Beta.* It looks like beta, he said, frowning. And I go, What's beta? Is that bad? I said, and he goes, Don't worry: it's not contagious. They eradicated it years ago. And I didn't know if he was being serious, so I ignored him, showing him another video.

This one, too, I said, playing another video for him on my computer. Because, at first, I thought maybe it was just that one, or maybe just my phone, but it's not, I said, taking out my computer. I turned it on, and then I pushed play, showing him this iMovie of me and Cam from last winter. I was sitting on his lap, in front of the computer, and I said, Oh, ha-ha, I'm Cam, and I'm so funny, slapping him, and then he got me in a bear hug, and Cam took one of my hands and made me slap myself, telling me: Theadora, quit hitting yourself. Quit hitting yourself. You silly girl, you silly teenage girl!

Knox started watching it again, and I said, Can we stop now? pressing stop. He looked embarrassed for a second, and I go, It's not that—we don't have sex or anything. It's just that every time I watch this, the image gets fainter. It gets more and more grainy every time. That's what I was trying to tell you. It's like it's decomposing, or rotting—I don't understand. Don't watch it again, he said, closing my computer, and I just looked at him, like, come on. He goes, No, seriously. Listen, can you burn me a copy? I go, Sure. But why? And he goes, I want to show it to a friend—I don't know jack squat about this stuff, so let me show it to someone who knows what they're doing. Is this the only one? Is this the only video that it's happened to? I shook my head and I go, No, there are others—all my videos.

He thought about it, sitting back, and then he goes, Okay, don't watch any of them, just burn me a copy, and we'll see what we can find out. I go, But you see what it looks like, like an old photograph, don't you think? It's like sepia, I said, and he looked at me, shaking his head, like what the hell is going on? Well, I told you, I said. You told me what? he said, and I go, I told you, I'm not the crazy one here. And he smiled and said, I beg to differ. He slid out of the booth, and then he said, Need a ride? I grabbed my bag and said, That's some quality detective work, right there.

We got in the car, and we didn't have much to say on the way home, until he pulled in front of our building, and then he said, Thea, there's something else I need to tell you. I was worried, and I said, Is it Mel? And he said, No, Mel's fine, and I looked, and he said, It's not Cam—we don't have any new information, I'm sorry, and I sighed, realizing that only left one other thing it could be. Ohmygod, I said, and he said, There were more videos posted on YouTube, and he looked at me, sympathizing.

Did you see? I said, and he nodded, and I felt my jaw lock up, getting ready for a fight.

I swallowed back, trying to calm down, and then I said, A video of what? And I could tell he'd been dreading this, but he came out with it. Knox goes, See for yourself, handing me his phone, and I took the phone, trying not to shake, and then I pressed play, and at first, you could sort of make out that it was a boy and girl, and they're having sex in a bathroom, right on the sink, and right away, I felt sick. It had gone high-def. It had been seen by four hundred thousand people. And it was me and Cam, real or not. That's what Foley was going to show me: I know he was, the perv.

I stared without staring at anything—there's a blindness that comes from emotion, from being overwhelmed, and it was like that. But I shook my head, and I go, I know how it looks, but Cam still didn't have anything to do with this. There's no way, I said, nodding, and Knox goes, Thea, listen. Every video posted, every picture, they've all been traced to Cam's website, and I snapped, So? Doesn't mean they're from Cam. And Knox goes, Do you really believe that? I could tell by the look in his eye, I could tell he thinks I'm crazy, or worse, I'm wrong, and he feels pity for me. I see it in his eyes, but I told him, I said, You know, I'm holding on . . . God, it was so hard to say it, but I had to get it out. Knox, I am holding on by *this much*, I said, pinching my thumb and index finger together. Don't take that away from me, and he nodded, dropping it. I cleared my throat, and I go, Three percent, and Knox goes, Sorry? I said, Did you know the human eye can only see three percent of reality? As sophisticated as our eyes are, that's all we register, and he said, Meaning? I go, Meaning, I don't care how it looks. I know Cam, and he'd never do that. *Never*, I said, and Knox nodded, putting his phone away.

Call me if you need anything, he said, tilting his head forward, looking at me in that way that told me he realized he wasn't going to convince me otherwise, and I nodded yes, that's right, now we're communicating. Then I said, You know what it's like, Knox? It's like those naked dreams—I had that dream once, a dream that I showed up for school in a sweater, but I wasn't wearing any pants or underpants, I said, and Knox sort of pulled away in that way he does when he doesn't like the fact that he's got visuals on me while I'm telling him something like this. Whatever. I said, I come to in the dream, and I'm just standing there, half-naked, in the middle of the hall, everyone standing around, heading for class, and I know I have two seconds before everyone sees me, and I'm thinking, *What the hell am I doing at school without any pants or underwear?* It's exactly like that, except that that's how my life really is now. Every day now, when I show up to school, everybody's seen something about me, and it's like I'm not just naked on the outside, I'm naked on the inside, too, I said. Knox took the back road, staring straight ahead, not saying a word—not avoiding speaking, just . . . what could he say, you know? What could he possibly say? So I said good-bye, opened the car door, and got out.

When I walked in, Mom was sitting on the couch, and her mouth fell open, seeing me home at that hour, and I go, I couldn't do it. I just couldn't do it, Mom. I got called to the office again, and . . . I couldn't even finish my sentence. Mom nods her head, telling me not to worry, and then I saw the people sitting in the chairs, across the room. She was sitting with this man and woman, and right when I'm figuring out what's going on, Mom stands up and introduces them to me, telling me the name of the firm they're with, Somebody, Somebody, Somebody, and Somebody Else. But right away, I knew what they wanted, why they were sitting in our sad little living room: money. There's money to be made, and they even had a computer with them, obviously online—the woman must've frozen the frame, hearing me walk in.

They both wore suits, so I knew they weren't from around here—I didn't even think they were from Albany. I didn't know where they were from—New York, maybe? The guy was fifty, maybe? I don't know, old, with a bald head—the kind with a ring of hair around his head, you know? The woman was younger, maybe thirty-five, tall and thin, and she'd set her long hair in rollers. The way she smiled at me, she had this air about her, like it was just between us girls, right? But plastic, and I'm like, I don't know you.

I didn't say hello, nothing. I just said, It's not true—those videos aren't me. And if it's not me, we can't sue anyone, so you're wasting your time, and then I turned back around. The man spoke up; he said, Thea, I'm sorry you've been dragged into this, but obviously there are legal issues to consider, since you're underage. There are statutory rape laws to consider, as well, the woman said, and I go, If that was me, maybe, but it's not. She goes, Thea, I'm so sorry to have to pry, but are you saying you didn't have sex with your boyfriend, John Cameron Conlon, on the afternoon of April 4? I turned around, and the man goes,

I'm sorry, Thea, I know this must be very confusing for you, and then I said, No, it's not confusing, because it's not me. He goes, But it's your room? Yes, I said, and he goes, Is the boy in this image your boyfriend, Cam Conlon? I don't know who he is, I said. He goes, The clock? Is that your clock? I don't know whose it is, either, I said. And the man goes, Well, then, can you tell us what you were doing at three forty-five on Monday afternoon, April 4? I go, I have nothing more to say.

See, this is where I get confused, Thea, the woman said. She nodded like she understood, and then she goes, Whoever it is, it certainly appears to be you and Cam, and these videos, all of them, are receiving tens of thousands of hits per day. Thea, we filed a cease and desist, and we're threatening them with a lawsuit. We have to put a stop to this, and I said, Stop *who*? And the man goes, Facebook, Flickr, Google, YouTube, iTunes—they're all showing these videos. And what? I said. You want to sue Google? Facebook? Yes, he said, dead serious. I go, For what? And he goes, For exhibiting videos of a minor performing sexual acts, in what is, technically, a case of statutory rape. *Rape?* I said, and I almost started laughing. I go, I never raped Cam, trust me. Thea, the woman said, we've been contacted by every major news agency in the world. CNN called and we feel—. *You feel?* Look, you have no business being here, I said, really getting angry with these people, and the woman smiled, like she felt sorry for me, and Mom goes, Thea, I retained their services two weeks ago. I had to—aside from the fact that your father left me little choice, we need legal counsel, she said. We? We who? I said, shocked she was just telling me this now, weeks after the fact. I'm sorry

I didn't tell you sooner, but I didn't want to worry you prematurely. Anything else you aren't telling me? I asked, glaring at her.

Immediately, the man said, Because there's more. More what? I asked. We can't understand how, but the resolution is getting sharper with every hit, every viewer. They can't seem to remove the tapes—or so they're saying, the woman said. They're claiming it's a virus unlike anything they've ever seen before. No kidding, I said, standing, ready to walk out. Please, I want you to leave now—or better yet, I will, I said, heading for the front door.

Thea, Mom said, look outside, and I could see not to push her any farther, so I walked over the window, and I twisted the blinds. I looked out the window, and there was a white van, a news van with a satellite dish on the hood—right in our parking lot. What happened? I asked, thinking there was an accident or a fire or something. Mom didn't know what to say, but the man spoke up. He said, That's what we're trying to tell you, Thea: *you* happened: you're big news.

When I was little, like three or four, Gram, my mom's mom, sent me this card for Easter with this bunny on it, and I thought it was the most beautiful bunny I'd ever seen. It was so real, too, like you could see its shiny hair and its little cotton tail and every blade of grass was so perfect, I became obsessed with trying to draw a bunny like that one. But I was so young, I couldn't even read yet, so my dad helped me look up the artist, online, and it was Albrecht Dürer, right, from like the 1500s, and when I saw all the things he'd drawn, I wanted to draw like that as well. I tried so hard, too. I worked and worked my little fingers to the bone, but I just couldn't come close to copying Dürer's hare with crayons.

A couple years later, when I was playing in Gram's attic, I was snooping around, and I found this old box. This was before my grandpa died, when he was in the hospital, and I found this collection of old *Playboys*, all the way back to the 1950s, even. I knew it was wrong, but I snuck a few of them, and then I spent like the whole day, looking at the centerfolds, trying to draw Playboy bunnies. I mean, I know that sounds weird, but I saw this show on TV that talked about figure drawing and how all the great artists learned to draw by drawing women naked, and I wanted to be a great artist, but I didn't know any women I could draw naked, you know? I must have been like five or six, because I could read by then, and I just thought it was so funny that the women were called bunnies, and for years I'd been drawing bunnies, so for some reason, I started drawing these totally curvy sixties Playboy bodies with pretty little Dürer bunny heads. And ever since then, I don't know, I've always drawn people with animal heads—eagles, tigers, badgers, you name it. I mean, I've always loved animals, but my dad's allergic to fur, so I could never have anything but fish, and that's not the same, but anyhow.

So after school one day, we were walking into 7-Eleven, and I was telling Cam how I was trying to talk my mom into letting me get a cat for my birthday. I know a dog is out of the question, especially in our apartment, but it's big enough for a cat, and I said I'd even keep the litter box in my room. God, I'd love to have an animal in the house—and it'd be so healthy—it's a fact, animals are good for your health. Really, I mean, there've been so many times when I couldn't feel anything, or I didn't feel for a long, long time, but even then, even at my worst, whenever I'd see an animal, I could feel what they were feeling. Like if they were happy, I'd remember how it felt to be happy. And if they hurt, I'd feel hurt. I didn't tell him that, but then Cam goes, A cat? What kind? And I go, Well, I know we should get a rescue, but I've always wanted one of those smoosh-faced ones, what are they called, and he opened the door. A Himalayan, he said, and I go, Yes! I want a Himalayan cat for my sixteenth birthday. In case you were wondering what to get me, I said, walking inside, and he whistled that whistle, like, pricy, because they aren't cheap, Himalayans, I know.

I went over to get something to drink, and we were horsing around. We have this running joke where Cam says, You know what Socrates said? It's just something he said once, fixing my computer, because I was just like, You are so brilliant, Cam, and he goes, Well, you know what Socrates said? And then he never told me what he was about to say, because without even thinking about it, I go, Bend over? Totally rude, I know, but it just became our thing. So ever since then, like as a comeback, totally dead-pan, Cam would say, You know what Socrates said? And I'd say, You're killing me, you bunch of dumbfucks, or whatever. So he said it, walking over to the counter to pay, and I was about to answer, when I saw the donation can. You know those cans they have at the register at convenience stores, the ones that have pictures of dogs and cats that have been tortured, starved, burned, and it's the most awful picture you can imagine? I leaned over the counter, laughing, about to answer, and there it was: a picture of this starving brown Lab who had been set on fire, so all its fur had been burned off its legs, and its skin looked like pink rice paper that's about to tear—you could see bone and . . . and I lost it. Instant waterworks, bawling right in front of the guy behind the counter.

Of course the guy was just like, Whoa, what's going on? So Cam paid and took me outside, pulling me by the arm, and then we stopped and he goes, Babe, what's going on? And I go, Didn't you see that can with the dog? I go, Cam, how could anyone *do* that? I just don't get it, you know; it's so fucking awful to do that, and I started sobbing. The worst part was the eyes—the dog's eyes were so gentle, but so scared, like she couldn't even trust the person taking her picture. She just wants to love you, but she's too scared to do that anymore. To do that to such a beautiful creature is truly evil, and I tried saying that, but it didn't make any sense through my tears. Cam held me, trying to calm me down, stroking my hair and whispering, Shhhh. . . .

The thing is, almost all my life, I used to feel things so strongly, I couldn't control it. And then, a couple years ago, I don't know what happened, but everything shut down. It's like the part of my brain that handles emotion, it bombed—not kidding, my brain bombed, and I couldn't feel anything. I'm better now, but when I see something like that poor dog, I fall apart.

We got in his car, and Cam handed me a bunch of those little take-out napkins to blow my nose, and I blew. I calmed down, and there were still tears in my eyes, but then I got so angry. I said, That's just so fucking *evil*, to set a dog on fire, I can't even— *can't*, I said, locking my jaw to keep from crying again. I know, he said, slowly nodding like he understood exactly what I was saying, but trying to calm me down, because I was getting upset all over again. So then I swallowed back, trying to get a hold of myself. He waited until I could breathe again, and I smiled, like, I'm fine. Really. Then, changing the subject, rubbing my leg,

Cam goes, Here's an idea. How about I take you home and we'll do something to cheer you up? He meant sex, right? Like he'd cheer me up by having sex with me, oh, lucky me. Which, to be fair, was our plan before I saw the horrible evil dog picture, but still, I was just like, *Seriously?* I was so annoyed, I snapped, How can you even *think* about having sex after looking at that picture?

Cam froze—his mouth open, realizing how bad that sounded—knew he was about to get himself in trouble. Then he goes, This is a trick question, right? I looked at him, my mouth hanging open, and he tried smoothing things over, saying, Babe, the way I see it, sex is going to happen sooner or later, so it might as well be—. *Uh-uh*, I said. I cut him off right there, and I said: The way *I* see it, babe, sex is not going to happen sooner or later, putting a stop to that. I couldn't even believe him, you know? He sat back in his seat, and he goes, I'm sorry—I was just kidding, and it was such bullshit, I shot him this look, totally disgusted, and I go, No you weren't. And Cam said, Well, not at the time, but I am now, and I gave him the look, you know, but I couldn't help laughing at him, and then, out of nowhere, I almost started crying again.

Cam reached over and put his hand on my cheek, and I said, I'm sorry I lost it; it's just that there are some really sick fucks in this world, and sometimes I can't deal with it. Tell me, how . . . how could anyone *do* that to an animal? Cam leaned over, grabbing my head, pressing his forehead against mine, and he said, I don't know, baby. I really don't know, he said, so I took a breath, one of those trembling breaths, and I was like, *Okay. Get a grip, Thea*, and I sat up.

Cam pulled out on the highway, then he looked in the rearview, adjusting it, and he goes, What do you feel like doing? And I go, I thought you wanted to have sex, no? He shot me this look, and he goes, For real? I go, *No.* Psych! I shouted, laughing, and Cam's face—ohmygod, priceless. Then I said, JYC—you know what JYC stands for? He bit the inside of his cheek, trying not to smile, because he was getting played like the player he is, and I go, *Jerkin' yo' chain*, that's what! Then I fell over, laughing, and he started paddling my thigh and my butt, slapping me across the seat: oh, I got him good. I'm sorry, I don't care how smart he is, the mind of a teenage boy? Talk about sick puppy.

## MONDAY, MAY 9, 2011
## (FIVE WEEKS LATER)

# 10:47 AM

I forgot how to do this, how to be alone. Every day now, I wake up, and I think, *Oh, yeah. I'm alone again.* It's like Saturdays now . . . Saturday used to pass in the blink of an eye, when I was with Cam. I was always like, *Why can't every day be Saturday?* But now, Saturdays just go on and on; the day feels like a week. And Sundays are even worse than Saturdays.

We used to drive, take our little day trips, just get on the road and figure out where we were going when we got there. I remember him saying that the first time he took me for a drive, and I said, Where are we going? And Cam shrugged: Guess we'll find out when we get there. Sometimes I get caught in class, spacing out, staring out the window, and then Mr. McConnell or whoever will ask a question, knowing I'm a million miles away, or a hundred, at least, and then I'll look up, snap back, and the whole class will be staring at me, waiting. Strange, how sound comes back at you, like through a wind tunnel, but time . . .

The other day, I was so far gone, Mr. McConnell couldn't even believe it. He just looked at me, like, You weren't even close to hearing what I just said, were you? Then he goes, Would you care to join us, Thea? And I couldn't answer, because I was so caught off guard, and because what I was thinking was, *No, actually, I would not*, but I didn't say it. I just looked at my notebook, and people started giggling, enjoying the fact that I'd been called out.

There was a knock on the classroom door, and Mr. McConnell said, Come in, and every head in class turned to look at me before the door opened: I knew; everyone knew it was for me. I'd seen Linda's face, peeking around the door, holding up her pink slip like a white flag so many times now, I could tell by looking at her that it was Foley. And because I pulled a runner, I could tell Linda had been told she had to escort me the whole way back. So I followed, ten paces behind her, back to the office, and we walked in, and she got behind her desk, without looking at me again. Cheesy came out of his office, hearing us, and he looked scared, but like I was the one scaring him, not the other way around. Seriously, people are beginning to look at me like I'm contagious.

Then Cheesy says, Special Agent Foley would like to ask you a couple more questions, Thea. I didn't even stop. I just nodded yes and walked straight down the hall, heading for the conference room. But then, when I got to the door, I froze, seeing

Foley's silhouette, seated at the table, perfectly framed, like Satan through the frosted glass, and I swallowed, before walking in. When Cheesy stepped up, behind me, I opened the door and walked in, but I didn't see Foley, all I saw was the black bag on the table, and I froze.

Foley goes, Good morning, Theadora. Please close the door, he said, and I did as he said. I realized my mouth was open, and I couldn't even shut it, hide it from him. He could tell, too, but he asked anyway, he goes, Do you recognize this bag, Theadora? And I nodded yes, and Cheesy assumed his perch, in the corner, like he was trying to say he wasn't really there, just act like he's not there, and Foley said, Where have you seen this bag before? There was something about his tone that made me feel like he might give me a little reward if I just answered a couple questions, so I said, Yes. It's Cam's backpack, I said, speaking to the bag, not Foley. It looked deflated and dirty, but it was definitely his. I knew by the band patches he'd sewn on, because they were his dad's.

I waited for what seemed like forever, until Foley said, We found it yesterday. And I said, Where? He said, In a tunnel, not far from here. Just behind the baseball field, he said, and I bit the inside of my lip. Cam? I said, and Foley said, Unfortunately, there was no sign of John. I looked at him, wondering what he wanted, and he goes, Would you please take a look at the bag, to be sure it's his? It's his, I said, and he goes, Please, to be sure, Theadora, meaning he wanted me to search the bag. There's nothing in the bag now, he said, slowly rotating his thumbs. John's phone and computer are still missing, as well, he said, then he reversed the direction of his thumbs, waiting on me.

So I unzipped the bag, feeling in each pocket, and—nothing. Like Foley said, there was nothing in it, but I just had this feeling like there was some little animal or spider that was going to bite me. Except for one thing, Foley said, almost smiling, the very second I felt it in my hand. Yes, we did find one thing in the bag, Foley said, and I knew what it was right away, before he said another word. Please, take a look, he said, as I removed my hand, seeing for myself. It was a baseball.

Does John play baseball? Foley asked, and I said, Not that I know of. Foley said, I didn't think so. But what's particularly odd is just how old this baseball is, and I looked at him, and then I looked at the baseball. It was really old, like a hundred years old, and it looked handmade. You've never seen this baseball before? Foley asked, and I shook my head no. Well, the plot thickens, he said, twirling his thumbs faster, like he was getting excited or something. Thank you, Theadora, he said, grinning at me. Freak.

Just when I thought the man was utterly and completely worthless, Cheesy says, Special Agent Foley, it's most unusual, isn't it, letting a piece of evidence be touched like this? Tampering, Cheesy said, remembering the word. Foley nodded, looking at Cheesy, like, what an astute observation. Then Foley said, Indeed, Principal Cheswick, it is most unusual to let a piece of evidence be touched. However, the most unusual part about it is that we now know there are two set of prints on this baseball: one set that belongs to John Cameron Conlon and another set that belongs to . . . Foley said, smiling at me: Theadora Denny. Technically, there's been no tampering, seeing as Theadora's prints match one set on the ball already. Whether or not it was true, Cheesy buckled, and honestly, my whole body went numb.

I have nothing more to say, except that I've never seen that ball in my entire life, I said, getting up from the table, and Foley raised a brow, Really, Theadora? he said, standing, and only then did I see that Foley was wearing white cloth gloves, and then he pulled a plastic bag out, from under the table, and he returned the backpack to the plastic bag, clearly marked EVIDENCE.

When I walked out of the conference room, I could barely feel my arms or legs. I turned to go back to class, but it was the first time I'd ever had anything like a panic attack. I mean, seriously, like not being able to move or breathe, even, so I stood there, just staring at the light of the front doors, at the end of the hall, and then the bell rang, and there were kids pouring out, everywhere, some looking at me, like, *What's her problem?* but I didn't care. I don't know how long I stood there, but long enough that the hall emptied again, and third bell rang, and then I started walking to the front door. And of course there was a voice that said, *You can't do this. Don't leave. You're going to get in so much trouble if you cut school again.* But I wouldn't listen, no, I put my hand on the front door, and I opened it, telling myself to shut up.

It was so bright out, I covered my eyes, stepping outside, and I didn't even have my coat, but I walked down the front steps. I don't know what I was thinking, but when I got to the football field, no one was there, so I walked to the top of the bleachers, and I started shouting, as loud as I could: Where are you?! *Cam, where the hell are you?!*

Nothing. Not a sound. Screaming like a tree falling in the forest. My throat hurt, my heart hurt, my head hurt, so I sat down on the top bleacher. Hoarse, sighing, I put my bag down, and stretched out my arms, about to lean back, then I felt something scratchy. I looked, and someone had carved 6001133, big—about six inches long and three inches wide, cut deep, using a pocketknife or something, and I leaned to the side, lifting my butt, and the numbers kept going. I stood up, and they went on and on, all the way down the bleacher. I didn't know what it was, but I had that feeling again, and I looked at the bleacher below me, and more numbers. I got up and walked to the bottom bleacher, far right, and there it was, starting: 3.1415926 . . . Ohmygod, I covered my mouth with both hands, seeing that the numbers went on and on, all the way across the first bleacher, the second bleacher, the third bleacher, every single bleacher covered in numbers, thousands and thousands of numbers, circling around and around, until I reached the very top again. I didn't know what the hell it meant, really, but I know π when I see it.

And then I heard his voice in my head, and I got such a chill, I had to cross my arms, nipping out: You do, too, know, Cam said. I'd almost forgotten about that night, the night he took me to the baseball field and he showed me the secret tunnel. After we got back in the car, Cam started to turn over the ignition, and then he changed his mind. Hunching over the steering wheel, he looked up at the hole in the fence, right above our heads. He just stared for like a minute or two, and the look on his face was the same look a little boy has, staring at a dump truck or a crane, lifting beams into the sky: pure joy, you know? Finally, I said, What're you thinking, boy genius? Cam sat back and he said, Numbers, Thee. Everything, absolutely *everything* in reality comes down to numbers and codes. Said it once, and I'll say it again: you break the code; you alter reality. That's the whole game, right there: just got to hack the code, he said, sitting back, beaming.

Rolling my eyes, I tsk-tsked, because he was basking in his own glory again. Christ, funny how that kept happening. So he raised his brow at me, and he goes, You disagree? I said, Everything, huh? Everything, he said, nodding yes at himself, and I said, Love, too? Is love just a code? He knocked his head backward, and then he goes, *Ohhhh!* And the crowd goes, *Rahhhhhh! Rahhhhhh!* he said, cupping his mouth with both hands: Thea Denny, ladies and gentlemen! Thea Denny hits a grand slam, right out of the park! I reached over to slap him with the back of my hand, but he caught my wrist, pulling me across the seat, holding me across his lap. Lying there, in his arms, looking up, I could see it, too, the dark hole in space and time that had Cam so smitten.

Cam kissed the top of my head, and smoothed my hair, and then he said, You know what pi is? And I said, No, and he gave me a smack on the butt. You do, too. Go on, tell me, he said, and I said, I know the *definition*, but I don't know what it *means*, and he said, Tell me the definition of pi, then, and I said, Cam, please. No more homework—. Tell me, he said, and I could tell he wasn't going to let it go, so I huffed, but I told him. I said, pi is the circumference of any circle, divided by its diameter, and he said, See? You know! No, Cam, I really have no idea what that means—. You do, Thee. Because pi is math's greatest love story—it never ends, infinite. Just like you and me, kid.

I could barely breathe, standing there, with my back to the football field, and I looked up, grinning at the sky, despite myself. *You smart-ass*, I thought, covering my face with both hands, because who else could have done this but Cam? No one: it had to be him. It was crazy—those numbers were completely crazy, but it was so beautiful. Cam always said math was beauty, and I got it—at long last, I got it—I saw how beautiful it is. And seeing Cam right there, plain as day, but nowhere to be found, I was laughing, but I was crying. Same difference.

I can always tell when they've had a fight, my mom and Rain Man. Like the second I walk in the door at night, or getting up, first thing in the morning on a Saturday, I'll know they've had a fight, because my mom always broadcasts the fact. Like if I walk in the door and she's playing Hole or Chrissie Hynde, that's a good sign: that's the sign that Mom's in her I-am-woman-hear-me-roar mode, and we have a fighting chance of her walking away from Raymond once and for all. But if I walk in and she's listening to the Afghan Whigs, I know I should turn back around and stay away for a couple days, let her burn the song off like a terrible hangover. Seriously, there's this Afghan Whigs song "My Curse," that she'll play over and over and over, all day long, and I just want to bang my head on the wall. Like, *Seriously, Mom, have you no shame?*

Reminds me of this story my dad told me once about how, in law school, he used to live below this woman who was up all night, every night, playing "Rikki Don't Lose That Number," over and over on the piano, right above his bedroom. Dad said he'd lie awake in bed, three, four in the morning, finally done studying, and night after night, just as he was drifting off, the piano part would start, and he'd shout at the ceiling: You have got to be kidding me! So, finally, one night, my dad had enough, and he got up and went upstairs to tell the woman to stop playing that song or he was calling the cops.

So he starts pounding on her door with his fist, demanding she open up the door, and turns out, the woman had cancer. She couldn't sleep because she was in so much pain, and looking at her, with a scarf wrapped around her head, totally gaunt and pale, my dad couldn't even speak. He looked at the poor woman, and then he turned and sulked back to his bedroom, completely ashamed.

The point is, I can't even yell at my mom, really, because it's so pathetic. I mean, come on, *I'm* the teenager—at long last, I made it to fifteen, right—and she's ruining it for me. I'm not kidding: every time she does it, I'm just like, *Now how am I ever going to spend an entire day, locked up in my room, listening to the same stupid sad song over and over again, feeling sorrier for myself than any girl in history, without thinking I'm just like my mom?* See what I mean? Ruined.

Even worse, she'll start smoking again, chain-smoking. Like Friday night, she'll decide she can have one cigarette with her vodka and cranberry or whatever, just one or two cigarettes, and by the next day, she'll be up to half a pack a day, easy. So of course she'll lose a ton of weight, and then, like clockwork, she'll break down and call Rain Man, because she hasn't eaten in days, so she's not thinking clearly, reassuring herself he's left a sufficient number of messages for her to dignify returning his call. And of course he'll tell her it didn't mean anything, whoever it was he was screwing on the side, or on his desk more like it, whatever.

I know because I hear it, every word. Every time they fight, I hear her in the next room, not all the words, necessarily, but the tone of her voice, all pleading and needy, and it's sickening. It is, that she needs so badly and doesn't believe she can do any better than Raymond at this point in her life, and it makes me so angry with her. It's hard because I know she did what she had to do, moving us here, because it was the first job she could get, and it wasn't about what she wanted, and I know that. But any confidence she used to have, it's gone. But more than that, sometimes I look at her, all curled up on the couch at night, drinking and smoking, and I'm like, *What is wrong with you? You're supposed to be the strong one: because you're the mom, remember?* Then I'll say something cruel, cutting, provoking her, because it's all I can do to get it out. And there are lots of ways to cut yourself, you know?

I remember this one time when she hadn't talked to Raymond in two weeks. It was the longest she'd ever gone, and I was so proud of her, but of course Ray kept calling her. So one night, he tried her cell phone first, and then he got bold and left a message on our landline. Bold because he knew I could hear him, and obviously he didn't care what I knew about him anymore. So, yeah, I heard his entire message, because we were watching TV, and he goes, I know you're home, Renee. Please, babe, pick up the phone? And you could see my mom twisting inside, like she was enjoying it so much that he kept pursuing her, and it would be a total mistake to speak to him, but, on the other hand. . . .

*Don't*, I said, looking her in the eye. Don't do it, Mom. Not this time. You ever think why he keeps making the same mistake? Maybe because you forgive him every time, I said, and she goes, I know you can't understand, Thea, and I go, Mom, you've been through this so many times now, so why do you keep going back to him? Do you really need a guy so badly? It was mean, I know, but I wasn't even that angry then, and she goes, I want someone in my life, Thea. Yes, she said, I do. I go, Yeah, well, me, too, but not someone who screws around on me. Do you enjoy being treated like you matter so little to him that he'll—. That's enough, Thea. She'll pull it together enough to put on the mom voice with me and say, That's enough, and I go, You said I can't understand, so explain it. Why do you keep going back to him when you know he'll just screw you over again? She goes, We aren't having this conversation, and I go, Fine. Call him back then, kiss and make up. But that's a hell of an example you're setting for me, Mom, thanks, I said, and I got up and went to my room.

I'm sorry, but I can't forgive him, even if she does. I mean, you want to know how she found out that time? She found out because she walked in on them—Ray and this girl, having sex in his office. And to have to think about my mom walking into some redneck commercial real estate office to find her loser fucking boyfriend going at it with some chick he'd picked up on his lunch hour, I have to block it out. Because aside from everything else I have to censor in that picture, to see the look on my mom's face at that moment? No, I can't. After everything that happened with my dad, I can't do it.

So I was mean to her, instead. Because I was afraid. Scared of the idea that you can spend half your life trying to figure out who you are, and just when you figure out who that is, that person is destroyed. Scared because if something like that could happen to my mom, it could happen to me, too. And I couldn't let that happen to me. I'm sorry, I love my mom more than anything, but it's just really hard to have to sit and watch her turning into this woman who is so much less than she used to be.

You know she was beautiful once, my mom. More beautiful than I'll ever be. And when she was in college, like when she met my dad, she was *gorgeous*. I'm serious, you look at pictures of her, and then you look at my dad from back then, and you think, *God, you got so lucky, dude.* I used to be really proud of her, proud introducing her to people. Saying, This is my mom. But when I look at her now, I think, *Who are you? How do I even talk to you anymore?*

Now, when I see her sometimes, turning her head in the aisle at the grocery store or getting out of the car at night, for a second, I see the beautiful woman she used to be, almost like this ghost that slips out for a second. And whenever that happens, I can't help thinking about those people, you know how parents say things about when adolescence hits, it's like aliens have abducted your children or something like that, right? The thing is, that can happen, no matter how old you get. Except in my mom's case, she wasn't abducted by aliens; it was just life.

Jenna Darnell: I knew the second she opened her mouth. Hello, Thea, she said, standing above me. I'd gone to Silver Top so I could be alone for a couple hours; I was trying to draw, but mostly just staring at the white pages, left side, right side, empty, and the bell rang above the front door. May I sit with you? she said, and I nodded. Okay, I said, not having much choice, really, but at least she cut to the chase.

She reached in her leather bag, pulled out a big envelope, and put it on the table, between us. I thought you should see these, she said, taking out a stack of color pictures. You know there's been a rash of vandalism in this town, she said. Between this, and the videos we all know about, and the vanishing tire tracks in the field, she said, looking at me like she was waiting for some response, but I didn't give her one. I had nothing to say. Thea, I can't help but wonder if this is all related, somehow, to your boyfriend, Cam, she said, tilting her head and giving me one of those sympathetic newscaster looks, but I stared at the table. I had a feeling she'd catch me in a lie if I said anything, so I didn't say a word.

She waited until it became uncomfortable, and then, finally, she said, Whether there's any connection between these events, people are very interested in your story, Thea—they want to hear what you have to say, and I hear there's even talk of a lawsuit involving some pretty big companies. But if and when you're ready, I would like to talk to you. I'm staying here now, in town, so we could meet anytime, she said. Her voice turned soft, sympathetic, and she leaned forward, across the table, and said, I can only imagine how difficult this has been for you, Thea, and I want to hear your side. I wanted to ask her what she was talking about, big companies, but I shook my head no, I have nothing to say, and she waited, staring at me. Thea, I'm running a story in the next couple days, and I thought you might want to take a look at these; she spread out all the pictures—graffiti from all over town, and I got the chills: **What would Socrates do?** tagged on a wall of the elementary school, right behind the jungle gyms. **I'M NOT LAUGHING!!!!!!!!!!!!** tagged across the front porch of the senior citizens home. Worst of all, 3%, tagged on a brick wall in the tunnel where Cam took me that night.

I have to go, I said, grabbing my bag and sliding out of the booth. Here, let me give you my card, Thea, she said, turning toward her leather bag. I said, That's okay, you already gave me your card, and she smiled, looking up at me: Yes, well, she said, in case you lost that one, here's another. Put it in your wallet, she suggested, smiling, and I left a few dollars on the table, walking away. But just as I walked past her, Jenna touched my shoulder, stopping me: Thea, there is a big, *big* story here; I can feel it, and I'm going to find out what that story is, she said. She wasn't threatening me, but she knew, I could tell; she smelled a story. So I said, Good luck, looking at her hand, then she let go of my arm and said, You, too, Thea. You take care, she said, but I'd already reached the front door.

I called my mom and asked her to pick me up at Knox's house on her way home. I knew Melody was at physical therapy, so I called Knox to tell him that I had to see him. When I got there, he opened the door and he was wearing a heather gray Jets shirt and his dad jeans. Friday casual already? I said, walking in, and before he could say anything, I told him about Jenna Darnell, cornering me at Silver Top, that she had pictures of all the graffiti that's been popping up, while he led me to his office at the end of the hall. I just got the pictures, he said, taking a seat at his desk. When I walked over, he had a still from a surveillance video onscreen: **I'M NOT LAUGHING!!!!!!!!!!!!!** I shivered, seeing it. He knew, too, even before he asked, but he asked anyway. He said, Thea, have you seen this before? I nodded and said, Yes, and then I pulled out Hubble, flipping to the page where I'd written that. I was going to hold the page up to the computer screen so he could see it was exactly the same as my handwriting, and just when I found the page, my notebook slipped, and I caught it, but the page tore.

*Ope*, Knox said, turning from me to his computer. What's wrong? I asked, and he shook his head. Nothing, I just hate that ball, he said, watching the spinning ball on his computer, and then he hit a couple keys, trying to get it to stop. Damn, he said, clicking back and forth a few times, and then, when the ball stopped spinning, returning to the freeze-frame taken at the old folks home, he balked. What is it? I said, turning to look, but a little upset about the torn page. When I looked, it was the same picture of the graffiti, except half the graffiti was gone; the words **NOT LAUGHING!!!!!!!!!!!!** weren't there anymore. Hubble, I said, and Knox said, Come again? I said, That's what we call it, our notebook, and then I held Hubble up to his computer, and the graffitied words were erased where I'd torn our notebook page. I looked at Knox, making sure he saw it, too, and he did.

Knox restarted his computer, not knowing what else to do, what else to believe, and I even wondered if that might change the image, but I knew better. Sure enough, the picture was the same; the words were gone. It only took a couple minutes, and then he got a text, a photo the cops had just taken. Knox held up his phone for me to see: the wall at the home looked exactly like it did on his screen, after I ripped the page—**NOT LAUGHING!!!!!!!!!!!!**— and I shuddered, crossing my arms and shivering, it scared me so much.

Listen to me, Thea. Listen, Knox said, more serious than I'd ever heard him sound before: it's that notebook. I don't know what the hell is going on, but whatever you do, don't let that notebook out of your sight. In fact, you should hide it, keep it here, and I said, No, Knox, I can't do that, and he sighed, knowing I wouldn't give it up. All right, but do not let it out of your sight, you understand? he said, and I nodded yes, grabbing my bag, hugging the notebook to my chest. I jumped, hearing my phone, and my first thought was Jenna Darnell, but it was just my mom, texting to say that she was outside.

I made it to the car and opened the door, and then I stopped, realizing what this might mean. Because if I could change something just by tearing one of my pages, what would happen if I tore one of Cam's pages, or scribbled on them, or erased them? You all right? Mom asked, and I nodded, buckling up, while she pulled out. How was the old Silver Top? she asked, smiling, because nothing changes at Silver Top. I told her. I said, That reporter showed up, Jenna Darnell, the one who's been covering all the stories about what's been going on in town.

Mom's mouth fell open, and then she furrowed her brow: What did she want? Did she try and ask you questions? Yes, but I said I couldn't comment on anything, and Mom started to say something, then she shut her mouth. So we drove a couple blocks, not saying anything, and then, waiting at the red light, she goes, You know what we should do tonight, babe? Let's go out to dinner, and I said, *Out?* Out where? Because we never go out to eat anymore, and Mom nodded her head side to side, thinking about it, then she goes, What about Indian? Remember how good it was?

There's an Indian family who moved to town last year and they opened this little place in this old strip mall behind Wal-Mart. The smell of curry and cardamom hit you the moment you walked through the door, and the food's so good, my mouth started watering. The owner came right over, the husband, soon as we walked in, and he was so genteel, I love him. Oh, good evening, ladies, he said, clasping his hands in front of him, and Mom goes, Good evening. Two, please? This way, please, the man said, holding out his hand, and Mom looked so happy, but once we sat down, I started feeling guilty, because I was thinking how big a splurge this dinner was.

I couldn't even stand to look at the prices on the menu, and then I started feeling angry with her, too, like why did she bring us here for dinner when we don't have the money? But I didn't say anything, I couldn't—Mom was smiling and she wanted to treat me to a nice dinner, just the two of us. She must've read the look on my face, because she looked up and said, Is this okay? You're not in the mood for Indian food? We could go somewhere else, she said. And the thing is, Mom looked so pretty again, like I remember her looking before our lives changed, before we moved here. This is great, I said, and she squeezed my hand, before ordering.

Once the food came and we started eating, we had such a good time, I forgot everything for a couple hours, all our problems. I can't tell you how nice that was, either, even for just two hours. For the first time in weeks, I went to bed feeling so much better, but then, I don't know if I ate too much or what, but I woke up in the middle of the night. I couldn't get back to sleep, so I just lay there, staring at my ceiling.

I felt so alone and it was so dark, I removed the Band-Aid from my shoulder, and I got up to look at the tattoo again in my bedroom mirror: TD + CC = TLA. It made me smile, but it was the painful kind of smile, the kind where the smile's pushing through, you know? And I don't know what made me think of it, but I went out to get the hand mirror from the bathroom, tiptoed back to my room, and opened my curtains so I could see outside.

Then I walked to the center of my room and turned my back to the full-length mirror while I held up the hand mirror, pointing the florescent reflection into the sky, like they do in Gotham with the Batman signal or whatever they call it. I stood there for at least a minute, waiting, but I don't think the stars heard me, because if they did, nothing happened. So I went back to the bathroom to put the mirror back in the drawer and put a fresh Band-Aid on.

That's when I felt it again, standing there, on the bath mat. It started at the back of my head, like when you get a headache that starts in your neck, and then it curls around your neck, like the headache's palming the back of your skull. So I opened the medicine cabinet, and I took out Raymond's razor, and I tiptoed back to my room, locking the door.

I stood there, staring at my rug, and I could feel it building. It's hard to describe, because it's like a headache, the pressure. Only it doesn't hurt the same, it's not that kind of pain; it's just the pressure of compulsion. Like you start to feel something pulling you like a wave. So you try to turn away or step around it, but it's inside of you. So you try to step around yourself, but you can't, because the wave is in your blood. And after our nice night out, I wanted to tell my mom, talk to her about it, but I can't because I'm not going back on drugs. I won't do it. I was just standing there, holding the razor in my hands, the pressure building behind my eyes. I wanted to cut so badly, too. I knew exactly where I would cut, and in my mind's eye, I was already taking off my clothes, readying myself. But there was so much pressure that when I reached to press my fingers against both my temples,

I dropped the razor; you couldn't hear a sound, but the motion triggered my computer, the screen lighting up. Immediately, I heard laughter—our laughter.

Before I even turned to look over, I knew what it was. There was a video on my desktop, even though I wasn't on YouTube. It wasn't sex: it was the two of us, goofing around. It was this video we took of ourselves on my computer last winter, after we went to New York. We got into this huge fight, because I got jealous and saw red and lost my shit, but anyhow. It was a video of the week after we made up, when Cam was teasing me about how I deal with my anger—my anger issues, yes.

I'm sitting on Cam's lap, and our faces and torsos are pretty much the whole frame, and right away, Cam grabs my hand like it's a paw, and he shakes my paw hand at the camera, saying, Hello, everybody! Hello, world! He's in this falsetto, impersonating me, right, and he goes, Hi! I'm Thea Denny, and I'm so angry, grrr! I'm so angry at my boyfriend, just to prove how angry I am, I'm not going to speak to him! I'll show my bad boyfriend how angry I am for doing whatever it was he did I'm not telling him about! he said, crossing his arms in front of me, squeezing both my wrists and then he said, I'm so angry I'm going to hit myself! Then he took my hands, flopping all over, and he started slapping me with my hands—lightly, just so silly, but he wouldn't let go when I tried to pull away. Then he goes, Thea, quit hitting yourself! Thea, quit being so angry that you hit yourself! he said, slapping me twice, on both cheeks, until I was laughing so hard that I couldn't even fight.

Of course, the moment we come close to having a moment, what's Cam do? He pokes me. In the butt. His erection, poking me in the butt! So I slapped him and was just like, Cam! And he goes, It wasn't voluntary! And I said, So? And he goes, Thea, take it as a compliment, and I said, Cam, you can't tell me it's involuntary, and then tell me to take it as a compliment, and he goes, Why not? Involuntary compliments happen all the time, he said, squeezing my knee. And I said, In your pants! laughing. That was us. That was real. And now that's all I have, and I stood there, smiling at us, tears in my eyes; my room glowing pink with the dawn.

It's so demented, because half the time, I worry who else has seen a video, and the other half, I worry that nobody has seen it. This time, I wasn't sure which was better, because it wasn't sex; it was a different kind of intimacy, not caught in the act, but caught in the heart. Who we really were, no cameras, no videos, no viewers, no one but us in the entire world. And we were happy, goddamnit. I didn't realize I was touching the screen, touching our faces, like he was right there.

I have no idea who else saw that video, I didn't even look to check the numbers; it must have been a lot of hits, because the resolution was so clear, so lifelike, but it didn't matter. All that mattered was the sign—that video was a sign from Cam that it was only a bad dream, to remember what was real, that he knew I was struggling. He was telling me to hold on, because I'm not alone. Yes and no, I said, staring at the screen: yes and no.

## SATURDAY, JANUARY 22, 2011
## (TEN WEEKS EARLIER)

4:56 PM

Cam's birthday is in January, and it was his golden birthday; he turned eighteen on January 18. So Karen made this fancy dinner, and a big cake, and we celebrated with her, of course, but then we had our own celebration, just the two of us. Because I'd been saving up since Christmas, and I surprised Cam with two tickets, and we went down to New York for a day, like a day trip.

It wasn't on his birthday, it was the weekend after, but we left early Saturday morning and drove to Hudson, then we took the train down, and we got to Penn Station just before noon. I wanted to go downtown, go see some galleries, go shopping, and I left all the directions to Cam, of course. We had so much fun, too. We ate noodles at this place near St. Mark's, and we took pictures of ourselves in front of the Joe Strummer mural by Tompkins Square Park. Honestly, we just asked this guy on the street to take it for us, but it's one of the best pictures we have.

Kicking up my heel, Cam's kissing the side of my face, so strong, hugging me. Makes me so happy, every time I look at it. Anyhow, we went window-shopping. I felt like we walked twenty miles that day, and then we went to this store I'd been reading about for ages, that's supposed to be like the coolest store in New York. I was so excited, because I'd been dreaming about that moment for a whole year, but when we walked in, it was a little intimidating. Place was way too cool for school, and none of the salespeople paid us any attention, so whatever.

Looking at the clothes, I pulled out this leather dress, showing it to Cam, and I was just like, Isn't this to *die*? Seriously, how can anything be so beautiful? And Cam pulled out the tag, and he goes, How can anything be so expensive? And I was just like, Philistine, and I put it back on the rack. Then Cam goes: What are you doing, Thee? Try it on, and I shook my head no, and he goes, Thee, we came all this way to see this store, and you aren't even going to try on a single dress? Who's the Philistine? And before I could say anything, he goes, You want to get me something for my birthday or not? I said, I can't afford anything here, and he goes, No, you can't. That's not what I want for my birthday, right? Well, I want you to try on that dress, he said. My mouth fell open, because I felt so embarrassed for some reason, and he says, You asked what I wanted. . . . And I did, too.

So I went to the counter and asked if I could try it on. I don't know why I was so scared to ask, but anyhow, the sales guy walked me to the back and opened up one of the dressing rooms for me, and I just stood in the room, holding this long-sleeve black leather dress up, then there was a knock. I go, Yes? It was

Cam, and he goes You'll need these, and I opened the door, and he handed me these pony-skin heels that were so gorgeous I died a thousand deaths.

Well, I managed to get the dress on, and it was so tight, all the way to my knees, and then I put the high heels on, and they fit perfectly. I really thought I'd gone to black leather dress heaven, and I walked out, looking for Cam, like, *Where are you?* Then I saw him talking to this salesgirl at the counter, and she was laughing at something he said. He didn't even notice me, standing there—he's totally flirting with her, or she's flirting with him, same fucking difference. She's tall and has this platinum blonde hair to her waist and she's like superskinny and I could hear her say something with this stupid cockney accent and leather hot pants and black tights, and I was just like, Whatever.

I felt so dumb, too, like some little girl playing little-rich-girl dress up, and all of a sudden, I wanted to cry. I don't even know what happened, but I got so angry, I walked back to the dressing room and took it off. The dress, the shoes, I took them off, put them back on the hanger, and I walked out. Cam didn't see me until the door opened, because it buzzed, and Cam caught up with me, outside, but I didn't speak to him the rest of the day. I didn't say anything the whole ride home, on Amtrak, and he kept saying he didn't understand what happened or why I was so angry, and I go, I don't know, Cam, why don't you ask your little blonde girlfriend? He started laughing, like it was a joke, and that just made me angrier, and then he told me I was completely overreacting. And then that just made me that much angrier, you know?

He was right, but I couldn't say it. Not just the fact that I was jealous, and I saw red, seeing him with this girl. The fact that I was so scared he'd leave me. That he didn't really love me. That I'd be alone. Everything, all of it, and all at once, something in me snapped, and I couldn't stop it. I told him: Don't talk to me right now. So for three hours, we didn't say a word. Not even when we got to my house, and I got out, and he got out, like he was going to follow me inside, and then I said, I told you, please leave me alone, Cam, and he stopped. It was only nine when I walked in, and Mom was on the couch, watching TV, and she goes, Did you have a good time? Tell me all about it, and I was just burning, in my chest, this sour, awful, teary burning, and I shook my head no. I said, New York sucks, and I went to my room and shut the door.

She knocked an hour later, when Ray showed up, and I said, Leave me alone, and she opened the door, and she said, Fine, but Ray says Cam's outside, and I felt it right in my chest, thinking about Cam sitting there, but I looked away. He's been outside since he dropped you off, she said, and I didn't say anything. She goes, So do you want to invite him in or should I? I stared at the wall, and then I go, Neither. Thea, she said, giving me that voice that told me I was about to get in trouble, and I go, What? Mom said, Come here, and she opened the door for me to follow her.

I walked to the living room, and then she opened the curtain so I could see outside, and there he was, in his car. Cam had been sitting out there, in the freezing cold, for more than an hour. Go, my mom said, so I grabbed my coat, and walked to the parking lot. I opened the door, and I got in his car, and it was freezing. I could see my own breath. I didn't know what to say, so I said, Are you hungry? And he said, Always, and I go, Ray brought pizza, if you want, and Cam nodded. He goes, Ray invited me, before he went inside. Are you still angry? he asked, and I nodded. He goes, We were talking about you, you know, and I said, No, I don't know, Cam. And he said, I'm telling you the truth, and I said, Great. Thanks. He nodded and sighed, then he goes, Are you going to speak to me again? I said, I'm speaking to you now, and he goes, No, you're not. You're yelling in a calm voice, he said, and I laughed, because he was right.

Why did you stay? I said, trying not to smile. Because I wanted to tell you something, he said, and I said, So. Tell me. Then he said, Look at me, and I looked at him, then I looked away. You aren't looking at me, and it's important, he said, so I turned to look at him, and then he said it. For the first time, Cam said it out loud: I love you, he said. He took my hand, and I couldn't say anything. He goes, Did you hear me? I nodded yes, but still, all I could do was stare straight ahead, while my eyes started tearing up. Then, smart-ass, he goes, Thea, do you have something you want to say to me? I nodded and I go, No. He laughed, slapping me, he goes, You are a terrible liar, and I go, Takes one to know one, and Cam goes, I've never lied to you, and I never will. All I could do was bite my tongue, because I knew what he was saying. He was talking about my dad, about how I could trust him, he'd never hurt me like that.

I couldn't say it then. Not even then, but I leaned over, putting my head on his lap, and I lay there, letting him smooth back my hair while I tried to figure it out in my head, trying to untie all the knots in my heart, one by one.

It's a kind of falling in love, having a new best friend. I mean, things like how you can't get enough of them. Like how you can spend the whole day together, and you do, every day, but it's not enough. Like you want to eat them up, every time you see them, and then, soon as you leave, you have to call them, because you thought of one more thing you absolutely have to tell them. And then, the second after you hang up, they call you right back, thinking of one other thing they absolutely have to tell you. And you aren't even doing anything special, you're just hanging in your room or whatever, but your room turns into the whole world. Mom always calls it a girls' honeymoon, when you share everything and you're totally inseparable, and that's how I am with Melody.

The thing is, at the beginning, I was the one showing Mel all these things, because she'd been living in a cave her whole

life, basically. Then, one day, I find out she's made her own dis-
coveries, without me, and I was like, *Wait, you did something
without me?* Like one day, I went over, after school, and I sat
down on the side of her bed, and Mel goes, *Ready?* She sounded
so excited, too, I go, Ready for what? She goes, *I've got an idea,
and I don't know if it'll work, but I want to try.* I said, Okay, tell
me, and we'll try, and she goes, *Well, I want to do a shoot, like
a photo shoot where I describe the pictures, but you take them
for us. Like I describe what I see, and you draw the pictures or
shoot them,* and I go, You mean I shoot what you explain to me?
*Exactly!* she said.

I thought I understood, but we'd never done it before. So I
go, What if I get them wrong? Because I was suddenly afraid
of disappointing her, and she goes, *Thee, you can't screw it up,
that's impossible.* All right, I said, a little embarrassed that all of
a sudden, I'm the one who's insecure. What's your idea? I said,
and she goes, *It's a movie.* And I said, Really? What's it about?
Give me the pitch, I said, leaning back, kicking off my shoes, and
she goes, *Well, it's a movie about a girl.* I go, Good start, and she
goes, *A beautiful girl—she's seventeen, eighteen, maybe, and
she's on the run.* And I go, Who is she running from? Mel goes, *I
don't know, but whoever it is, she has to totally reinvent herself.*
I said, *Reinvent herself?* She's seventeen, Mel, and Melody goes,
*Exactly. So she runs away to Paris, because what better place to
run away and reinvent yourself? And she has a look that's sort of
exotic and otherworldly, too. She has this sort of Paris 1968 vibe,
or wait, wait—no, no, I know—maybe she runs away, back in
time? That's it, that's it!*

I've never seen Mel so excited, she was holding up her hands, like she was asking me to let her think it through, and then she goes, *I've got it: What if she runs back in time? What if she gets ID pictures taken in a photo booth, and bang, flash, she's gone! When she steps out of the photo booth, she's traveled back in time—because isn't that what a photo booth is, a time machine? So when she steps out of the booth, she finds herself in Paris, in April, 1968.* I was just like, Ohmygod, that's *so good*, and Mel goes, *Now you go, Thea: Your turn. Tell me what you see*, she said, and I could see it. I could see everything she was describing, and I said, But does she have a name? Mel beamed, almost squealing, and she goes, *Yes! Violaine. Her name is Violaine!* Soon as she said that, I could totally see the girl's face, too, like her long, dark, straight hair and black-and-white photo booth pictures. I said, So she's got a whole new identity, right? *Yes*, Mel said: *new life, new identity, finds a time machine in a photo booth and she runs away, back in time, to Paris, 1968.*

I was just like, *Wow*. So she runs away, back in time, to Paris, and then what? I go, What does she do? Mel goes, *Oh, easy: She goes to the Louvre every day, where men stare at her. She wears this fitted coat with sort of a swing skirt bottom, like Dior meets Vivienne Westwood coat, and five-inch heels. And leather gloves, of course. But no make up—Violaine doesn't really do make up, and she doesn't need to, and she goes to the Louvre every day, because it's so conspicuous, it's inconspicuous! Isn't that genius?* If you do say so yourself, I said, laughing. I swear, I have created a monster—the most beautiful monster in the whole wide world, but still.

*Seriously,* Thee, she said. *Can't you just imagine her apartment, and her clothes, and her closet, and the balcony off her bedroom, where she has some plants and the most outrageous view of Paris? She steps outside, one morning, waking up, and watching her do that, just that bit, your first thought is how fucking good it is to be this girl, excuse my French,* she said. I was putting a pillow under my head, but then I almost fell off her bed, I was laughing so hard. But Mel was on a tear: *Then Violaine turns back inside, and you see her vanity with her perfume bottles and her jewelry, and there are gorgeous shoes everywhere, and records and books and magazines. . . .*

Listening to Mel, it really felt like she was giving me a tour of this girl's life, and I could see it, but all I could think was, *Where is this all coming from?* She goes, *Oh, and it's slow, and sexy, and the whole film follows her exploring all these bars and jazz clubs in Paris, and that's how we learn what she's running from, starting a life in Paris.*

I go, You're right, it's genius. Violaine is running from her past by going back in time. Clever, very clever, and Mel goes, *Of course: Violaine is a revolutionary, a Marxist.* I go, What kind of Marxist hides out in the Louvre, wearing five-inch heels? Mel said, *Ohmygod.* She goes, *Why, a Miuccia Prada Marxist,* and I had to laugh. *Wait, wait—there's our title,* she said. *The Prada Marxiste!* she said, clapping. *Can't you see it, Thee?* And I could, too. It was like a brainstorm, only stronger, the way she was describing everything. I could see all the pictures in her head just like it was a movie.

Okay, but wait, I said. How do we figure it out, whatever it is she's running from? And she goes, *I don't know. What matters is that her life—Violaine's life is . . . different than ours. I mean, can't one teenage girl in this world create a charmed life for herself that we can all dream about and share? Doesn't someone get to escape reality and live an incredible life somewhere, in some dimension, even if it's only for a couple hours in a movie theater? Because if that's not possible, how else are we going to get through all this, you know?*

I didn't say anything, thinking it over, and then I just had to ask again, But what's she running from? Mel goes, *Something awful she did,* and I go, Give me an example of something so awful she could have done that would make her run away all the way back in time? Mel goes, *I don't know. Maybe she screwed around on her boyfriend and got pregnant from another guy and she had an abortion and then her boyfriend found out, and he was completely devastated—.* Okay, easy, I said, holding up my hands, not at all prepared. *I'm just saying,* she said, and I go, I know, but that's pretty intense. Mel goes, *Well, there has to be a clear motive why she would give up her entire life and go back in time. Because the thing about time travel is, there's no guarantee she'll make it back to her old life ever again. There might be no way back to the future, you know, so it'd have to be something pretty intense, right?* Maybe she's traveling in Ghost Time, I said, thinking about what it could be, what a person could do that would be so horrible they'd leave their own time forever, and Mel perked up. *What's Ghost Time?* I didn't even realize I'd spoken out loud. Nothing, I said, smiling, trying to think of what to say to change the subject, but I couldn't think of anything. It was okay, though; she left it alone. I don't know how Mel knew, but I could see on her face that she knew it was something to do with Cam. Sometimes she's really good at knowing when not to ask a question—not often, but that was one of those times.

Knox knocked and stuck his head in the door before I even had a chance to say come in, so annoying. Then, on second thought, I said, Knox, you're just in time, actually, and he looked curious, smiling, included. I said, We're working on a script about a completely gorgeous girl who goes back in time, changes her name to Violaine, and lives in Paris in April 1968. And being a cop, you'd have some idea, so, the questions is, what is something so awful that a girl could do that she'd go back in time, never to see anyone she loves, the people she most loves in the entire world, ever again? He smiled, sort of chuckled about that one, because there I was, trying to bring him in and share, which is what he wanted more than anything, to be included. On the other hand, he deemed the entire situation completely fucked up. So.

Let me ask you this, he said, and I could tell he was changing the subject, but whatever. Why does this girl go back in time instead of forward? *Got this one, Mel*, I said. *There are lots of reasons why she goes back in time, but, mostly, because that's the only direction she can go. The only way you can get somewhere that's never been is with art, so she has to make art or go back in time, maybe both, we'll see!* Honestly, until that moment, I didn't even know how much that picture with Cam truly meant to me, but I know now.

Because *The Future Is Unwritten*! I said, clapping my hands, grabbing my phone from my bag. I had the picture—I showed Knox the picture of me and Cam, standing in front of the Joe Strummer mural on his birthday. Mel goes, *Show me! Show me, Thea—what are you doing, showing my dad first?* I laughed and said, Mel, I only showed him first because he was closest, but she was right, so I jumped over and showed her. It was only then that it dawned on me that I'd never offered to show her a picture of Cam. And I felt terrible about that, too. I mean, she never asked, but I never offered. I guess because I felt like I was always looking at pictures of him.

Here, I said, holding the camera up for her. And she inhaled so deep, like she was flapping her face, unable to breathe, excited, and she goes, *Ohmygod, Thea! Cam is so cute!* I laughed, blushed. Part of me was like, Oh, here we go again, even my own best friend is going to wonder what he's doing with me, so let's be done with it, already. But then part of me was just giddy. I said, Yeah, he is really cute, isn't he? When I say cute, I mean really fucking cute, like I just want to eat him up! I said, bobbling my head, cooing at the picture of us, and immediately, I feel a flare up in the corner: Knox telling me to watch my language. I was just like, This is *our* world, *our* domain, Knox, you want in or not? I didn't say that, because there was no point: you know he wouldn't have known how to answer. Did he want to be included in our world, really? Maybe. Gee, sounds good on paper, honey, but . . . I'm sorry, but dads and their cafeteria-style intimacy, you know? When I watch Knox, I get it, though. He just doesn't have a clue. Anyhow.

Then Knox goes, Hey, you two, what do you say about going to get something to eat? Mel goes, *No, thanks*, and he goes, I didn't have a chance to shop, and Mel goes, *Not again*, and he said, So we'll pick something up before we take Thea home, and I just looked at her, and I looked at Knox, and he goes, What? I shook my head, never mind.

We got in, got Mel situated, pulled out, and Knox started to say something, and Mel goes, *Here we go*, and Knox goes, I know it's nothing fancy, but how's McDonald's sound? And I just shrugged, like, whatever, it's up to you guys, but then Mel goes, *No*. I turned around to look at her, and Knox looked at her in the rearview. And I said, What's wrong? She goes, *Never mind*, and she sighed this heavy sigh. Knox looked at me, and I shrugged, like, I don't know.

So we got to the drive-in, and Mel goes, *Thee, I want you to tell my dad something*. I turned and looked back at her, because she hadn't said anything the whole way, and I was like, What's up? And she goes, *I want you to tell him that I'm a vegetarian*. Knox looked at her in the rearview again, and he goes, What's up? He could tell, so I told him: There's something you should know about Melody. He goes, Sounds serious, and I said, It is. To Mel, I said, and Knox goes, All right. Let's hear. Then he turned to face her, and he said, Let's have it. I sighed, and then I spit it out: Mel's vegetarian, and Knox laughed, and he goes, She's *what*? So I told him, I said, She's vegetarian. She doesn't eat meat—wouldn't if she had any choice, I said.

He looked at me, he looked at her, and he chuckled, then he goes, You got to be kidding me, vegetarian, turning back around, facing front. No how, no way: *capisce?* he said, turning back to look at Melody again. Then Mel goes, *Ohmygod, seriously, Dad? You've never noticed? Tell him—Thea, tell him,* she said, and I go, Knox, why do you think she throws the worst fits when you're feeding her? What are you feeding her? And he goes, She throws fits every night for god's sake, and I go, Because you force her to eat meat every night! Didn't it ever occur to you? I asked, and his mouth fell open. Finally, in this stern dad voice, he goes, No. No, it didn't. And she needs the protein.

I said, Please, you can get protein in other ways, and he goes, Not in my house you can't. I said, Knox, Mel believes in reincarnation: she believes people can come back as animals, and if you eat them, who knows who you're eating, and he goes, This has gone too far—this, is this your doing? And I said, *My doing?* No. And she's been on my case, too, so I've quit eating all red meat, and I'm thinking of giving up chicken, too. Maybe just fish. He goes, Oh, so people can't come back as fish in the next life, and I go, She's right: everyone agrees it's terrible for the environment. Knox goes, No, everyone does not agree: *I* do not agree. Then the girl came on the intercom to tell us our total and Knox pulled through, paying for his food.

I didn't say anything until he pulled out and parked, then I go, Just don't ever say I didn't tell you. And don't say you don't know how she feels. And most of all, don't kill the messenger and eat me in my next life, I said, looking back at Mel, and she goes, *Meat is murder,* and I nodded, Such a great album, right? What's that? Knox said, shoving a bit of bun in his mouth. Mel goes, *Meat is murder,* meaning that she wanted me to translate, so I said: Meat is murder, Mel says, and Knox pulled out his drink and took a long sip, not the least fazed. Then Mel goes, *Honestly, Thee, I don't think it'd make any difference if I could talk—I think he'd be just like this*, and I go, Totally, and she goes, *But, like, are all dads lame or just my dad?* And I go, All of them, pretty much. I mean, I'm sure there are exceptions, but I don't know any, I said, looking back, and in a flash, I saw her. I saw the beautiful Melody, locking her jaw, angry, staring out her window, and it hit me right in my gut. Course Knox knew we were talking about him, but he just finished his burger, before heading to my house.

Mel's so funny, though, she started singing, she goes, *I am the daughter and heir, of nothing in particular*, and I started laughing. Of course Knox goes, What's funny? And I shook my head, never mind, and he goes, Tell me, and I go, You won't get it, and he goes, Try me. Mel laughed, and she goes, *Yeah, try him, Thee*, and I go, Mel was singing, *I am the daughter and heir*, and Knox waited, like there must be more, and I go, It's a line from the Smiths: *I am the son and the heir*, and Mel was singing, I am the daughter and the heir—playing on *son*, you get it? Knox just looked out his window.

That night, after they dropped me off, walking upstairs, to our apartment, all I could think was, *What could a person do that would be so terrible? I mean, besides, say, killing somebody?* I got out my key, opening our door, and soon as I stepped inside, I got a text with a YouTube link. So I went to my room, turned on my computer and typed in the link, and of course it was another video. But for once, it wasn't a video of me and Cam.

No, this time, the reason I started shaking was because someone posted a video of Mel and me, and the whole conversation we'd just had, not even an hour before. It was like someone was in the room with us, like there was a ghost with a handheld camera.

Except in the video, all you can see is me sitting on the side of Mel's bed, looking at her, talking to her. I mean, I look like a total lunatic, babbling on with her. The whole time, Mel just sits there, in her chair, her head tilted to the side, and she doesn't say a word. Because she can't speak, and we were talking in my head. Watching us like that, I couldn't breathe, but I sent Knox the link, and he wrote me back, What's up? I wrote him back and said, Did you look at it? And he said, Look at what? I go, The link I sent you. And he wrote me back, No link, so I went back to check my sent mail, and he was right: there was no link: there was no e-mail. Honestly, I think I'm losing it, I really do.

Without even thinking about it, I still draw my old room some-times, every detail I can remember. It's so hard to remember, though, because now I know all the things that I didn't know about, and then something in my head clicks, and I don't feel anything. I just shut down. Honestly, I have to laugh when I think of all the times that my dad called me sensitive, how he was always like, *You're too sensitive. You gotta grow some thicker skin, Thea!* And then, one day, I lost it. The night my parents told me they were splitting up.

Isn't it strange how you can know something, hearing the phone ring or walking through a door? You feel it, and you just *know.* I don't remember what day, but it was November, and it was cold that night, and I remember I had on boots, a scarf, and a hat and gloves, and walking home, I was so pleased with being all bundled up. And I still remember unlocking the front door, and that wave of heat, stepping inside, and then it was like some other light was on. Not the overhead, something else. Because when I closed the front door, behind me, looking up and seeing my mom and dad sitting in the living room, waiting for me to walk in, I knew. It was a trap—they'd set a trap for me in the living room—don't ask me how, but I knew the moment I laid eyes on them, and all I could say was, No.

I stood there, between the front hall and the living room, and they both looked at me, waiting for me to come in, so it could begin, and I stared, hoping they'd change their minds. They didn't, of course, they just kept looking, waiting on me, and then I said it again, louder this time; I said, No. For a second, I thought maybe . . . maybe I could actually close the door and sneak out. Like maybe if I was fast, faster than sound or light or time, I could stop this from happening, as if I'd triggered everything, walking in.

Don't, I said, standing there, in my coat, holding my bag, nodding at them. Don't do this to me. I don't want to go, I said. I could hear myself, but I remember that feeling of watching myself, something splitting, and Mom goes, Thee, come in, and I knew she knew, because tears were welling up in her eyes. No, I said, and I turned around, making sure there was no other way out, but there wasn't. Thea, come sit down, my dad said, but all I could think about was my room: because I grew up in that room. It wasn't rainbows anymore, it was wallpapered in tons of pictures and drawings—mine, my room. It was *my room*, and I'd never lived anywhere but there, and it was gone. In that moment, our house was gone, my room was gone, my family, everything I had: gone. Really, how is it possible you're a family one minute, and then, what, it's just over? I mean, if family's so sacred, tell me, how is that possible?

Standing there, knowing my room was gone . . . unless you've stood there, you can't say it's cynical to think families are no different than cars or houses or boats, things that you can buy and sell. They can have expiration dates like anything else, and I felt so sick, figuring that out. Sit down with us, Mom said, patting the seat next to her, on the couch, trying not to cry. No, I repeated, then I looked at my dad, sitting in the opposite chair, leaning forward, staring at his hands. He couldn't look at me, and I waited, but he wouldn't dare, coward. I knew everything in that second; it was like I'd read an entire book, and I knew exactly what he did. Somehow, I swear, I even knew who the woman was he was leaving us for. I thought I was going to puke, and I dropped my bag and ran to the bathroom, and I made it just in time, retching.

Mom came, knocking, asking if I was all right, and when I opened the door, she tried to hug me, and I pushed her away. Don't touch me, I said, stepping back, and so angry, it was like this fire in me, pushing up from the floor to my ankles, and my ankles to my knees. It kept rising, and she saw it, too, raising her hands and stepping back, hands off. So I went to my bedroom, locked the door, and I stood there, looking around at all these things that I loved so much: all my pictures, my drawings, everything I thought was mine. . . . It took me a moment, but I knew what I had to do. Then I started tearing it apart, my whole room. The curtains, the bedspread, everything I had, I broke. They were just things, right? Just like us. And that's when I heard my mom shouting, calling my name. She'd heard me, and both my parents were banging on my door, demanding I let them in. I don't know how much time had passed, but when I stopped throwing things, when I could hear sound again, I looked around, and my room was a disaster. Broken glass, down feathers, dozens of triangles of tape on the wall, where all the pictures had been ripped. . . . I snapped back, and I was like, *Ohmygod*. It was such a mess, I couldn't believe I'd done that. I really lost it, too. But, honestly, I have to say, looking around, I felt better. I felt like at least one person in our family, what was our family, could still be honest: me.

My dad kept pounding. That's all he knew how to do, pound on the door, so I walked over, and I remember feeling so calm as I unlocked and opened the door. I'll never forget the look on his face, or my mom's face, seeing what I'd done. He looked like he was going to fall back, and then he stepped forward, shocked, but still demanding an explanation. And I looked at him, thinking, *Who are you to look at me that way? Like you don't know the answer?* And then I told him, I said, I hate you.

We stood there, the three of us, frozen. And then, for the last time, covering his mouth with one hand, he turned to my mother, needing her, and I'll never forget this, how calmly she said it, just like a mom. She looked at him, and for the last time, she said, I'll get the broom.

A few days later, you know what he did? He offered to take me out, and you know where he took me? Chuck E. Cheese's. He took me to Chuck E. Cheese's, okay? I mean, just when you thought it couldn't get any worse, Dad announces he wants to have a father-daughter talk. And of course he didn't tell me where we were going, either; he just said he had a special place in mind. So when we got there, and he parked up front, my jaw dropped into my lap, watching him unbuckle his seat belt, turning to look at me, like, *Surprise!* And I was like, *Tell me you're just kidding.* Here we are, he said, not kidding, and I go, We who? He goes, I thought we could get something to eat and talk, and I go, Knock yourself out, looking out my window, crossing my arms. Then he goes, Thea, how many times have you begged me to bring you here? He was so proud of himself for remembering the name of the place, and I said, I was *six*, I'm twelve, Dad. Twelve. All right, he said, sighing, turning back to face the wheel, clearly annoyed. You want to go somewhere else, then tell me where, he said, like I was being the pain in the ass, right.

*Home.* Didn't even think about it, the words came straight to mind: *Home, I want to go home, Dad, but it's not there anymore.* I thought it over, and in the end, I was just like, *What's the difference?* Let's just get this over with, I said, opening my door.

I thought I could do it, too, but when we walked through the door, I wanted to cry. It was awful, beyond awful. Because it was like seven o'clock and the whole place was full of kids, happy kids, running around, chasing each other, spazzing out on sugar and fried food and who knows what else. I just watched the kids, but it was impossible not to think, *Enjoy it. Because one day, you might walk through the door and poof! It'll all be gone, kid.* I felt like I should have a T-shirt: My parents went to divorce court, and all I got was dinner at Chuck E. Cheese's.

What do you want to talk about? I asked, soon as the waitress brought our drinks, wanting to get the show on the road. Too painful: the whole thing was too painful, so let's be done with it, right? So my dad takes a deep breath, looking all sorrowful, and he goes, I want you to know you can hate me, but I'm still your father. I mean, so rehearsed and so lame, I was like, Wow, you find that line in a Cracker Jack box, Dad? I said, You what, you're leaving me and Mom for another woman, and I'm supposed to be like, Oh, good, at least you're still my father? He goes, Thea, it's not that simple—. You tell me you're still my father, and you want to talk about simple? I said, looking away. And at that moment, all these bells and whistles started as a birthday party for twenty-five seven-year-olds got under way, and looking at the night sky, I thought, *Lightning bolt, right here: please, just kill me now.*

I pushed my plate away, refusing to touch the food he'd ordered for me. God, I was so angry, I almost started bawling, thinking, *This is love? This is your idea of love?* Then he said it again, he goes, I'm still your father, and I just rolled my eyes to keep from crying. Thea. Look at me, he said, and I looked at him, glaring, so I wouldn't cry. He had no right to see me cry. Then he said it again: I am still your father, Thea, and I love you, and I waited until I knew my voice wouldn't crack. I swallowed and said, Lucky me. Did you hear me? he said. I love you, he said, moving like he was going to take my hands, and I go, Oh, and you know what love means, right?

The waitress walked over to ask if we needed anything else, and my dad said no, we were fine. Seeing I wasn't talking, he took a couple bites of his burger, before he set it down, wiping his fingers, individually, with the silly paper napkins. Are you ready to go? he asked, getting out of the booth, pulling out his wallet. Let's go, he said, dropping a few dollars tip on the table; talk over. Looking outside, at the black sky, I knew that nothing would ever be the same between us again. While in the window, I watched the reflection of children playing, not a care in the world.

And that was it. Talk over. The funny part is, next day, my parents made me see a shrink. *Me.* I had to see a shrink. Okay, I went a little bonkers in my bedroom, I get that, but come on, you're telling me I'm the one who doesn't know how to communicate? My dad cheats on my mom, leaves her for some twenty-three-year-old, then he takes me to Chuck E. Cheese's to have the Talk, and I'm the one who needs help?

A week later, the van was there when I got home from school. My dad was staying at a hotel by then, and my mom was handling all the packing alone. The plan was: I go home after school, the last day before winter break, and as soon as the movers were done, we'd follow them to the storage unit Mom had rented. She'd been offered a job as a paralegal in some town, upstate, so she drove up one day to meet with them. Of course I was praying she'd hate it there, so we could stay in Poughkeepsie, but no such luck. When she came home that night, she tried selling me on it, moving to some place called Fort Marshall, and I said, Indiana? We're moving to *Indiana*? Mom laughed and goes: No, that's Fort Wayne, baby, but I didn't even care. I was just like, Ohmygod, last time I wanted to live in a place called Fort anything, I was five. Honestly, I didn't like the sound of it from the first moment, and I didn't try to hide the fact, but Mom smiled and said it was just a couple hours northwest of Poughkeepsie. When she said that, I was like, Just a couple *hours*? Canada's just a couple hours northwest, too, so why don't we move there? She ignored me, going on about how beautiful and safe and clean it was, this town I'd never ever heard of in my entire life, and when clean is a selling point, you know it's bad, really bad. I couldn't even look at her, listening to her going on about how we'd stay in a motel or whatever until we got settled, and that we'd go apartment hunting together, like how fun, right? It'll be a whole new life, she said, and I said, Can we not talk about this right now? We were eating pizza at our kitchen table, the night before we moved out, and she looked hurt. But I didn't care: I loved my old life, and just because she didn't, I'm sorry.

We'll give it a year and see what happens, she said, returning to the table with a beer, and for a moment, I don't know why, but out of nowhere, I just wanted to hurt her. I got up to carry my paper plate to the trash, which at that point was a black Hefty bag on the floor, in front of the back door, and the rest of the kitchen was packed. There were boxes stacked everywhere, all very clearly marked in my mom's perfect handwriting, and it looked so sad. I didn't understand our things, boxed like that, but then again, I didn't understand anything.

I looked at her, and I was just like, What? I go, What, Mom? And she goes, Come here, and I stood on the staircase, wanting to say no. Thea, come here, she said; I was so annoyed, I wanted to scream. I don't know why, really, but I was annoyed with her all the time by then. So I rolled my eyes, turning around and walking back into the dining room. *What!* I said, not asking her, telling her, making sure she knew how irritated I was. Good night, she said, looking like herself again for a second, with that look in her eyes, telling me I knew better, because we always said good night, especially the last night in our own home. Good night, I said, turning around.

I think that was the last time I saw my mom. I mean the woman I remember her being. It didn't hit me until I grabbed the rail, and then, walking upstairs, I felt like I was going to cry all of a sudden. I made it to my room, and closed the door, and I wanted to—I even sat down on the side of my bed, ready for it, but nothing came. Guess my tears got packed, too.

The next day, when I got home from school, the movers only had a few boxes left to load into the truck. It took about five minutes for them to finish up, while Mom and I stood in the living room, looking at it, nothing to say. So when we heard them open their doors, we locked up for the last time and we got in Mom's car, ready to follow the moving van to the storage unit. I'd been thinking about that moment for a couple weeks, and to be honest, I was glad they'd taken the boxes away, because it was too painful. But once I got in the car and put on my seat belt, looking at our house one last time, I couldn't do it. I wasn't ready to go.

Wait, I said, and I told my mom I had to pee. I held my breath while she reached for her purse and took out some Kleenex and handed them to me with her set of house keys, because I didn't even have my own keys anymore. I don't know if she knew or not, but I didn't have to pee; I wanted to be in our house, alone, for a few minutes. I wanted to say good-bye in my own way.

The thing is, when I walked in, it didn't feel like our house anymore. I'd never seen it like that, so empty and naked and . . . *lonely.* Our house had never been lonely before; it always had us there. It was too much, so I went upstairs, heading toward my room, but before I got to the end of the hall, I stopped in my parent's bedroom, their old bedroom, whatever, facing the driveway. The curtains were still there, because Mom was just too burned out by the very end to pull them down, and she didn't want things from that room anymore, anyway, she said. So I walked over, and I stood, looking out the window. My mom had gotten out of the car, and she'd turned her back to the house, leaning against her car door.

She was smoking. She'd started smoking again. We'd gotten into it a few times, and then she gave me, Who's the mom here, you or I? I said, If you have to ask, that's a problem, don't you think? She knew, at the very least, she couldn't smoke in the car, because I get carsick, but still. It was gross, and it was needy, and to me, it seemed like she was turning into this sad, old divorced woman, overnight, and it made me so angry. Everything was making me so angry, and then, catching her, sneaking in another smoke, I wanted to knock on the window, yell down at her, but I didn't. I just stood there watching her leaning against the car, smoking, and I was just like, *Who is this woman, and what have you done to my mother?*

You know they must do something, real estate agents, to get the old juju or mojo or whatever you want to call it out of house—us, how to get *us* out. I mean, you don't just walk into an empty house where people have lived twelve years and not feel their presence. It's not the same as ghosts, but it's haunted in a way, because if you ask me, the living can be as haunted as the dead. And looking around their bedroom, I thought, *How do I say good-bye to my own life?* You want to know? I'll tell you how: in as few words as possible.

You know, to this day, after everything that's happened—the divorce, moving to this town, my breakdown, the hospital, all of it, my mom still tries talking to me about it sometimes. Like when my dad calls and I won't return his calls, she's always telling me that I'm the one being eaten up by my anger. She always says I'm the one who pays the price, and she might be right, but I'm just like, Well, the thing is, I can afford to pay right now. I mean, I'm fifteen, I'm *allowed* to hate my dad, you know? And the truth is, I can't forgive him for what he did to us, not yet. And honestly, I know it makes me sound like a terrible person, but I'm not sure if I ever will forgive him. It's like, I know forgiveness is divine, but maybe I don't need to be divine, maybe I just need to be a girl.

## TUESDAY, MAY 17, 2011
## (SIX WEEKS LATER)

It was nice out, so when I got to their house, Knox helped Mel out of her chair, and I spread out a blanket, even though Melody never liked lying on the blanket. So we lay on the blanket until Knox went inside, because he didn't like her on the grass and he wouldn't listen. Anyhow, after he went in, I slipped the blanket out, beneath her, so she could feel the grass.

*You want to hear a new scene I'm working on for* La Marxiste? she said, knowing the answer was yes. That's what we decided to call our film, *La Marxiste,* the story of Violaine, the beautiful runaway time-traveling teenage girl. So I'd bring Mel playlists, and she's tell me about a new scene she'd come up with. We had at least twenty *La Marxiste* soundtracks, and some days we spent the whole time listening to a new playlist and talking about what actress could play Violaine in the movie. I was thinking Taylor Momsen or Emma Watson, maybe, if she can do an

American accent, but she's so big, we talked about finding a complete unknown. *This is a role that's going to make her a star, whoever she is,* Mel said, and I laughed, and she was like, *What?* I mean, I totally agreed, but it was just funny. These days, Mel's the only person who can make me laugh, and seeing her is the only thing keeping me sane. Or as close I get, at least.

The one thing that's really hard with her is that all I wanted to do after school was to forget about school, and when we're together, all Mel wants to hear about is my day and what high school's like. Mel's completely obsessed with high school, just like I was, until I became a freshman. She wants details so badly, too. If it were up to Melody, I would've been wired up with a video camera, filming my every move—which I feel like I am, actually, but I never tell her about that. Me and Knox, we have an agreement that we don't talk about that with her, because . . . because I don't want her involved, that's why. Anyhow.

Mel loves watching reality shows on MTV. *Teen Mom, My Super Sweet 16.* Anything with teenagers, and then she'll ask me if it's true. *Is it really like this? God, I'd love to sit in a desk, just once,* she said. *Walk down the halls, carrying my books, have people bump into me, not noticing me because I'm a freshman. Buying new school supplies, getting a new locker,* and I go, I know what you mean, but believe me, the excitement wears thin before you even learn your combination.

She goes, *It's not just school, it's everything, Thea. I want to know how it feels to skin your knee, to climb trees, to cry yourself to sleep over some guy who was a total dick to you—.* I go, Yep, you're really missing out And she goes, *I am! I am missing out!* We'd reached that point where she could be joking, half joking, or she could be angry. I didn't know where we'd fall, or what to say. Not because I was afraid of her being angry, really, I just didn't always know how to deal with it. I mean, I barely knew how to deal with my own anger, you know? So I didn't say anything, and she got quiet.

I could tell she'd been wanting to ask me something, and then she finally did. She goes, *You aren't popular, are you, Thea?* I go, Whatever gave you that impression? And she goes, *Because if you were, why would you be here, with me?* I cocked my head at her, like, Stop. *You know you could be, if you wanted to,* she said, and I go, Mel, I don't care about being popular, I really don't. I used to, but not anymore. Mel said, *Wouldn't school be so much easier if you had friends?* I shook my head no and said, Mel, I had friends, and believe me, it wasn't easier. She goes, *Why don't you try, at least?* I said, Because I'm not like you. *Social,* I said, clarifying. *Yeah, I'm so social,* she said, *look at me.* I go, You are, Mel, you're much more outgoing than I am, even if I'm the only person who knows that. *Tell me why,* she said. *Seriously, Thea, why don't you have any friends?*

I knew she wasn't going to drop it, so I decided to get it over with, tell her what happened. I go, I don't try anymore because I had friends, or people I thought were my friends, but turned out, they weren't. Those girls weren't my friends at all, and so it's just easier to hang on my own, instead of pretending. I mean, everything changed after I met Cam, but I don't know . . . some people are good at school or sports or singing, and some people are good at people, and I'm not good at any of those things, I said. And

I'm okay with that. Really, I've made my peace. She goes, *What happened? Tell me, Thee,* she said, and I knew she wouldn't drop it, ever, so I finally told her.

I said, It's hard to explain, but last year, freshman year, I got the flu and I missed a slumber party, and I guess some things were said about me. I don't know what, really, but by Monday morning, my friends didn't like me anymore. She goes, *Wait, because you missed a party, your friends didn't like you?* I said, It doesn't really make sense, but wait. Let me just tell you what happened, and then you can ask, all right? *All right,* she said. I go, Because that's how it happens with girls sometimes. One night, someone smells blood, and they all get in on it. And the thing is, these girls, this group of girls, I told them lots of things about myself. So they knew where I was coming from, and they did it anyway, they kicked me out of the circle. I thought if I pretended nothing had happened, that I didn't notice anything different, they'd forget about not liking me, and things would go back to normal. Then, about a month later, we all went to a party, and I thought we were all friends again, and I was so happy, and then someone spiked my drink. I honestly don't remember anything that happened after that, but I found out I was hanging all over the guys, taking my shirt off, dancing on a table. My friends, the girls I thought were my friends, knew who did it, but they never told. Because they were already in so much trouble for what went down at the party, I said.

Mel didn't know what to say, because it was one of those situations she doesn't understand. And I could tell she felt like she should really say something, but it was one of those moments when you realize no matter how much teen drama you watch on TV, that doesn't help at all when it's happening to you, when the problem is real and even your best friend doesn't have a clue how to help. Finally, she spoke up: *So what you're saying is you weren't always a loser? Is that what you're telling me, Thee?* No, I said, trying to laugh off her teasing. Believe it or not, I was popular once. For a long time, but . . . I said, shrugging: that was then, and this is now.

After that party, it was such a mess at school, I quit sitting with my friends, quit going to the cafeteria at lunch. I'd find a corner in the library and draw, I said, and Mel goes, *So they're still in school with you? These girls?* And I go, Yep, I see them every day. We still say hi, whatever, I said, but rolling my eyes, because it was so fake. *Did they ever apologize?* she said. *For lying about the boys?* No. Never, I said. Actually, they got really hostile with me for a while after they lied. Like they were trying to convince themselves it was my fault, that I was the one who lied about the guys who spiked my drink, saying that I showed up at the party screwed up. I mean, they'd practically hiss, seeing me in the hall. My so-called friends, I said.

The next morning, Saturday morning, after that party, I woke up, and I felt *awful*. Not just hungover, different. I thought I had a flu, maybe, and I told my mom I had the flu again, and she looked at me, and she didn't believe me, but she couldn't be certain. So she told me to stay in bed, but she wasn't really as sweet as she is when she knows I'm sick-sick, you know? But I was definitely sick, and I stayed in bed all day. So I didn't notice, really, until Sunday that no one called me all day. Not a text, nothing. And then, by Sunday night, no one answered my calls, either.

Monday, heading to Stella's locker, when they turned to look at me—all three of them, Leila, Stella, Danielle—I knew it was over. I was out, but the thing is, I couldn't remember anything about Friday night, after we got to the party. I remember drinking a beer, and that's it. The rest is a blur. And whatever I did, I just wanted someone to tell me, you know? Like no matter how awful, no matter how totally mortifying it was, I wanted to hear it, because it was actually worse not knowing. So when they three of them turned their heads, looking at me, and I said, Hey, I saw it pass through them. This current of . . . hatred.

It's one thing I'd never ever wish on you, knowing how that feels, I said. If I'm grateful for anything, it's that you could never be hurt like that. She goes, *That's not a silver lining. And if I could walk, I wouldn't care*, she said. Yes, you would, I said. You'd just be able to walk. It's humiliating, Mel: that's the part I wouldn't want you to feel, I said. *Because I wouldn't know about that, would I?* she said. I said, That's not what I mean, Mel, and she goes, *No, but it's true, and you know what I'm saying*. I go, I know what you're saying, all right. And I'm not trying to compare, I'm just trying to tell you that I wouldn't want anyone to be mean to you, I said. Melody didn't say anything, and I knew I was digging a deeper hole.

*So what happened after that?* she said, wanting to hear the end of the story. I go, Nobody talked to me most of the week. And then, one by one, people started looking at me strange in the halls, laughing at me, or more like snickering. I remember walking around, thinking, *This is bad. This is really, really bad.* You know how I finally found out what happened at the party? Raymond, I said. He was friends or worked with one of their dads, with Stella's dad, and her dad heard all about it, when everyone got busted for the party.

Melody goes, *Wait, how did they get busted?* I said, Oh. The pictures. Someone took pictures, and then there was like a thirty-second video of me, too, and it made the rounds, all over school, all over the Internet. I was such a mess, too, dancing, screaming, taking my clothes off. I'm telling you, all I can remember is talking to Leila, and then Spencer walking over, bringing us our drinks, that was it. But no one believed me. I'm not even sure my mom believed me, I said, and Mel goes, *Your mom saw the video, the pictures?* I go, She had to. All the parents were called in. All the kids, all the parents, we were all called in with Principal Cheswick, I said.

You have no idea how hard it is to go to school, knowing everybody has seen you in your bra, pulling your pants down, showing your ass, ohmygod . . . I could barely look anyone in the eye for the rest of the third quarter of school, not even my teachers. Then my grades dropped, and things started going haywire again, and that's when I shut down, I said, and I almost told her about the hospital. I almost told her that that's when I really lost it, cutting myself, and my mom found me, the whole story. But I didn't. Maybe it's dishonest or cowardly, I don't know, but there is a part of me, a real part that just wants to protect her. Except, I'm not even sure what that means anymore.

I go, When I met Cam, I think I was so cold to him for so long because I knew he would see those pictures, one day, that someone would show them to him, and if he did actually like me, he wouldn't after he saw that. How could he like me after he saw me acting like that, you know? And she goes, *But he did—Cam did like you.* And when she said that, I got another knot in my throat, and all I could do was nod yes. He did, but . . . I couldn't finish my sentence. *But what?* she said, and I go, But it was really hard, trusting him, and I could see she didn't understand. I go, It's hard to trust somebody, because it's easier not having something than to have something and have it taken away, you know? *Thea,* she said, and she sounded so serious, I felt better for a second, because I thought she was going to tell me something secret about herself. And she did, but not what I was expecting at all. I go, What? Tell me what you want to know, I said, and then she said, *What's it feel like?* I knew, right away, but I didn't say anything, so she said it, point-blank. She looks at me and straight out she goes, *Tell me what sex feels like.*

I didn't know what to say, because it's hard for me to talk about it with Melody, about Cam and sex and intimacy, what it's like, how it feels. Because she really wants to know, and it's so honest and brave the way she asks and says what she really means—it's hard to say those things, I know. I totally understand, because everyone wants to know what it's like for other people, because no one really knows. I mean, you can read all about it, see as many movies as you want, and you're still there, in your body, all alone. Well, more or less, but you know what I mean.

The thing is, I wanted to tell her. I wanted to try and answer all Mel's questions, but then I would look at her and think about the fact that she won't have that experience; she'll never know how it feels. So I told her the truth. I said, Honestly? Sorry to disappoint you, but it's awkward. It's really awkward and kind of stupid, I said, and all you do is pretend you know what you're doing, because you don't have a clue, so the whole time, you're thinking, *Am I doing this right?* And, *Will you still like me if I'm not very good at this?*

One night, we were watching TV, eating in the living room, my mom and I. And my mom's really into this new drama *Starting Over*, about a single mother, who has just gotten divorced, and she has this teenage son—sound familiar? Anyhow, it's the two of them, the mother and son, and they've made this big move across country, and they're starting over. Also, the mother's just gone back to medical school; she's in her first year, I think, and her son's in high school, so it's all about them going through the same struggles, or parallels between their lives, whatever. I'd never seen it, but Mom turned it on while we were sitting on the couch together, eating the pizza she picked up.

There's this scene where the woman's at school, working late on a lab or something, then there's this whole thing where one of the other students, who's obviously like ten years younger than the mom is, has the hots for her—so predictable. I shouldn't have rolled my eyes, I know, because my mom likes it, but it's dumb, and I couldn't help it. I know my mom deserves a few simple pleasures, and I have no right to be critical of my own mother, but it's stupid. I mean, why, when we could watch a good movie, did we have to watch this crap?

Anyhow, the woman's son has a girl over to study the night his mom's working late, and I mean, come on, who ever has anyone over to study in their bedroom? Anyhow, the girl—they're both supposed to be my age—and the girl, who's blonde and looks like she's about twenty-five, even though you know for a fact, in real life, a girl that hot would not be dating scrawny high school boys, but whatever. They're in his room—I remember, his name's Cody, the son's name is Cody. They're sitting in Cody's room, the two of them, with their books open, and the girl's sitting on the floor, and Cody's sitting on his bed, and then you see the girl look up from her book at Cody, who's got his nose in the book, studying. Like, he's all, Gotta keep that GPA up, get into the right school, who has time for sex? Please. So I'm trying not to roll my eyes, I really am, but it's so lame.

Then the girl, she looks up at Cody like she's ready to pounce. I mean, she looks at him like, here comes sex kitten, ready or not. So she closes her book, ready to make a move, and she crawls over to the bed on all fours, gets up close to him, right in his face and then, trying to sound all sultry, the girl says, Tell me what you want me to do to you. Honestly, when she said that, I totally burst out laughing. And it wasn't nerves, because I felt uncomfortable, watching some teen sex scene with my mom there; I laughed because it was so stupid, that's why. I was just like, *Ohmygod, I wish Cam were here. . . .*

You know what's true? For me, at least. The truth is, the first time with Cam, the whole time, all I could think was, *Am I doing this right? Do you like this? What should I do?* My head, all four limbs, two hands, my whole body felt like two left feet. And if I was sweaty, it was because I was so nervous! I mean, show me *that*—show me the real girl. You have writers, you have actors, you have camera crews, so why is it so hard to tell the truth?

I don't know. Hopefully, you get better with age. But still, deep down, don't you always carry that fifteen-year-old boy and girl around, and don't they come out when you really like a person, if you truly want to please them? I mean, wouldn't it be sad to lose that first time, altogether?

Every time I think about it, it blows me away how much Mel's never seen or heard before. I mean, can you imagine never having heard the Smiths? Seriously, Mel told me, in their house, music begins and ends with the Indigo Girls, and I was just like, *Are you kidding me?* I hate to say it, but I don't think cerebral palsy's her only disability; I think it's that she's been deprived of so much art and film and music her whole life.

I mean, driving home, Knox reached to turn up the radio, and Mel goes, *Please don't,* and I laughed, and I told him what she said, Please don't, and he lowered his hand, looking in the rearview, and he goes, Thea, can you—I need you to give me a sign when she's speaking. It's driving me nuts, and I go, It's driving *you* nuts? Knox goes, Could you just, I don't know, raise your hand when Melody's speaking? I go, What, like, *How, white man?* He goes, I don't care if you want to stand on one leg and rub your stomach, just do something so I know who's talking, okay? I go, Okay, okay, and I thought about it. How about one hand? I raise one hand, I said, raising my right, and that means I'm talking for Mel. And he goes, Great. Perfect, and I was like, Cool.

I sighed, and then I turned to the backseat, and I go, Glad we got that settled, speaking to Melody, and Knox goes, Can I ask you something? And I said, Sure, shoot. And he goes, Does she hear what you're thinking? looking at her in the rearview mirror. Mel started laughing, and I had to laugh, too, and I go, No, it doesn't work that way. I mean, she might know what I'm thinking, because we're friends, but I need to tell her in words, I said, and he shook his head, staring ahead. What is it? I said, because I could see he wanted to ask something else, and he goes, Nothing. It's just I've never heard anyone say that, and I go, Say what? Knox said, I've never heard anyone call her their friend. I'm glad—I'm glad you're friends, he said, speaking to Melody in the rearview, and she goes, *Okay, okay, let's not get carried away*, and I laughed.

Knox got this look on his face, and he had to look away for a second, then he goes, Thea, when you hear Melody's voice? He looked in the rearview, at her, so she'd know he was asking us both. Yes? I said, waiting, and he goes, No, just—what's it like, her voice? What's her voice sound like? She sings beautifully, I said, turning to the back, telling her, because she was being so quiet. Knox goes, She sings? I go, Oh, all the time, and he goes, What, like songs or does she hum? I go, Yes, songs. She loves music, you know—not your music, but good music. He goes, Hey, hey, and I go, I don't just hear her, I see her, too, Knox. I didn't explain it this way, but it's like bifocals—I see one girl sometimes, one girl other times, and once in a while, I see both girls at the same time. I go, I see the girl she really is—and I'm not just saying this, okay—but Mel's the most beautiful girl I've ever seen, and Knox looked in the rearview at her, and he goes, Me, too. Most beautiful girl in the whole world, if you ask me, and Mel goes, *Dad, please. That's so gay!* I started laughing, and he goes, What did she say? I shook my head, like, Don't ask, even though he already did.

*Grandma Lois has a beautiful voice*, she said, and I raised my hand, repeating: Grandma Lois has a beautiful voice, and then Knox pulled over to the side of the road. *What's going on?* Mel said, and I said, What's wrong? And we waited, but Knox just stared ahead in a total daze. For like a whole minute, and then he raised his hand, warding me off. I . . . I just needed a moment, he said. I tried to get my mind around it, and sometimes I actually think I have. And then, other times, I don't—I don't understand one damn thing about what's happening, he said. Just give me a minute here, he said, staring off.

I know how hard it must be for him to get his head around it, but I don't feel like he ever stops to think what it's like for me, hearing his daughter's voice in my head and being able to see her like she's a normal, healthy, beautiful girl, so I told him. I said it: What, you think it doesn't make *me* feel crazy sometimes? You think I don't lie awake in bed at night, wondering if maybe they were right about me and I really should be locked up? I mean, seriously, sometimes, listening to you two talk back and forth, inside my head, outside my head, I feel like I'm gonna throw up, like I'm getting carsick—it's not easy for me, either, you know? I said, covering my eyes with my hands, then sitting up straight again. Knox's mouth fell open, then he swallowed back, before turning and looking me in the eye, hearing what I was saying. I knew I shouldn't have said that out loud, especially in front of Mel, but I did. I needed them both to know, because it's like, this isn't easy for any of us—not for Knox, not for Mel, not for me.

So we just sat there, silent, like a wet wool blanket was thrown over the whole car, and then Mel said, *I'm sorry, Thee. I'm so sorry about how hard this must be on you, with no one you can tell, no one you can even talk to,* and I turned right around, looking at her, both girls, both Mels, bifocal vision: Never, I said. Don't ever be sorry, because I can talk to you, more than anyone, and I wouldn't give that up for the whole world, I said, smiling, but my chin puckering because I felt so teary. Which, thankfully, knocked things back into place by making Knox uncomfortable, readjusting himself in his seat and putting the car back in gear. Even so, we were all pretty quiet the rest of the way to my house.

Soon as I got out, I can't—I can't explain how I knew, but walking up the back stairs, after Mel and Knox left, from the moment I walked through our front door, I knew there was something there for me, a message. I could feel it, and I was so certain, I didn't bother taking off my coat at the front door, I just walked straight to my room, turned on my computer, and I was right. There was an e-mail from Cam, or Cam's address, at least. I don't know who it is, but all the subject headers are some inside jokes, something only Cam would know, like the subject header will say, You know what Socrates said? I open them because Cam is the only person in the world who knows the joke. Except this one was different, it was a time code, *5:57 PM, May 10, 2010,* and it said, *Unedited.*

Somehow, I knew—I mean I didn't know what, exactly, but I knew what day that was. I'd lived with it for a whole year. It was video taken at that party, at Spencer Perry's party, last spring. The video starts when we showed up at his house, because things got started right after school. The four of us, we went to Leila's house to change, and we got to Spencer's by five, but the video's shot in a way that it's like there was someone else with us, walking between me and Dani and Leila and Stella. The four of us, we walked in alone, and the way the video looks, it's like there was someone else with us, almost in the middle of the whole group. When I saw that, the way it was shot, I nodded and said, No, out loud. But on the other hand, everything else is exactly as I remember it happening.

Stella and Dani went to the kitchen, and I stayed with Leila, outside, in the backyard. And then Spencer came over, and he brought me a drink, saying he'd make another for Leila when they went inside. I remember drinking it, and the hardest part, watching it again, was remembering how close I felt to all my friends that night, because these were my best friends. Maybe I didn't choose this town, and it was hard getting used to it, but this was my home now, you know? And then—I remember this now, watching this video—slurring, I told Leila and Spencer: I feel so dizzy and buzzy!

It was snowing, too. It was so weird because we had a huge storm that week, in March. Spencer's parents had left for the Bahamas or Bermuda, I don't remember. Just that we went inside so Spencer could make us some more drinks, I walked to the back windows of their kitchen, they had these big bay windows, and I looked at all the kids, outside, playing in the snow. And a few of them started spinning around, holding back their heads, and then all I know is they started morphing into multiples. Like two, three four of each kid appeared, and they all started spinning around, like florescent whirling dervishes. And it was beautiful, watching it snow in this big backyard. I think that was the happiest day I'd had in years, like for the first time since I'd moved, I belonged. Then the video stopped, and I realized the amazing thing was that it was exactly what happened to me. But how could anyone have shot exactly what I saw?

I went over and sat down on the side of my bed, but I felt numb. Because when I think of everyone being called into Cheswick's office to discuss the party; all these kids, all their parents, everyone getting so busted. And they all wanted a scapegoat. And I was new, and I was the one dancing on the coffee table, clearly I was the bad apple. And I'd never been in trouble like that, I'd never been singled out for any inappropriate behavior, but then everyone was so relieved to be off the hook, they had to dedicate themselves to believing their own lies.

Still, sitting there, with my coat on, and my bag twisted around my shoulder, I smiled at the screen, feeling that moment all over again. I mean, it was the first time I'd ever really sat and thought about it, without crying or turning away, feeling sick. I'd gone through so much embarrassment, so much teasing and shame that year, but this time, I could actually watch without turning away. Honestly, I felt better, because that's what really happened, and somehow, there was someone who knew the truth, too.

Then, the very next day, I got another text with a link, right after I got home from school. The thing is, whoever sent it to me, they sent it to the whole school. I almost had a heart attack when I saw that, at first, and then I watched it, because I had to know what it was everyone was seeing. So I watched it, and right away, I knew everyone would be freaking out. Because it tells the rest of the story, what happened that night. At first, I thought it was a copy of the same video from the night before, because it starts with the four of us, Leila, Dani, and Stella and me, showing up at Spencer's party. So right after we all walk into the Perry's kitchen, then it cuts to Spencer Perry and Brandon Firth standing in one of the rooms, down from the kitchen, where you turn to their laundry room. Then you see Brandon peek his head out to see that we're there, while Spencer's standing over a cup, doing something you can't see, but whatever they're doing, you're thinking, *They're up to something, those guys are definitely up to something.* . . .

The strange thing is, watching it, I knew it was going to be okay. Or I knew at least I wasn't the one who had to worry, because it's like someone's taken my memories and made a movie out of them, and you see exactly what I was seeing that night, living. After you see Spencer and Brandon in the laundry room, the next thing you see is my point of view, and I'm stumbling all over, holding my hands out for balance, wasted, as a bunch of us pile into a couple cars and drive to Shecky's.

Shecky's is this local chain, kind of like IHOP, that stays open late on Friday and Saturday nights. The whole way there, I was in the backseat with Brandon, making out with him—*ugh*, so gross.

A good minute of tongue and tongue close-up that's sloppy and pimply and stomach-turning. I'd rather watch animals humping on *National Geographic*, I really would. All my friends are grossed out too, all of them shooting each other looks, but I have no idea what's going on. I couldn't remember it for so long, but when I saw it, with my own eyes, the two of us, me and Brandon, going at it in the backseat, I felt sick. Because it was true, that's what really happened, and I'd seen a little worse than that, the Monday when it got out about the party, and there were pictures of us in the car.

I stopped the video and closed my computer. I don't know how long I sat there, totally shocked, maybe an hour before I heard my mom walk through the front door, and she called my name. Then she knocked, and I said, Come in. Hey, she said, still holding the doorknob, standing in my doorway, and I said, Hey, seeing she hadn't even taken off her coat. All right, she says, slapping both hands on her thighs. She goes: Principal Cheswick called me this afternoon and told me there's a new video of the party from last year—a video of what really happened at that party, she said, and then she held up her hand, seeing my mouth fall open. She said, I saw. I watched them already. And I just want to say I'm sorry, Thea. I'm so sorry I didn't believe in you more last year, despite how things looked, and she really did look so remorseful. Principal Cheswick would like to meet with us tomorrow to talk about it, she said, and that's what we need to discuss now. There are a lot of things I want to talk to you about tonight, before we have that meeting, she said.

I said, Mom, I told you I don't want to talk about the party anymore, throwing my head back. She goes, Lots of things, Thee—there are lots of things I want to talk to you about. And the way she said that, I knew something happened: What happened? I said. Let me take my coat off, she said. You might want to do the same, she said, looking at me as she stood from my bed. And only then did I realize I'd been sitting there, in my coat, too, that whole time.

Let's sit at the table, she said, and I followed her into the kitchen and sat down. She got a beer out of the fridge, then looked at me: You want one? she said, holding the bottle up. So something pretty bad happened, I knew, watching her pouring her beer in an iced glass. It's the one thing Mom still does that we'd done when my dad was around: she always has good beer glasses that she keeps in the freezer. Now, though, our freezer is so small, she has to turn the glasses on their side.

Looking at her, I thought, *You're so pretty. Despite everything, you are still so pretty, Mom.* I don't notice it much anymore, but she is, she's beautiful. I thought about telling her that, too, then she took a sip of beer and said, They're cutting back at work, and I said, But they already cut back. She nodded. More, she said, and I said, You lost your *job*? It was so awful, my mouth fell open. Not exactly, she said, but I'll be working part-time now, which is better than nothing. I said, I'm so sorry, Mom, because I didn't know what else to say.

My mind started reeling, trying to figure out what we'd do, where we'd go, what I could do. I'll try to get a job, after school, I said, and I knew it sounded dumb, because if there were any jobs, my mom could get one, too. Thanks, babe, she said, smiling, but not wanting to talk about that yet. Looking at her face, I felt so bad, because I spend so much time keeping her out of my life, keeping away from her in every possible way; I forget how much I need her. But the thing is, I'm almost afraid of how much I need her since she just isn't very strong anymore.

What else? I asked, sensing she hadn't told me everything, and she dropped her head side to side, shoulder to shoulder, a few times. You've gotten lots of offers, Thea, people offering a lot of money for your story, Thea, and then I knew, seeing the look in her eye. She lost her job, and we needed money, and people wanted to pay me to talk about Cam and me. To tell my story, right, but how could I do that? On the other hand, look at our house. Look at where we are. How could I say no, knowing how badly we needed money? So, I said, there, almost laughing, almost crying, just covering my mouth: *What do I do?*

## TUESDAY, DECEMBER 28, 2010
## (FOUR MONTHS EARLIER)

I must've seemed like a prude, I stopped him so many times. I'd finally told him just about every secret I have to tell, but I still wouldn't let him touch me. For like two months, soon as he'd reach under my shirt or touch my skin or just about anything, I'd tense up. Like even my sleeves, anything above my knees, I'd pull away. Like it was fine if he touched me over my clothes, but never under, and I'd always turn out the light, too. Then, one night, after I told him about Spencer's party and everything with the hospital, Cam goes, Thea, why won't you let me see you? And I said, You can see me.

He goes, No. You won't let me see you; you won't let me touch you, he said, and he wasn't pushing—Cam never pushed. He just wanted to understand what was going on with me, and he could tell—I mean, of course he could tell, when I wouldn't even let him touch my bare arms, something's not right. So, finally,

I decided I'd told him that much, I might as well show him. So I sat up, and I turned on the light, and I got up. I go, I don't let you see me, and I don't let you touch me, because I have scars all over my body, and he looked at me, and I took off my sweatshirt, so he could see the scars up and down the inside of my biceps, both sides. Then I took my shirt off and let it fall on the floor. And I unbuttoned my pants, starting to pull them off, and he reached—I'll never forget that, that he reached to stop me, like I didn't have to do that, and I shook my head no. I did have to do that, because I needed him to see. I needed him to see me, all of me, not just 3 percent.

So I took my jeans off, and I stood there, in my bra and underwear, and I turned around in a full circle, so he could see them all. He was sitting up, on the side of my bed, then he reached for my hands, pulling me to him, and he goes, Oh, baby, what happened? And I thought about it, where to begin, then I told him: Me. I happened. I did it to myself. That's why they sent me to the hospital, my mom and dad, I said. Because I couldn't stop cutting myself, and they couldn't get the drugs right.

I didn't tell him, but at that moment, I remembered what Brandon had said about me, after that night, that party. He told everybody I looked like I'd been in a slasher film, naked. God, the way Cam was looking at me, the moment he brushed a tear away from his eye, on the back of his hand, and then he said, Come here. I swear, I don't know what I was more afraid of, that he would touch me or that he wouldn't. Come here, he said, in a softer voice than before, so I stepped forward. I felt so brave, but only for a second, and then I got a chill, and I'm standing there, covered in goose bumps and scars: *gross*. I felt as sexy as a raw chicken breast, and I laughed, because I was so nervous, so naked. And then I felt choked up, looking at him, holding my face in his hands, looking into those big gray eyes of his, thinking, *What's happening? How or . . . where do I know you from?*

Please, let me look at you, Thea, he said, putting his hands on my hands, pulling them away from my chest. He looked at every inch of my body, and I rolled my eyes back, trying so hard not to cry, and then he stood up, right in front of me, and he said, Beautiful . . . I think they're beautiful. My scars—he meant my scars. I mean, there I am, so ashamed, I'm shaking, hiding myself, and there he is, telling me they're beautiful, that I'm beautiful, and that's when I started crying, asking him, How can you say that? Cam said, Because they're part of you. And then, *ugh*, I don't know if I've ever cried like that, and he just held me the whole time, smoothing my hair. Look at all my scars, Thee—we match, he said, and I said, You got those from skate-boarding—it's not the same. And he opened his mouth, about to say something, then he nodded no, tilting his head. Doesn't matter, he said. When I stopped crying, he goes, Thee, I know I can't stop you, but I don't want you to do that to yourself anymore. Please, he said, listen, and he swiveled around, something serious to say to me, I could tell.

Listen, he said, grabbing both my hips. Shit like that's always bound to come up at you again, sooner or later, and I can't stop you, no one can, I know that, Thee. But you've got to fight.

Promise me, if you ever feel the urge to do that, to cut yourself, Cam made himself say, so I'd know he could say the words—he wasn't afraid of saying what I am, really. Promise me that if I'm not there—. Where would you be? I asked him, suddenly worried, and he said, Promise, you'll put up a good fight? Okay, I promise, I said. Good. Say it again, he said, and I said, I promise to put up a good fight, laughing and exasperated. And it felt so good, knowing that he could love me exactly as I am, who I really am, but the trick is, now I had to be that person. Real. I blushed, actually, realizing that as messed up as I am, he could love me, and as screwed up as I am, he would never judge me. And then he reached out, grabbing my wrist, pulling me to him.

He sat right there in my computer chair, in front of me, pulling me forward, pulling down my underwear, leaving nothing, not a stitch. He still had his jeans on, it's just me who was naked. What I remember most clearly is holding his head in my hands, how bristly soft his hair felt, and looking down, watching him, running his tongue down my right tit—watching the hairs on my arm stand on end, getting the chills, completely erect, when he sucked my nipple, and then slowly kissed his way across my chest to the other nipple. I didn't even think I liked pretty boys, and watching his face—god, he's so pretty—I had that spasm again, where I can't believe how beautiful he is, and yes, I did want to take a picture of his face, slightly in profile, kissing across my chest. But I didn't: I just watched him, thinking, *You are so beautiful, and you are so . . . tender.* I really had no idea what that word meant until then, *tender.*

People always talk about your first time. The thing is, there isn't just one first time, there are many first times, if you really love that person. I mean, there's the first time between your legs, with your body, but there's the first time inside your chest, in your heart, too. And that was our first time.

I kept drawing. I kept working on Hubble, drawing and writing in it every day, because what else could I do? Who else could I talk to? Even if—even if Cam was dead, and I know he's not, but even if he was dead, he'd still be the only person I could talk to. So I wrote like I always had, like he'd read it tomorrow, when I handed it back to him before first period. I told him everything he was missing, whether it was funny, or I was angry or scared or both. I told him, *I wish you could see my face now. Every day, I wish you could feel what I feel, even though I know you can't. And you couldn't yesterday, or the day before that, or last week, and chances are, you won't feel what I feel tomorrow or the next day, either. But I still can't stop wishing that you could. So what is it, chemical? Really, is hope just another chemical? I don't know, I really don't. Whatever.*

*You know there are videos of us all over the Internet? Or at least there are videos of people who look like us—exactly like us, you and me. Someone sent me a new one yesterday. From that night we went to 7-Eleven? Remember that time we went and I got so upset because they had that can at the counter for donations for abused animals? And it had that picture of that dog and the cat, and we were having so much fun, but that picture almost made me cry? It was a tape from the security camera, right above the counter. It's black and white and grainy, and you can't hear very well, but I remember the color, the live version, and I, I remember everything.*

*That was an easy one, too. Most of the videos aren't easy, not even close to the ones of us in my bed. And I know it's not you, that you couldn't have taken them, but the way they're shot, the only person that close to me was you. Seriously, the only person who could have shot them was you. Because there's a camera pointed in my face, at my neck, looking downward, pointed at my crotch, your crotch, and it shows everything. It makes me sick, watching the two of us, in my room, in my bed. It's you and me, and I can't even stand to watch us, you know?*

*All I know is, I almost hope . . . I almost hope . . . I'm sorry, but I almost hope something happened to you. I'm sorry, but it's true, because it's like I don't think I'll ever be able to forgive you if you just ran away like that. No, not if you left me here, alone. Because I shouldn't have to deal with this alone—with school, my mom, your mom, the whole town, the whole world, every day. I keep my phone turned off all the time now, and I* can barely stand to open my computer anymore, the messages people leave, the things people post about me, e-mail me. No one deserves that, but I definitely don't.

So I don't know what people see or don't see, except when they make comments in the halls. Do you know how paranoid it makes you, someone sending you a video of yourself that only one person could have taken, but knowing there's no way? I tell them, too—I tell my mom, Knox, the lawyers, that it's impossible. You couldn't have shot that, because you would have had to have a camera in your hand to get that close. So I don't understand, because it's just not possible. But it's there, online. Everyone at school has seen it—the whole world's seen it. They try to take it down, Apple does, YouTube does, but every time it gets a hit, the image becomes clearer. Even that 7-Eleven surveillance video of us, that'll be high-def by the end of the week.

Every day, every single day, there's a moment when I think I'm going to lose it. Why would you do this to me? But I have no idea what to believe, what's true, if it even matters anymore. The real joke is that everyone knows who we are now. We're big news, right? We're celebrities, Cam. And then, sometimes I think about sending you a postcard that says: We're famous. Wish you were here.

I stopped there, looked at the words, and closed the book. I checked my calendar, wanting to date the page, and I don't pay much attention to days of the week anymore. I mean, yesterday, tomorrow: same difference. So I put Hubble away, and I went to bed, sometime around four, I think, and then, next thing I know, Mom's knocking on my door, and of course, I panicked.

It just reminded me so much of Karen knocking, and I got up, right away. It wasn't early, though, I'd just been up late, writing. Actually, it was almost noon, and I opened the door, and Mom said, Wash your face, and come to the living room, and then she turned around.

I could tell it wasn't Cam, so I put on my slippers, washed my face and brushed my teeth. Then, pulling a sweatshirt over my head, I walked to the living room, thinking we were going to have another talk about the book offers. So, no warning, whatsoever, I walked in, and then I froze. Because it wasn't the lawyers again; it was worse: It was my dad. Sitting in our living room.

I didn't recognize him at first, because I was so unprepared to see him there, but he looked just the same, but a little older, a little richer. He was wearing a gray cashmere V-neck sweater, dark Levis, loafers, and a big new watch that probably cost more than my mom makes in a year now. He looked tan, too—probably took a two-week vacation with his new family in the Bahamas, and I thought, *Take a good look around: because this is what you did to us.* He stood up, smiling, and said, Hello, Thea. I'm so glad to see you, and I looked at him, then I looked at Mom, and then I said, *Get out.* Get out! Get out of our house! My mom told me to calm down, but I wouldn't listen. I just started losing it, and it all came back, this wave of rage. At my dad, my mom, at Cam, at the whole fucking world, and I remember my mom putting up her hands, walking over to touch me, and I said, Don't you touch me! Get out, and go to hell, I said, clenching my jaw. Then I turned and went back to my room, and I slammed the door.

I didn't come out of my room all day, not until my mom forced me to, sometime after six. She knocked on my door and I said, What? Then she opened the door and she goes, What are you doing? I was sitting at my desk, trying to work, and I go, What's it look like? She goes, Well, it looks like you're glaring at me. Dinner, she said, and I said I wasn't hungry, and then she said, I don't care. Get out here, Thea, now. I know when I can push, but I could tell by her voice it wasn't one of those times.

So I walked out, fuming, and sat down at the table, thinking, *You can't make me eat.* And then, before she could even say anything, I started in. I said, He has no right to be here. And she goes, He does. He has a legal right to see you, Thea. I go, Not here, not in my house! She goes, Thee, when are you going to forgive him? I said, When I'm ready. That's when, I said, pushing my chair away from the table, standing up, and she goes, Sit. *Down.* Sit your ass down, right now, young lady, and eat your dinner, she said, so I parked it.

She brought over a bowl of soup, and she said, I want you to eat before you leave this table. I go, I'm not hungry, and she goes, I didn't ask if you were hungry—in fact, I didn't ask you anything. Eat, she said, speaking to me like I was three years old. I said, Please, Mom, I'm not hungry. She goes, Thea, you're losing weight. You don't go out; you barely leave your room—. I *can't* go outside, I said, and she goes, I know. But I want you to start taking care of yourself. I didn't argue, Thea—I didn't say a word about you missing school—I know perfectly well how many classes you've been skipping, and I haven't said a word. Because I know you need space; it's got to be hell, I know. But you're going to eat something. Right now. Come on: four bites, she said, and I looked at the bowl.

I pushed my spoon around, and I tried, but the smell of food was so disgusting. I said, I can't, Mom. I can't do this—I can't do any of this anymore, and I started crying. I didn't think she'd budge, and then she stood and walked to my chair, before hugging me.

It's going to be all right, she said, kissing my head. I looked at her, and I said, How can you say that? She tilted her head, side to side, then she goes, Good question. I don't know, sweetheart. . . . I guess, I guess you just have to believe, like it or not, she said, hugging my head to her stomach. Made me so angry, too, I raised my voice again, and I go, Believe in what, Mom? In what? She took my chin in her head, and she lifted my face, and then she said, In you, Thea. I believe in you.

There were parties all week, and Cam kept asking me to go, but I wouldn't. I just couldn't stand the thought of someone saying something, making a dig—anything would have set me off. But finally, he was just like, Thea, what's the deal? I mean, we'd gotten so close, and I think he thought I was pushing him away. Maybe I was, but then I decided to tell him. I knew he must have heard something, so I told him all about the party, what happened, the hospital, how one thing lead to another, you know?

It got really bad after Spencer's party, after all my friends turned on me. That Monday, after the party, I can't describe it, but soon as I walked in the door, I knew something had changed, and whatever it was, I knew it had something to do with me. It started building like a headache, little by little. After a few days, I didn't feel anything but pressure, all day long, from the moment I opened my eyes, until I closed them. Even in my sleep,

I felt pressure, building and building, and the only way to relieve the pressure was to cut it out—I had to get it out. That's what happened. One day, after school, right before spring break. I cut too deep, and I got blood everywhere. When I passed out, seeing all the blood, I hit my head on the side of the bathtub and gave myself a concussion. I was completely out, when my mom found me, and then she freaked and called an ambulance, and they rushed me to the hospital, wheeling me behind these curtains, cutting off my clothes. . . . It was so awful.

After the doctors told my mom how I just missed an artery in my thigh, and how scarred up I was, they had to call in Social Services to be sure it wasn't child abuse, and they contacted my dad. When my dad found out what happened, how my mom found me in the bathroom, about the ambulance and everything, he gave her an ultimatum. He said if my mom didn't take action, he would, and not only would he have me institutionalized, he said he'd sue her for full custody. And that he'd win. God, I hate lawyers.

She signed the papers that day. They kept me overnight for observation, but my mom committed me that day, and she didn't even tell me—I had no idea what was going on. So when we got home, the next day, I walked into my room, and she'd already torn my whole room apart, like I did that day my parents told me they were getting a divorce. She searched every inch of my room, looking for razors, anything I might have hidden—my computer, my phone, all my notebooks. She even cut the lock off my foot-locker, my hope chest. The place where I keep all my treasures safe, like that Easter card Gram sent.

Every time I told Cam something about me, every single time I shared a secret, I thought that would be the end. I thought as soon as he saw me for who I really am, in a day or two, he'd move on, and that time, for sure—I was so sure that'd be the end, but it wasn't. No, Cam put his arms around me, hugging me for the longest time, rocking me until I wasn't tense, and then he put both his hands on my face, so I'd look at him. There were tears in his eyes, and I knew then—I knew he loved me, because I could see the girl he sees in me. She's so beautiful, too, it reminded me of that saying: Beauty is truth, truth beauty, which sounds great, right? The catch is no one ever said truth is easy to look at.

Cloud porn. We were driving to the playground, because Melody was dying to go to the playground, and just before we got there, she looked out the window and she goes, *Look! Cloud porn*, and I just started laughing, thinking, *Oh, here we go again*. Because we'd seen it on Flickr, something about the best Cloud Porn photos or whatever, and Mel got on a roll with it; *Oh, look: tree porn! Oh, look: squirrel porn! Oh, look: cookie porn!*

But you knew about porn before that, right? I asked, and Knox's head turned so fast, I'm surprised he didn't give himself whiplash. Not you. *Mel*, I said. Mel, where did you hear about porn? I said, and Knox balked: Excuse me, and Mel ignored him: Nickelodeon, she said. I laughed, turning around in my seat to face her. *What, you never heard of kiddy porn?* she asked, and I bonked my head against the seat back, laughing. No, seriously, though, I asked, and I could feel Knox's jaw lock shut, preparing something to say if the conversation went any further. *Only everywhere—I watch TV, you know,* she said. *I know I live in a bubble, but I still hear things. I have ears, Thee.* I know you do, I said, I'm sorry, just as we pulled into the parking lot.

So we got out and pushed Mel over to a bench, beneath a tree, and Knox and I sat down on each side, with her chair backed up against the bench, between us. *You know what?* Mel said, and I go, What's that?, watching a kid fall into the sand. She goes, *I want to sit in the grass,* and I was like, The grass? looking down. She goes, *Yes. I want to sit in the grass. You won't get hurt,* she said, and I looked at her, ha-ha. She wants to sit in the grass, I told Knox, because he was waiting. Where, here? Knox asked, same reaction I had, right. Mel goes, *What is wrong with you people? You can sit in the grass, and you'd rather sit on a bench?* she asked. All right, all right, I said.

We'd been looking at pictures all week; Melody had this huge folder of pictures of girls lying in flowers and grass, and she said it was something she wanted to do, too, to lie in the grass and stare at the clouds like a real girl. *I should be able to do that much—I mean, you don't have to move, right?* she said, and I rolled my eyes at her. So Knox got up to push her, and we walked over to the nicest part of grass we could find. It didn't look all green and beautiful like the pictures she'd chosen, but it was as close as we were going to get, and it was shaded. Knox started to spread out a blanket for us, getting down on his knees, smoothing it out, but then Mel said, *Not on a blanket, Dad, I want to feel it.* So I told him, She doesn't want a blanket, she wants to feel the grass, and he pursed his lips. I don't know, he said, and then Mel goes, *You two are such sissies. It's grass*, she said, and I translated, raising my right hand: You are such a sissy, Knox: it's grass.

He looked at us, sighing, and then smiled, knowing he was being silly. He started folding up the blanket again, and then he said, Screw it, throwing it over his arm, before unfastening Melody. She never let me help with this part, she didn't even like me to look, so I turned away, while he picked her up. Even though the truth is, every time I see him do that, even out of the corner of my eye, I try to remember the last time my dad picked me up and carried me, but I can never remember when that was.

Knox set her down, and he goes, Is that okay? making sure her face was in the shade. Then Mel goes, *Lie down with me, Thee*, so I did, scooching myself backward, putting my head next to hers. Then I go, You know what, Mel? and Knox turned, looking at us. Here, I said, grabbing my camera. You want to try? And she goes, *How? You know I can't move*, she said, and I hated that fear in her voice. No, I didn't *hate* it, but I had to put a stop to it. Easy, I said: you tell me when, and I'll push our fingers down. Let's try, so you can feel it, just once? I asked, and she smiled, giving in.

I pointed the camera upward, and then I took her right hand, curling her index finger and thumb around the lens. I moved it back and forth so she could see and feel the movement, and I told her to tell me when to stop, when the picture looked right. Stop, she said, and I peeked, and it was right. Now, tell me when to take the shot, I said, feeling a breeze start, and she waited, and then she goes, *Now!* Then I pressed as fast as I could. Look, I said, showing her, and it was good. Way better than my first picture, I said.

I leaned up, and out of the corner of my eye, I saw this kid with a backpack, and I was like, Oh, hey, it's Ricky. So I called out: Ricky! And I waved at him, and he turned, so I waved him over. Hey, he said, looking a little suspicious—I don't know if it was us or Knox, but probably Knox. Ricky stepped closer, and I said, What's up? And then Mel goes, *Who's this?* And I go, Oh, sorry, Ricky, this is Mel. Mel, this is Ricky. And this, I said, meaning Knox, not sure what to call him, and Knox said hello, as suspicious of Ricky as I've ever seen him of anyone. What are you doing? I said, and Ricky shrugged. I had to take some books back to the library for my brother. Oh, I said, smiling, not sure what else to say.

*He's kinda cute*, Mel said, and I almost started laughing in front of him. Well, see you around, Ricky said, and I said, See you later, and he walked away. Knox looked at me, and I sort of slapped Mel for making me laugh. *What? He's cute, don't you think?* I said, You think so? And she goes, *Totally! And did you see how he was looking at me? He wants me,* she said, and I busted out laughing. *He's not popular, is he?* she asked. Not really, but he's cool, I said. Thankfully, Knox's phone rang and it must have been work, because he got up to answer it, walking away.

*Is he a loser?* she asked. He's more popular than I am, I said. *Well, that's not saying much, is it?* Ha-ha-ha, I said, pinching her arm, and she said, *Are you friends?* Kinda, I said, shrugging, and she said, *Tell me,* and I said, We used to hang out last year, after everything went down with that party, you know? *Like you hung out at your house?* she asked, so inquisitive. No, no. At school. Lunchtime, the library—. *Why doesn't he have any friends?* He has friends, I said. *But?* But he's got epilepsy, I said, and I could tell she wasn't going to drop it, so I told her the whole story.

Right after I moved to town, he had a really bad seizure, standing right in line in the cafeteria. He had a full tray and the food went flying everywhere and people started yelling—I'll never forget seeing him fall down, and . . . no one knew what to do. Someone said he had to put a belt or something between his teeth—. *That's not true*, she said. *That's totally false—you can strangle someone having a seizure if you block their airway*, she said, genuinely upset. I know, I said. Ricky told us afterward. I mean, after we started talking. It was humiliating for him, you know, I said, and it was the first time I realized why he and I had so much in common. And I didn't tell her this, but it was the first time it crossed my mind, and I don't know why, but it's so much easier to be sympathetic of someone else's shame than your own. Mel, how do you know that about epilepsy? I asked, and she said, *Drrr. I've spent more time in hospitals than you have, remember. Anyhow, he's hot*, and I snorted, watching Knox kneel back down to sit with us. Knox looked at us, shaking his head the way he does, inside, without moving on the outside. We should get going soon, girls, he said. *Think my dad would let me go out on a date?* With Ricky? I said, and out of the blue, Knox goes, No. Both our mouths fell open, and we just looked at him—he didn't know exactly what we were talking about, but he knew something and he wasn't having any of it.

It was such a good day, I forgot all about Cam for like three hours—well, two maybe. On the way home, Mel goes, *Thee, Thee! Play him our song, play my dad our song*, and I turned to Knox and I go, We have a song, me and Mel, Our Song. You want to hear Our Song? I said, and Mel started laughing. Knox goes, You two have a song? I go, You bet we do, then I plugged in my iPod, and pulled it up. Ready, Mel? I said, and she goes, *Born ready!* I started laughing, and then I hit play, and I turned to face Mel, so she could see me dance, shimmying my shoulders, right when it kicked in: Buht, buhn . . . buh-nuh-but-nuht-nuht! *Sweet sixteen in leather boots! Body and soul, I go crazy!* Knox pulled over.

I'm not kidding: Knox pulled over, on the side of the road, and I looked at him and said, Chill, Daddy, chill! Then, all choppy, he goes, *What* the *hell* is *that?* I told him, That's Iggy, Knox—*Sixteen*, get it? We're going to be *sixteen*, that's why it's Our Song? And Mel goes, *Ohmygod, Dad, this song's only like fifty years old*, and I go, Seriously, Mel loves the Stooges, and Knox goes, No. Oh, no, no, like he's putting his foot down, and Mel goes, *He'd rather I listened to Foreigner*, and I gasped. My mouth fell open, and I said, Knox, you don't honestly listen to Foreigner, do you? He turned to the backseat, knowing exactly who told me, but still, I was so embarrassed, I had to cover my face, blushing. I go, Ohmygod, that's like worse than finding out your dad watches porn, and Mel goes, *Don't even get me started.* And I looked at Knox, like, *Eww.* I said, Please tell me you don't listen to the Indigo Girls and watch porn at the same time, and his chin fell open, and I said, I'm sorry, but that's disgusting.

Mel goes, *Come on, Thee, sing it with me: I wanna know what love is, I want you to show me.* . . . I had to stop laughing before I could sing that line with her, because that's all I knew, and then it hit me again. I keep reaching out, wanting to share these things, these moments, with Cam, and I keep getting bitch-slapped by reality. I shut my mouth while Knox pulled back on the highway, and Mel goes, *Thee, you okay?* I nodded, but I didn't turn around. She goes, *You want to talk?* I shook my head no, oh, no. Knox looked at me, I could see him looking at me, and then he looked in the rearview. Just then, we reached the turnoff to my building, and I could see a couple news vans—I saw the satellite dish on a news van, and I said, Pull over.

I still forget—I keep forgetting anyone knows, that anyone cares, about reporters, waiting around our building. Then, for a split second, when I see them there, I still can't believe it's happening, that there are all these people waiting to take my picture, ask me questions, you know? But as soon as I saw them, I said, Stop. Knox saw them too, at the same moment. Let me out here, I said. It's fine. Really, it's fine, I said, and I didn't say it, but he knew. I didn't want him to drive any closer to our house because Mel was in the car. I didn't want her to see this, all these people, waiting for me to show up. *What's up?* she said, and she couldn't see them, but she knew something was going on. I'm getting out here, I said, as Knox pulled over, off the highway, but he didn't turn in.

*Here? Why here?* Mel asked, and I turned around. I smiled, trying to let her know it was okay, even though it wasn't. Because, I said, and I started to say something, but I didn't even know what I was going to say. I'll tell you later, okay? It's nothing, but I just don't want to get into it right now. Please? I said, and she didn't like it, but she listened. Of course I knew she'd be angry that I was trying to protect her the same way Knox was always trying to protect her. The way that didn't let you live life, that treated you like a child, or worse, in her case, an invalid. It's not fair, I know. Then again, in this case, in this situation, that's how it had to be. And I know Knox wanted to walk me to my door, but Mel had to come first, and we both knew it.

So I got out, on the side of the road, and I waved good-bye, waiting for them to leave before I took my phone out to call my mom, heading upstairs, taking the back way. There was nothing she could do to make them go away, but it was something for me to focus on, when I walked into the building. If they saw my mom there, sometimes people were better behaved, but they would still ask me anything they want, whether my mom was there or not. Like, *Are there more sex tapes, Thea? How do you feel about being called a teenage porn star? Do you think your boyfriend's dead?*

Sometimes, the storm's worse inside than outside. When Mom opened the door for me, I got inside, and what did I see? The lawyers—the lawyers were back again, sitting on our couch. I looked at my mom, disgusted, and before I could say anything, the man goes, Hello, Thea. You mother called to discuss the video, from the party last year. I go, What's there to discuss? He goes, Do you intend to press charges? I go, Press charges? He said, Whether or not you decide to press criminal charges, the DA—. No, I said, and my mom goes, Thea, that's not up to you, and I go, Leave me alone, all of you! I yelled, then I went to my room and slammed the door.

I felt it again, building up, the pressure, it kept building. I had to fight it—I couldn't let it win. I couldn't go back, I didn't want to go back. Then I heard myself, realizing I spoke out loud: Please, I said. *Please?* I didn't know who I was talking to, but I said, Please help me. Because I didn't want to go back ever again, but I didn't have any energy left to fight.

I'd never had a boyfriend before, so I had no idea how stressful it was, the whole gift thing. I mean, at first, I didn't really think about it, because, well, I didn't think it would last more than a couple weeks, and then Cam would want to see other people. So I never thought about Christmas, until Black Friday, and then, seeing all the commercials on TV, I was just like, *Oh, shit. Guess maybe I should get it together, huh?* And once I started thinking about it, I thought of a thousand things he'd love. Only problem was, I didn't have any money. And even if I wanted to, there was no work anymore—there weren't even babysitting jobs around here anymore. So, basically, there was nothing I could afford to buy him, and after a couple weeks, it put me in a mood.

Every day we got closer to Christmas, the more it bummed me out—showed, too. One day, after school, I got so worked up about it that we almost had a fight. I mean, not a fight-fight, but we were sitting in our booth at Silver Top, one day, and Cam's like, All right, enough with the attitude and mopey face, Thee. Seriously, what's the problem? So I just told him, Look, I'm sorry, but I'm stressed out about Christmas, because I don't know what to get you, since I don't have any money to get you anything, and—. He cut me off, and then he goes, This is what you've been pouting about? I go, I haven't been pouting, and I cocked my head, and he goes, You've been a bit prickly, Thee. I was like, Cam, what do you expect? I'm stressed, okay. I told you. Cam goes, This is what you've been stressed about? I said, Yes, and he goes, I thought you hated Christmas? And I said, I do, but that doesn't mean I don't want to spend money I don't have like everyone else, and that got him. He laughed, sitting back.

Come on, Thee, let's just forget about Christmas, and instead, how about you stop moping and getting all stressed out about what you can't get me that I don't really need anyhow? I said no. No, I said, shaking my head, no way, out of the question. Why not? he said, and I said, Because, and he said, Because why? So I told him, Because I've never had a boyfriend, and it's my first Christmas with my first boyfriend, and I've never had anyone special to get stressed out about, and I want to get you something really excellent, just so unbelievably fucking cool you remember it for the rest of your life, that's why! *Duh*, I said, really practically kicking my foot against the opposite side of the booth, pushing myself back into my seat, folding my arms.

Cam looked at me for a moment, seeing I wasn't kidding, and he goes, Okay. Listen, he said, you know those times when you say you don't understand why I think you're crazy and you want me to name one time you were ever crazy? Well, this is one of those times, he said, leaning over the table, reaching for my hands—making a joke out of it, right? It's not funny, I said, turning away. Good. Because I wasn't joking, Thee, he said, sitting back, and I looked at him, totally unamused. Hey, how about this? How about we celebrate Christmas by not giving any gifts? How about our gift is no gift, meaning the gift of no stress? Because right now, I think that sounds like a perfect gift, he said. No, I said, shaking my head no, no, that's not okay. And he goes, Then why don't you draw something for me, give me one of your pictures—. Cam, I give you drawings and pictures *all the time*, that's not special! I whined, and he looked at me. And the look in his eyes said so many things; there was no need to open his mouth.

I mean, of course it's special, I said, apologetically, and he goes, What about the picture you took last week? I hate that picture, I said, like no way, and he goes, I love that picture, and I go, Why? He goes, Because you aren't posing, you aren't self-conscious, you're just you—it's gorgeous. And I was so flattered, so touched he said that, but still. No way, I said. And he goes, Why is it always about you? He was joking, and then Sharon came over to our booth to check on us. Fill 'er up, honey? she said, seeing Cam's empty glass. Sharon loves Cam, and he knows it, too. Thanks, Sharon, he said, pushing his empty extralarge brown plastic diner glass over. You betcha, hon, she said. Thea, you doing all right? I'm fine, thanks, I said, smiling. All right, then, she said, leaving us alone again.

Cam leaned forward, grabbed both my hands, and he goes, You're serious about this? Do I not look serious to you? I asked, and he goes, Well, then. If you really want to give me something special—. Then I totally cut him and his dirty mind off; I go, Oh, here we go, slouching in the booth, my arms still crossed, biting my tongue between my incisors. Because I'll tell you exactly what I want, he said, and I was trying so hard not to laugh, not to smile, pulling away, like, get your dirty brain and your filthy hands off me.

I go, Actually, you know what? No presents, I said. Brilliant idea: no presents, no gifts, no giving. Cam reached over and grabbed my hand, like it or not, pulling me forward, and then he turned my hand and bit the side, waiting to see what I'd do. Doesn't hurt, I said, watching him, and then he bit harder. Nothing, I said, taunting him, and then he bit hard enough his teeth were showing. I just held still, watching his front teeth making a mark, feeling them reaching the bones in my hand. Still can't feel it, I said, and I knew it should hurt, but I still didn't feel a thing. Nope, I said, and watching his lips pull back, I knew he was about to bite as hard as he could—.

Cameron, let me get you a menu, son, Sharon said, stepping forward, and Cam released my hand, wiping his mouth with the back side of his hand, and I pulled my sleeve down, over my wrist, so Sharon wouldn't see how deep the teeth marks were. Have a sip of this, and cool yourself off, honey, Sharon said, setting down Cam's second refill of lemonade. We didn't take our eyes off each other the whole time, and I knew he knew what I was thinking:

*Didn't feel a thing, bite as hard as you like. I wasn't going to cry uncle.* Ah, young love, Sharon said, sighing, and I had to look out the window, biting the inside of my lip to keep from laughing. It was almost dark, and I could see Cam's reflection, his beautiful face grinning back at me in the diner window, and just above his head, the first star in the sky.

I looked like a bag lady. Then, when Knox opened the door, seeing me, standing there with all these bags of clothes, Knox's face looked like he had this terrifying thought that I was going to ask him if I could move in with them. I said, Relax. I'm giving Mel a makeover, that's all.

Knox had to work late, and Heather's mom was really sick, so she was out of town every weekend, so I asked if I could hang with Mel. At first, I didn't think Knox would agree, but then he helped me rearrange the furniture so I could set up a table for makeup and a mirror. All set, I said, meaning he could leave, and then he gave Mel a kiss good-bye, telling her to be good. Thea, if anything happens, he said, warning me, and I go, Knox, nothing is going to happen—come on, you don't do anything when someone does your hair and makeup: you just close your eyes and chill. When he finally left, I was just like, Mel, ohmygod, your dad, and she goes, *Don't get me started*, so I didn't.

Anyhow, I think it was really calming for her—it feels good, having someone do your makeup, brushing your hair. Kind of like a massage, and Melody has such beautiful skin, too. Porcelain, and she always says she has such white skin because she's like human veal, ha, ha, ha, but that's not it. They take her out more than I'm ever outside, trust me. No, she just had that really beautiful white, white skin. Her hair would be great, too, if you set it in rollers. So that's what I decided to do, set her hair in rollers while I did her makeup.

Honestly, I couldn't believe how beautiful she looked, so I took all these pictures. I wanted to put her in all these different outfits, too, and I did, but it was a lot of work. I almost broke a sweat, changing her, and I know it was hard for Mel, letting me do that, changing her clothes for her. It's this horrible thought that she's a burden, and it passes through me, this jolt, when her muscles tense, like she's trying to protect herself, but she can't. And when I feel her body do that, I see her again the way the rest of the world sees her, but still. That night, when I turned her around, in front of the mirror and I did the big reveal, she gasped, saying, *Ohmygod, is that me?* That's you, I said, and for once, I knew how Cam felt, showing me that girl I didn't see. And I wished so badly he was there, so I could tell him, but then I had to turn away, because my eyes got all teary.

*Thee, I want to ask you something*, Mel said, when I sat down again. I knew what she was going to say before she asked. And I knew there was no getting out of it, either. I tried to hide them, covering myself when I got undressed, but I knew she must have seen. And she knew, somehow she just knew, and I guess I just hoped she'd leave it alone, but no. *How could you do that?* she said, and I looked at my hands. *How can you take a razor and do that to yourself?* That's the thing, I said. It won't make sense to you, because the same force you feel not to do that to yourself, whatever that instinct is, self-preservation, whatever, I felt the opposite pull to do it. I *had* to do it: it wasn't a choice anymore than breathing. Sometimes I didn't even want to do it, but I had to. *Did you ever ask for help?* And I knew she didn't mean to sound so snotty, I know, but she did.

Look, Mel, you got your bad wiring; I got mine. I mean, why do you think we're so different? *Because I would never do that to myself*, she said, and I said, How can you know that, Mel? Seriously, I'm not asking you to understand, but I am asking you not to judge me. She goes, *I don't judge you, Thea*, and I go, Well, you should hear yourself in my head. *I'm just telling you how I feel*, she said. *Thinking of you doing that to yourself, it hurts. That's what I'm trying to say*, she said, and I go, You don't understand, and she goes, *No, I don't, so tell me.*

I just sighed, so not wanting to get into it, but needing to, at the same time. I said, It's just this, this pressure that used to build. At first, it feels annoying, like you have a splinter, and you want to take it out—drives you crazy, and you have to get it out. Except that the splinter starts getting bigger, all this pressure starts building, and it's like you feel it right beneath the skin, but it won't come out on its own. I never know where I'll feel it, because sometimes it's my thigh, or sometimes it's my arm, but it's this huge piece of glass, and I have to cut it out or I feel like I'll lose my mind. It's so crazy-making, and all I care about is making the cut so my head doesn't explode, I said. I stopped talking, and I shivered—just talking about it, telling her even that much, I could feel it closing in again, and it scared me.

*Thea*, she said, and I knew she was about to say something I'd never be able to escape. And then she did; she said: *Promise me you won't do that anymore?* All I could do was let out this big sigh, hearing those words, her voice in my mind. Because it doesn't work like that. You can't ask someone to do something for you that . . . I don't know, it doesn't work like that or everyone could just make a promise not to hurt themselves or others. But who in this whole world can make that promise? I was about to argue, but she didn't care. *Promise me*, she said.

I've never wanted to be so honest with anyone. Like even more than Cam in a way, because I never felt like I had to protect him—not when we were together, at least. But with Mel, it's different. She's the last person in the world I ever want to hurt, you know? But I had this terrible feeling she'd be the person I hurt the most, the worst. I didn't know how or why, except that it's just—me. That's just me.

I can't even explain what I saw, looking at her then. I reached for my camera and I focused, taking a picture of her, in profile. Her perfect little nose, her beautiful white skin, hair all curled and her lashes curled and lips glossed. She looked like a girl getting ready for a big date on Friday night. What could I do? I promise, Mel, I said, putting my camera down for a second, sure

I got the shot. *Thank you*, she said. *Now show me*, she said, her voice changing, sounding excited, wanting me to show her the pictures I'd just taken.

I think she knows now. I mean, when I showed her some of the pictures I took of us, Mel couldn't even believe it. She didn't say anything, looking at them, but I knew. I mean, I knew it was a lot for her to take it, a lot of thinking was changing, seeing herself so differently, and she does the same for me, too. Honestly, Mel showed me things about myself even Cam had never seen. Like just because you make some mistakes . . . I mean, even really bad mistakes, and you hurt so many people, being stupid, that doesn't mean you can't make it right, do good—change, even. Then she goes, *Thee, I'm tired of all this hiding, all the secrets. I want my mom to know—we aren't doing anything wrong, and I don't want to hide anymore.* I thought about it, and I go, I don't blame her, really, for wanting you to stay away from me, my life, and Mel said, *I do. I blame her every day.*

I said, Mel, you have no idea, and she goes, *I have no idea? You're wrong: I have a very good idea, and when do I get to have a life, too? A few hours every week, don't I deserve that much?* I said, Mel, of course you do, and she goes, *I want to talk to my dad, when he gets home. Tonight*, she said. I go, All right. But you know what he's going to say, and she said, *I do. But he has no idea what I'm going to say, does he?* I go, What are you going to say, Mel? She said, *That he has to tell my mom about you, everything.* She was so serious, I took a deep breath. Then I said, I know what you're saying, but I don't know that it's that simple.

*I disagree*, she said. *If he wants to live a lie, that's his decision, but he has no right to make that choice for me.* I knew what she was saying, and she was braver than me and Knox combined. That's when I realized that I needed Mel much more than she needed me. Then she goes, *So are we going to talk to him or not?* All right, I said, let's get ready.

So I set her up in the living room, and we took our positions, waiting for Knox to get home. *We almost look like twins, don't we?* she said, and I had to laugh. We'd taken one shot in these matching dresses, and I did our hair the same, sort of. Mel's hair is a lot longer, but we looked identical. We are twins, I said, meaning our birthday. Mel and I have the same birthday, and we were even born the same hour—crazy, huh? Then she goes, *Hey, Thee? What should we do for our birthday?* Funny, because I'd been thinking about that, too, and then someone knocked on the front door, and I looked at Mel, and she looked at me, and then I thought maybe Knox couldn't find his keys, so I walked to the door and opened it. Then my mouth fell open, seeing him, standing there: Foley. It was Foley.

Strange thing is, he didn't seem at all surprised to see me there, much less all dressed up. Foley smiles and he goes, Hello, Theadora. What a surprise, he said. *Who is it?* Melody asked, but I didn't answer. I just looked at Foley, but I couldn't tell if he heard her or not. Is Detective Knox here? he said, and I go, No, grabbing the door so I'd have something to hold on to more than anything. And he looked like he was about to ask what I was doing at Knox's house, but he didn't. He goes, Oh, I see. Do you know when he'll be home? I go, I don't know when, and he said, Are you here alone, then? looking around me, into the living room, and I stepped to the side, so he couldn't see Mel.

Just then, Mel called my name, *Thee? Who is it?* And then Foley leaned to his side, talking around me, and he said, Just me—Agent Foley, and I had to clench my jaw so hard to keep it from falling. He heard her—I swear Foley heard Mel speaking to me. Did you say something, Theodora? he asked, smiling like we had some inside joke, and I shook my head—too fast, I started shaking my head too fast. I didn't say anything, I said, and he smiled, Sorry, I thought I heard something. Well, anyhow, you should call him, I said, and Foley goes, Thank you, I'll do that, smiling his special pervy smile, and then I closed the door, right in his face. *Thea? Thee, who is it?* Mel asked, and I just stood there, staring at the door, knowing he hadn't moved, either.

After I closed the door, when I walked back into the living room, I felt so dirty, I wanted to take a shower. I really did. And I wasn't sure, but I'm pretty sure he saw Mel, because you can see from the door into the living room, and I had her seated, situated on their couch so she'd be the first thing Knox saw, when he walked in the door. Knox got home literally, like, one minute after Foley left. He pulled in the drive, walked straight across the path, and opened the front door. One look and he knew something was wrong. What's wrong? What happened? he said, following me into the living room. He balked, seeing Melody, and then he held up his finger, like we'll get to you in a second, and he waited for me to say something, make sense of whatever was going on. Tell me what's going on, Thea, he said, and I go, Someone came to the door, so I answered.

Here? he said, and I said, Yes. I thought it was you, I said, and then I felt bad, because you should always ask before opening the door. I knew that; everyone knows that. He could trust me, alone, with his daughter, you know? At least when it came to answering doors. Just not tonight, maybe, and he goes, Who was it? And I winced, and then I told him: Foley, I said. He knew before, though, like the second before, Knox saw it. What did he want? he said, setting down his keys. He had a file in his hand, I said, putting it together. He was going to deliver my medical file to Knox.

Knox was frowning, and he goes, Did he say anything? I go, No, he asked for you, and Knox goes, What did you tell him? I go, I told him you were out, and he should call you, I said. That's all? Knox said, and I go, That's all I told him, Knox, yes, and it wasn't right, both of us knew something wasn't right. And then Mel goes, *What's going on? Would someone please tell me what's going on?* I didn't even have a chance to tell her before Knox walked in, and part of me didn't want Mel to know. *Please tell me what's going on*, she said, and Knox could tell she was talking to me. Mel, I don't know, I said. I don't know what's going on, except that Special Agent Foley decided to pay your dad a house call, and he had a folder in his hands. All right, Knox said, sighing. He didn't know what to do, but he didn't want to talk about it either.

*Thee, let's talk to him now*, Mel said, acting like this was our golden opportunity. I need to take a bath, I said. I'm not kidding: I feel so gross, you have no idea—. Whoa, whoa, whoa . . . back up. First of all, Knox said, and then Mel said, *We have to tell him now. It's the perfect time, Thee*—. First of all, Knox said, what's with all this makeup on Melody's face? *Ohmygod, Dad*, Mel said. *You aren't really going to start in because I'm wearing makeup?* He goes, Thea, you didn't tell me you were going to paint—. *You have got to be kidding me*, Mel said. Stop, I said. Paint her face like that, he said. *Is that your idea of a compliment, Dad?* she said, and I couldn't take it anymore: Stop! I said, stop, both of you. Quiet—would you be quiet? I need to think, I said, and believe it or not, they shut up. They both shut up, and they looked at me, waiting.

I took a deep breath and said, Knox, Mel wants to have a talk—she wants you to have a talk with Heather, tell her Mel and I are friends. She also invited me to spend the night. Is that cool? I said. *Tell him we can have the talk or he can just say yes*, Mel said. I raised my right hand: Talk with Heather or sleepover, which would you rather have? Knox made this little huff, puffing his lips, knowing it was two against one, and then he said, When you put it that way, I'd rather we all went to bed.

So we took Mel upstairs, and I helped her get dressed for bed, and then I left them alone for a moment, waiting outside her room. Get some sleep, girls, Knox said, stepping out of the room. I got in bed, and I was so careful, lying down beside Mel, and I pulled the covers up, tucking them in around her body. Good night, I said, looking at her, and she goes, *Hey, Thee?* I sat up, so she could see me, and she said, *I've decided I'm going to get my hair cut. For my birthday—for our birthday.* I could tell she was serious, too, so I go, Then do it, and she goes, *I will. You'll see, Thee: I'm not afraid of what my parents will do.* I said, I know you aren't afraid—you're the bravest person I know. *Are you just saying that?* she asked, and I said, No. I mean it. Now go to sleep, I said, giving her a kiss on each cheek, lying down beside her.

I shut my eyes, and then she said, *Hey, Thee . . . you know you never really talk about him*, and of course I knew what she was saying. Really? Maybe because I'm always thinking about him, I feel like I talk about him all the time, even if I'm not saying it out loud, I said. Mel didn't ask, but I told her, the only person I've ever told. I said, The last thing Cam said to me, he was leaving my house, and he asked me the craziest question. He said, What if God was a teenage girl?

Mel balked, then turned to look at me, almost squinting. She said, *Literally, you mean? Like, what, like, And on the seventh day, teenage girl God created the shopping mall?* I smiled and my head fell back, shaking, because Mel's *dying* to go to a shopping mall, and I told her she's not missing anything, but she said she doesn't care, so I promised her we'd go sometime. I said, Honestly, I don't have a clue what he was talking about—that's just Cam. He had all sorts of crazy questions, crazy ideas—everyone thinks I'm so crazy and he's so sane, right, and they've got it all wrong, I said. *Has*, Mel said, quietly. Sorry? I said, looking up. *He* has *all sorts of crazy ideas*, she said, smiling. Has, I said.

Anyhow, I have no idea what he meant, but that question keeps coming back to me, I said. Like he was trying to tell me something, you know? *Yeah, well, that's kind of big, whatever it was he was trying to tell you*, she said, and I just had to laugh. Kinda, yeah, I said. You want to hear something else he taught me? I said, propping myself up on my elbow. And Mel said, *Tell me*, and I said, You know what the Butterfly Effect is, how, like if a butterfly flaps its wings in Japan, it can start a hurricane in Kansas or whatever? *Um, not really . . .* And I said, Anyhow, Cam used to say the same thing about butterfly kisses. He called it the Butterfly Kisses Effect, that you couldn't possibly know the magnitude of a single action. Watch, I said, and then I leaned over her, giving her butterfly kisses until she squealed. Now go to sleep, I said, resting my head on my pillow, waiting for her to close her eyes.

After she fell asleep, I decided I better get up to pee, so I wouldn't wake her in the middle of the night. Knox heard me, walking out of the bathroom, and he called up to me: Thea? Yes? I whispered, peeking down the stairs, and he nodded his head, wanting me to see something in the living room, and to be quiet about it. So I walked down, and before I could ask, Knox cocked his head across the room, holding the remote control in his hand. I was watching the news, he said, and there's something you should see, Thea. My first thought was, *Ohmygod, they can't show porn on the eleven o'clock news, can they?* And then he hit play, and the news segment started. It was footage taken at night, an aerial view, and it took a few seconds to come into view, the reporters talking about some private jet that had recorded a most unusual sight in the quiet town of Fort Marshall, which had been experiencing some rather bizarre events recently, and then they flashed back to a clip of the tire tracks that ended in the middle of an endless field.

In that same field, the woman said, we now have this, and then a fluorescent image came into focus. Flying directly over the field, the jet had videotaped this enormous heart with an arrow through it—someone tagged the whole damn field with a fluorescent green heart that read, CC + TD = TLA! First thing I did was reach for my tattoo, and I took the Band-Aid off—I've been wearing one of those huge Band-Aids made for heels or whatever, and I tried shading my shoulder, but I couldn't see it. Knox, look: look, I said, and I got up, walking to the end of the hall, where it was dark. He got up and walked over, and I showed him, pulling back my T-shirt. All you could see, just barely, was the scar on my shoulder, but no tattoo. Where is it? he said. It's gone, I said, shaking my head. Knox, my tattoo is gone—it's in that field now.

Knox exhaled a thick sigh, not like one I'd ever heard before, and he turned, heading back into the living room, needing to sit and think about this a second, I could tell. When I followed him back into the living room, I saw that he had a bottle open. Whiskey, scotch, I don't know the difference. Especially when the bottle's almost empty. Maybe that's why he really didn't want me sleeping over. I couldn't really deal with that, too, at that moment, while Knox hit play, returning to the end of the news story.

All I could think about was my tattoo—you could see it from a mile above ground. Isn't that something? the guy reporter in the studio said, and I shivered, crossing my arms. Police say that they don't have a suspect yet, but they do have a few leads, said the chick—what's-her-name, the one who gave me her card. Leads? I said, and Knox said, The authorities don't have a fucking clue, trust me—we don't have any leads. He stifled a belch with one fist, and then he said, Excuse me.

He was sloppy, but still on the job. Has anyone else seen it? Your tattoo? he said, trying to act as sober as he could. My radioactive tattoo? I asked, and he said, Yes, and I said, No. I taped it up. I covered it with one of those jumbo Band-Aids—no one's seen me, I said. He scratched the side of his cheek for a moment, thinking it over, and then, finally, he said, This is some fucked-up shit. I don't know what the hell is going on, here, but I do know some fucked-up shit when I see it. I knew he was drunk: Knox never swears. Then he nodded, agreeing with himself, and then he said, Go on, cocking his head toward the stairs. Off to bed with you, he said, still staring at the TV, so I got up and said good night, passing him. I'd walked halfway upstairs, when Knox called after me, Thea? I could feel him on the other side of the wall, sitting on the couch, staring in the opposite direction, toward the TV. Yes? I said, and then he said, Sweet dreams.

I crawled back into bed as quietly as I could, but Melody was awake. *Thee?* she said, and I pulled the covers over my shoulder, turning to her, inches from her face. *Is my dad awake?* she said, and I said, Yes. *He's drinking*, she said, matter-of-fact, and I said, Yes. *Every night*, she says. *He must drink a bottle a night, easy. Sometimes, I'll wake up, hearing him crying. Because of me*, she said, and I said, No—it's not you, and she said, *It is. I know it is.*

*He can't stop wishing I were healthy, normal, and it tears him up, because he loves me. You know he always says, You're perfect, my perfect girl, and I don't know who he's trying to convince. I just wish . . . ,* she said, then she stopped; her eyes welling. You wish what? I said, Tell me. And Mel said, *Some people believe everything happens for a reason, but I don't know about that. I think, honestly, sometimes things just happen and we make of it what we will. But whether there's any reason or not, I just wish my dad could forgive us both for being who we really are.*

I don't know if Mel could see the tears in my eyes, but I wiped them off my cheek, then I hugged her arm in mine and closed my eyes. I didn't say anything, because the one thing I've figured out is that there are times you have to find the courage to say everything in your heart. And there are times you cannot possibly say everything in your heart, so you have to find the courage to be quiet and still in the dark.

Karen wanted a picture. That's what she asked for for Christmas, one of my drawings or a photo. It freaked me out, too, because Karen used to own a famous frame shop in Los Angeles, like she knows Sally Mann—she's framed Sally Mann's photographs, okay? If that wasn't bad enough, when Karen invited us over for Christmas, I didn't know what to say, because, well, for one thing, she'd already had us over for Thanksgiving, and it's not like I wanted to have them over to our place, because we wouldn't all fit for starters. So when Karen said, Thea, I was hoping you, your mom, and Raymond could join us for Christmas brunch, I looked at her like, *Eeesh, not so sure about that.* Because Karen knows how I feel about Raymond. I mean, I haven't told her everything, but she knows.

It was about two weeks before Christmas, and we were in her little shop—that's what she calls the back room, off the patio.

She's set up in there, and the room's just big enough for framing, and I went over one day, when Cam was out, skating, so we could work on framing the pictures I was giving him. We were choosing mattes, and then she said, Thea, I called and invited your mom and Raymond for Christmas, holding up one of the pictures I'd chosen for my mom, and my face fell.

For a moment, I felt really annoyed with her, too. Because she knew how I felt, and she invited Ray anyway. What's that look? she asked, smiling in that motherly way like she was about to reprimand me, but it wouldn't hurt too much, because I'd see the wisdom of it. She goes, I know you don't understand, and I said, You're right, I don't. I mean, I'm sorry, but I can't stand the guy, how he treats my mom, and he makes things so much worse with her, and whatever. I didn't want Ray there, period, and it was the first time I'd had a really hard time talking to Karen, and she goes, Thea, it's Christmas, and it's the right thing to do. I go, Karen, trust me, there's nothing right about Ray, whatever day of the year, and she goes, It'll be easier on your mother, and then we heard the front door open in the house. Cam was back. I just stared at the ground, not sure what to say.

You don't want him here that badly? she asked, sighing, covering the photographs I'd brought. I go, Honestly, no, I don't want him here that badly, and her face fell. I go, I'm not a bad person because I don't want him in my life or my mom's life, and because I don't want to spend Christmas with Raymond, playing nice because it's Christmas, I said, feeling my throat swell. Now my boyfriend's mom would know I was not this sweet girl, you know? Listen, she said, grabbing my hand, taking it in hers.

Karen said, Thea, all I'm saying is there are times we have to take the high road, and I think this is one of those times. If you don't want him here, all right. It's your choice, she said, and I stared at the ground, then Cam walked in, and he had this look, like, Whoa, what's going on? Because he could see we were in the middle of something.

I told him about it on the way home, but he's like Karen. Meaning, they're bigger people than I am, I guess. Seriously, it was so painful at Thanksgiving, watching Ray looking at Karen's artwork with that buffoon look on his face, like, *WTF, dude, this looks like scribbles, my nephew could do that.* . . . So when I got home that night, I almost said something to my mom, too, telling her Ray wasn't invited, so if she didn't want to go to Karen's house on Christmas, that was her decision. But then, looking at her, sitting at the table, taking out the few ornaments that were light enough to hang on the Charlie Brown fake tree we put up in the living room, I couldn't. Because she was smiling, and I didn't see her look that way much anymore.

Christmas Day, Ray picked us up, and we drove over at noon, but the whole way, I was trying to steel my mind. Telling myself, *You're not going to snap. You're not going to roll your eyes. And you're not going to let Rain Man piss you off and make a scene in Karen's house, because this is her house, and you love her, and you are going to behave. Whether anyone knows it or not,* I thought, *this is my gift to you all. So I hope you love it, because it might be the last time ever.*

It was fine. Really, it wasn't great, but it was fine. The food was amazing, and Karen and my mom were laughing, and

Raymond was embarrassing, but not as bad as usual, because he was out of his element, so he actually kept his mouth shut. Cam kept checking in, squeezing my shoulders every few minutes, reassuring me it was cool, right. By the time gift time rolled around, I was so excited, I asked if I could give Karen her gifts first. Cam helped me choose a picture for her, and I handed it to her, and she shook the box, like she didn't know what it was. Then she started opening it, all delicate, until I said, Karen, rip the paper! So she tore it open, and she took the photograph out and opened up the matte frame I'd made. . . . She looked at it for a good minute, then her eyes started welling, and she goes, *I love it*, and she gave me a kiss.

So Karen held up the photograph, so everyone could see, and Raymond's face . . . ohmygod, Rain Man, I swear, his mouth fell open. Like he was standing there, holding his beer in his hand, with that wide-leg stance he takes, and seeing this picture of me in my underwear, he balked, like he wasn't seeing it right. It's me, I said, so proud that Karen approved, and she wasn't just saying she loved it to be nice, either. Cam sat in his chair, grinning at me, because it was really scary, giving Karen that picture, and he swore it was the right one, and he was right.

It's beautiful, Mom said, squeezing my shoulder, and I felt really happy, but then, hearing my mom, Raymond looked at her, like, *What?* Like, you could see the wheels in Ray's head thinking, *Drr. Her feet are blurry, why are her feet blurry? And why is she sitting on a chair in her underwear?* Karen caught my eye, and then she goes, Raymond, can I get you another beer? Right on cue, Cam sprung up from his chair, saying, I'll get it. Anyone else? I followed him, and then Karen followed me, and we barely made it to the kitchen before we burst out laughing.

Took a few minutes to gather ourselves, but then we carried our drinks back into the living room. For a minute there, it was good, and I was thinking maybe Christmas isn't so bad, after all. Then, at that moment, at that very second, my phone rang, and everyone turned. I knew, so I let it go to voice mail, because I knew it was my dad calling. Cheers, everyone, Karen said, holding up her drink, so we all held up our drinks, toasting. I took a big drink of my eggnog, waiting for the burn to pass in the back of my throat, and then I grabbed another square box, and I looked over and smiling this big smile, I said, Ray, ready to open your gift?

Mel's obsessed with chairlifts. Don't ask me how we got on the subject, but it came one day when we were driving past Silver Top. I sighed, looking out the window, and I said, Look, Mel: There's Silver Top, and she goes, *Let's go.* And I said, You want to go in, really? And she said, *Why not? My mom won't be home for a couple hours,* so I said, Knox, Mel wants to go to Silver Top, and he raised his brow, looking at her in the mirror, and she grinned that grin that he can't resist. Mel has this smile that turns Knox to putty, like total daddy dough, and she pulled that number on him, all right; he knew he was beat, and he pulled over.

So we went in and sat at our table, the booth Cam and I always took, and it was strange, because I wanted them to sit there with me, but I didn't at the same time, because I can't seem to juggle both sides of my life, you know? Anyhow, Mel's totally hooked on Flickr, and she has this thing for chairlifts, so I found this picture for her and I showed it to her after we sat down. It's not one of those pictures people take during the wintertime, when you can see snow everywhere and people are sitting on chairlifts, with their skis dangling in the air. The one I chose for her was this shot of a single chairlift—must be in the summer or the fall, maybe, because there was no snow and the people were all gone. It was a picture of this big empty chairlift, high up in the air, and the first time I saw it, I knew how badly Mel would want to sit on it like a swing, with the whole sky to herself.

So we're sitting there, and Mel was saying how she wanted to go on a Ferris wheel, too, how cool it would be to feel her legs dangle, when this black SUV drove by. I caught it out of the corner of my eye, and right away, I felt this chill run up and down my back before I even knew why, and then it registered: it was Foley.

Knox saw it, too, and then Mel saw there was something wrong, so she asked, *What is it?* Nothing, I said, squeezing her hand. But my hand was clammy, and I think she knew. And if she didn't, a minute later, the bell rang over the door, and Foley walked in. He saw us through the window, I know he did. Knox had his back turned to the door, but he saw my face go pale, and just as he was turning to look, Foley came straight for us, smiling. He goes, Detective Knox, and all I wanted was to throw my body over Mel like a blanket and protect her. But there was nothing I could do, you know, except stare at the table, feeling Foley walk straight over.

Agent Foley, Knox said. He didn't offer his hand, he didn't say anything. Hello, Theodora, Foley said, and Mel still had her back turned, and then Foley bent over to look Melody in the eye, and said, And who is this? I didn't say anything, and Knox didn't say anything. At that moment, I think we both wanted to jump Foley and strangle him. This is my daughter, Melody, Knox said, and Foley goes, I didn't know you had a daughter, Detective Knox. *Melody*, Foley drawled, sort of singsong. What a beautiful name. And what a beautiful girl, he said, leaning around to face her, and I shuddered. Then Foley did the most vile thing: he took Melody's right hand and shook it. I swear, I almost stabbed him in the neck with my fork.

Melody, I almost feel as though we've met before, Foley said, eyeing me, meaning the night he went to their house, looking for Knox, and I shook my head. I don't believe you've met my daughter, Knox said, intervening, and Foley said, No, I certainly wouldn't forget her if I had, acting all suave, and Mel goes, *Gag!* Foley smiled and said, What's that? My jaw dropped, and all I could do was look away, staring at the table, trying to breathe. Mel picked up on it, too, because she said, *Thee, can he hear me?* She was thinking out loud, in my head, and Foley touched her arm, standing up again. He did—I swear Foley heard Mel, speaking, and it was all I could do to sit there, clenching my fists beneath the table.

Have you two been friends a long time? Foley asked me, and I couldn't even find my voice to answer. We were just giving Thea a ride home, Knox said. It's been a difficult week, he said, reaching for Mel's arm and telling Foley to back away from his daughter. I imagine so, yes, Foley said, still looking at me. Well, nice to see you all, I just came in for the coffee. Really, who has better coffee than Silver Top? Good-bye, Melody, Foley said, leaning around her chair again, looking her in the eye. Such a pleasure to meet you. Theadora, he said, and then he stepped away, taking all the oxygen in my lungs with him.

Neither one of us said anything, Knox or me, and then Mel goes, *Who the hell was that?* Long story, I said, and then she convulsed, her whole body. We thought the same thing, Knox and I, and then she goes, *Disgusting*, like practically hissing. I started laughing, and then, I lost it. Because Foley is so disgusting, and I almost fell out of the booth, I started laughing so hard. And then Melody said, *Is that the one, Dad? Is that the guy?* Without even thinking, I raised my right hand, speaking for her, and I said, Is that the one, Dad? Is that the guy? And then I realized what I'd done, talking loud enough for anyone to hear. Automatically, I turned to see if Foley had heard, and he was sitting there, at the counter, looking at us. The way he was looking at us, if I didn't know any better, I'd think he knew exactly what was going on. Shall we, ladies? Knox said, squeezing out of the booth, taking out his wallet.

No one really had anything to say the whole way back to my house. We took the back road, because it was quieter, and I could still slip in and out of my building easier. When Knox pulled over, I started to get out, and then I stopped. I need to tell you something, I said, and Knox sighed a sigh I'd never heard, like an *I'm not getting out of this, am I?* sigh. So I just came out with it: Foley has my medical records, I said. How do you know? Knox said, frowning. I just know he does, I said, and Knox shook his head and he goes, Are you sick? I couldn't help smiling, and I said, Sometimes. My stomach was all twisted, so I just spit it out:

I was in a hospital for a few months. Psych ward, I said, and all I could think was, *He's never going to let me see Mel again; he's never going to believe me . . .* But Knox didn't say anything for a minute.

What happened? he said, and I smiled, remembering Cam say that. Me, I said, I happened. I have a problem sometimes, I said, and it was so hard, saying it, but I did. I go, I cut myself—not anymore, but I used to. And for a while, I couldn't stop. I know he knows. Foley knows, I said. And I know he's going to use it somehow, so I want you to know. I go, Knox, I've never lied to you, ever. But tell me, how did you, how did your family? he said, trying to figure out how it all went down. I didn't want to tell him anything, but after everything that's happened, I don't have any more room for any more secrets, you know? So I told him, straight out.

One afternoon, I was in the bathroom, and I cut too deep, and I felt blood on my leg, and I had to turn and look, because I was afraid I'd get blood on the floor. And when I saw it, I fainted. Wait, you fainted from cutting too deep? he said, looking confused. No, I fainted because I can't stand the sight of blood, I said, and he goes, Thea, you're telling me you're a cutter, but you can't stand the sight of blood? I said, Stranger things have happened, and he looked at me like he didn't know what to say to that. I go, I can't watch horror movies, I can't watch blood being taken at the doctor's office without feeling faint. I'm not kidding, if there's blood in my dream, like even if I have a dream with blood in it, I'll pass out—in my dream. Then I'll wake up, I said, and Knox covered his eyes with all his fingers, letting out this slow sigh, like, just when he thought he'd heard it all.

So what happened? he said, leaning back, exhaling. My mom came home and found me like that before I came to. She must've been right at the door, and I didn't hear her coming in, and then she called an ambulance, and then there was nothing I could do. He didn't say anything, and I was trying so hard to brace myself for whatever was about to happen next, like, if he was going to tell me I wasn't allowed to see Mel anymore—I don't know what—but he didn't. He sighed once more, but more like a huff, then he reached over and grabbed my hand and squeezed it, and he said the nicest thing he'd ever said to me before. Knox said: I'm sorry, Thea. I'm so sorry.

## MONDAY, NOVEMBER 22, 2010
## (FIVE MONTHS EARLIER)

Looking at him, sitting across from me, his eyes, I grabbed his hands, and I had this urge to put them in my mouth, eat him whole, when Cam pulled me forward by the wrists, and he said, That reminds me. I know it's a little late, but my mom wanted me to ask if you and your mom and Ray would like to join us for Thanksgiving dinner? Mom'll take care of everything, he said, and I pulled away, saying, You know . . . that's so sweet, really, but I don't think so. I shook my head no, smiling, very sweet, but no, and Cam goes, Why not? You guys have plans? And I go, Yeah, see, the thing is, we don't celebrate Thanksgiving in my family: it's against out religion. Thea, seriously, he said, my mom's so excited, and she wants to meet Renee—. I go, Cam, I don't think it's a good idea, and he goes, Why not? I go, For lots of reasons, and he goes, Name one, and I go, Your mom's educated, for one thing.

He leaned back, against the booth, and he goes, Please. Your mom is educated, I go, No, not anymore. Not since she met Rain Man. Sixteen years of education: gone, in a single loser, and Cam gave me this look like I was overreacting or being too harsh or whatever, and I said, Look, your mom went to Berkeley. She studied film. She's traveled. She's sophisticated. My mom looks forward to *Grey's Anatomy* reruns at nine o'clock. And Ray, do you really think your mom would have anything to talk about with Ray? He goes, Listen. She's not inviting Raymond for Raymond, and it's one meal, and my mom wants you there. It'd be rude not to accept her invitation, and you know it. I said, Cam, I see what you're saying, but what I'm saying is, it's actually a sign of great respect that I'm trying to get out of this meal. Two o'clock, he said, telling me, not asking me.

Cam goes, Listen. You know what makes this the best Thanksgiving ever? You know what I'm most grateful for this year, Thee? And of course I thought he was talking about us, or more specifically, *me*, about having me in his life, right—he so set me up, too. So I smiled and I go, No, tell me, Cam. What makes this the best Thanksgiving ever and what are you most grateful for? Then he lets out this big, heavy sigh and he goes, Well. What I'm most grateful for is that the LHC and the ATLAS detector have started up, right now, as we speak, he said, tapping his finger on the table. At this very moment, Thee, they're collecting data that will expand the boundary of all knowledge way beyond our current understanding. Do you *know* what this means for the Standard Model of Particle Physics? I think my face fell, I really do, because I looked at him, then he reached over to grab my hand

and he goes, And I'm grateful for you, of course, he said, and I pulled my hand away, like don't even touch me right now. On cue, Sharon walked up. How you kids doing over here? she asked, and Cam goes: Peachy, Sharon. We were just making Thanksgiving plans, is all, and I just looked away, thinking, *Great.*

So, as if it wasn't stressful enough, of course we got in a fight in the car on the way over. Big surprise, right? But I have to say, you'd think Raymond would've learned by now, except for the fact that he hasn't learned a damn thing about me. I mean, we're halfway to Cam's house, and I had nothing to say to either one of them, and then Ray looked at me in the rearview and he said, Did you talk to your dad today, Theadorie? I go, *No.* Why would I, Raymond? I asked, looking at him in the rearview, and he goes, You're a little hard on him, don't you think? I said, No. I don't think so, Raymond. And I don't think it's any of your business. Raymond, my mom said, reaching across the seat; Thea, she said, turning back, like she was calling a truce, but I just rolled my eyes at her, and looked out my window, and no one said anything else the rest of the way.

So we got there, and Karen met us at the door, and Cam came down the hall. He'd just shaved his head again, and he was wearing a black turtleneck sweater and flat-front chinos—he got all dressed up, and Mom goes, *Oh, Cam . . . don't you look hand-some!* I turned to her and I go, Please? Karen put her arm over my shoulders, and then Cam took all our coats before he went to get everyone drinks. It was fine, I guess, but then, once we sat down in the living room, Raymond goes, So what brought you to these parts, Karen? And I wanted to crawl under the table. I excused myself to get something in the kitchen, and Cam followed me. What's wrong? he whispered. So what brings you to these parts, Karen? I repeated, and Cam goes, He's just making conversation, and I said, He sounds inbred, Cam. I told you you'd hear the *Deliverance* banjo when we walked through your door, didn't I? Yes, he said, you did, you're right. But no one's blaming you, babe, he said, poking me in the rib, and I turned away. Come on, chill out, he said, and I go, You know, nothing pisses me off like being told to chill out when I'm not chill, Cam.

Breathe, he said, rubbing both my arms. Or does nothing piss you off like being told to breathe when you look like you're about to explode? I go, I told you this was a bad idea, and he goes, All right. You told me. So, now, here we are in the middle of a bad idea. Let's just get through it, okay? Okay, I said, knowing he was right, that I was just throwing a fit. But I couldn't let it go, either: Store-bought, I said. She said they'd handle the pie. My mom told Karen we'd handle the pie and they got store-bought? Cam goes, Thea. It's not a big deal, but I wouldn't listen. I go, First time we meet your mom and we buy a pie from Priceline? I said, completely humiliated. Of course we got into it in the car, I said, and Cam goes, Because of the pie? No, because Rain Man butted his nose in. Your dad called, Cam said, knowing right away. I go, Oh, no, my dad *texted*: he never calls. Cam goes, Maybe he's afraid—. Yeah, that tends to happen when you're a coward. Seriously, what did deadbeat dads do before texting? Cam grabbed my arms, squeezing, not saying anything.

Finally, he goes, I'm sorry. Me, too, I said. It's like, your dad's been dead for ten years and you're closer to him now than I am to my dad, and he goes, Do me a favor? I said, What's that? He goes, Could you just try to have a little fun today? Just a little, he said, squeezing his thumb and index finger together. Then Karen and my mom walked in, smiling at us, like the two teenagers isolating themselves in the kitchen, silly kids. But still, looking at the two of them, both dressed, trying to make this nice day for us all, what could I do but smile? I turned back to Cam, and I nodded yes, I'll try.

## MONDAY, MAY 30, 2011
## (EIGHT WEEKS LATER)

I saw Karen today. She came over—didn't call, didn't text, she just knocked on our door. I hadn't been over to see her in weeks. Mostly because it was so hard for me to go outside anymore, but also because it made me so sad, seeing her, how much she'd changed, sunken, ashen. Or maybe how much I'd changed, and now there was this tension between us—the reporters, cameras, cops, the FBI, the lawyers, the threats.

Anyhow, she caught me off guard, coming over first thing in the morning. She could tell I was totally surprised to see her, too, because, before I could say anything, she said she had something for me. I asked her if she wanted to come in, and she shook her head no, then she opened her canvas duffel and pulled out this big cardboard envelope, maybe twelve-by-seventeen, big. She handed it to me, and I asked her what it was, and she said they were photos, Cam's photos.

My mouth fell open, and Karen said, Cam never told you, did he? And I said, Probably not, no. So what didn't he tell me this time? I said, and then she told me that Cam always wanted to be a photographer when he was a little boy. She said that he used to take pictures all the time, but his favorite was whenever the three of them, Cam and his mom and dad, would take trips, road trips.

I didn't know what to say, because he'd never told me that. She just looked at me, and I couldn't even believe the bags and dark circles under her eyes—it wasn't Karen I was talking to. But I said no, he'd never said a word and Karen goes, He was shy about telling you, Thea, and I almost flared up for some reason, and she saw it. Believe me or don't, but I'm telling you, Cam admired you and your talent so much, I think he was afraid you'd think less of him, or maybe even be embarrassed in some way if you didn't like his photography, she said, this tiny puff of a laugh escaping her lips, looking at the photos.

I couldn't help smiling when she said that word, afraid. But you know what? That's bullshit. All the times he pushed me to open up, all the things he said about being brave, taking risks, sharing my work, and he didn't even tell me he took pictures of his family? I believed him, too. Everything he told me, I believed every word. And do you have any idea the mess he'd made of my life? I was just like, Karen. Did you see all those people, outside, when you walked in here? Some people think Cam's alive, some people think he's dead. Same difference, the way everyone looks at me. It's become a sick joke: the rumors, the videos, the sex tapes, everything. And guess who has to listen, every day, all day? Me, I said: me.

I didn't say that, but all I could think was how I start and stop letters to him all the time, all day, every day. I kept writing in our sketchbook, drafting e-mails. I typed and erased or I wrote things, crossed them out, scribbled over and over: *Who are you?* That's the one thing that kept coming back, every time I held a pen in my hand. I kept spacing out and snapping back, realizing I'd scribbled *WHO ARE YOU?* a thousand times. Seriously, seems like I didn't know anything about him, really. I mean, maybe I knew the person he showed me, but that's not who he really was, was it? I'm sorry, but the more I learn about him, the more I realize I didn't know Cam at all.

What can I say? One day, I find out my boyfriend was an aspiring photographer, and he never mentioned any of this to me. Karen even said he won some awards for his photography. Imagine how that feels, hearing that my boyfriend won awards for pictures he took, and it's all news to me. I mean, I told him things, things I never told anyone, and he didn't trust me? So when Karen handed me the envelope, she said she wanted me to have it, and I started to look at them, all of Cam's pictures, and then, when I was done, I just handed them back to her.

Why now? I said. Why are you giving these to me now? She goes, Was there a better time? not taking the envelope. I go, Yes. Yes, there was a better time. Like when Cam was here, when he was— I said, and then I had to catch myself. I mean, I didn't say it, but I almost did. I almost said, *When he was alive.* She knew, too. Karen knew exactly what I meant, and she goes, Now, because he'd want you to have them. Even if he didn't tell you, she said. And it hurt, it scared me, like even Karen was giving up on him. I go, If he'd wanted me to have these, he would've shown them to me, himself. Like I did with him, I said, and she started to say something, then she stopped.

It was so awkward for a minute, and then she said, I know you don't understand, and you're hurt that he didn't share these with you, but I think Cam didn't share these with you because he quit taking pictures. I said, Karen, I don't know what to say to that, because he never told me any of this, and the expression on her face wasn't surprise, it was pain. I said, You're surprised, how much he hid from me? No, she said, her head falling to one side. Not really. Boys have a problem sometimes with these things. I go, Life, you mean? She said, That, too, and for some reason, I felt so angry with her. Maybe because she was all I had to be angry with, and I said, That's a bullshit excuse. She goes, Maybe, but the fact is, Cam quit taking pictures after he met you because he said he loved the *idea* of taking pictures, but you loved doing it. He said he loved watching you take pictures more than he'd ever loved taking a single shot, she said, smiling at me like that made it better. She goes, You can hold it against him, but he changed a lot, after he met you, Thea.

I stared at the rug, trying to figure out what to say. When did he quit? I asked, trying to understand, but mostly feeling numb. First week of school, after he met you, she said. No, we didn't meet until the end of the first month of school, I said. I didn't know him the first week. No, but he knew you, she said, turning away, about to open the door, to leave. There was more to it than she was saying, that's all I know. That's how Karen had become since Cam disappeared. Like there was this side of her now, and I didn't really know her anymore. She looked at me for a moment, exhaling through her nose, and then she said, Do what you want with them, Thea, but I know Cam would want you to have them, and then she walked out, closing the door behind her.

I went to my room, and I opened the envelope, pulled them all out, on top of my bed. And they're good—he's really good. There were some great shots that he must have taken on their drive across country, when they moved here. The last picture, though . . . the last picture made my heart stop. It was a picture of me, when my hair was still long, just before I got it cut. I knew exactly when and where it was taken: it was the week before school started, and I'd gotten in a fight with my mom, and I'd gone to the park for the afternoon. I was looking at the sky, because this huge storm was coming in, the whole sky was gray, almost as angry as I was, and I remember—. This is so silly, but I remember thinking, *Bring it*. You can't see my face, just the back of my head, my hair's blowing everywhere, but I know it's me, and Cam was right behind me, watching me, even then.

Karen had a yard sale in late October. Cam and I had been going out for a month or so, I guess, but that was the first time I ever met Cam's mom. Cam said she had some things she thought I might want, and that she wanted to meet me, and I didn't know what to say, really. But his mom was having a yard sale, and a lot of it was junk, Cam said, but there was one thing I might want. What's that? I asked. You'll have to come over to meet her and find out, he said. If I meet your mother, I'll get a surprise gift? So you're bribing me, basically, is that right? I asked. Yes. Is that a problem for you? he asked, sitting back in his seat, and I thought about it.

No, not really, I said, taking a sip of my Diet Coke, staring out the window of Silver Top. I mean, of course it was a problem, and my stomach gurgled just thinking about it. She's cool, he said, laughing at my stomach. You'll like her. And she'll love you, he said, smiling. So what's the gift? I asked, trying to sound all nonchalant. Not telling, he said. You can't be bribed, I said. I never said I couldn't be bribed, he said, before looking up, smiling at Sharon, who was bringing our plate of fries. Anything else, hon? Sharon asked. No, thank you, Sharon, I said. She was speaking to me, Cam said. You're welcome, doll, she said, speaking to me, but nodding her head at him, always amused by Cam and his lines. My mom wants you to come over for dinner, Friday, and then we can look through the stuff she's selling before dinner. Okay? he asked, grabbing the red plastic ketchup bottle, giving it a good hard shake. I watched him squeeze it out, thinking it sounded just like my stomach felt, and I nodded yes.

I actually lost sleep over it, too, Thursday night, trying to figure out what to take over, what to wear. Getting ready for dinner that night, my room looked like an explosion had gone off in my closet, leaving clothing shrapnel and shoes everywhere. Saturday, Cam offered to pick me up, but he was helping set up for their yard sale, so I asked my mom. She was in one of her good moods that she gets in when I do something or have one of those coming-of-age moments, and she gets all misty on me. But I'm glad I asked her, and I probably should've invited her in, but she knew. So I got out, and I walked up their walk, and I turned back, and my mom was leaning over the wheel, peeking, and I waved her off, like, *Stop, would you? Go!* She knew what I was saying, too, but she just sat there, waiting for me to knock, waving. I was just like, *Ohmygod, Mom, could you be any more obvious?* I mean, I wasn't really annoyed, I was just nervous.

So I walked up, I took a deep breath, and I knocked on the door. I swear my hand was shaking, knocking, too, and then I heard a woman's voice that had to be Cam's mom, answer, Coming! Then the door opened while I was still trying to swallow. And she was beautiful. That sort of long, curly white-blonde hair. Fine nose, light freckles, tall, thin. And she has this gap between her two front teeth, but Nordic looking. Nothing like me. Kind of intimidating, and nothing like me at all. *Hello!* You must be Thea, she said, opening the screen door. Yes, I said, not sure if I should call her Mrs. Conlon, because you know some mothers don't like that, because it makes them feel old or something; it's complicated. So I didn't call her anything, I just said hi and held up my hand.

Come in, come in, she said, smiling, standing back so I could walk past her. Cam? Thea's here, she called, and then she asked to take my jacket. I had a whole breakdown about what to wear, and I settled on a black dress and flats, and then I saw myself in the hallway mirror and I looked a little Tuesday Addams. That's what my mom called the look, Tuesday Addams, Wednesday Addams's older sister, ha, and I almost lost it with her, too, because I heard it enough at school, you know? Thea, I love your dress, Karen said, and I smiled. She goes, Is it vintage? And I said yes, smiling. Honestly, I wanted to fall on my knees and thank her for saying that, because I'd changed like twenty times, trying to figure out what to wear.

Hey, Cam said, walking down the front hall. You're here, he said. I'm here, I said, trying to smile, but feeling like my lips were doing something strange, pursed, I don't know. Come sit down, Thea, Karen said, turning and then turning back. Oh, do you want me to hang your bag? she asked. No, it's fine, I've got it, thanks, I said, following her into the living room, and Cam following behind. I took a seat at the end of the couch, and I looked around the room, and it was . . . stylish. I didn't see many stylish rooms. Style, period. In magazines, yes. But here, in this town, people chose floral wallpaper and matching drapes and carpeting and American Colonial dining room sets. But this, this was, this was stylin'. I wanted Karen to decorate our place. Except that I never ever wanted her to see our apartment.

Cam, why don't you get her something to drink? she said. What would you like? he asked. Anything, I said, realizing how stupidly agreeable I sounded, and he nodded. Coming right up, he said. I love your house, I said, smiling at Karen, sounding stupid again, wanting to pound my head against the wall first chance I got. Thank you, she said, smiling, still taking me in. I brought you something, I said, remembering why I'd held on to my bag. I didn't have any money to bring anything, and Nanna drilled it into me, you always take something with you when you're invited to someone's house, so I drew her a picture of flowers. I looked up a bunch of things online, and I chose the flowers, just like I would if I actually had the money and we had a posh florist who'd have flowers like those. I didn't have a chance to go to the flower shop, so I drew these instead, I said, suddenly realizing how dumb I sounded.

Cam walked in then, holding two glasses of something with bubbles, and I wanted to run out of the house. Oh, look at that, she said, looking at the picture, really looking at it, and then looking up at me, like she was looking to see if I'd really drawn it, myself, and then looking at the picture again. Thea, this is so much better than real flowers, she said. And I love real flowers, don't get me wrong, but this is just beautiful. Thank you, she said, beaming, showing it to Cam. And then he looked at me, looked at his mom again, and then handed me my drink, smiling.

Cam told me you're *very* talented, she said, smiling, still looking at the picture. Thank you, I said, taking a sip of my drink. Cherry seltzer. Made me burp, but I hid it. Cam, go grab the box, will you? Karen asked, taking the drink from him. Cam stepped out of the room and returned with a big cardboard box, setting it down by me. We saved a few things for you, things Cam said you might want. So take a look, Karen said, please. I peeked inside the box, and I saw right away: it was a Super 8 camera and a box of film, and I pulled it out, no idea what to say.

You like it? Cam said, and I nodded yes, yes! I've *always* wanted a Super 8, I said, totally blown away that she was giving it to me, and Karen smiled. Well, just so you know, there are a couple pieces missing, but I'm sure anyone with an Internet connection could track them down with a little effort, she said, but looking at Cam, not me. If you want to keep it, I said, thinking maybe Cam had been eyeing the camera for himself, but then he shook his head. No, he said, I want you to have it—even if it doesn't work. *Yet,* Karen said, winking at me, before excusing herself, leaving us alone.

Go on: check it out, Cam said, handing me the camera, and I looked through the lens, turning to him, wishing it worked and had film. When's your birthday? he said, and I lowered the camera. June, I said, biting the inside of my lip, and he said, June what? And I said, June 16. Ah-ha, he said, curling his tongue between this teeth. It's your sweet sixteen, right? he said, and I said, Why do you ask? And he shrugged, I don't know, it's just that we don't buy gifts in my family; birthdays, Christmas, you have to make something. So I was thinking maybe I'd fix this for you for your birthday. We'll see, I said, raising my brow, trying to act all cool, but all I could do was stare at my feet, kicking the heel of my Converse against the toe of my other shoe.

What, Cam said, you don't believe me? Fifty bucks—no, make it a hundred—a hundred bucks, he said, making me a bet. I said, A hundred bucks, what? And he said, A hundred bucks says I'll get this thing working and give it back to you for your sixteenth birthday. If you're nice, maybe I'll even throw in a projector, he said, and I couldn't help smiling—couldn't even look at him, that bitter feeling in my cheeks. Still staring at my feet, a voice in my head started screeching, *Please don't make me any promises you can't keep, Cam, because it'd break my heart,* and I think he saw it, too, because then he reached for my hand. He took my left hand in his and he shook my hand, looking me in the eye, shaking on it. Deal? he asked, and I smiled: Deal, I said.

He let go and then he handed the camera back to me, Hold that for a sec, will you? he said, getting up and heading for the kitchen, and I got up to follow. Standing there, in the doorway, watching them together, I knew I'd always remember the day I met Karen for the first time, looking at the two of them through the lens of a Super 8 camera.

## WEDNESDAY, JUNE 1, 2011
## (EIGHT WEEKS LATER)

The lawyers came over to tell us there was some film company making a made-for-TV movie about my life. I guess they're saying it was based on a true story, and they weren't saying it was me, but it was obvious it was me: *When an upstate New York girl's boyfriend disappears, her life is turned upside down.* That's the description, okay: tell me that's not me. Even better, they sold the deal for more than half a million dollars, and now they're getting some big actress to play the role of this mysterious upstate girl, and when Mom told me that, I couldn't even ask who was going to play the me they weren't saying is me.

Mom said the lawyers said it was happening, whether we liked it or not, and there was only so much they could do, and of course, if I didn't agree to the book deal or anything being offered, like *right now*, I might never get another chance. So, basically, they're telling me my days as a hot commodity were numbered, and I'd have to live with other people making money off my story. I got a headache, sitting at the table, listening to her tell me what the lawyers said. I mean, not a real headache, the pressure, because I can't . . . I can't take it anymore. I can't do this anymore. Seriously, I just wanted to disappear, find an island without any Internet or TV, and never be heard or seen again.

Thea, there are some offers you need to consider, whatever you decide, and I said, No. I want you to go now, speaking to the lawyers. I won't have this conversation without Cam—I'm not talking to anyone without Cam here. She said, Thea, please, baby, you've got to face—. Face what? I said, clenching my jaw, I've got to face what, Mom? She shook her head no, she didn't mean that. But she did—I could see it in her eyes, she was this close—this close to telling me I had to face facts. I knew what she was thinking, and maybe I was in denial. All this time, maybe that's how I've been able to function, because I was in denial about Cam, about the people outside our front door, about being on the nightly news, about becoming the teen porn queen of the Internet. If it hadn't been for denial, I think I would have truly lost my mind. But there still comes a point when you can't avoid it anymore, and you have to ask yourself, What if Cam is dead? And how long—what, three months, six months, a year? How long are you going to wait before accepting that whether he's alive or dead, you have to go on without him? There's no avoiding it, but so far, there was only one answer: Not today. I'm not going on without him today.

I told my mom I needed to think and when I went back to my room, I closed the door, and I could see how bright it was outside, almost eleven o'clock. I had to close the curtains all the time, because people would take pictures through our windows. Crazy, you know? Still, looking out the window, you could just feel how nice and warm it was outside, what a beautiful day it would be to go for a picnic or do something in the park, call Mel and Knox, see if they could pick me up, maybe?

But then I remembered. I couldn't even step outside my front door these days. There were camera crews that actually spent the night in the parking lot, in front of our house, in case I walk outside. People were actually camping in our parking lot, and sometimes I wanted to go out there and ask them, Do you honestly care about this story? Seriously, do you care enough about my life or is this just money to you? Because I didn't think they cared at all. Really, you know how they say people see what they want to see? I'm not really so sure about that. Because the thing is, I haven't seen anything I want to see. And now there was a movie being made, based on a true story, no matter what I do or don't do. All I want to know is, what's the true part?

## SATURDAY, OCTOBER 23, 2010
## (SIX MONTHS EARLIER)

That first time, the first time Cam kissed me, it wasn't really what I'd imagined. What I mean is, it didn't happen the way I thought it would, with us sitting in his front seat or standing at my door, or even standing on the stairwell, in front of the building, where it's dark. That's where I always thought he'd kiss me, when I thought about it, but of course that's not how it happened.

What happened is, on Saturday, when Cam picked me up, I got in, and he asked if I wanted to go for a drive. I said, Sure, where did he want to go? He said, Let's take the back roads and see where we end up, and I couldn't have cared less where we went or what we did. The thing is, I've lived here for three years now, but driving with him, it was like I'd never seen any of those towns or roads or ever been anywhere before. I took my old Nikon, and we talked, but mostly, we drove and watched. I didn't feel stupid that I had nothing to say, I didn't feel like I had to ask him questions about himself or do anything. I could just be there, sitting beside him, and for once, I didn't worry.

So we drove all afternoon, and it was strange, you know? Like those times when, suddenly, you feel so close to your parents again after so many months of not getting along, fighting, bickering, whatever, and then for some reason, you remember how much fun you can have with them, how much you love them? It's just a flash, but there's this moment when you see how badly you treat them sometimes, how much you take them for granted. Driving with Cam that day, that's how I felt about Fort Marshall and all the other towns, and this whole part of the country. It's so beautiful here, and I take so much for granted. All I could ever think about was getting the hell out of this place, and maybe that's not the only direction, you know?

When we got back, it was about six, just getting dark. So we stopped at Silver Top, and when we walked in, Sharon smiled. We'd been there a few times by then, but she could tell it was different. When I walked in, sat down at our booth, I swear there was a halo around me, I was so happy. I ordered a grilled cheese and Cam had a burger, and we just sat there, talking. I don't remember what we were talking about: I just remember the moment I looked up, and two hours had passed. And I had to pee so badly, having had two huge Diet Cokes, because my mouth kept getting dry. So for like an hour, I just crossed my legs and squeezed, because I didn't want to break the spell.

But then, finally, I had to go; I was dying. Actually, Cam was the one who pushed himself off the table, squeezing out, saying,

I'll be right back, heading for the men's room. So then I waited, and we switched off. When I returned to the booth, he said, We should get you home, and I smiled, even though I so didn't want to go home. Then I took out my purse to get money, and Cam said, I already paid, and he stepped back, waiting for me to go first out the door. That's when I finally realized, like, *Wow, is this a date?* This sounds so dumb, but I swear even the old bell, over the door, was happy for me.

The whole way home, I couldn't think of a thing to say, because I kept wondering if he was going to kiss me when we got to my house. And my stomach reminded me of an old neighbor of ours, back in Poughkeepsie, whose cat had a litter. I remember holding one, how this teeny tiny kitten kneaded its paws against my stomach, while I cradled it. I felt like I had that kitten with me, but on the inside, kneading me on the inside, in my intestines, all the way down to my butt. I'm sorry, but it's true, everything kneading and gurgling and nervous.

When we got back to my place, he parked up front, and said, I'll walk you in. You don't need to, I said. No, I want to, he said, so we got out, and he followed me toward the stairs. My mom's home, I said, seeing the lights on in our living room, before we reached the door. You want to sit down for a minute? he asked, nodding at the rail. Sure, I said, because I couldn't invite him inside, with my mom there. So we sat on the second floor, with our legs dangling through the metal railing, watching the cars on the highway. And as ugly as it is, as much as I hate to look at it in the daytime, the highway and the strip mall on the other side, I was thinking there's something so beautiful about red and orange taillights at night. I smiled, so happy to be exactly where I was, and then Cam leaned over and kissed my cheek, smiling back at me. I looked at him, not sure what he was doing, or what I was supposed to do back, after he kissed my cheek, and then he laughed, seeing the look on my face. No rush, he said.

And then I kissed him. I leaned over, and I kissed him. Not, you know, intensely or anything, just . . . light. It wasn't conscious or whatever, that's just how it happened. I mean, I thought it'd last longer, you know. It was sweet, and his lips were so soft and warm and didn't shake, like mine, tense and dry-mouthed. When I leaned back, my stomach gurgled, and it was so embarrassing, because he heard. But the best part of it was, actually, it was over. I kissed him; it was done, and I could quit worrying about it. Then my stomach growled again, even louder, and I crossed my arms over my stomach, Ohmygod, I said. When Cam stopped laughing at me, he ran his finger around my ear, pulling my hair back, then he reached his arm over his head, alley-oop, and pulled my head on his shoulder, holding it there. I took a deep breath, and the smell of his neck made me want to bite him, suck him, give him a hickey—just the most awful burning and fluttering in my stomach, my mouth, my head.

And sure enough, who pulls into the parking lot? Rain Man. Couldn't believe it. I mean, the fact that Ray was there at all, which meant I'd have to deal with him on Sunday morning, and then, just to make matter worse, he'd expect me to introduce him to Cam. Which is the last thing I wanted to do. Gotta go, I said, grabbing the rails with both hands, pulling myself up. Why? Cam said, standing up. My mother's boyfriend is here, I said, and I can't. I'm sorry, I said. No problem, he said. Call me tomorrow?

Sure, I said, smiling. All right, he said, and he leaned over and kissed me, and we were standing far enough back that Raymond couldn't see, and then he touched the side of my face, and left. I stood there, waiting, and I leaned over the rail to see what would happen. Ray had gotten out of his car, and first thing he did was walk over, checking out Cam's car, and then he balked, seeing Cam head for the car, taking out his keys, making it clear it was his car. The best part was when Cam gets to Raymond, and then he breezed by him, not a care in the world. Hey, Cam said, raising his hand, being cool, but looking at Raymond, like, *Dude, mind if I get in my car now?*

Hey, Raymond said, stepping back and pressing the alarm on his car, standing there, waiting for this kid, who obviously wasn't from around here, to acknowledge him. And Cam was perfectly nice, chill about the whole thing. Take it easy, Cam said, shutting the door, and I started laughing, knowing Raymond wanted to ask Cam who he was, but not being able to, because Cam wouldn't give him the opening Raymond needed to ask about the car. Ohmygod, it was so funny, I leaned over the rail, my shoulders shaking. And I thought Cam would leave, drive off, but he didn't. He just sat there, watching me laugh, waiting for Ray to walk upstairs.

Hey, Theadorie, Ray said, reaching the top stair, heading toward me, for our door. Ray, I said. Friend of yours? he asked, looking over his shoulder at the parking lot. But I didn't answer, didn't turn around. I just smiled at Cam, watching him start his car. Bye, I said, mouthing the words, and he held up his hand, pressing it against the inside of the front window. I held up my right hand and spread my fingers wide apart. When I think about the first time we went out, the first time we kissed, what I remember most is watching my hand, steady in the dark.

It was a Monday. For some reason, it was just me and the IV Babies, the Garner twins, standing at the bus stop. It'd been raining all night, and the sky was still gray, and there were all these worms on the road. The twins used to bother me a lot more, but then I thought they were kind of funny, because they'd always freaked Cam out. The first time we saw them we were at the store. Mom called and asked me to pick up some toilet paper on my way home, this list of things we needed, didn't matter. I was with Cam, and as long as we got to spend more time together, I didn't care what she needed me to do. So we were walking around, trying to find the paper products, and we turned the corner, and Cam almost screamed. Not like I scream, but like a guy screams, because the freaky twins were just standing there, in the middle of the aisle, like they'd been waiting for us. Lucy and Lucas, that's their names. They didn't say anything, either. They just stared at us, and I pulled Cam away, turning back down the aisle.

Thee, he said: did you see that? Did you see those kids, the way they were just standing there? Yeah, they ride my bus, I said. Freaky, right? It's that skin, they have that skim-milky-blue skin. They never talk, either. They just stare at you, I said, opening my eyes, staring at him like the twins stare. They remind me of those twins in *The Shining*, he said, shuddering. Remembering that, I couldn't help smiling at them at the bus stop, standing shoulder to shoulder, staring at the worms on the road. When they heard me laugh, they turned and stared, just like always, except I couldn't take it anymore.

Why do you always stare at me? I said, and I waited, but they didn't say anything. Finally, I snapped, Speak! And in unison—in perfect unison, I swear, they go, We know. Their voices had this metallic sound, and I think it was the first time I ever heard their voices, and it was so weird, hearing them, it took me a minute before I understood what they'd just said. You know what? I said. And they go, Lots of things, and I go, Oh, yeah? What things? And they said, Things about that boy, and I knew they were talking about Cam, but I go, What boy? And they go, The boy who's missing. Your friend, they said. We saw him. Right away, I go, *When?* When did you see him? I said, and my heart started pounding so loud, I swear they must have heard. They go, That day. The day he disappeared, they said in metallic unison, and I said, Tell me. What did you see?

They go, We saw him get in his car and drive away, and I

said, How do you know? And they go, We were playing outside. In our yard, they said, and if I hadn't been so upset, I would've been totally freaked that these kids talk entirely in unison, like every word. Still, I go, Did you tell anyone? No, they said. I said, No one? No, they said. Not even your Mom? I said, and they repeated: No one. Good, I said, don't. Ever. It's not safe, you understand? Yes, they said in unison, staring me right in the eye. I said, Did he come back? They shook their heads, and I go, Are you *sure*? And they said, Yes, and I said, How can you be sure? And they go, Because we don't like him. He drove off, and then the car came back, they said. Wait, you saw him drive back? I said, and they go, No, just the car, not the boy.

My stomach was in my throat, thinking maybe Cam came back to tell me something, like Foley said, or maybe he was coming to warn me. When? I said. When did the car come back? Later, they said, and I was like, An hour, two hours? No, in the night, they said, and I go, Don't lie to me, and they both raised their voices: It's true! We woke up, and we saw his car, and he got out of the car, but then another car came and that boy ran away, they said. I go, What time was it? And they go, Told you: it was late, and I go, What were you doing out of bed? And they go, We had to pee, and I didn't even want to think about that. Okay, but the other car, was it like an SUV? I said, and they said, Yes. An SUV, they said, nodding in unison. Could you see in the windows? I said, and they shook their heads. No, the twins said. It was all black; the windows, too, they said, and then I about screamed, because Mason honked the horn, behind us. I didn't even notice he'd pulled up, right behind me, the whole bus was waiting.

Mason opened the bus's sliding door, and said: Morning, kids! My hands were shaking when I got on the bus, and my hands were still shaking after school. I thought about them all day long, but then, just as I was getting on the bus, I heard a voice calling me, Hey, Thea! Thea! I turned around, and it was Ricky. He never takes the bus. He's had to deal with so much bullying, his mom always drives him to school and picks him up after, but anyhow.

He was out of breath, running to catch me, and I said, Hey, what's up? And right away, he goes, There's something I didn't tell you about my dream. I didn't know what dream, and he said, My seizure, remember what I was telling you? It was a seizure, but it was like waking up in a dream. And in the dream, I was in this empty house somewhere. There was nothing in the house, no furniture, nothing, but all the walls were tagged, everywhere, he said. And as soon as he said that, I got the chills. Then he goes, I didn't tell you that when I stepped back—when I was in that empty house, and I stepped back, looking at all the graffiti on the walls, it was like that art thing, what do you call it? Like when up close it's just dots but you step away and you see what the picture really is? Impressionism, I said, and he said, Yeah, that. When I stepped back, looking at all the 1s and 0s, I could see what it said. It was a word, see, the entire wall was one big word, and I said, What word? Ricky furrowed his brow like it was the craziest thing, and he said, Forever. The wall said, FOREVER. My mouth fell wide open, and I almost screamed when Mason yelled, Yo! Thea, let's get a move on! Because everyone was waiting on me, the whole bus, and I couldn't speak. I said, I, I . . . I've got to go, I'll talk to you later, Ricky. Later, he said, turning, walking away.

By the time I sat down, I'd forgotten all about the IV Babies, what they said about seeing Cam. I just sat there, slumped in my seat, flipping back and forth, looking at all the pages of 1s and 0s he'd drawn, remembering what Cam told me it really said. At first I thought maybe if I took a picture of each page, I could print them all out, assemble them, like Ricky said, see if it was true, but I didn't want to take a chance of piecing it together. I was just so stunned, you know, because all day long, I thought I was going to sit with the twins, ask them more questions on the way home, but they weren't on the bus, after school, and I didn't even think of it until I got off the bus.

When I got home, I walked over to their house, across the street, and they weren't playing outside. Didn't look like anyone was home, either. No lights on, no sound, no car in the driveway. So the next morning, I got up early and walked over, thinking I'd see them, at least. I don't know why, but I just needed to see them, but no one was home. At seven thirty in the morning, too. They were gone. Finally, after school, I walked straight over to their house, instead of going home. They weren't on the bus, and there was no one home. I walked right up to the door, listened. Then I walked around back, looked inside. No one there.

I couldn't deal with going home, either, so I decided to walk to Silver Top, and I called Knox before going inside. What's going on? he said. Will you call the elementary school for me? I said.

Why? It's about the twins, Lucy and Lucas Garner. I haven't seen them in a few days, and no one's at their house, and I want to be sure they're all right. Will you call now, before the office closes? All right, hang on, Knox said, reaching for a pen. Go on, what are their names? he asked. Lucy and Lucas Garner, I said, twins, and probably in the first grade. Call you back, he said, and I walked around the corner of Silver Top, trying to catch my breath while I waited for him.

He called back two minutes later, catching me red-handed. Thea, you told me they'd been gone a few days, and the school secretary said it's only been one day, he said. Listen, Knox, I just—I have a *hunch*, okay? A hunch about what? he said, and I said, A hunch that something's wrong, Knox, and then, totally deadpan, he goes: You *think*? My mouth fell open, because it was so snap! and I didn't know he had it in him. Then he goes, You're a regular Nancy Drew, aren't you? Anyhow, the secretary said the mother called to say they'd be out of town this week.

Did they say why? I asked. Family emergency, that's all I know, he said. Why? And I was just like, *Where do I begin?* Nothing, I said, hanging up. I was standing behind the diner, near the Dumpsters. I don't know why, really. Just that I like to stay away from the road now, because the last thing I needed was to see Foley driving by. I heard the bell of the front door open, and just as I turned, I saw this fresh black tag on the big blue Dumpster, and I froze, because it was my handwriting, and it said, **You're no Che Guevara!** Right away, I knew what it was: it was from a note I'd written in a corner of one of Cam's pages in Hubble. He was going on and on again about his hacking prowess, and then

I doodled, You're no Che Guevara! And here it is, spray-painted on the trash Dumpster. I just reached for Hubble, about to pull it out, find the page, and then I almost jumped out of my skin, hearing footsteps, but it was just Sharon, I could tell. So I walked over, and we almost ran into each other, both turning the corner at the same time.

She said, Thea! I'm so sorry, I didn't mean to scare you, darlin', but I thought I saw you walk by, didn't know what happened to you. Is everything okay? I said, trying to walk forward, get her away from the trash Dumpster. I just wanted to tell you something came for you. In the mail, she said. I said, *For me? What is it?* And she goes, I don't know. It's in a padded envelope. I go, Where is it? I put in the office, she said, heading back inside, so I followed her, and then I realized I'd never been in her office before. All this time, and I'd never been in the kitchen, and it felt . . . it felt sort of like a special privilege or something to be walking straight through the Silver Top kitchen.

In here, Thea, she said, and I walked in. The office was tiny, with fake wood paneling and some kitschy things, but I tried not to look around too much. Here it is, she said, handing me this large yellow padded envelope. It's not marked, I said, studying the postage. I saw that, she said. You want to open here or wait? I don't know, I said, looking at the handwriting, but it wasn't Cam's. Well, then, sit down, she said, nodding at a tiny couch on the opposite side of the office: I'll let you have a little privacy, she said. Thank you, Sharon, I said, trying to smile. Get you something to drink? she asked, opening the door. No, thank you, I said, smiling. She was so kind. Well, then, I'll be out front if you need me, she said.

I sat down on the couch, and I felt the envelope, and it was soft. So soft, too, I was just like, *What could it be? Clothing?* My hands were shaking, but I couldn't wait until I got home, so I tore it open, peeking inside . . . the stars. I couldn't tell what it was at first, and then I turned the envelope upside down, tried to shake it out, but it was stuck. So I reached inside—freaked me out, too, putting my hand in the envelope, like maybe there was something in it that might bite me or something or a white powder in the envelope, like Anthrax or I don't know what. But I reached in and pulled out the padding, inside, whatever it was, and it fell to the ground, just this big white wad. Looked like the rag bag my mom saved for cleaning.

Took me a minute and then I realized what it was—it was the stars from the flag. It was all the stars that somebody cut out of the flag in front of the high school. They were all there, all fifty, and they were perfect, too, not one loose thread. But what really upset me was that I saw them on Cam's ceiling—they were there. That night I stayed over, slept in his room, when I looked up, all fifty stars were on his ceiling—I touched them, with my own hands. I covered my mouth with both hands, because they were right there, last time I was at his house, so how could they be . . . ?

I heard Sharon walking through the kitchen, so I gathered the stars and shoved them back in the envelope. They didn't quite fit, so I put the envelope in my bag, upside down. The funny thing is, I was a little nervous, carrying the stars around, because it's a crime. I thought, *What if someone stops me, finds out I'm carrying the flag's stars? Could I go to jail?* Seriously.

Anyhow, I slipped out, while Sharon was talking on the phone, taking an order, and then I called back, Thank you, bye, and I ran outside, before she could say anything. I waited until I got to the parking lot, and then I called Karen. She didn't answer, though, not at home or her cell, and I stopped, not knowing what to do. When I reached the road, I decided to go over to their house anyway.

## TUESDAY, OCTOBER 19, 2010
## (SIX MONTHS EARLIER)

Cam loved it. I mean, we're talking love at first sight, the day we drove over, after school, seeing his face as he looked up at the sign, the original sign, which was older than my mother, even, and read, Silver Top. It's called Silver Top, he said, in awe, and I had to laugh. The diner's called Silver Top and it has a silver top, he said, stunned. Tricky, huh? I said, walking past him. That's *brilliant*, he said. Brilliant? I said, and he said, No, really, how often is what you see what you get in this world? he asked, beaming, as I opened the door, waving him in: Welcome to Fort Marshall, California boy, I said. He followed me in and I took the booth in the corner, farthest from the old men, who'd stopped talking to stare.

This all right? I asked, taking a seat, the seat with my back turned to the old men, of course. Perfect. This is perfect, Cam said, sliding in, cheeks flushed. Honestly, he was so enamored with its what-you-see-is-what-you-get-Americanness. He bought it, hook, line, and sinker. These places where time stops every day. Look at this: this, this, here, is America, he said, all but pounding his fist on the table. And you've never seen America, before? I asked, trying not to laugh, but not having any luck. Not this one! He goes, Thea, this is the perfect, perfect first-date spot. And then I snapped, This is not a *date*, not even realizing I was bristling, right through my shoulders, too.

Yeah, whatever, he said, looking at the counter and his mouth falling open, seeing the glass pie case. That's right: homemade lemon meringue pie. Every day. Lucky us.

How's it going? he asked, leaning to the side, holding one hand up at the old men, the Elders, and I looked at him like, *What are you doing? No one new waves at the old men.* Trust me, the old men didn't know what to make of it, either; all they could do was stare at the kid, trying to wrap their heads around it. But then, seeing he was genuine, like it or not, they couldn't say he wasn't real in his boyish enthusiasm.

One thing: I just wish she were wearing one of those old uniforms, he said, and I said, Who, Sharon? And he said, Sharon! Yes, that's the one thing I'd change, but nothing else. Not one thing, he said, and the way he looked at me, grinning, I knew he meant more than Silver Top. He meant us, the two of us, together, that moment. Will you just look at this view, he said, turning his head, looking over his shoulder at the motel satellite dish, across the parking lot. He goes, Who needs Paris? And I said, Very funny, and he goes, I'm not kidding, Thea, then he folded his hands on top of the booth. Don't move—don't move!, I said, grabbing my sketchbook, and I started drawing his hands. When I finished, I turned the book around, holding it just above his hands, so he could compare the two, and he looked at me. I couldn't take it, ten, fifteen seconds, okay, but finally, I had to ask: What, already? And he goes, You're amazing, and that's when I blushed. Can I look? he asked, meaning my sketchbook, and I shrugged sure, pushing it toward him.

He looked at every single picture, and I just tried to stare out the window, pretend I didn't care, and then, finally, like twenty minutes later, he sat back, shaking his head, and he goes, You should put these up—you got to put these up—I'll help you set up a Flickr account tonight if you want, and I just looked at him, like, Drr. I said, I know how to set up a Flickr account, okay? Just because I'm not good at geometry doesn't mean I'm a complete moron, and he goes, Then do it! I go, No. I don't want to, or I would have by now, and he goes, You're so good—these drawings are so fucking good, why don't you show them? And I go, Because I don't want to, that's why. He goes, Thea, come on—I'm sorry, but you gotta show your work—you're too good not to, and I said, Excuse me, but I don't have to do anything. It's mine, they're mine, not yours, okay? All of a sudden, I was so angry, and I didn't even know why.

So Cam sat back, and I could see in his eyes he knew he crossed a line. He goes, You're right, nodding in agreement with me. It's yours, your work. But can I ask why you don't show it? If I could draw like that, Thea, and I go, Because. Because this, I said, touching my notebook, folding it up: this is private. This is the one place I have all to myself; it's mine, and it's . . . it's safe. When I'm here, I'm . . . I'm okay. So leave it alone, all right? He goes, I'm sorry, and he started leaning forward, pressing his hands on the tabletop, and for a second I thought he was going to grab my hands or something, and I was just like, *Dude. No moments: I'm not having a moment with you. Let's just get that straight.* Sharon came over to check on us: How you kids doing? she said, and Cam gave her this big old smile and he goes, We're perfect.

You know, it had gotten to where I couldn't go outside, and I couldn't answer my phone, and I couldn't check my e-mail—Mom neither—neither one of us. Our life had become a circus, it really had. We'd become prisoners, and let me tell you, you don't need an island to get lost. Anyhow, we were sitting at the table, eating dinner—I was trying to eat dinner, and mom was drinking—and she brought it up again, saying Dad called. He keeps calling, I guess, but right away, I go, Mom, it's my life, and it's my dad, not yours, okay? She let out this heavy sigh, putting down her glass, then she got up and left the room, and she came right back, carrying a stack of three shoe boxes.

She put them on the table, and she goes, These are for you, and I go, Are they yours? Because if they were from my dad, I wasn't touching them. They were mine, she said, but I've been saving them. Go on, open them, she said. So I pulled the boxes over and took off the lids, and they were full of hundreds of mixed tapes of all these old bands from the eighties and nineties. All these punk bands, new wave, hardcore, and the inserts had been doodled on, designed in markers, all these colors of ink.

I didn't know what to say, it was such a goldmine. She'd never mentioned it to me, either, and I was just like, *Wow, this is so cool!* Then she goes, I wish you could've known him—I don't know, when we were younger. I don't how to explain, really, except that I wish you had known him at his best. I'm sorry you didn't, but you see these? He made half of these for me, and I made the other half for him, she said, but I didn't know what to say. Then Mom smiled and said, You know he was in a band when I met him? I just looked at her, stunned, and she goes, See? You didn't know that, did you? I go, No one ever told me, and before I could ask why not, she said, They were called the Tesla Coils, and then her head fell to the side and she started laughing. *Ewe*, I said, wincing. Yeah, she said, they called themselves synth punks, and I go, Mom. Please, stop.

She goes, They wore matching leather jackets—. I go, Okay, now I'm losing my appetite, but she wouldn't listen, oh, no. She goes, They did this cover of the Stranglers' "Peaches," and I just about swooned, she said. Don't know it, I said, nodding, relieved. Yes, you do: *peaches on beaches*, Thee? And I was just like, *Oh, is that what they're saying?* I thought it was, *bitches on beaches*. She started laughing, and she goes, They wore eyeliner, and I go, Ohmygod: stop, Mom. You have to stop, I said, getting up, about to take my plate with me, and she grabbed my hand, not letting me go. So I sat down again. She goes, But the tapes he made me, that was as close as your dad ever got to writing me poetry, and I go, Mom, are you drunk? She goes, It's called survival, Thea—I'm a survivor. I said, Okay, but that's, that's just *disgusting*. So unless you're offering me a drink, I said, standing again. Oh, sit down, and eat your dinner, young lady, she said, and I sat down, still shivering, *ugh*.

It gets better, or worse, she said, and I was just like, No. I go, No, Mom, please don't, because I knew it was going to be really, really bad, and I said it again, No, and then she said it. The Cod Pieces, that was his other band, she said, and I screeched, *Ew, ew, ew!* It was so gross, you know, like all I could do was shake my hands, it was so gross, and then I blushed, and Ohmygod, no wonder, you know? No wonder I am the way I am: I never had a chance.

Now, she said, and I knew she was going to start in again about me and my dad, and I cut her off. I go, Mom, after all he's done, how can you forgive him? She leaned forward, and grabbed my hand, and she goes, Because I don't see it as a choice. The way I see it, forgiveness isn't a choice, it's a necessity—not for him, for *me*. Because it's the only way I will ever truly be able to get him out of my life, she said, and I knew she was about to talk about me, too, why I needed to forgive him, but fortunately or unfortunately, her cell rang. I go, Saved by the dumbbell, knowing it was Rain Man, and I thought she'd go get her phone, but she just let it ring. Because we were talking, and honestly, I was so grateful she stayed with me, that we came first, that I came first.

I pulled out one of the tapes, ready to make a joke, and then I saw the heart—it was a boy's writing, my dad's. He'd drawn this little red heart with his initials and my mom's initials, and a big arrow through the heart. He used all these different color pens, red, black, purple, blue, and for the songs, the playlist, he wrote out in all these different funky letters, like his own typography, whatever, and the whole playlist was written out: Siouxsie Sioux, Bauhaus, New Order, Love and Rockets, the Cure, the Smiths, Cocteau Twins, Wire—a goldmine. I don't know why it made me tear up, but it did, because . . . because I don't understand why—why my dad . . . I don't understand him or why he did what he did. Really, I don't understand people. And I don't know what's happened to my boyfriend or what the hell's going on and nothing makes sense. For like one moment, one beautiful hour, I loved and I was loved and I believed, heart and soul, and this world was such a good place, and now it was gone.

Just all of it, everything, it's too much, you know? And my dad, fuck—*ugh*, I couldn't stop crying, and my mom came over, and put her arms around me, and hid my face in her stomach, holding me, while she smoothed my hair. Like we used to be. And I cried.

Finally, when I stopped, Mom kissed the top of my head, and then she goes, I've got something else for you. She went to the bathroom, and I heard her unroll some toilet paper, because I needed to blow my nose, but then she went to her room. I didn't know what she was doing, but she goes, Close your eyes, so I did. And she came back in, and she said, Hold out your hands, so I did, and then she put something heavy in them, and she told me to open my eyes. When I did, I saw what it was, but I still asked, What is it? It's a Walkman, she said, shaking her head at me, like, you silly girl, and I said, I know, but—. How else are you going to listen to all these tapes? she said, handing it to me. It was heavier than I thought it would be, and looking at the Walkman's yellow plastic case, the words got caught in my throat. Finally, I said, Mom, I don't . . . I'm sorry, but I don't want to listen to these, and she smiled, Yes, you do—you might not want to forgive him, but I *know* you want to listen to these tapes.

When she said that, I remembered Cam once saying I should forgive him, too. It was after Christmas. We were talking about my dad leaving me another text, and Cam said, Forgive him—not for him, for you. But I nodded no way, and Cam said, Thee, what if I did something? I cut him off: You aren't my dad—you aren't *anything* like him, Cam, and he goes, But what if I did something terrible, would you still love me? I said, Always. I've always loved you, and I always will, and he goes, Promise? And he took my pinkie finger in his and I swung our fingers: Promise, I said. Mom looked at me, waiting to hear what was on my mind, and I just shook my head no, nothing.

I go, Mom, he hadn't even talked to me in a year and he wanted me put away, and she said, Thea, he didn't want you to hurt yourself, and he didn't know what else to do—neither of us did. I said, Oh, *please*: he didn't want me to hurt myself, but he didn't seem to care how bad he hurt me, did he? She couldn't argue with that, but she still found a way. She goes, Thea, I'm sorry to say this, but the truth is, you aren't hurting him half as much as you're hurting yourself by not forgiving. I go, I'm not, Mom, I'm not hurting at all, and she goes, Oh, but you are, baby. You are—just because you can't feel it now doesn't mean a thing. Make your peace. I know it's hard to know how or where to begin, but you got to try, she said, walking over, putting her hand around my head. For you—not for him, for you, she said, and then I hid my face in her stomach again, because I felt so . . . angry.

Thea, try to understand, she said, meaning about my dad, right, but I snapped at her, Mom, that's all I do! All day long, I try to understand! Really, how could she even say that to me? And she goes, I know, I know, I'm sorry. Just listen, then. Try to listen, whenever you don't understand, and I got so annoyed with her all over again for saying that. Then she goes, Make your peace, Thee, and if you can't do that—if you can't make your peace, call a truce, and I go, What if I can't call a truce? And she goes, Baby, you can do anything you put your heart to, then she took my face in her hands and she pulled my chin up and said, I love you. She kissed my forehead, and each of my eyes, and then she went to her room, closing the door, leaving me alone with the Walkman and a box of mixed tapes.

## THURSDAY, OCTOBER 7, 2010
## (SIX MONTHS EARLIER)

The first time it happened, the first time that time stopped, was in the woods. Cam offered to give me a ride home from school, maybe the third time we met after school, and when we got in his car, he was about to turn the ignition, and then he stopped and he looked over and he goes, Can I show you something? He said it wouldn't take long, and we didn't have to stay. Think of it as a field trip, he said, and I go, A field trip? He goes, A surprise, how's that? I started to ask him where we were going, and then I decided it didn't matter, because I wanted to stay with him as long as possible.

And I'm not even into cars, really, but Cam's car is so *bitchin'*, I literally had to bite my tongue to keep from giggling, getting in. Seriously, I was trying to play it off, hard as I could, but I couldn't help myself: I felt so fucking cool. Trust me, that never happens. I mean, when he pulled out of the parking lot, I had the strangest feeling, and I didn't know what it was at first. Sort of like when you feel a swelling in your throat, and you touch your neck thinking, *Am I getting sick?* Except I wasn't getting sick, I was just . . . happy. I didn't care where we were going until we pulled down a dirt road that I knew, heading to this place in the woods. When we got to the end of the road, Cam parked and he goes, I wanted to bring you here, Thea. Right here. Why? I said, looking around, and Cam said, Something I want to show you. Two minutes, he said, seeing the look on my face, because I'm not really into the woods. Two, he said, holding up both fingers. That's all I ask, he said, and then I opened my door, getting out of the car. I followed him down the path, and there was a view of the river.

We walked for about five minutes, and then he stopped, finally. This is it, he said, opening his arms to the view, and I go, This is what you wanted to show me? And he said, I thought you might want to sit and draw for a while. Sit and draw, I repeated, and he goes, I thought you might want to draw something besides men in tights, he said, because I'd been doing all these silly drawings of famous men modeling for American Apparel ads, spoofing, whatever. I said, Why on earth would you think such a thing? He goes, You want to go back? And I shook my head no; We're here now, I said. You want to keep walking? he asked, and I nodded, fine. Is that a yes? he said, and I smiled: Yes, I said.

Just over there, he said, pointing at a clearing, down a hill, and then up a couple hundred yards. Up for it? he asked. Okay, I said, following closer behind him, as we made our way down the hill, grabbing old branches to steady myself. We made it all the way across what must've been a dry riverbed, and just then,

I stepped on a patch of wet leaves, and just as I slipped, there were his hands. You okay? he said, holding on, and his grip was so strong. He's so thin, I never thought about how strong he is. Yeah, I'm fine, thanks, I said, pulling away. But then he didn't let go of my hand, and everything changed in that moment, seeing the way he looked at me.

What I remember most was that I had the craziest thought in my head—even for me, it was crazy. Because I remember thinking, *He loves me. And he's always loved me.* Like I said, crazy, even by my standards. Really, I met this guy a couple weeks ago and didn't know him from Adam, but in that moment, I kept thinking, *How do I know you? Why do I feel like I've met you before?* And I knew I loved him, that I'd always loved him, too. Seriously, for the first time in my life, I thought, *Wow, I am truly nuts, aren't I?* You okay? he asked, and I said, yeah, fine— thanks, pulling away, looking away as quick as I could. He saw it, though—I could tell he'd read it in my eyes. I think that was the first time it ever really occurred to me how many ways there are to be naked in front of someone. I'm fine, I said, almost snapping at him, caught red-handed.

It's there, he said, pointing at an overlook with a couple dry boulders about a hundred feet ahead. All right? Yeah, I'm fine, I said, brushing off my hands, because I didn't what else to do with them. This is it, he said, taking a seat, and I sat down beside him. The rocks were warm; it felt good, as good as I'd imagined, even. So we sat down and stretched out our arms and legs, like we were making snow angels without snow. Sunset angels, I don't know what you'd call them, but they were ours to make. Staring at the sky, I couldn't help imagining the vantage point the trees had, looking down on us, the striped shadows their branches cast.

I have something for you, Cam said, sitting up, scooching himself back a bit, reaching in his bag, pulling out a small box. What is it? I said, sitting up beside him.

Open it and find out, he said, laughing at me, like, drrr. So I opened it, wishing he'd quit staring at me, but so grateful he didn't, and then I took out a tiny box, turning it around to face me. I made it, he said, opening the box, and then he removed a pinhole camera. Thought you might be inspired, he said, but I stared at the camera, not sure what to do. I made it for you, he said, waiting for me to take it, to say something, at least. I don't know what to say, I said, taking it, furrowing my brow. Not because I didn't like it; but because I couldn't remember the last time anyone made anything for me.

Take some pictures for me, and we'll be even, Cam said, and at that moment, I wanted him to take it back. I wanted to tell him, Listen, don't give me anything. It's just something more I couldn't stand to lose. Then he shook his head no, just shook his head, looking at me, like, *You crazy girl, you don't understand anything I'm trying to tell you, do you?* It's a gift, he said. Even if you don't take it, it'll still be a gift. Thank you, I said, unable to take my eyes off it. But even then I knew we'd never be even, no matter how many pictures I took. Really, how many times does someone give you their hand; catch your fall twice in one day? You ready to head home? he asked, bending his knees, leaning forward like he was ready to stand. For the first time, I spoke my mind, I told him the whole truth: No, I said, not yet, and then I took a picture with his camera.

When I look at that picture . . . when I look at his face in the light, I feel Cam's hand that day, reaching for me, catching me. I feel the blood in my cheeks, seeing him hand me a camera he made for me. I feel him seeing me blush, bright red, and knowing exactly why, how uncomfortable I was to be seen, even though there was nowhere else in the world I wanted to be. I feel my heart, despite myself. But most of all, I feel time stop for the first time in my life. Some people don't believe photography is art. Then again, some people don't believe in magic, either. How tragic.

## THURSDAY, JUNE 9, 2011
## (TEN WEEKS LATER)

I was dreaming. I was having one of those dreams where I knew I was dreaming, but I didn't want to stop, and I was with Cam, and we were laughing, and we were in a field, somewhere warm, and everything was blooming and sunshine. . . . Then my mom knocked on my door. She was in a mood, I could tell, because she said, Thea, get dressed and come into the living room, and I rolled over, planning to ignore her, when she goes: *Now.* So I put on some sweats and washed my face, and I could feel people in the living room, with her, but it was quiet. Then, when I walked in, I almost shrieked: it was Foley. Sitting in our living room. The lawyers were there, too.

When I saw him, in our house, on our couch, it was like: Bam! Like I'd run into a brick wall. What do you want? I said, and Foley goes, Hello, Theadora. Please sit down, he said, returning his attention to the computer, resting on our coffee table, in front of him. Just received this one about an hour ago, Theadora, and I wanted your mother and counsel to see. Then Foley played another video of us, but not a sex video—just us. It was grainy, handheld, Super 8. It was right before sunset, and I was standing in the middle of this huge field of purple flowers, it was like purple shag carpeting, so thick, though, it was up to my ankles. And I was just jumping around, dancing around, rolling around in the flowers, being a complete idiot, and it's exactly like I imagined it would be, purple clover, wall-to-horizon, smelling like lavender, only sweeter. Lying on my back, I looked up, at the sky, and the sky's gray, silver gray, like when the sky's charging, that whole scene looked just like I saw it when Cam described it to me. And then it began raining, pouring down, but so warm, I sat up, and my shirt was getting soaked, and I was just screeching, kneeling, trying to stand in a thunderstorm in the middle of Death Valley. It was 100 percent girl, it was hopelessly sweet and adoring, and there was only person who could have shot that video of me, seen that part of me, and that's Cam, and I started shaking my head again.

Even my mom balked, looking at that freaky computer screen of Foley's, trying to figure out how or when I could have been in Death Valley with Cam; how could that be possible? Foley turned to me and said, When were you in Death Valley, Theadora? I said, I've never been to Death Valley. And he said, But that certainly does look like you, and the boy filming it does sound like John Cameron, and the girl who looks like you answers to the name Thea. I said, Foley, how could it be us if we've never been there before? Foley clapped his hands together: Bingo, Theadora!

Bingo! he said, more animated than I've ever seen him. I wanted to puke, it was so gross the way he said that, bingo, I actually felt slimed. That is precisely what I was thinking, Theadora. How could it be you if you've never been there before? Perhaps in another life or another dimension, I said, and completely uncharacteristically, Foley perked up, all excited. Really, what was most upsetting was watching Foley beam at me, welling up, hearing my comment. He was telling me something in his own sick way, letting me hover over some psychic landmine, and he was savoring this moment for all it was worth.

This is what you came for? To show me this? I asked, cocking my chin at his scary black computer. Still seated, Foley practically bounced, clapping one hand on top of the other in his lap, and he said, No. No, thank you for reminding me. The main reason I'm here is that I wanted you to know that we received the results of your blood test, and we're certain it's not your blood, he said, and I said, I told you it wasn't my blood, and Foley smiled. Yes, well. We've actually had your test results for some time, but I didn't want to say anything while we were cross-checking our database, going back quite a few years. What's most perplexing is that the blood found in Cam's trunk matches the blood type of a little girl who died over five years ago in a fire in Southern California that was started by a boy named Jeremy Naas, a twelve-year-old arsonist. Which, statistically, is one of the first signs exhibited by serial killers, he said, leaning back, smug as could be. Jeremy Naz, I said, almost laughing, and Foley said, Naas, Theadora. N-A-A-S. The name is German, or in this case, more likely Norwegian in origin, and you know what it means?

Naas means fiery—purely coincidental, I'm sure, if you believe in coincidences. I said, I believe in coincidences, Foley; it's you I don't believe.

He just stared at me, so I stared back, looking at him, like, are you insane? I said, Foley, what are you talking about? And Foley said, Theadora, I'm very sorry to have to tell you this, but the boy you know as John Cameron Conlon was born Jeremy Naas, and he and his mother, Liv, changed their names ten months ago, when Jeremy was released from prison, after serving five years in a juvenile correction facility for the arson of a warehouse building that resulted in the death of a security guard's four-year-old daughter. Apparently, the guard was a single father, and he had no choice that night but to take his little girl to work with him. No one knew she was sleeping in the man's office, that he'd locked her inside, to be sure she was safe while he did his rounds, Foley said, twirling his thumbs.

No. All I could do was say no, no, no. . . . I don't believe you, I said, no fucking way. Foley goes, The boy you knew as John Conlon was in a serious lockdown facility, believe it or not, Theadora. And I have to say, it couldn't have been easy for such a pretty boy, being in prison, and I cut him off: I don't believe you, I said, not a word. Foley nodded his head, sympathetically, and he said, Maybe not, but doesn't it make you wonder how much you truly know about the boy, Theadora? Then he pulled a file out of his briefcase, this huge manila file, and he opened it, showing crime scene photos of the warehouse, what appeared to be a little girl's body, hidden under a white sheet, and I had to look away, disgusted. No, I said, it doesn't make me wonder. Why should I believe you, anyway? Because I'm here, Theadora, and I have the proof, he said, showing me a picture of Cam, his police photo, headshots. Go on, Foley said, pushing the folder across our coffee table: look for yourself. No, I said, glaring at him, because he was enjoying this. Foley had known all along—he'd been waiting for this moment, telling me, and I felt so, so *violent*, my hands clenched in fists as I was gritting my teeth.

It was so absurd, but Foley just sat there, calmly, watching me, nodding. When I stopped, he goes, Also, Theadora, as I mentioned when we first met, there were two NSA agents on their way to arrest a renowned hacker named Jeremy Naas, alias John Cameron Conlon, when he left your house, here, on the afternoon of April 4, and I said, If that's true, Foley, then why don't you ask the agents where he is? And Foley said, Because they're dead. Both NSA agents are dead, Theadora, he said, and my jaw dropped, *clunk*.

I looked at my mom, the lawyers, none of them could look me in the eye, but I didn't care. I managed to shut my mouth, and then I said, That's not funny—that's not funny at all, and Foley raised his brow, tilting his head to the side. He said, I couldn't agree with you more, Theadora. It's not funny that your boyfriend is missing, and two federal agents are dead. It's not funny when local authorities handling the missing person's investigation, Detective Knox and his colleagues, failed to discover blood in the trunk of John Conlon's car that is not John Conlon's blood, which matches the blood of the girl he inadvertently killed, six years ago. I said, If that's true, about the agents, then why isn't it in the news? Foley nodded, like he was overflowing with compassion, and he goes, We've kept it under wraps—can't have it on the nightly news or going viral on the Internet, can we? Thea, first things, first. If you don't believe me, what I'm telling you about John Conlon, or Cam, as you call him, why don't you ask his mother? Ask Karen Conlon who Jeremy Naas is. Jeremy Naas: N-A-A-S. Ask her, he said, folding his hands.

I thought I was going to be sick. I felt vomit building in my chest, my throat, heading for my mouth, and I turned and ran for the toilet. But I didn't make it, and puke ran down the side of the toilet, the floor. My mom knocked and came in, but I didn't turn around. I rested my head on the toilet seat: Let me be. Please, I said, and I could feel her open her mouth, then she changed her mind and quietly close the door, leaving me alone.

I waited in the bathroom until Foley and the lawyers left. Then I brushed my teeth and told my mom I was going out for some air—I think she knew, because she offered to give me a ride, and I said no. I slipped out the back, and when I got there, Karen was in the backyard, weeding, and I set down my bike, knocking on the gate. Thea! Well, hello, stranger! Come in, she said, taking off her gloves and giving me a kiss. You look like you've seen a ghost, she said, and I said, I need to talk to you about something. All right. Can I get you something to drink, Thee? she asked, opening the porch door, while I followed her inside. No, thank you, I said, having a hard time speaking. Please, sit down, she said, looking a the porch swing. Give me just a second to wash my hands and I'll be right with you. Sure you don't want some tea, something?

No, thank you, I said. Well, then, she said, sighing and smiling, walking back out on the porch. She looked tired, pale. What is it? she asked, smiling, sitting down beside me and grabbing my hands. Who is Jeremy Naas? I asked, practically pouncing. It hit her like a slap across the face, and she goes, Who told you that name? I go, Is it true, Karen? Is it true? I said, waiting, and until the very last second, I prayed she would deny it. But then she didn't say anything, and I kept waiting. I said, Tell me it's not true, Karen, please, and she almost stuttered, swallowing, and then she almost stuttered, swallowing, and then she said, I am so sorry.

I walked right past her, opened the screen door, and stormed down the hall, throwing Cam's bedroom door open, staring at the ceiling—they were gone. The stars were gone, and Karen stood in the kitchen, her mouth wide open. Neat trick, I said, practically hissing, walking back outside, no idea what I was even doing. Karen closed the door behind her and then held up both hands, patting the air, telling me to calm down, and she said, Thea, what are you talking about? Now slow down, and talk to me, she said, and I said, *Talk to you?* How am I supposed to talk to you when, when I don't . . . I don't even know who you are? And she goes, I know how it must seem, and that was it: I snapped.

I go, You lied to me? All this time, you've been lying to me? She goes, Please, let me explain. I said no and she goes, Thea—he wanted to tell you. And I go, Not enough to tell me—and you—you! Everything I've been through, and you knew all along? She goes, He was afraid—we were both afraid, but then he met you

THURSDAY, JUNE 9, 2011

and he didn't want you to know. I said, Tell me the truth. You could at least have had the decency to tell me the truth. What did he do? What did Cam do? Tell me, I said, and she goes, He started a fire—yes, he was very young, and he knew what he was doing, but he had no idea that . . . It was an accident, she said, looking down, and then I knew. She died, I said. And she nodded. I said, It's true, then, that a little girl died in that fire? She nodded yes, again, and I reached for my bag and I took out my phone and I texted him, sitting on the swing with Karen, reading my text out loud as I typed: You *lied* to me. You're a fucking liar!

I grabbed my bag, got up, and ran for the door—I bolted, Karen calling after me, Thea, please wait? I couldn't get the door open, because it's a little sticky, and because my hands were shaking so badly. Karen walked up, behind me and she said, Thea, I am so sorry, and I turned around and I looked at her, and I said, Sorry? You're sorry? How can you be sorry when I don't even know your real name, Karen? And then I walked out.

I got on my bike, and I knew exactly where I was going: the grocery store. To buy razors. And then the gas station, on my way home. To use their bathroom. I wanted it out, I wanted the pressure out, I had to get it out, and I didn't even realize I was talking to him, until I heard my own voice say, Motherfucker, you motherfucker! No more—you lie to me, I'll lie to you! And then my foot slipped, and I almost fell. I banged my shin on the pedal so hard, I had to get off, pull my bike over, off the street, then I just threw it down, on somebody's yard, kneeling down on the sidewalk, and I bawled. Heaving, shaking, on my knees, the sobs couldn't even find their way out. An old man wearing suspenders and a madras shirt stopped watering his lawn, watching me, not knowing what to do, and I didn't care. I didn't care about any of it. Really, the one, the one person . . . Jesus Christ, the love of my life, that's what I thought he was, and it was all a lie.

I lay there, on the ground, for I don't know how long, but almost until sunset. And then I sat up, balancing on my elbow, looking around, and then I saw something, icing on the cake. Just down the sidewalk, about five feet away from where I was sitting, they'd just poured new cement in the sidewalk; it was fresh, and someone had written—not my writing, some little kid, someone who must have seen it on TV, they wrote TD + CC = TLA in a big heart with an arrow shooting through it. Looking at it, I grabbed my left shoulder, where my tattoo had been, and part of me wanted it back to keep. But another part of me wanted it back just so I could cut it out. I looked around in the grass, trying to find a stick, and I did, then I crossed it out. I had to really scrape, because it was almost dry, and I don't know why, really, but I drew an anarchy symbol over the heart, and then I picked my bike up. Go to hell, I said.

We were watching something on TV. I don't remember what. I didn't even care. I was sitting at the end of the couch, with my sketchbook open, remembering the moment I felt him standing there, behind me. I was thinking about the moment I felt him standing over me, watching me draw. I was thinking how odd it was that someone was standing over me, and I couldn't imagine who, but I didn't feel scared, either—no, I felt . . . I felt like he knew me. Like instead of waking into a dream, where you know everything that's going on, but you don't know how? For the first time, I felt like that, but waking into my own life, you know? Weird.

Honestly, it felt more like I'd been waiting for him all this time, so long I couldn't remember when, and then, at that moment, when I finally looked up: seeing his face, his eyes. I swear, he is the most beautiful boy I have ever seen—like how can a boy be that beautiful? Thea? Mom said, and she startled me. Like she'd been saying my name, but I didn't hear her. Maybe she had. *What?* I snapped, then Rain Man goes, You're smiling. He wasn't teasing me, really, more like he'd never seen me smile before. Still, I go, *Shut up*, closing my sketchbook. Ray goes, What did I say? That's when I knew my mom knew something was up. Not just because I'd been sitting there, staring at the television with some goofy smile on my face, but because she didn't scold me or use that stern voice she puts on, when she's saying, Don't push your luck, kid. I think she knew I was thinking about a boy, and I think she was happy.

Just as I was leaving the room, we heard something, the strangest sound coming from my bedroom. Leave it to Ray to open his big mouth and insert his big foot again: What's that? he said, looking around the room. I go, My phone, even though my back was turned, and Mom goes, It's Thea's phone, and I couldn't see her, but I could tell she was giving him the eye: *Tell you later.* I didn't even care what look she was giving him at that moment. It was all I could do not to sprint into my bedroom. I have a text, *I have a text*, I thought, closing my doors, rattling my fists to silence the squeal in my throat. And only then, shoving my hand in my bag, fishing for my phone, did it occur to me: *What if it's not him?*

My heart stopped for a second, then it started again: because I knew. Of course it's him: ha! I blew on my knuckles: ha, and I wiped them against my chest, and then I wiped my hand against my tights, because my palms were sweaty. I don't know where the words came from, but all I could think was, *Finally! It's beginning—my life's finally beginning!*

## THURSDAY, JUNE 9, 2011
## (TEN WEEKS LATER)

7:02 PM

I made it to the end of the block, and then I stopped and hid behind empty trash and recycling cans, thinking I was going to be sick. I expected . . . I expected Karen to tell me it was insane, it was a lie, both. She didn't. Because it wasn't—it was insane, but it wasn't a lie, and I got dizzy for a second, had to bend forward, taking deep breaths before I could stand again.

I didn't know where to go, and I couldn't go home, I just couldn't. So I started walking to Silver Top, and halfway there, I got a text. From Jenna Darnell. She said she had something she very much wanted to show me, alone; it would only take a minute. I told her to meet me in ten minutes. I didn't even care anymore: What, another sex tape? Another fantasy? Another dream for the whole world to see? I couldn't feel anything, my whole body was buzzing, inside, outside. Seemed as good a time as any to see whatever it was, this breaking news.

She came alone. She had one of her news suits on, camera-ready. The Elders stopped talking, soon as she walked in, and she said hello. I don't know if they greeted her or what, but she didn't waste any time, either, sliding into the bench. We're running a story tonight, and I wanted you to see it first, she said, pulling out her computer, pressing a key. The bus depot, the school bus garage—every bus in our entire school district was tagged. Every single bus in the fleet was tagged, she said, showing me individual photos that she took or one of her camera guys took. It looked like gibberish, if you just read a few of the words on each different bus. But it looked familiar, too, even though I couldn't put it together right away. Not yet, she said, watching the buses pull out, fall into formation. Still nothing, just a dozen buses with white big black tags, a few letters, exclamation points, and then she pressed another key. I was getting impatient, like, whatever. Wait, she said. Now look here, she said, pulling up video from the camera in front of the high school. This was just this morning, she said, and then she hit play, so you see all the buses pulling in front of the high school, weaving in and out, and then, snap! She hit pause. And you could read the billboard the twelve buses made. You could read the gibberish, now that they were all lined up, it was a page from Hubble. Each bus had a few words, but together, in tableaux, you could read an entire paragraph from our notebook, what I wrote to Cam.

It was my handwriting, it was exactly what I wrote him the day my dad showed up at our house: *I wish you could see my face now. Every day, I wish you could feel what I feel, even though I know you can't. And you couldn't yesterday, or the day before that, or last week, and chances are, you won't feel what I feel tomorrow or the next day, either. But I still can't stop wishing that you could. So what is it, chemical? Really, is hope just another chemical? I don't know, I really don't. Whatever.*

I didn't say a word. I just stared, biting the inside of my cheek as hard as I could without showing it. It's almost as though it was torn from a girl's diary, Jenna said. No, I said, and she looked at me. You don't think so? she asked, and I said, No. Meaning no comment. I'm not supposed to talk to reporters, I said, doctor's and lawyer's orders. She looked away, scratching her temple, seeing her plan didn't work. She nodded, sliding out of the booth, grabbing her computer. Well, I'll e-mail you a copy of the still, if you like. I wanted it, and then, on second thought, I said, That's not necessary, but thanks. She smiled, All right, then. Good to see you, Thea. You, too, Ms. Darnell, I said, and I looked away. I waited until the bell over the front door rang, and then I slid across the booth and rested my head against the front window. I ducked down, so the Elders wouldn't see me crying, while hoping, if Cam was out there, he could see me now, and I closed my eyes, thinking, *Nice trick. I'm touched, really. And I know you're out there, watching me. But the thing is, how do I trust you if I don't even know who you really are? The person I loved, he never really existed, did he?*

I felt so betrayed. I can't even put it into words, how that felt, and a moment later, Sharon left something on the table, and I saw she'd brought me napkins to dry my face. I nodded my thank-you, and I didn't feel sick anymore, and I didn't feel sad or scared or angry or anything. I'm sure it was shock, but still, I almost laughed. After all, the joke was on me, because in the end, turns out, I thought right: I just made him up in my head.

I hate American Apparel. Okay, I'll shop there, but I hate their ads. Seriously, if I have to see another chick, bent over with her ass spread . . . And it's always chicks, too. You never see a guy with his butt or his legs spread at the camera. Which was why I'd been working on a series, swapping men for the girls. I had an entire folder of American Apparel ads and Xeroxes of famous men I'd been working with. Some of them were pretty good, actually. Bill Clinton, that was good. But George Bush and Dick Cheney in matching micromesh bodysuits were probably my favorites. And if nothing else, it made social studies a little more interesting.

I was working on a new ad, when I realized there was someone standing over my shoulder, staring at my drawing. And I remember . . . I remember the exact moment I stopped drawing and I looked up at him, and then he stood straight, stepping back, realizing his bad manners, staring over my shoulder. It's so stupid, but I remember the moment the image of his face clicked in my brain, like the picture was taken, and I realized he was, quite possibly, the most beautiful boy I had ever seen. And for some reason, I wasn't at all surprised to find him there. I'm sorry, I didn't mean to stare, he said. Yes, you did, I said. You're right, he said, but I didn't mean to be rude. Despite leaning over my shoulder, staring at my notebook, I said. Well, there's staring, and there's staring—. Yes, and you were staring, I said, looking at him, like, come on. That's what I'm trying to say. Exactly. And who knew? he said, tilting his head, taking one last peek at my drawing: Really, who knew Stephen Hawking was so flexible?

That was it: that was the moment. I thought I'd find a way to discount him, to write him off, dislike him, maybe even loathe him and his beauty, but then it hit. It doesn't happen but once in a blue moon anymore, but still. You know there's an operation they can do to cut your blush out? Snip, snip: no more blushing. Me, it'd take more teams of surgeons than those conjoined twins, because they'd have to start disconnecting me at my hipbones. Maybe even my kneecaps. And at that moment, I felt it coming, blood like a tsunami ocean. He took a seat at the same moment I stood from the table: I need to get a drink of water, I said. No problem. I'll be here, he said, putting his bag up on the table. Great, I said, and then, thankfully, he couldn't see me wincing at my stupid comeback: *great*? How fortunate that I was carrying my notebook, too, because otherwise, I would've held up my hands at myself: *What was that?* Great, I said, walking into the hall. That's just great, Thea. . . .

## THURSDAY, JUNE 16, 2011
## (ELEVEN WEEKS LATER)

4:45 PM

We kept it quiet. For like three weeks, I didn't see her, didn't ask about her—I didn't even want to *think* about Mel for fear that somehow, some way, someone would find out. That one day I'd get some text or I'd go home and find a video on YouTube and Knox would never let me see her again. No way: it was *our* birthday, so we kept it to ourselves for almost an entire month.

So when Mom asked me what I wanted for my birthday, I told her I wanted to be left alone. I didn't want any lawyers, I didn't want any videos, I didn't want any reporters or awful phone calls or e-mails or missing boyfriends. I asked if we could have dinner the next night, and if I could just have the apartment to myself for a night? I told her I didn't want her to buy me anything, I just wanted some space. It was mean of me—I don't even know why I was being so mean to her, but I couldn't stop, either.

Anyhow, we made a plan. I offered to stay with Melody for

a couple hours in between the time Knox had to go to work and Heather came home, and since it was our birthday, he talked Heather into letting me spend a few hours with her, alone. When I got there, we waited until he left, and then I called a cab. I'd never called a cab before, but I told them I had a friend in a chair, and they sent one of those little vans and even had a lift. I guess for all the old people in town.

After I hung up, I got the strangest feeling. Well, probably because I knew we were going to get in trouble, but I'd been hauling my bag around all day. So, right before the cab came, I put it down and pulled out Hubble, and I said, Mel, do you think I could leave this here? She shot me this look, and she said, *Are you sure?* It was strange, I know, because I've never let our notebook out of my sight, but I just had this feeling I shouldn't carry it around the mall with me.

*Hide it under my mattress*, Mel said, and I said, You sure? Then she got the strange feeling, too, I could tell, because she changed her tune and said, *Positive. Leave it here. What safer place could there be in this town than my bed?* she said, and I just nodded, I'm not touching that. She goes, *No, seriously, no one will ever find it if you hide it between the bottom mattress and the bedspring*, she said. So I folded back her mattress, and I placed Hubble just under where her pillows were, then covered it back up, making sure her bed was perfectly tidy before we headed back out.

The cabdriver got out to open the doors for us, and when we got in the cab, we just started giggling, Melody and I. She goes, *We're going to get in so much trouble*, and I go, I know. Isn't this great? Then I turned off my phone. I told the driver, I said, It's our birthday, and he looked at me in the rearview, and he goes, Yeah? You two sisters? And I go, *Twins*—Mel said it at the same time, and I go, Jinx! And she said it, too, same exact time. Like I said, grinning, I was so happy. She made the guy nervous, Melody did, I could tell. Which is good, because he ignored us the whole way. I had to ask her again, I go, Are you sure about this? And she goes, *I'm sure*, and I used the money she had in her piggy bank, like she told me to, but I saved her a surprise.

I waited until we got there, and then I saw this bench that was free, so I wheeled her there, and she goes, *What are we doing?* And I go, I got you something, and she goes, *No! Thee, no—I thought this was our gift*, she said, meaning our trip to the mall, right? I go, It is, but I got you a little something, and I pulled her gift out of my bag. It was small, soft, wrapped. I made the wrapping paper—I drew a picture of her on Kraft paper and I showed it to her. *Thee*, she whined, because she felt bad, and I go, You want me to open it or not? She just grinned at me, and then she goes, *Open it!* So I undid the piece of tape at the back, saving her drawing, and I opened her gift and showed it to her, holding it up.

She goes, *Ohmygod. Oh. My God.* I go, You like it? It's vintage, and I looked at it, holding it up. Took me eight days of hand-to-hand combat bidding on eBay, but I got her an original Meat Is Murder T-shirt. I even kept the envelope it was mailed in, I said, it came all the way from Manchester. She goes. *No!* I go, It's true. I'll show you, and she goes, *I can't believe it!* I go, You want to wear it? And she goes, *Yes, yes!* I go, Over your shirt? And she goes, *No, I hate this shirt! Burn it!*

So I took her to the bathroom and we changed her clothes, and I didn't burn it, but I threw her shirt in the trash—I did—she told me to. Then Mel goes, *I'm ready—let's do this.* I couldn't help laughing, but I go, Let's, and we went back to the mall, and she goes, *Thee?* I stopped and bent over her, looking at her upside down, and she goes, *I didn't get you anything*, and she felt so bad. I go, *You did, too—you got me my best friend forever*, and then I leaned forward, giving her butterfly kisses. Then she goes, *Ohmygod, Thea, that was so sweet, I think I gagged.* All right, enough. Let's do this already, I said, ignoring her, pushing her toward the front doors.

When we got into the mall, the center of the ring, Mel freaked out. Just total sensory overload, you know, and she clenched her jaw, and she goes, *Thee, people are staring at me.* I go, Don't flatter yourself: they're staring at me, and Mel goes, *You know, you're very funny for a sixteen-year-old girl*, and then it hit me. I was just like, *Wow, I'm sixteen.* I go, Mel, we're sixteen, can you believe it? And she squealed, *I know!* Gave me the chills. I go, Seriously, it's not you, it's your shirt: they don't get many vegetarians in this neck of the woods, Mel, and she started laughing. People were gawking, it's true, but I was just like, What's your problem? She's in a wheelchair and you've got a fat ass, so what? Then, out of nowhere, Mel goes, *Woo hoo! Sixteen in leather boots!* I almost fell on the ground, laughing. I can't even remember the last time I laughed like that. Honestly.

Anyhow, we looked at the mall map, and I cruised her around to the three places, and she chose the one she liked, then we went in and waited our turn. When the stylist came over, the one handed our appointment, she had jet-black hair—sort of like that guy from Flock of Seagulls, except one side of her head was shaved and she had a nose ring, and seeing, like, eight piercings in the ear on the shaved side of her head, I was just like, I've done some really crazy things, but I don't think I could ever do that, but Mel goes, *She's perfect.*

So the girl, the stylist, whatever, comes over and she looks at Mel, saying, Hello! All singsong like people do when they see this poor girl in a wheelchair, right? I mean, I know they don't mean to condescend, but it annoys me. I go, My sister wants her hair cut in a bob, and she leaned over, smiling at Mel, and she goes, What kind of bob? I go, Like Siouxsie Sioux, and the girl goes, "Spellbound"? And I go: Snap! And Mel goes, *Told you.* I go, You ready? And Mel goes—smart-ass, Mel goes, *I was born ready.* So I wheeled her over to the girl's chair, and the woman unfolded a cape, then she wrapped it around Mel's neck. I told her we could skip the wash, because it would be too hard in the wheelchair, so after the girl wet down Mel's hair, I took Mel's hand and squeezed, watching the stylist make the first cut, five inches of hair, falling to the floor.

It took forever with the blowout, but when she finished, I was just like, Ohmygod, Mel, look at you! She looked so incredible, I was just, like, speechless. Looking at herself in the mirror, Mel goes, *I can't believe it's me,* and I go, It's you—it's the new you. And she goes, *Thee, for the first time, I feel sixteen, not six!* You look so gorgeous, I told her, and she said, *Thee, we aren't done yet.* And I said, Makeup? And she said, *Yes. But first, I want my ears pierced*, and I go, Mel, no—. And she goes, *Thea, I'm not a child—you told me your mom let you get yours pierced when you were eight!* And I go, I know, Mel, but, and she goes, *It's my birthday, and I have a right to choose, don't I?*

So I took her to the piercing place at the end of the mall. It was a shop that sold earrings, and the woman had a piercing station at the back. When she saw us, of course she assumed it was for me, and I go, No, it's for her, and before she could say anything, I took out the money to pay her. I mean, the place was dead, she couldn't say no, really. So she sterilized Mel's ears with alcohol, and I go, You're so brave, and held her hand while the lady put the gun to her ear—I think it hurt me more than it hurt her when he shot the stud through her lobe, and her entire body spasmed. She goes: *Fine, I'm fine*, and I was like, Oh, shit, Mel, you sure? And she goes—get this—she goes, *Thee, don't worry, I have a very high pain threshold.* And then she started singing, *I am the daughter and the heir. . . .*

An hour later, Melody had a new hair cut, pierced ears, and professional makeup. I don't know why the mall makeup artists always plaster it on, but anyhow. I took pictures, showing her on my phone, and then Mel goes, *Ohmygod, I look so retarded!* And I said, You look like me, and she said, *I repeat*, and I said, Hey, hey, it's my birthday: be nice, and she said, *I know. Sorry, now I'm acting like you.* I put my phone away, rolling my eyes at her, and she goes, *It's just that I can't focus my face, I can't—*, but I cut her off. I said, Mel, I can't listen to this today. And you know what? I said, leaning over the chair, looking at her upside down: You're beautiful. She is—she's so beautiful, and then I heard these voices—a voice in my head and a voice in my heart, saying, tell her, say it, and I opened my mouth to say, I love you, and then I heard this voice say, Girls. I knew before I turned around, but I still turned, and sure enough, this mall cop stepped up, and I knew we were busted. Mel knew, too, because she goes, *Uh-oh*, and the cop spoke into the walkie-talkie on his shoulder, and I go, Party's over.

He was one of those bland mall cops, a big guy, not quite overweight, with pink skin and pudgy fingers and a crew cut. He didn't say anything, but you could tell by the way he tiptoed around us that we were in big trouble. And the whole time we were sitting there, waiting for Knox to show up, the guy was trying not to stare at Mel, but he wasn't doing a very good job. So finally, Mel goes, *Dude, look or don't look—god, you'd think you'd never seen a palsied girl with a Siouxsie Sioux haircut and a Meat Is Murder shirt before*, and I started laughing. And then Mel did, too, and I had a feeling it would be the last time we laughed together for a while.

When I heard Knox's footsteps, outside, Mel goes, *You ready, Thee?* I looked at her, smiling, and I go, Born ready, and I clasped her hand, standing up, watching the door open. When Knox saw us, Mel goes, *Thee?* And I go, Yeah? And I looked at her—she was Melody, my Melody—the real girl, holding my hand in hers, standing beside me, shoulder to shoulder. Mel said, *No matter what happens, this is the best birthday I've ever had*, and I had to swallow and roll my eyes—I kept it together, though, and I go,

Me, too. And we knew this would happen—it was part of the plan—that's what we planned all along. Not just no more lying, no more secrets, hiding from her mom. Mel always wanted to be a teenager—to break rules, get caught, to know how it feels—to live. She wanted to live, on the inside and outside, and we did. Still, ohmygod, we were in such trouble, I was really scared.

Knox couldn't even look at me, he was so angry, walking in, and then, when he saw Melody, his face turned beet red. I've never ever seen him so angry, and I thought he was about to explode, but he managed to get out of the office, and we got to the parking lot, and he got Mel situated in the back. The mall was closing; it was almost ten o'clock, and when I got in, I was about to apologize when Knox lost it. He said, Do you, do you have any idea how much trouble you're in? Heather lost her shit when she found out I'd left Mel alone with you, and she called the cops—she reported Melody missing. Mel goes, *Oh, Jesus Christ, Dad!* And I raised my hand: *Jesus Christ, Dad.* And Knox shouted, I trusted you! How could you do this, Thea? How could you do this to my daughter! Then Mel started yelling back at him, *Why are you yelling at her?* I raised both my hands, Why are you yelling at me? Melody goes, *This is what I wanted, this is what* I wanted, *and I have a right to be a girl like every other girl!* I didn't even realize for a moment I was yelling along with her, word for word, and Knox just stared, his mouth hanging open.

I raised my hand and told him exactly what Mel said, word for word: *Every day, all day, all night, you wish I was normal, a normal healthy girl, and then, when I act like a normal teenager, you wish I was a vegetable again!* And he goes, Don't say that—don't ever say that! And she goes—I spoke for her: *It's true. It's true, Dad! Every night, you drink. You drink and you feel sorry for yourself and you blame your family and blame the war—you always find someone or something to blame!*

*Don't you understand, Dad?* she said, and I raised my hand, saying, Don't you understand? She goes, *Don't you see? It's nobody's fault, what happened to me, Dad. Nothing could have been done to stop it—it's a disease, and it's just what happens in this world sometimes to some people and I know it's not fair. I know, I do, and I try to accept that—every single day; I have to accept that the world's just not fair, but you don't want to accept that. You think I don't know? You think I don't I hear you at night, Daddy? I know the truth about you. And you aren't protecting me from anything: Jesus, you're so upset over, what? I cut my hair?* God, it's just hair, I said, raising my right hand, yelling at him, but he wasn't listening.

I can't believe you, he said, speaking to me, and I go, Me? You're the one, I said. You *like* controlling her, you like that she's never going to grow up! Mel started yelling, and I started yelling for her: *Quit feeling so sorry for yourself, quit blaming everyone and everything, quit drinking and pretending you don't wish I'd never been born!* Knox goes, Take it back, and she goes, and I raised my hand, No, I said. *Because it's true! You tell everyone I've taught you more about love than you ever knew was possible, but you wish that weren't the case—you'd rather have a normal daughter than know anything about love!* Knox swerved, pulling off the road, just before we reached our building.

The car snapped, like a rubber band snapped the air, and no one said anything. He looked at Melody, and then he looked at me again: I said, *take it back*, he said. And then, I raised my hand, like I was taking an oath, and I told him exactly what she said: *Fuck you.* Knox's mouth fell open, then he raised his hand and slapped me—he slapped me across the face. There was a sharp, cracking sound, and then Mel started screaming and flailing in the backseat, and Knox yelled: She's having a seizure! I yelled back at him, She's not! It's not a seizure! And Mel was yelling in my ears: *Don't touch me! Don't touch me, you bastard!* Knox got in the back and held her down until she stopped kicking, and I just watched, waiting for her to calm down. She did—a few minutes later, Mel stopped, didn't say a word, and then, when Knox sat back, tears started streaming down her cheek. Black tears, mascara.

Knox hid his face in his hands for a minute, then we heard this roar. *What's going on? What's happening? Thee, what's going on?* Mel was beginning to panic, and I was beginning to panic, and Knox said, *Holy fuck*, seeing the crowd of reporters in front of our building. *Thea, what's happening—tell me what's going on*, Mel said, twisting her head to see, and I said, Me. I'm happening. Just then, Knox got back in the front and he said, Get out, as someone in the crowd pointed, seeing us, and people started to turn. Some people started walking toward us, a few at a time, and then, almost the whole mass of them started moving straight for us. Get out! Now! Get out! Knox yelled at me, before leaning over and throwing open my door, unfastening my seat belt, almost shoving me out of the car. *No! No, Dad, no!* Mel screamed. I almost fell, and Knox closed the door, and I got up, pounding on the window, Please, I said, barely able to talk: please don't leave me! I held my breath, waiting for him to turn around, but he didn't. So I started screaming at him, down the highway: Come back! Don't leave me! But they didn't turn around. He just left me there, feeding me to the wolves.

Trying not to cry, trying to hold on, I turned and I started walking back to our building. Steeling myself, I looked at the crowd, but the only person I recognized was Jenna Darnell, and she saw me right away, and she actually looked scared, just this look in her eyes, and then everyone started streaming around her, rushing toward me. All these reporters and cameramen, and all I could think was, *Now what? Haven't you people seen a sex tape before?* I thought they would stop, let me through, but they didn't. I made it to the middle of the parking lot, before they surrounded me, and it was like a storm hit, with lights flashing and flashing, voices shouting and shouting, Thea! Thea! Thea, over here! Thea, is it true . . . Blinding, deafening, couldn't breathe. Let me go! Let me go! I said, trying to push my way through.

I was crushed, literally crushed by people pushing against me, unable to breathe, starting to panic. The thing is, when I saw them, I thought they'd stay back, because why would they push like that, why would anybody behave like that unless it's an emergency? But it was not an emergency; it was just news. I'm the news, being swarmed by this crowd of reporters, all asking questions, and I kept trying to follow their words, but I couldn't see who was talking, because they were shining lights in my face, and they all kept pushing, and I was trying not to trip or step on anybody, thinking, *This isn't really happening.* You see it so many times on TV, you think you'd know how to deal with it, but you don't, trust me. No one knows how to deal with a stampede.

I couldn't hear, couldn't see, so I started shouting, I can't breathe! Please, I can't breathe! And then a hand grabbed my arm, and turning, I screamed, because it was Foley. Don't touch me! Get your hands off of me! I yelled, but he wouldn't let go, pulling me through the crowd, bulbs flashing everywhere, and Foley said, Theadora Denny, you're under arrest. Arrest for what? I said, covering my eyes as more flashbulbs went off, and there were so many people shouting; I could barely hear Foley answer: You are under arrest for the kidnapping of Melody Knox. Her mother is pressing charges, and your mother is waiting for us at the police station, Foley said, and then he started reciting my rights, and I said, You're joking—you must be joking, but he wasn't. He led me to the black SUV and opened the back door, covering my head with his hand and pushing me inside. Once the door closed, it was silent, and it was dark, inside. I could open my eyes again, hearing Foley get in the cab, up front, and then, very carefully, the driver pulled out.

We reached the highway, about to turn, and sitting on the side closest to our building, I looked up, at our empty doorway, remembering the last time I saw Cam. Then I closed my eyes, and I told him the truth, thinking, *You are the very best thing that has ever happened to me. And I am the very best me when I'm with you. If we'd never met, I wouldn't know what it is to love with all my heart, and I would never have met Melody, the best friend I've ever had, and I never would've seen how beautiful I am, through your eyes. But right now, at this moment, if I could do it all over again, if I had a choice and I could go back in time? Honestly, Cam, I love you more than anything in this world, but if I were God and I could do anything, if I could do it all over again, I would never meet you. No, we would never meet again.*

There was a black glass partition between the front seat and the backseat, so I didn't have to look at Foley, and then I opened my eyes, seeing something flashing in the glass, something right behind me. Then I saw that it wasn't behind me: it was me: I was flashing again. Leaning my head against the window, my sweater had fallen down, and the scar on my shoulder was glowing green again, and I could see the reflection in the opposite window. But it was a different shape—the big heart with an arrow through it had turned into an anarchy symbol, and it was flashing: dot dot dot; dash dash dash; dot dot dot . . . SOS.

## THURSDAY, SEPTEMBER 23, 2010
## (SEVEN MONTHS EARLIER)

Another year. I can't believe I'm back here again. I can't believe how everything and nothing changes, but that's high school, I guess. It's funny, though, because people keep double-taking, looking at my new haircut. At first, they look all excited, like maybe there's a new girl in school from some faraway place—you can totally see it in their eyes. But then, when they see that it's me, they're like, Oh. Oh, yeah. It's that crazy girl. And I'm just like, That's right. So stay the hell away from me, because you don't know what a crazy girl might do, now, do you? I don't care anymore. I really don't; let them stare.

I was so bummed, though; because of all the school I missed at the end of last year, they'd already set me up for tutoring. Like seven hours a day in class wasn't enough, I had to stay an extra hour twice a week? Whatever, let's just get it over with. So I went to the library right after last bell, because I wanted a table at the back. I should've sat in the front, where I could be seen, clearly waiting for my new tutor, but I was like, *No. He's the one getting paid, so let him find me, and if he doesn't, I'm outta here.* I took out my sketchbook—I've been working on this American Apparel series, using all these famous men as models, and once I started drawing, I forgot all about school. For a few minutes, and then I felt someone standing over me.

All I could see were his feet. He was wearing Vans and Levis and he looked tall, thin. Maybe because he was standing right over me, staring at my notebook, but when he said, Who knew Stephen Hawkins was so flexible? all the hair on the back of my neck stood on end, and out of nowhere, I could feel the blood heading straight for my cheeks, and I didn't even know why. Just this feeling in my guts and tingling between my legs. Then the strangest thing happened, because there was this voice in my head that said, *Don't turn around, Thea. Whatever you do, do not look at him. Just get up, take your books and walk away.* Then there was this other voice in my head that said, *Look— look at him, because your life's about to change forever.* I mean, I just sat there, gripping my pencil, no idea where these voices were coming from, and I knew it was completely crazy to think looking at some kid could change my whole life, but crazy as it was, deep down, I had to believe that anything was possible.